'You're right, you know,' Molly said with a sigh of regret. 'We've absolutely nothing in common. What on earth would we talk about on a date except the Abberwick Foundation?'

'I don't know. Want to find out tomorrow night?'

Molly felt as though she were standing on the brink of a giant bottomless whirlpool. She was gathering the nerve to dip one toe into the swirling currents when she suddenly remembered a previous engagement. She was amazed at the degree of disappointment she felt.

'I'm busy tomorrow night. I'm going to take my sister shopping for her college wardrobe. She starts her freshman year in the fall.'

'Friday night?'

Molly took a deep breath and prepared to jump into the whirlpool. 'All right.' Panic set in almost immediately. 'But this will be just a test date. First, we find out whether or not we're going to bore each other silly over dinner. Then we'll decide what to do after that.'

Harry smiled. 'I won't rush you into anything. I'm the slow, methodical type, remember?'

**Jayne Ann Krentz** has, in her dazzling career, captured nearly every award for romance writers. She is the author of historical romance novels under the name Amanda Quick. She lives in Seattle with her husband, Frank.

**Also by Jayne Ann Krentz**

Silver Linings
Perfect Partners
Family Man
Wildest Hearts
Grand Passion
Trust Me

# Jayne Ann Krentz

# Absolutely, Positively

ARROW

Published in the United Kingdom in 1998 by
Arrow Books

5 7 9 10 8 6

Copyright © 1996 by Jayne Ann Krentz

First published in the United Kingdom in 1998 by William Heinemann

Arrow Books Limited
The Random House Group Ltd
20 Vauxhall Bridge Road, London SW1V 2SA

Random House Australia (Pty) Limited
20 Alfred Street, Milsons Point, Sydney,
New South Wales 2061, Australia

Random House New Zealand Limited
18 Poland Road, Glenfield, Auckland 10, New Zealand

Random House (Pty) Limited
Endulini, 5a Jubilee Road, Parktown 2193, South Africa

The Random House Group Limited Reg No 954009

A CIP catalogue record for this book
is available from the British Library
www.randomhouse.co.uk

Printed and bound in Great Britain by
Bookmarque Ltd, Croydon, Surrey

ISBN 0 7493 2391 4

For Edna and J. L. Krentz,
With love and affection

# Absolutely,

# Positively

# 1

$\mathcal{H}$arry Stratton Trevelyan allowed himself few certainties in life, but during the past month he had become absolutely, positively sure of one thing. He wanted Molly Abberwick. Tonight he intended to ask her to have an affair with him.

This was a major decision for Harry. But then, most decisions were major for him.

The opening sentence of his latest book could have served as his personal motto: *Absolute certainty is the greatest of all illusions.*

As a general rule he applied that principle to his work and to his personal life. A man had only one reliable defense against illusions in both arenas, and that defense was caution. Harry made it a habit to be very, very careful.

Harry's past as well as his current occupation combined to ensure that he viewed the world with what some people called a marked degree of cynicism. He preferred to call it intelligent skepticism, but the result was the same.

The good news was that he rarely got conned, scammed, or fleeced.

The bad news was that a lot of people thought that he was cold-blooded. That, however, did not bother Harry.

By training and inclination, Harry demanded hard, solid

1

proof in virtually every arena of his life. He had a passion for it. He preferred a logical approach to all things.

Once in a while, however, his finely tuned brain seemed to skip the usual methodical steps and leaped straight to an insight so shatteringly perceptive that it sometimes scared him. *Really* scared him. Nevertheless, for the most part, he took satisfaction in exercising his razor-sharp intelligence. He knew that he was much better at thinking than he was at handling relationships.

Thus far he had moved slowly and carefully toward his goal of beginning an affair with Molly. He did not intend to make the mistake he had made with his ex-fiancée. He would not become involved with another woman in a desperate attempt to seek an answer to the ·dark questions about himself that he could not, would not put into words.

He would settle for sex and companionship this time.

"Will that be all, Harry?"

Harry glanced at his part-time housekeeper. Ginny Rondell, a plump, pleasant-faced woman in her late forties, hovered on the other side of the long granite counter that separated the kitchen from the living room of the high-rise condominium.

"Yes, thank you, Ginny," Harry said. "An excellent meal, by the way."

Molly Abberwick, seated on the black sofa facing the wall of windows, smiled warmly at Ginny. "It was fantastic."

Ginny's broad face suffused with pleasure. "Thank you, Ms. Abberwick. The tea is ready, Dr. Trevelyan. Are you sure you don't want me to serve it?"

"Thanks, I'll handle it," Harry said.

"Yes, well, I'll say good night, then." Ginny came around the edge of the long counter and trundled toward the green-marble-tiled hall.

Harry waited with an unfamiliar sense of gathering impatience as Ginny opened a closet door and removed her purse. He waited while she put on her sweater. At last she let herself out through the front door.

An acute silence fell on the condominium.

Alone at last, Harry thought, wryly amused at his own eagerness. He hadn't felt this way in a long, long time. He could not even recall the last occasion. It had no doubt occurred at some point in his youth. He was thirty-six, but he had been feeling very ancient for the past eight years.

"I'll get the tea," he said as he got to his feet.

Molly nodded. There was an expectant look in her wide, sea green eyes. Harry hoped the expression boded well for his plans for the evening. He had turned off *both* phones for the night, an unheard-of course of action. Ginny had been astounded.

True, he generally switched off the business line in the evenings or when he was engaged in intensive study, but he never threw the switch on the family line when he was at home. He was always available to both sides of his feuding clans.

Harry got to his feet and walked to the granite counter. He picked up the tray containing the pot of tea and two cups. He had ordered the very expensive Darjeeling after having made it his business to discover Molly's personal preference. No sugar. No milk. Harry was good with details.

Covertly, he studied Molly as he carried the tea tray to the glass table in front of the sofa. There was definitely an undercurrent of excitement stirring in her. He could almost feel it lapping at him in tiny waves. His own anticipation surged.

Molly sat somewhat primly on the sofa, her attention caught by the lights of the Pike Place Market down below and the dark expanse of Elliott Bay. It was summer in the Northwest, and the days seemed to last forever. But it was after ten o'clock, and night had finally arrived. Along with it had come Harry's opportunity to begin an affair with his client.

This was not the first time Molly had seen the sights from Harry's twenty-fifth-floor downtown condo. He worked out of his home, and Molly had come here often enough on business during the past month. But this was the first time she had ever seen the lights at night.

"You have an incredible view from up here," she said as he set the tea tray down on the coffee table.

"I like it." Harry sat down beside her and reached for the teapot. Out of the corner of his eye he saw her smile. He took that to be another good sign.

Molly had a very expressive face. Harry could have watched her for hours. The angle of her brows reminded him of a bird on the wing. The image was a good metaphor for Molly. A man who wanted to catch her would have to be very fast and very smart. Harry told himself that he was both.

Tonight Molly was dressed in a businesslike, moss green pantsuit complete with a one-button jacket and softly pleated trousers. She wore a pair of demure, suede pumps. Harry had never before paid much attention to women's feet, but he found himself captivated by Molly's. They were perfectly arched with delicate ankles. All in all, a marvel of engineering design, he thought.

The rest of Molly was well designed, too.

Having given the matter a great deal of close consideration in recent days, Harry had finally concluded that Molly was slender, but definitely not skinny. She practically radiated health and vitality. He was extremely healthy, himself. He had the reflexes of a cat, and he actually felt turbocharged when Molly was in the vicinity.

There was an appealing roundness to certain portions of Molly's anatomy. The jacket of the pantsuit skimmed over high breasts that Harry knew would fit nicely into his hand. The pleats of the trousers flared to encompass full, womanly hips.

Although he found her figure eminently interesting, it was Molly's vibrant face that commanded Harry's most serious attention. She was spectacular, he thought with satisfaction. Not spectacularly beautiful, just spectacular. She was unique. Special. Different.

Intelligence shimmered in her green eyes. Harry acknowledged that he was a sucker for brains in a woman. There was strength and fortitude and character in the delicate yet determined lines of her nose and high cheekbones. Her honey brown hair had a mind of its own. It exploded around her head in a short, thick, frothy mass. The style emphasized the tilt of her fey eyes.

It occurred to Harry that with those eyes, Molly could have made her living as a carnival fortune-teller. It would have been a simple matter for her to convince any likely mark that she could see straight into his past, present, and future.

The realization sparked a flash of renewed caution in Harry. The last thing he needed was a woman who could see deeply into his soul. That way lay madness.

For the space of perhaps three heartbeats he seriously questioned the wisdom of getting involved with a woman whose gaze held such a disconcerting degree of perception. He did not do well with women who were inclined to probe his psyche. His disastrous experience with his ex-fiancée had proved that much. On the other hand, he had no patience with bimbos.

For a few seconds Harry let his future hang in the balance as he contemplated his next move.

Molly gave him a questioning smile, revealing two slightly crooked front teeth. There was something endearing about those two teeth, Harry thought.

He took a deep breath and consigned his qualms to hell with a breathtaking recklessness that should have alarmed him. It would be okay this time, he told himself. Molly was a businesswoman, not a psychologist. She would take a rational, levelheaded approach to what he was about to offer. She would not be inclined to dissect him or try to analyze him.

"I would like to discuss something with you." Harry poured tea into her cup with calm deliberation.

"*Yes.*" Molly gave a little shriek, made a small fist, and pumped it wildly. Her eyes glowed. "Hot damn, I knew it."

Harry looked up, startled. "You did?"

She grinned as she picked up her teacup. "It's about time, if you don't mind my saying so."

Enthusiasm was a good thing in a woman, Harry assured himself. "Uh, no. No, I don't mind. I just hadn't realized that we were on the same wavelength here."

"You know what they say about great minds thinking alike."

Harry smiled. "Yes."

"I realized when you invited me to dinner tonight that this was a special occasion, not an ordinary business consultation."

"Right."

"I knew that you had finally made a decision."

"I have, as a matter of fact." He eyed her closely. "I've given the matter a great deal of thought."

"Naturally. If I've learned one thing about you during the past few weeks, it's that you give everything a great deal of thought. So you finally concluded that Duncan Brockway's grant proposal is worth funding. About time."

Harry blanked for a split second. "Brockway's proposal?"

Molly's eyes sparkled with satisfaction. "I knew you'd approve that one. I just *knew* it. It's so original. So intriguing. And the potential is absolutely unlimited."

Harry narrowed his eyes. "This has nothing to do with Brockway's grant proposal. I wanted to talk about another matter."

The excitement in her eyes dimmed slightly. "You did look it over, didn't you?"

"Brockway's proposal? Yes, I did. It's no good. We can go into the details later, if you like. But right now I want to discuss something more important."

Molly looked honestly baffled. "What's more important than Duncan Brockway's grant proposal?"

Harry set his teacup down with great precision. "Our relationship."

"Our *what?*"

"I think you heard me."

Molly's cup crashed back into its saucer. "That does it, I've had it."

Harry stilled. "What's wrong?"

6

"You have the nerve to ask me what's wrong? After telling me that you're not going to approve Duncan's proposal?"

"Molly, I'm trying to conduct an intelligent conversation here. However, it seems to be falling apart. Now, about our relationship—"

*"Our relationship?"* Molly erupted from the sofa with the force of a small volcano. "I'll tell you about our relationship. It's a complete, unmitigated disaster."

"I wasn't aware that we even had one yet."

"We most certainly do. But it's ending here. Now. Tonight. I refuse to continue to pay for your services as a consultant, Harry Trevelyan. Thus far, I have not received one damn thing for my money."

"There seems to be a misunderstanding here."

"I'll say there is." There was green sheet lightning in Molly's eyes. "I thought you invited me to dinner tonight to tell me that you'd approved Duncan Brockway's grant proposal."

"Why in hell would I invite you to dinner just to tell you that Brockway's proposal is a scam?"

"It's not a scam."

"Yes, it is." Harry was not accustomed to having his verdicts questioned. He was, after all, a leading authority in his field.

"According to you, every single one of the one hundred grant proposals that have been submitted to the Abberwick Foundation have been scams."

"Not all of them." Harry preferred accuracy to gross generalizations. "Some were just plain bad science. Look, Molly, I'm trying to discuss something else entirely here."

"Our relationship, I believe you said. Well, it's over, Dr. Trevelyan. This was your last chance. You're fired."

Harry wondered if he had accidentally stepped into a parallel universe. This was not going according to plan.

He had made his decision regarding Molly with great care and consideration. True, he had wanted her from the start, but he had not allowed himself to be swept away by physical

7

desire. He had worked from a very basic premise. Following the demise of his engagement over a year ago, he had given his future sex life a great deal of serious contemplation. He had concluded that he knew exactly what he needed in a woman. He wanted a relationship with someone who had a lot of interests of her own, someone who would not require constant attention from him.

He required a woman who would not take mortal offense when he was consumed with his research. A woman who would not care if he locked himself in his office to work on a book or an investigation. A woman who could tolerate the demands of his personal life.

Most of all he wanted an affair with a woman who would not question his moods or suggest that he get therapy for them.

Molly Abberwick had appeared to fit the bill. She was twenty-nine years old, a competent, successful entrepreneur. From what Harry could determine, she had virtually raised her younger sister single-handedly after her mother's death several years earlier. Her father had been a genius, but as was usually the case with the obsessively creative type, he had devoted his time to his inventions, not his children.

From what Harry could discern, Molly was no fragile flower, but a strong, sturdy plant that could weather the worst storms, perhaps even those that occasionally howled across his own melancholy soul.

As the proprietor of the Abberwick Tea & Spice Company, Molly had proven her ability to survive and flourish in the tough, competitive world of small business. In addition to running her shop, she was the sole trustee of the Abberwick Foundation, a charitable trust established by her father, the late Jasper Abberwick. Jasper's inventions were the real source of the wealth in the Abberwick family. It was the business of the trust that had brought Molly to Harry a month ago.

"You don't want to fire me," Harry said.

"It's the only thing I can do," she retorted. "There's certainly not much point in continuing our association. Nothing is getting done."

"What, exactly, did you expect from me?"

Molly threw up her hands in exasperation. "I thought you would be more helpful. More positive. More *excited* about the various grant proposals. No offense, but waiting for you to approve one is like watching trees grow."

"I don't do excited. I take a deliberate approach to my work. I thought you understood that. That's why you hired me in the first place."

"You're deliberate the same way a stone wall is deliberate." Molly clasped her hands behind her back and began to pace the carpet in front of the windows with long, angry strides. "Our association has been a complete waste of time."

Harry watched her, fascinated. Molly's whole body vibrated with outrage. The volatile emotion should have worried him, but it only seemed to add yet another intriguing dimension to her riveting face.

*Riveting?* Harry frowned at the thought.

"I knew you would probably be difficult." Molly turned her head to glower furiously at him over her shoulder. "But I didn't think you would be impossible."

Definitely riveting, Harry decided. He could not recall the last time he had been *riveted* by a woman. *Rivet* was a word he generally reserved for other areas of interest. A discussion of Leibniz's claim to the invention of the calculus was *riveting*. Charles Babbage's design for an analytical engine was *riveting*. The ramifications of Boole's work in symbolic logic were *riveting*.

Tonight Harry knew beyond a shadow of a doubt that Molly Abberwick had to be added to the list of things that could rivet him. The knowledge made him deeply uneasy even as it fed his hunger for her.

"Look, I'm sorry that you think I'm difficult," Harry began.

"Not difficult. Impossible."

He cleared his throat. "Don't you think that's an overly personal way to characterize my professional decisions?"

"Calling Duncan Brockway's grant proposal fraudulent is an overly personal way to characterize poor Duncan."

"Forget Brockway's proposal. I only did what you pay me to do, Molly."

"Is that right? Then you're overcharging me."

"No, I'm not. You're overreacting."

"Overreacting? *Overreacting?*" Molly reached the granite counter. She whirled around and started back toward the opposite wall. "I'll admit that I'm fed up. If you want to call that overreacting, fine. But it doesn't change anything. This relationship of ours is not working out at all the way that I thought it would. What a disappointment. What a waste of time."

'We don't exactly have a relationship," Harry said through his teeth. "We have a business association."

"Not any longer," she announced triumphantly.

From out of nowhere, Harry felt the dark, brooding sensation descend on him. He should have been thanking his lucky stars for a narrow escape, he thought. A relationship with Molly would never have worked.

But instead of a sense of relief, he knew a hint of despair. He recalled the day Molly had walked into his office-study for the first time.

She had announced that she wished to hire him as a consultant for the Abberwick Foundation. The trust had been established by her father to make grants to promising inventors who could not get funding for their work. Jasper Abberwick had known the problems such people faced all too well. He and his brother, Julius, had labored under financial difficulties for most of their careers. Their cash flow problems had not been resolved until four years ago, when Jasper had succeeded in patenting a new generation of industrial robots.

Jasper had not been able to enjoy his newfound wealth for long. He and his brother, Julius, had both been killed two years ago while experimenting with their latest creation, a prototype design for a man-powered aircraft.

It had taken a year to get the Abberwick Foundation up and running. Molly had invested the money very shrewdly and was now eager to use the income to make the kind of grants her father had wanted her to make.

As the foundation's sole trustee, she was required to handle a wide variety of problems. She was adept at dealing with the vast majority of them, specifically the ones that involved financial decisions. But, unlike her father, she was a businesswoman, not an engineer or a scientist.

Evaluating the merits of the grant proposals submitted by desperate inventors required a sound, working knowledge of scientific principles and cutting-edge technology. In addition, it demanded historical perspective. Such judgments could only be rendered by a trained mind. The Abberwick Foundation had required the services of someone who could judge a proposal not on the basis of its potential for immediate industrial application, but for its long-term value.

Beyond that, Molly had also needed someone who could weed out the frauds and con artists who circled wealthy foundations such as hers like so many sharks in the water.

Molly had many impressive credentials, Harry acknowledged, but she did not have a strong technical background. She was a woman with half a million dollars a year to spend, and she needed help. Specifically she needed Harry Stratton Trevelyan, Ph.D.

Thus far Harry had perused over a hundred grant proposals for her. He had not approved a single one. He was chagrined to realize that he had not understood how impatient Molly had become during the past few weeks.

His attention had obviously been focused on other things.

He had been curious about her from the moment she had made the appointment to interview him as a consultant. He had recognized her last name immediately. The Abberwick family had produced a long string of eccentric but undeniably gifted inventors over the years.

The Abberwick name was not exactly a household word,

but it was certainly a familiar one in the commercial world. There it was associated with a variety of machine tools, control system components, and, in recent years, robotic devices.

As an authority in the esoteric field of the history and philosophy of science, Harry had had occasion to learn something about the various Abberwick contributions to technology.

The family had a history as old as the nation itself. One early colonial Abberwick had made a significant improvement to printing press machinery. That particular device had made it possible to double the output of certain inflammatory tracts and newspapers, which had, in turn, helped shape public opinion concerning a revolution in the American colonies.

In the 1870s another Abberwick had made a major advance in steam engine design. The result had been increased efficiency for the railroads, which had, in turn, influenced the development of the western regions of the United States.

In the late 1930s an Abberwick had invented a control mechanism that had made assembly lines more efficient. The increased efficiency had impacted wartime production of tanks and airplanes.

And so it went. The Abberwick name was sprinkled about the history of American invention like so much popcorn on the floor of a theater. And it was noticed in much the same manner. One didn't really see it until one stepped on it.

But Harry had made a career of stepping on such odd bits of information. Invention shaped history, and history shaped invention. Harry frequently studied the way in which the two meshed, mingled, and influenced each other.

He gave lectures on the subject at various universities and colleges. He wrote books that were considered classics in the field of the history of science. And somewhere along the way, he had become an authority on scientific fraud.

Harry frowned as he watched Molly fume. It alarmed him that he was still looking for an excuse to pursue an affair with her. An intelligent man would back off at this point, and he was nothing if not intelligent.

"Let's be realistic, here, Molly," he said. "Firing me would be an extremely foolish move on your part. We both know that."

She spun around, brows beetled. "Don't you dare call me a fool."

"I didn't call you a fool. I merely said that it would be foolish to end our business arrangement. You need me."

"I'm beginning to have serious doubts about that." She aimed a finger at him. "You're supposed to advise me, but so far all of your decisions can be summed up in a single word. And that word is *no*."

"Molly . . ."

"It doesn't take any great talent to say no, Dr. Trevelyan. I'll bet that I can find lots of people who can say it. Some of them probably charge a good deal less than you do, too."

"But will they say yes when they should say it?" he asked softly.

"All right, so maybe another consultant will screw up now and then, and I'll make some grants to the wrong people." She dismissed that possibility with a wave of her hand. "You know what the French say, you can't make an omelette without breaking a few eggs. At least something will get done."

"Half a million dollars a year is more than a few eggs. You're assuming that you can even find another academic specialist here in Seattle who possesses the historical perspective as well as the scientific and engineering expertise to advise you."

She looked down her strong, assertive little nose at him. "I don't see why it should be so difficult to find someone else to do this kind of consulting."

Harry realized with a sense of amazement that he was actually getting angry. He quickly suppressed the sensation. He would not allow Molly to set a match to his temper.

"You're welcome to try, of course," he said politely.

Molly's soft mouth tightened. She tapped the toe of one suede pump and regarded him with an expression of simmering irritation. Harry said nothing. They both knew that her odds of finding anyone else with his peculiar combination of qualifications was bleak.

"Damn," Molly said eventually.

Harry sensed a minor victory. "You're going to have to be patient, Molly."

"Says who? I'm the sole trustee of the foundation. I can be as impatient as I want."

"This argument is degenerating."

"Yes, it is, isn't it?" Molly brightened. "And you know what? It feels good. I've been wanting to say a few things to you for days, Dr. Trevelyan."

"Harry will do."

She smiled grimly. "Oh, no, I wouldn't dream of calling you just plain Harry. Harry doesn't suit you at all, Dr. Harry Stratton Trevelyan, Ph.D., author, lecturer, and noted detector of scientific fraud." She threw out a hand to indicate the three copies of his latest book that sat on a nearby shelf. "You're much too pompous and arrogant to be a mere Harry."

Harry became aware of a faint, unfamiliar staccato sound. He looked down and discovered that he was drumming his finger against the arm of the sofa. With an effort of will he made himself stop.

He was an idiot even to contemplate trying to salvage his tenuous connection with Molly. He had enough problems in his life.

But the thought of never seeing her again suddenly conjured up an image of a glass bridge stretched over an abyss. It was an old and terrifying mental picture. He pushed it back into the shadows with every ounce of will at his command.

"Why don't you sit down, Molly?" he said, determined to regain control of the situation. "You're a businesswoman. Let's discuss this in a businesslike manner."

"There's nothing to discuss. You said no to Duncan Brockway's grant proposal, remember? And your opinion seems to be the only one that counts around here."

"I vetoed this particular funding request because it's clearly a scam. It's an obvious attempt to defraud the Abberwick Foundation of twenty thousand dollars."

Molly folded her arms beneath her breasts and regarded him with belligerent challenge. "You really believe that?"

"Yes."

"You're certain?"

"Yes."

"Positive?" she asked far too sweetly.

"Yes."

"It must be nice to be so sure of yourself."

Harry did not respond to that goad.

Silence fell.

"I really liked Duncan's proposal," Molly said finally.

"I know."

She flashed him a quick, searching look, as if sensing weakness. "There's no hope at all?"

"None."

"Not even a shred of a possibility that Brockway has hit upon a fundamentally new concept?"

"No. I can run the proposal past a friend of mine at the University of Washington who is an expert on energy sources, if you want confirmation. But he'll back me up. There is no valid scientific basis for Brockway's concept of generating power from moonlight in any manner that is even remotely analogous to the collection of solar power. The technology he proposes to use does not exist, and the theory behind the whole project is pure bull."

Amusement briefly replaced the anger in Molly's eyes. "Pure bull? Is that some kind of specialized technical jargon?"

"Yes, as a matter of fact, it is." Harry was thrown off-balance by her sudden shift of mood. "Very useful jargon. It can be applied to any number of situations. Save the foundation's money for a more deserving applicant, Molly. This Duncan Brockway character is trying to take you for twenty grand."

Molly gave a resigned-sounding groan and threw herself

back down onto the sofa. "Okay, I surrender. Sorry I lost my temper. But I'm really getting frustrated, Harry. I've got a lot of things to do. I can't spend all of my time trying to get grant proposals past you."

The storm was past. Harry did not know whether or not to breathe a sigh of relief. "Being a trustee of a foundation is time-consuming."

"Brockway's plan seemed like such a brilliant idea," Molly said wistfully. "Just think, a battery that can generate power from moonlight."

"Con artists aren't brilliant. They just have an incredible amount of audacity." Harry eyed her with sudden speculation. "And charm."

Molly winced. "All right, so I liked Duncan Brockway. He seemed very earnest and sincere when I interviewed him."

"I don't doubt that." So the bastard had tried to sweet-talk her into giving him the money, Harry thought. It came as no surprise. Nevertheless, it annoyed him. "Brockway was very earnestly and sincerely trying to get twenty thousand dollars from the Abberwick Foundation."

Molly scowled. "That's not fair. Duncan's an inventor, not a con man. Just a dreamer who wanted to make his dreams come true. I come from a long line of such people. The Abberwick Foundation exists to help them."

"You told me that the mandate of the foundation is to fund serious inventors who can't get government or corporate backing for their projects."

"I believe that Duncan Brockway is serious." Molly lifted one shoulder in an elegant little shrug. "So maybe his plans were somewhat overenthusiastic. That's not unusual in an inventor."

"And he seemed like such a nice man," Harry muttered. "Well, he did."

"Molly, if there's one thing I know, it's con artists. You hired me to weed them out for you, remember?"

"I hired you to help me select the best grant proposals and to choose funding applicants who present innovative concepts."

"And to ferret out the scams."

"Okay, okay. You win. Again."

"This isn't supposed to be a battle," Harry said wearily. "I'm just trying to do my job."

"Sure."

"I know that the foundation money is burning a hole in your pocket, but there will be plenty of opportunities to give it away."

"I'm beginning to wonder about that."

"You don't want to be too hasty. Selecting legitimate applicants takes time. It should be done cautiously and deliberately." The same way a man should select a lover, Harry thought.

"Uh-huh." Molly glanced at the crammed bookcases that covered two walls of the large living room. "How long have you been doing this kind of consulting?"

"Officially? About six years." Harry frowned at the sudden change of topic. "Why?"

"Just curious." She gave him a sublimely innocent smile. "You've got to admit it's an unusual career. There aren't a lot of people who specialize in detecting fraudulent grant applications. How did you get started?"

Harry wondered where this was going. The woman changed directions faster than alternating current. "A few years ago an acquaintance who was overseeing a government-funded project became suspicious of some of the test results. He asked me if I would take a look at the methodology the grant recipient claimed to be using. I did. It was immediately clear that the outcome of the experiments had been rigged."

"Immediately clear?" Molly's eyes widened with sudden interest. "You realized the guy was a fake right away?"

"Yes."

"Just like that?" She snapped her fingers.

Harry did not want to go into a detailed explanation of just how it had become evident to him that an elaborate fraud had been perpetrated. "Let's just say I have a feel for that kind of thing."

**17**

"A feel for it?" Molly sat forward, obviously intrigued. "You mean you're psychic or something?"

"Hell, no, I'm not psychic." Harry grabbed the teapot and forced himself to pour more of the Darjeeling into his cup. He was pleased to see that not so much as a single drop splashed on the glass table. His hands were as steady as ever. "That's a crazy thing to suggest. Do I look like the kind of person who would claim psychic powers?"

Molly settled back against the sofa. A thoughtful expression lit her eyes. "Sorry. Didn't mean to offend you."

Harry assumed his best professorial tone. "I'm a student of the history and philosophy of science."

"I know."

He gave her a hooded look. "In addition to my doctorate in that field, I have undergraduate degrees in mathematics, engineering, and philosophy."

She batted her lashes. "Wow."

Harry ground his teeth. "My background gives me insights which those who have specialized in only a single field tend to miss."

"Ah, yes. Insights."

"Exactly. As I was saying ..."

"Before you were so rudely interrupted," she murmured.

"To answer your question concerning my career path," Harry plowed on steadily, "one consulting job led to another. I now do a handful every year, provided that they don't get in the way of my research and writing projects."

"Your research and writing are more important to you?"

"Absolutely."

Molly propped one elbow on the arm of the sofa and rested her chin on the heel of her hand. "So how come you agreed to work for me? I'm sure I'm not paying you nearly as much as you can get from a contract with the government or a big corporation."

"No," he agreed. "You aren't."

"Why, then, are you bothering to consult for the lowly little Abberwick Foundation?"

"Because you're willing to do what government and industry won't do."

She tilted her head to one side. "What's that?"

"Waste money on interesting, intriguing projects that don't have any immediate, obvious application. You're willing to invest in the unknown."

Her brows raised. "That's why you agreed to work for me?"

"That's why I agreed to consult for you," he corrected coolly.

"Same thing."

"Not quite."

She ignored that. "Why are you so eager to fund a bunch of crazy inventors?"

Harry hesitated and then decided to try to explain. "I've spent my entire career studying the history of scientific and technological progress."

"I know. I read your latest book."

Harry was so surprised by that revelation that he nearly choked on his tea. "You read *Illusions of Certainty?*"

"Uh-huh." Molly grinned. "I won't pretend it was the hottest bedside reading that I've ever done, but I admit that I found it unexpectedly interesting."

Harry was amazed to discover that he felt flattered. He glanced at the book on the nearby shelf.

*Illusions of Certainty: Toward a New Philosophy of Science* was not the sort of volume that made best-seller lists. A lengthy, meticulously researched discussion of historical and societal constraints on scientific and technological progress, it was aimed squarely at the academic market. It had sold very well as a college text for students in the history of science, but it had not been meant for the average reader. Of course, Molly Abberwick was hardly average, he thought ruefully.

"*Calculated Deceptions: A History of Scientific Frauds, Swindles, and Hoaxes* was much more popular," Harry said, striving for modesty. *Calculated Deceptions* had been his first stab at writing for the lay market. It had done surprisingly well.

"I read that one, too."

"I see." Harry got to his feet, embarrassed. He went to stand at the window. "Well. Thank you."

"Don't thank me. I was doing research on you."

"Research?"

"I was trying to decide whether or not to hire you as my fraud detective."

Harry winced. He gazed out into the night and tried to reassemble his fragmented bits of logic. So Molly was not quite what he had expected. So there were some unplumbed depths in her. Some surprises. So what? He was thirty-six years old, but his Trevelyan reflexes were still very good. He could handle an affair with Molly, he decided.

"Go on," she prompted.

"What?"

"You were about to tell me why you're taken with the idea of funding inventions that don't offer any obvious payback."

Harry contemplated the night on the other side of the wall of windows. "I told you, I've made a career of studying the history of invention and discovery. In the course of that study I often find myself asking certain questions."

"What kind of questions?"

"Questions such as what would have happened if Charles Babbage had gotten funding to build his analytical engine in 1833, for example."

"The history of the computer would have to be rewritten?" Molly suggested.

"Undoubtedly. If he had been able to create his vision, the world might have headed into the computer age a hundred years earlier. Just think how much farther along we'd be by now." Harry turned away from the window, suddenly caught up in the passion he felt for his subject. "There are a thousand other examples of brilliant concepts that languished for lack of money and encouragement. I could name—"

He broke off as the front door opened.

"What in the world?" Molly glanced toward the glass-block barrier that divided the front hall from the living area. "I think someone's coming in, Harry."

Harry started forward. "Ginny must have forgotten to lock the door on her way out."

The intruder suddenly appeared. He was a tall, lanky young man dressed in jeans and a blue workshirt. He stopped when he saw Harry, braced his feet apart, and raised his arm. Light gleamed on the steel blade in his right hand.

"This is the end, Trevelyan," the newcomer snarled. "I've finally tracked you down. You won't escape this time."

"My God." Molly leaped off the sofa. "He's got a knife."

"So he does." Harry paused.

The intruder drew back his hand with a lethal, practiced movement.

"*Look out.*" Molly grabbed the teapot.

"Hell," Harry muttered. "Some people have no sense of timing."

The intruder hurled the blade.

Molly shrieked and threw the teapot in the general direction of the glass blocks.

First things first, Harry thought. He grabbed the teapot as it went sailing past.

"Do something," Molly yelled.

Harry smiled wryly. He cradled the teapot in one hand and opened his other hand to show her the knife he held.

Molly stared at him, open-mouthed. Her gaze went from the knife to the intruder's empty hands.

"You snatched that knife right out of thin air," Molly whispered.

Harry glanced down at the gleaming blade. "Looks that way, doesn't it?"

## 2

"*N*ice, Cousin Harry." The stranger clapped appreciatively. "Very nice. Your timing is as great as ever."

"Unfortunately, I can't say the same about yours." Harry set the teapot and the knife down on a nearby table. "I'm trying to conduct a business meeting here."

Stunned by the quick shift of events, Molly stared at Harry. "What's going on? Who is this?"

"Allow me to introduce my cousin, Josh Trevelyan." Harry eyed his relative with resigned disapproval. "He has a flair for the dramatic entrance. It runs in the family. Josh, this is Molly Abberwick."

"Hi," Josh said cheerfully.

Molly found her voice. "Hello."

Josh was young, Molly realized, perhaps two years older than her sister, Kelsey. That made him twenty at the most. He bore more than a passing resemblance to Harry. Same midnight black hair, although Josh's was not yet showing the hint of silver that marked Harry's. Same lean, elegant build. True, Josh had not yet developed Harry's look of sleek, controlled strength, but Molly had a hunch that would come with time.

The chief difference between the two men, other than their ages, was in their faces. It was a significant discrepancy.

Josh Trevelyan was undeniably handsome in the traditional sense established by Hollywood. With his long black lashes, dark, romantic eyes, and finely chiseled nose and mouth, he could have walked straight off the silver screen.

Harry's features, on the other hand, were unabashedly, gloriously fierce. He had the face of a hardened ascetic, a man who had spent years gazing into the depths of an alchemist's seething flask in search of arcane truths.

Harry looked like a man who had practiced self-control and self-denial for so long that those qualities had been absorbed into his very flesh and bone. It seemed to Molly that some very old fires burned in Harry's amber eyes. His powerful, long-fingered hands promised the possibilities of both great art and great despair.

"Next time, try knocking," Molly suggested. She sank down onto the arm of the leather sofa. She could not have remained standing a moment longer. Adrenaline still surged unpleasantly through her veins.

"I'm sorry about this, Molly." Harry looked at his young cousin. "Ms. Abberwick is a client of mine. She's got a point. Next time, knock first."

Josh chuckled, apparently oblivious to Harry's irritation. "Didn't mean to scare the daylights out of you."

"I'm delighted to hear that," Molly grumbled.

Still shaken by what she had just witnessed, she looked at Harry for an explanation. His ferociously intelligent eyes met hers with an expression of rueful chagrin. She got the distinct impression that he was not quite sure what to do next.

Molly was briefly intrigued by that insight. At no time during the past month had she ever seen him betray so much as a hint of uncertainty. Until tonight he had exhibited an almost Zen-like self-assurance. It was a little unnerving.

His unshakable control and bird-of-prey patience together with his undeniable brainpower had combined to make Molly wary. And deeply, inexplicably curious. A moth and flame sort of thing, she had concluded. Very dangerous. Especially for a woman who had always been too burdened with responsibilities to take risks.

She had been flabbergasted to discover that she was attracted to Harry. As soon as the realization had hit her—a momentous event that had occurred the day she met him—she had made a valiant effort to conceal it. She had needed time to decide how to handle it. She was still working on the problem.

Harry Stratton Trevelyan could have been a swordsman, an artist, a monk, or a vampire. With such a range of career options, Molly found it intensely interesting that he had chosen a scholarly vocation.

At first she had rationalized Harry's impact on her senses as a function of the fact that she was just not getting out enough these days. Aunt Venicia, her sister, Kelsey, and her counter assistant, Tessa, were forever telling her that she ought to get a life.

*Easy for them to say,* Molly thought. What with raising Kelsey, running her business, sorting out the complex legal tangle of her father's affairs, and establishing the Abberwick Foundation, there was not a lot of room for a private life. There never had been.

Molly dated occasionally when she had the time and the opportunity. A year ago she had thought she might finally settle down into a contented relationship with Gordon Brooke, the owner of an espresso shop located near Abberwick Tea & Spice. She and Gordon had a lot in common, and Gordon was an attractive man. But that possibility had evaporated months ago.

For quite a while now, Molly had found herself far more consumed by her busy routine than she was by thoughts of passion. Lately even her quarterly business tax forms seemed more interesting than the men she met. She had begun to wonder if her female hormones had gone into permanent hibernation.

That particular concern had vanished the day she had looked straight into Harry's amber eyes. All of her hormones had sat bolt upright and immediately launched into a stirring rendition of the Hallelujah Chorus.

Her common sense did not join in the refrain, however. It had several pithy things to say on the subject of Harry Trevelyan. They all boiled down to a loud warning to stand clear. Unfortunately, while she had not inherited the family genius for invention, she had gotten a full measure of the other infamous Abberwick family characteristic: curiosity.

And Molly had never been more curious about anything in her life than she was about Harry.

She scowled at him. "Do you Trevelyans always greet each other in such a heartwarming fashion?"

Harry looked pained.

Josh laughed as he sauntered forward. "That bit with the knife is part of an old carnival act that Harry and I run through once in a while just to stay in practice."

"Carnival act?" Molly took several deep breaths to finish metabolizing the remainder of the adrenaline in her bloodstream. She looked at Harry. "What you just did was impossible."

"Not for Cousin Harry," Josh assured her. "Fastest hands in the family."

"What on earth does that mean?" Molly asked.

"Pay no attention to him." Harry put down the teapot. "Snatching a knife out of midair is nothing more than an illusion. My father taught me the routine. I taught it to Josh. Which, upon reflection, may have been a mistake."

"My grandfather says Harry's dad had one of the best working knife acts in the business," Josh said. "Harry knows all of his secrets."

Molly glanced at Harry. "It's just a trick?"

"Yes," Harry said.

Josh gave him a reproachful look. "It's a lot more than a trick." He glanced at Molly. "Hasn't Harry told you about his great gift?"

"No, actually, he hasn't." Molly raised one brow. "I have a feeling that there's a lot Harry hasn't told me."

"Cousin Harry has the Trevelyan Second Sight," Josh

confided. His eyes gleamed with laughter at Harry's expression.

"Second sight?" Molly turned back to Harry.

"Josh has a distorted sense of humor," Harry said. "Take my word for it, the knife-catching trick is an illusion, pure and simple."

"Hah. That's just where you're wrong, Harry." Josh smiled wickedly. "It's definitely not simple. You gotta be fast. And you're very, very fast." He winked at Molly. "He's also got the Trevelyan reflexes, y'know."

"Fascinating," Molly murmured. Coming from a family of inventors, as she did, she was accustomed to odd pranks and unusual practical jokes, but this one was definitely unique.

Harry gave Josh a disgusted look. "Show Molly the knife that she thought she saw you throw."

Josh was genuinely horrified. "I can't do that. It's against the rules."

"I make the rules around here," Harry said. "Show her the knife."

"Only if you promise that you won't tell Cousin Raleigh or Aunt Evie."

"Believe me, you have my word on it," Harry said.

"Right." With a theatrical flourish Josh plucked a gleaming blade from beneath his shirtsleeve. He grinned at Molly. "Now you see it." The blade disappeared under his cuff. "Now you don't."

"Amazing." Molly was impressed. "I could have sworn I saw you throw it."

"That's the whole idea," Josh said.

Molly turned to Harry. "Where did you get the knife that you pretended to catch in midair?"

"From an ankle sheath that he wears," Josh explained.

Molly stared at Harry. "Good grief. You carry a knife?"

"Family tradition on his side of the clan," Josh said easily. "Show her, Harry."

"This is not how I had intended to spend the evening," Harry muttered.

Molly watched, fascinated, as he crouched in one of those

incredibly fluid movements she had come to associate with him. He calmly slipped the knife into a small leather sheath strapped to his ankle and brushed the cuff of his trousers over it.

Molly shook her head in wonder. "I never even saw you remove it."

Harry shrugged. "You were distracted by Josh's grand entrance."

Molly studied him intently. "Are you two ex-stuntmen, by any chance?"

"Not exactly." Josh slid Harry a sly glance. "Sounds as though my cousin hasn't told you much about us Trevelyans."

"No, as a matter of fact, he hasn't."

"Harry's father, my Uncle Sean, used to own an amusement show," Josh explained.

"Those days," Harry said softly, "are long gone."

"Don't let Aunt Evie hear you say that," Josh cautioned. "She's already pissed off enough as it is because of the way you turned your back on your heritage."

"What heritage?" Molly asked, enthralled.

"Good question," Harry said.

"Come on, now, Harry, I'm shocked at your lack of respect for the Trevelyan traditions." Josh turned to Molly. "Trevelyans have been doing carnival psychic acts and motorcycle stunts, telling fortunes, throwing knives, and racing cars for generations."

Molly was dumbfounded. The notion of Harry Stratton Trevelyan, Ph.D. and all-around know-it-all as a descendant of a long line of carnies, stuntmen, and race-car drivers was mind-boggling. "This is a joke, right?"

"It's no joke," Josh assured her. "Look at me. I'm carrying on the proud tradition, myself. At least until the end of summer. I go back to the University of Washington in the fall."

"What's your summer job?" Molly asked.

"I set up and operate rides in the Smoke & Mirrors Amusement Company," Josh said. "Aunt Evangeline owns the business. Several members of my family work in it. My grandfather travels with the show, too."

"Your grandfather?"

"Right. Grandpa's been involved in racing all of his life." Josh glanced briefly at Harry. "Smoke & Mirrors is doing a fair in Hidden Springs at the moment. There's stock car racing in the evenings. Grandpa is one of the best mechanics around. He works in the pits."

"I see," Molly said. "Where's Hidden Springs? I don't think I've ever heard of it."

"That's because it's so well hidden," Josh said smoothly. "It's about an hour's drive from here. North and slightly east toward the Cascades. Farm country. Smoke & Mirrors always does well there. The poor townies haven't had any real excitement since we played their local fair last summer."

"Speaking of which," Harry interrupted. "What are you doing here tonight? You're supposed to be working."

"Aunt Evangeline said I could sneak over to Seattle to see you, Harry." The good-natured amusement faded in Josh's eyes. "I wanted to talk to you about some stuff. Sorry I interrupted your evening."

"You should have called," Harry said.

"I tried." Josh shrugged. "I got the answering machine."

Harry's mouth twisted slightly. "I turned off the phones."

Josh looked surprised. "Yeah? You always take calls from family when you're home."

"I made an exception tonight, okay?" Harry said coolly. "Why didn't the doorman use the intercom to tell me you were on the way up?"

"I told Chris that I wanted to surprise you," Josh said.

"Hey, don't worry about it," Molly said quickly before Harry could continue to grill his cousin. "I was about to leave, anyway."

Harry's amber eyes gleamed with impatience. "There's no need for you to leave. We haven't finished our business."

Molly winced. "No problem. We can discuss it tomorrow."

She'd hoped that in the excitement of Josh's arrival Harry had forgotten that she'd lost her temper and fired him. What in the world had gotten into her? she wondered. Firing Harry meant never having an excuse to see him again.

That thought sent a chill through her bones. She got to her feet.

"Don't leave on my account." Josh backed hastily toward the front door. "I'll just go down to the lobby and read or something. Chris won't mind. He likes the company."

"Nonsense." Molly briskly straightened her jacket. "It's nearly eleven. You two obviously have personal things to discuss, and I need my sleep. I've got a business to run. Harry, will you call a cab?"

Harry's jaw tightened. "I'll drive you home."

"There's no need. A cab will be fine."

"I said, I'll see you home," Harry repeated evenly.

Molly met his implacable eyes and thought better of debating the subject. "If you insist."

"I insist."

Maybe he had decided to let her fire him after all, Molly thought. She wracked her brain for a way to forestall that possibility.

He was irritating, arrogant, and downright stubborn, but for some reason the last thing she wanted to do was fire Harry.

Molly's home was on Capitol Hill, some twelve blocks from Harry's downtown condo, but the short drive through the city streets was one of the longest trips she had ever made. She could not decide if Harry was angry or merely brooding.

Whatever his mood, Harry drove the sleek, hunter green sports car with graceful precision. Molly was unfamiliar with the make and model. She had, however, been raised in a family of mechanical geniuses, and she knew expensive engineering design when she saw it. She made a note to ask Harry about his car. But not tonight.

At the moment, she was enthralled not with the car, but with the way Harry handled the gear shift and clutch. She realized that he derived a subtle, sensual pleasure from the smooth, perfectly timed manipulation of the vehicle's controls. He drove the car the way he would have ridden a horse.

"Did you actually travel with a carnival?" Molly finally asked when the silence lengthened.

"No. My father did. As Josh told you, he owned an amusement show. But he sold it shortly after he ran off with my mother. He took the money and opened a dive shop in Hawaii. That's where I grew up."

"I guess I sort of assumed that you came from a long line of academics."

The streetlights revealed Harry's bleak smile. "I'm the first member of the Trevelyan clan since the first Harry Trevelyan to make a living doing something other than telling fortunes, racing cars, or throwing knives."

"When did the first Harry Trevelyan start the tradition?"

"Early eighteen hundreds."

"And your mother?" Molly asked.

"She was a Stratton."

The significance of his middle name finally clicked. "One of the Seattle Strattons? The commercial real estate development family?"

"Three generations of money, business influence, and political clout," Harry agreed in a voice that lacked all expression.

Molly thought about that. "An unusual combination," she said delicately. "Your father and your mother, I mean."

"A carny and a socialite? *Unusual* is one word for it. The Trevelyans and the Strattons have used a whole thesaurus full of other words. Most of them unprintable."

"I take it neither family approved of the match?"

"That's putting it mildly. The Trevelyans were furious because after the marriage my father sold the show. As far as they were concerned, he'd turned his back on his family, most of whom were working in said show at the time. The new owner had his own crew."

"Instant unemployment for the Trevelyans, hmm?"

"Right."

"And the Strattons?"

"Let's just say that my mother was supposed to marry a wealthy, well-connected Stanford grad. Instead she ran off with a carny." Harry slanted Molly a derisive glance. "How do you think most families would have reacted under those circumstances?"

"Not very enthusiastically, I suppose."

"You've got that right."

"So? What happened?"

Harry's brows rose slightly. "You're very curious."

"Sorry." Molly was embarrassed. "It's a family failing. I come from a long line of inventors, remember."

"I know."

"Look, you certainly don't have to answer if you'd rather not. I didn't mean to pry."

"The Strattons did everything they could to dissolve the marriage. Parker Stratton, my grandfather, tried to force an annulment. When that failed, he pushed for a divorce. One of the reasons my parents moved to the islands was so that they could put a large chunk of ocean between themselves and their families. It was the only way they could get some peace."

"Did things cool down after you arrived?"

"No. The feud continues to this day."

"And you're caught in the middle?"

Harry's shoulder lifted slightly. "That's the way it goes sometimes."

On the surface, he sounded incredibly casual, even dismissive of the family situation. But Molly flinched against the pain implied by his words. It hit her in a wave that made her catch her breath. Whatever Harry felt toward the Strattons and the Trevelyans, it was anything but indifference. But she also understood that he kept his emotions relating to that subject under lock and key.

"Do your parents still live in the islands?" Molly asked.

"My parents are dead. They were murdered by a couple of armored car thieves nine years ago."

Harry's voice was infinitely soft and infinitely cold. But

Molly stilled beneath the deluge of powerful emotions that emanated from him. She could not even begin to identify the complex and dangerous brew. Rage? Despair? Remorse? All those and more, yes. This was the stuff of nightmares.

"My God." Molly could not think of anything else to say. "My God."

Harry was silent.

"I'm so sorry," Molly offered, feeling helpless.

"Your folks are both dead, also," he pointed out, as if they had that much in common.

"Yes." It was Molly's turn to fall silent for a while.

Her feelings were not nearly as complicated as Harry's. Whenever she thought about her parents these days, she experienced a straightforward sense of wistful loss. The initial grief had faded over time. So had the anger and fear that she'd once had difficulty admitting to herself. She no longer lay awake at night wondering how she would make the mortgage payment and see her sister safely raised. She had managed to shoulder the responsibilities that had once seemed so overwhelming.

Molly peered through the windshield as the lights of what her sister mockingly called "the Abberwick family mansion" appeared. "Well, here we are. Thanks so much for seeing me home."

"I'll take you to your door." Harry brought the car to a halt in front of the massive wrought-iron gates.

Molly hastily rummaged around in her purse for the card key. When she found it, she handed it to him. Harry lowered his window and inserted the card into the lock. The heavy gates swung inward.

"Good security," Harry remarked.

"My father designed it." Molly tilted her chin to indicate the night-shrouded gardens. "He designed the sprinkler system, too. He was always tinkering with things around the house. My sister, Kelsey, is following in his footsteps. She got the Abberwick genius for scientific and technical stuff."

"What about you?"

Molly chuckled. "I got the bills."

Harry drove slowly along the curving driveway and stopped in front of the steps. He switched off the engine, removed the keys from the ignition, and opened his door. A brief smile came and went on his hard face as he surveyed the old, ramshackle mansion.

Molly had no trouble guessing his thoughts. Her home looked like the work of a seriously deranged architect. It was a bizarre collection of Gothic arches and Victorian flourishes. The perfect setting for a mad scientist.

"Interesting," was all Harry said as he opened Molly's car door.

She smiled as she got out. "Be honest, it bears a striking resemblance to Dr. Frankenstein's castle. What can I say? It's home."

"Were you raised in this house?"

"Yes, indeed. You're looking at the ancestral manor. My parents bought it during a brief spell of Abberwick prosperity thirty years ago. Dad had just patented some new machine tool. He fell in love with this place. Said he needed the space for his workshops. The money didn't last long, of course. It never did with Dad. But somehow we managed to hang on to the house."

"I see."

Molly gave Harry a second card key. He took it from her as they went up the steps to the front door.

Molly tried to think of a polite way to end the evening.

"We didn't finish our earlier conversation," Harry said as he opened the door.

"No, we didn't, did we? But we can conclude it some other time. I'm sure you're anxious to get home so that you can chat with your cousin."

"He'll keep." Harry surveyed the vast hall. "I believe you misunderstood something I said earlier about our relationship."

Molly stepped over the threshold and turned to face him with her brightest smile. "Don't worry. I've decided not to fire you."

Harry propped one shoulder against the doorjamb and folded his arms. "Is that a fact?"

"Yes, it is," Molly said briskly. "You're right when you say that there's not a lot of choice when it comes to the sort of consulting expertise that I require."

"I'm glad to know that you're aware of that."

"So it appears I'm stuck with you."

"Nothing like feeling needed."

"However, I want to make it clear that things cannot continue to go on as they have for the past month. We must make some real progress."

"I agree." Harry moved.

Molly was in his arms before she even realized his intention. He covered her startled mouth with his own and crushed her close to his lean, hard body.

For an instant she was too surprised to react. She inhaled the warm, male scent of him. It acted like a powerful drug on her senses. She could feel the strength in his arms and the sleek power in his body. She could also feel the hard bulge in his close-fitting trousers.

Harry wanted her.

The knowledge inspired the choir of female hormones that had been humming inside Molly all evening. They burst into full-throated song once more.

Molly wrapped her arms around his neck and leaned into the kiss with a soft sigh of delight. Harry groaned softly and tightened his hold on her. Excitement welled up within her. A delicious warmth stole into the lower portions of her body.

"Inside," Harry muttered into her mouth. He urged her back through the doorway.

Molly grabbed his shoulders to steady herself.

"Let me get the door closed," Harry said hoarsely.

Molly ignored him. He was nibbling on her ear, and it felt wonderful. Nothing had ever felt so terrific. She heard the door finally crash shut.

Harry swung her around and crowded her up against the nearest wall. He leaned over her and planted his strong, elegant hands on either side of her head, caging her. He kissed her throat and the hollow of her shoulder.

"*Molly.* I knew it would be good, but I didn't realize . . . God, I want you." Harry deepened the kiss.

Molly thought she would collapse. Harry thrust his foot deliberately between her ankles, easing her legs apart. Molly felt herself grow damp even though he still had his hands flattened against the wall. She shivered.

She was quivering. Trembling. The sensation awed her. She had never actually trembled with desire. She had assumed the phrase was nothing more than poetic imagery. Harry seemed to be shaking a little, himself, which was even more interesting.

He trailed kisses along the line of her jaw all the way to her ear. "Take off your jacket." His voice was that of the devil at midnight, dark, seductive, infinitely compelling. "Please."

Molly nearly went under for the third time. Somewhere in the distance the rational part of her brain was struggling to be heard. She thought it was yelling something along the lines of *get a grip,* but it was difficult to be certain. An utterly alien sensation of pure, wild recklessness held her.

Years of being careful, responsible, and generally too exhausted to take a chance washed away in an instant.

She lifted her hands to ease her jacket off her shoulders. All she could think about was getting closer to Harry.

A soft whirring noise sounded in the hall.

"What the hell?" Harry broke off the kiss. He swung around with feline speed.

The small dusting robot rolled to a halt less than twelve inches away from Harry's foot and beeped in an aggrieved tone. Its sensors seemed to glower at the object in its path. It waved its dusting sponge as though seeking a target.

Harry fitted his hands to his hips and studied the plastic and metal household robot for a long moment. Then he switched his attention to Molly. "Your chaperon?"

Molly giggled. She *never* giggled, she thought, appalled. She was actually feeling giddy from the effects of Harry's kisses. She swallowed and took a deep breath in an effort to regain some semblance of self-control.

"It's a patented Abberwick Duster," she explained. "There's one on each floor. My father designed them. I set it to dust while I was out this evening. It's just finishing the baseboards. You're in its way."

"Too bad. There's only room for one of us in this hall, and I'm not ready to leave."

"I'll take care of it." Molly hastily bent down and punched a button to send the duster back to its closet.

The little machine obediently swiveled around and hummed off down the hall.

Harry watched it disappear. "Sort of takes the magic out of the scene, doesn't it?"

"To tell you the truth, I'm so accustomed to the cleaning robots that I hardly notice them. I grew up with machines like that around. Every year while my father was alive there were newer and fancier models. My sister continues to experiment with them. Frankly, I wouldn't know how to keep house without them."

Harry exhaled slowly. The ancient fires in his eyes still burned, but he had turned the heat down to a bearable level. "Maybe the interruption was for the best. I've been trying to have a discussion about our relationship all evening. I'll be damned if I'm going to go home without finishing it."

Molly's mouth fell open. "You were talking about this kind of relationship? You? Me? Us?"

"Yes." Harry eyed her with moody consideration. "Us. A relationship."

"Good grief." Molly put a hand on the wall to steady herself. She started making her way very cautiously toward the kitchen. "I had no idea. I thought you were referring to our, uh ... well, you know."

"You thought I was talking about our business relationship. I'm not. I'm talking about this kind of relationship. Does that really strike you as such a bizarre concept?"

"Uh, well ..."

"Correct me if I'm wrong, but I got the impression from

that kiss that you might have done some preliminary thinking about the possibilities."

Molly's flush deepened. Fantasy was one thing. Reality was quite another. "Well . . ."

Harry ran a beautifully sculpted hand impatiently through his dark hair: "Look, I know we're not exactly a perfect match."

Molly finally located her tongue. "You can say that again. I'm from the business world. You're the scholarly, academic type."

He nodded, obviously in total agreement. "I'm analytical and logical by nature. You're inclined to shoot from the hip."

"You're stubborn."

"You're impulsive."

"You're slower than a turtle when it comes to making decisions," Molly said, getting into the spirit of the discussion. "You wouldn't last five minutes in the business world. The competition would devour you."

"Is that so?" Harry eyed her thoughtfully. "For your information, you wouldn't have made it in the academic world. Don't get me wrong, you've got the basic intelligence, but your thinking processes are undisciplined."

"I say *tomayto* and you say *tomahto,*" she chanted in a singsong voice.

"What?"

"Never mind." Molly contemplated the tantalizing prospect of having the floor-cleaning robot assault him with a mop. "We seem to have established that we were not meant for each other. That didn't take long. Now, then, what was your point, Dr. Trevelyan?"

He frowned. "My point was that I would like to suggest that you and I have an affair."

"You're serious, aren't you?"

"Yes."

She stared at him in disbelief. "I don't believe this. What about that little duet concerning tomatoes that we just sang together? We're opposites."

He shrugged. "Opposites attract."

"Come off it, Dr. Trevelyan. Don't give me that nonsense. I expect better logic from someone with a Ph.D."

"It's not nonsense. It's a basic principle in the science of magnetism."

Molly lifted her eyes toward the high ceiling. "We are not a couple of magnets."

"Look, I'm not suggesting that we get married," Harry said quietly. "I'm suggesting an affair. What's so damned difficult about that idea?"

"You don't think it sounds just a tad cold-blooded?"

Harry hesitated, as though he sensed that he was on dangerous ground. "I think it sounds like a rational way to establish a relationship. We're obviously attracted to each other physically."

"Yeah, but we don't communicate too well, do we?" Molly retorted with grim relish. "If nothing else, I think we established that fact this evening."

"What of it? According to the shrinks, men and women rarely do communicate well."

Molly was intrigued. "You read those pop-psych books?"

"I was engaged to a psychologist for a while a year and a half ago. You hang out with shrinks, you pick up a few things."

"Nothing contagious, I trust. Look, Harry, I don't think your idea is a particularly brilliant one."

"Why not?"

She sighed. "Because I'd probably drive you crazy."

An odd, unreadable expression flashed in Harry's eyes. It was gone in the next instant. "I've thought about that possibility," he said dryly. "But I think that I can handle the situation."

"Gosh whiz, I can't tell you how relieved I am to hear that." She glowered at him. "What about me? You're just as likely to make me crazy, too."

"Are you telling me that you don't think you can cope with my pompous, arrogant, stubborn ways?"

For some reason, that annoyed her. "If I can cope with

business competition, rude customers, and the mountain of tax forms I'm required to file just to keep my shop running, I can probably cope with you."

"Is there someone else?" Harry asked softly.

She grimaced. "No." She paused to slant him a sidelong glance. "I take it you're not involved with anyone else, either, or we wouldn't be having this conversation."

"You're right. There's no one else. There hasn't been for quite a while."

"Same here. Doesn't sound like either of us leads an exciting social life, does it?"

He smiled. "I'm hoping to change that."

"You're right, you know," Molly said with a sigh of regret. "We've got absolutely nothing in common. What on earth would we talk about on a date except the Abberwick Foundation?"

"I don't know. Want to find out tomorrow night?"

Molly felt as though she were standing on the brink of a giant, bottomless whirlpool. She was gathering the nerve to dip one toe into the swirling currents when she suddenly remembered a previous engagement. She was amazed at the degree of disappointment she felt.

"I'm busy tomorrow night. I'm going to take my sister shopping for her college wardrobe. She starts her freshman year in the fall."

"Friday night?"

Molly took a deep breath and prepared to jump into the whirlpool. "All right." Panic set in almost immediately. "But this will be just a test date. First, we find out whether or not we're going to bore each other silly over dinner. Then we'll decide what to do after that."

Harry smiled. "I won't rush you into anything. I'm the slow, methodical type, remember?"

*Except when you're plucking knives out of thin air,* Molly thought.

# 3

Josh wandered into the kitchen shortly after seven. He was dressed in jeans and a green pullover. His hair was still damp from the shower. He yawned, dropped onto one of the black wire-frame chairs in front of the granite counter, and reached for the French press coffee pot. The rich aroma of the Gordon Brooke Special Dark City Roast blend wafted through the air.

" 'Morning, Harry. Sorry about interrupting things last night."

"Forget it." Harry spread the *Post Intelligencer* out on the counter. He handed the sports section to Josh and then turned to the headlines.

Both men fell into a companionable silence as they munched cereal, drank coffee, and read the morning paper. The routine was a familiar one. They had observed it together ever since Josh had come to live with Harry at the age of twelve.

The pattern had altered when Josh had started college at the University of Washington. He could have continued to live at home with Harry and commute to the UW, but both of them had known that it was time for Josh to have his own place.

Nevertheless, the condominium was still home. Josh

showed up at the front door during school vacations, some weekends, and not infrequently in the evenings if he happened to be at loose ends or wanted to talk about his studies. The unplanned appearances were rarely a problem. Harry was almost always home alone with his books. Last night had been an anomaly.

But Harry was no longer irritated by Josh's unannounced arrival the previous evening. To his quiet astonishment, he was feeling remarkably cheerful in spite of the fact that it had taken him much longer than usual to get to sleep. The prospect of tomorrow night glimmered on the horizon, casting a pleasant glow over the entire day.

Josh finished his first cup of coffee. He looked up from the sports page, a speculative gleam in his dark eyes. "Been a while since I've come home unexpectedly and found you making out with a date."

"I was not making out with her." Harry frowned over an article on inflation. "We were discussing business. I told you, Molly's a client."

Josh helped himself to a second cup of coffee. "I got the feeling she's more than a client. You two been seeing each other long?"

"I've been doing some consulting work for her for about a month."

"Consulting?"

"Right." Harry turned the page.

"Help me out here, Cousin Harry." Josh grinned. "I'm a little confused. Are you dating her or not?"

"Since when did you become so interested in my love life?"

"Since I discovered that you had one again. It's been over a year, if my calculations are correct. Congratulations."

Harry said nothing.

"It's about time you started dating again." Josh's tone grew serious. "You've been living like a monk since Olivia broke off the engagement."

"How would you know? You aren't here most of the time these days."

41

Josh waved his fork in a vaguely menacing manner. "Ve haf vays of knowing these things."

Harry frowned. "What ways?"

"I recognize that box of condoms stashed in the bathroom cupboard. It's been there ever since you stopped seeing Olivia. The same number of little packets inside, too."

"Hell, I don't believe this." Harry sank his teeth into a slice of toast. "Talk about an invasion of privacy."

"I worry about you, Harry. You have a tendency to brood."

"I don't brood. I contemplate things for long periods of time. There's a difference."

"Call it what you want." Josh shoved bread into the toaster. "I know you better than you think."

"That possibility makes my blood run cold."

Josh's eyes widened innocently. "I only have your best interests at heart."

"I'll console myself with that thought."

"Molly Abberwick seems nice."

"She is."

"You got back here early last night after you took her home."

"Yes."

"Going to see her again soon?"

"As a matter of fact," Harry said, "I'm taking her out to dinner tomorrow night."

"Aha. Don't forget to move the box of condoms back into the drawer beside your bed."

Harry refolded the paper with painstaking care. "Last night you said you wanted to talk to me. Is something wrong?"

The amusement vanished from Josh's eyes. "It's Grandpa."

"Again?"

"Yeah. He's giving me static about going back to school in the fall. Says I'm wasting my time. Two years is enough college for any Trevelyan. He wants me to join his pit crew."

"That sounds familiar."

Josh buttered a slice of toast. "I was wondering if you would talk to him. Make him understand."

Harry gazed absently at the clouds that were moving across Elliott Bay. "I'll talk to him, but I can't promise to change his mind, Josh. You know that. He's stuck in a time warp."

"Yeah, but he'll listen to you. I tell myself it doesn't matter what he thinks. I'm going to finish college and go on to grad school regardless of his opinions." Josh shrugged. "But sometimes he gets to me."

"I know."

"If Dad were still alive things would be different. It would sort of take the pressure off me. But as it stands, I'm all Grandpa has left."

Harry said nothing. Unlike Josh, he had no illusions on that score. He knew that there would have been more, not less pressure on Josh if his father had still been alive. But Wild Willy Trevelyan, daredevil motorcycle stunt driver, ladies' man, and unofficial poster boy for the macho, hard-living lifestyle, was dead.

Wild Willy had been killed seven years earlier when he had tried to ride his overpowered cycle across a mountain of cars that had been set ablaze. A thousand spectators, including his twelve-year-old son, Josh, had witnessed the engine explosion that had caused Wild Willy's death.

Josh had gone into a state of shock. No one in the family knew what to do. Josh's mother had been killed in a carnival accident shortly after he was born. His reckless, embittered grandfather, Leon Trevelyan, was no fit parent for a young, deeply traumatized boy. Most of the other Trevelyans were too broke to assume the responsibility of an extra mouth to feed.

Newly arrived in the Northwest, Harry had also been present in the audience the day Wild Willy had been killed. He had recognized the dazed look in Josh's eyes. In the months since the death of his own parents, Harry had grown accustomed to seeing that same expression every time he had looked into a mirror.

Harry had brought Josh back to Seattle after the funeral. No one in the family had argued about the decision. They had all been vastly relieved to have Harry take charge of the boy.

Josh had eventually begun to recover from his grief, but it was obvious by the end of that first summer that there was nowhere for him to go. Fall was approaching. Harry registered him in a Seattle school.

It became clear very quickly that Josh was highly intelligent. Under Harry's guidance he had developed a passion for math and science.

For his part, assuming responsibility for his young cousin had given Harry a badly needed sense of focus. Things had settled into a stable routine that had worked surprisingly well for several years.

Then, one day shortly after Josh's sixteenth birthday, Leon Trevelyan had appeared at the front door of Harry's condominium.

Leon had wanted his grandson. He intended to teach the boy how to drive a race car.

Fortunately, Josh had been at school that day. Harry had taken his uncle Leon into his study, closed the door, and proceeded to wrestle with the devil.

Harry had known from the outset that he could not afford to lose. Josh's future had been at stake. Failure would have meant consigning the boy to the path his father and grandfather had traveled. It was a dead-end road.

Harry had won the battle.

He pushed aside the old memories. "Don't worry," Harry said. "I'll deal with Leon."

Josh looked enormously relieved. "Thanks."

Harry went back to his paper.

"About this date you've got for Friday night," Josh said.

"What about it?"

"No offense, Harry, but from what I saw last night, you're a little rusty."

"Rusty?"

Josh grinned. "In exchange for getting Grandpa off my back, I am prepared to give you some advice."

"I don't think I need any advice."

"Don't be too sure of that," Josh said. "It's a jungle out there these days."

Tessa Calshot was refilling a glass container of whole cloves when Molly walked into Abberwick Tea & Spice Company on Thursday morning.

" 'Morning, Molly." Tessa hoisted the plastic sack of cloves. The sleeve of her faded, 1930s vintage thrift-shop dress fell back to reveal the elaborate tattoo that decorated her right arm. "Be careful when you go into your office. Kelsey's in there. She's experimenting with a new version of her ground spice dispenser."

"Thanks for the warning."

"Ever vigilant, that's me. Especially so since that little episode with her tea-brewing gizmo." Tessa shook the last of the cloves out of the sack. "Took me most of the morning to clean up after the explosion, if you will recall."

"Only too well." Molly grinned at her assistant.

Tessa spent her nights playing lead guitar for an all-female band called Ruby Sweat, but as far as Molly was concerned, her true talent lay in the marketing and merchandising arena. She had a natural genius for the field, although few traditional businesspeople would have recognized it. Tessa was not exactly the conservative type.

Her spiky hair was rarely the same color two days in a row. This morning it was neon green. Her lipstick was brown. She favored pre–World War II era dresses that hung oddly on her short, sturdy frame. She paired them with large, clunky platform shoes and a number of small steel chains. There was a gold ring in her nose and another through her eyebrow.

Molly wouldn't have cared if Tessa came to work stark naked. Tessa was a natural saleswoman. She could have made a fortune in commissions at Nordstrom if she had been willing to dress to suit the corporate image of the sophisticated fashion store. Fortunately for Molly, she refused even to consider the notion.

Tourists, who comprised a large share of Molly's customers, found Tessa fascinating. They frequently asked to take her picture after they had made their purchases. They couldn't wait to show the photos to their friends back in Kansas. Pictures of Tessa constituted proof positive that things really were different out on the Coast.

Seattleites, on the other hand, long accustomed to the colorful off-beat *barristas* who operated the city's innumerable espresso machines, felt comfortable with Tessa. She reminded them of the counter assistants who sold them their daily lattes. The connection between the familiar world of the Seattle coffee culture and that of the more exotic realm of tea and spices was a subtle one, but it was effective. Molly and Tessa had deliberately exploited it.

"How did the meeting with T-Rex go last night?" Tessa asked as she closed the glass container.

"It got complicated," Molly said.

Tessa leaned her elbows on the counter. "So? Did you fire him like you promised?"

"Not exactly."

Tessa looked surprised. "You mean he finally approved a grant proposal?"

"Not exactly."

"What, exactly, did happen?"

"Let's just say I changed my mind."

"No kidding?" Tessa arched black brows that appeared to have been drawn with a wide-nibbed marking pen. "When you left here yesterday afternoon you swore that T-Rex would get no more chances to savage one of your precious grant proposals. You said that turning down the Wharton Kendall proposal was the next-to-the-last straw. I distinctly heard you say that if Trevelyan nixed Duncan Brockway's grant, the man was definitely road kill."

"Things change." Molly decided there was no point being secretive. "I've got a date with him tomorrow night."

Tessa's eyes widened in shock. "A date with T-Rex?"

"Kind of a stunner, isn't it?" Molly paused beside a shelf to rearrange a collection of designer teapots. "You know, maybe it's time to stop calling him T-Rex."

"You told me he was cold-blooded and utterly ruthless. You said he shredded the work of innocent inventors as if it were so much raw meat. You said that hiring him to help you vet grant proposals had been the equivalent of hiring Tyrannosaurus Rex to baby-sit small, furry mammals."

Molly thought about Harry's mouth on hers. She could still feel the heat he had generated. It was more intense than any of the thirteen different varieties of chile peppers she stocked.

"Let's just say I was definitely wrong about one thing," Molly said. "He's not cold-blooded."

"I don't believe it." Tessa shook her head. "The guy talked you into a date?"

"Sort of."

"Aren't you worried that you'll die of boredom?"

"I don't think boredom will be a problem," Molly mused. "And that's another distinction that must be made between T-Rex and Harry Trevelyan. From all accounts, dinosaurs had tiny little two-watt brains. The same cannot be said of Dr. Harry Trevelyan. He's what they call a polymath these days."

"What's a polymath?"

"The modern term for a Renaissance man. Well-versed in a wide variety of subjects."

"Oh." Tessa looked dubious. "Brainpower does not necessarily make a man an interesting dinner companion."

"Harry is plenty interesting, believe me." Molly inhaled the scents of fine teas and fragrant spices. She glanced around the shop with proprietary pride. Automatically, she checked to see that all was in readiness for the day.

The ritual was a familiar one. She had been going through it faithfully since the first morning she had come to work. That had been when she was twenty years old, the year her mother had died. Molly had been forced to drop out of college to support herself, her sister, and her father.

The Abberwick fortunes, never stable, had taken another serious downturn that year. Jasper had borrowed twenty thousand dollars to finance the development of a new invention, and the bank wanted its money back. The loan officer had been under the impression that Jasper had intended to use the cash to make household improvements. He did not take kindly to the discovery that the money had been poured into a failed design for robotic control systems.

Jasper had been educated as an engineer, but he was constitutionally incapable of holding down a regular job. The compulsion to design and invent always got in the way of even the most liberal corporate routine. Jasper had chafed under any sort of restriction. He had to be free to pursue his dreams.

Molly's mother, Samantha, had loved her husband with patience and understanding. She had also been practical. It was Samantha's steady paycheck that had kept the family afloat during lean times.

Things changed with Samantha Abberwick's death in a car accident. Kelsey had been only nine at the time. The family had been devastated, both emotionally and financially.

. Molly had missed her mother desperately, but there was scant time to grieve. Too many things had to be done. Kelsey was Molly's top priority. And then there was the family's fragile financial situation. Without the income from Samantha's job to rely upon, disaster loomed.

Jasper Abberwick was the epitome of the absentminded inventor. In the days following his wife's death, he could not deal with the realities of the family's cash flow problems. He took refuge in his basement workshop, leaving Molly to confront the crisis.

Molly had assessed the situation, and then she had done what had to be done. She had left college for the working world.

The shop she now owned had not been named Abberwick Tea & Spice in those days. It had been called Pipewell Tea in honor of its owner, Zinnia Pipewell.

It had been located in a dingy hole-in-the-wall near the Pike Place Market. Business had not been what anyone would have called brisk. Seattle was a city addicted to coffee, not fine tea. Zinnia could barely afford an assistant.

Molly had suspected from the start that the older woman had felt sorry for her. She knew Zinnia had hired her in the middle of a recession out of compassion, not because she actually needed a counter assistant.

Molly had been determined that her new employer would not regret her act of generosity. She had plunged into the task of working full-time with the same energy and enthusiasm that she had once reserved for her studies. There had been no other option.

Within a week of working at Zinnia's tea shop, Molly had realized that unless something was done, the business would not last the year. With it would go her job. After some research, Molly suggested that Zinnia add a full line of spices to be sold in bulk. Zinnia had gone along with the plan.

Seattle was what gourmets and restaurant reviewers liked to call a *foodie* town. Molly knew that exotic spices were of interest to a lot of people. After locating and contracting with various sources for a steady supply of everything from dried New Mexican chiles to Spanish saffron, Molly had turned her attention to packaging and advertising. The shop changed its name to Pipewell Tea & Spice.

Instead of opting for a trendy, Euro-modern image, which the espresso bars favored, Molly had chosen an old-fashioned, antique design for the shop. The result had been a store that captured the feel of an early nineteenth-century tea and spice traders' dockside warehouse.

Business had picked up rapidly.

Molly expanded carefully. She offered a mailing service so that out-of-town customers would not have to carry their purchases home in their baggage. She provided recipe books and prepackaged dip mixes. She developed catalogs. She installed a tea bar in the front window.

Molly capitalized on the new research reports that promoted the healthful aspects of tea drinking. She pursued health food junkies and jaded coffee drinkers with clever marketing schemes. When that proved profitable, she started marketing to the New Age and meditation crowd. She hired an instructor to give lessons in the ancient art of the Japanese tea ceremony.

The bank got its money. Jasper borrowed more. Life went on. Somewhere along the line Molly realized that she was never going to go back to college to finish her studies.

Zinnia made Molly a partner in the business. With a view toward her own retirement, she had suggested that the name of the shop be changed to reflect the future. Molly had never forgotten the thrill of pride she had experienced the day the Abberwick Tea & Spice Co. sign had gone up over the door of the shop.

A year later, Molly bought out Zinnia's half of the business. The lease was up for renewal. Molly decided to move to a new location. She chose spacious, airy premises midway up a broad flight of fountain-studded steps designed to channel tourists to the waterfront. It was a perfect location for attracting both the tourist crowd and the office workers who often ate their brown bag lunches on the steps.

Zinnia went on a long cruise.

Jasper finally managed to take out a lucrative patent on his industrial robot systems. At Molly's suggestion he had licensed the rights to an aggressive young Oregon firm. Money had poured into the Abberwick family coffers.

There was suddenly so much money that even Jasper and his brother could not manage to blow it all before they were killed in their man-powered aircraft experiment.

Jasper left his daughters a sizable patent royalty income that promised to continue for years. He had left the huge headache that became known as the Abberwick Foundation to Molly.

Tessa busied herself brewing tea for the window service bar. "Tell me more about this hot date with Trevelyan."

"There's nothing to tell," Molly said. "I haven't gone out with him yet."

"Ruby Sweat is playing the Cave on Friday night," Tessa said ingenuously. "You could take him there for an evening of fun and frolic."

"Somehow I don't think the Cave is Harry's kind of place."

"I still don't get it. What made you decide to date—"

A thundering crash interrupted Tessa's question.

Molly spun around to gaze at the closed door of her office. "Oh, no, not again."

She rushed forward and threw open the door. Her sister, Kelsey, looked up from the wreckage of her latest prototype device, a gadget designed to dispense ground spice. Molly could barely see her through the cloud of powdery sage.

"What happened?" Molly demanded.

"There was a small problem with the design," Kelsey gasped. "Cover your nose, quick."

It was too late. Sage wafted through the air. Molly started to sneeze. Tears formed in her eyes. She hurried into her office and slammed the door shut behind her to prevent the spice from getting into the outer shop. She seized a tissue from the box on her desk and breathed through it while she waited for the finely ground sage to settle.

"Sorry about this." Kelsey sneezed into a tissue. "I was real close this time. Next time for sure."

Molly had heard those words a thousand times over the years. Her father and her uncle, Julius, had both used them like a litany. *I was real close this time. Next time for sure.* Molly had considered inscribing those words over the door of the Abberwick mansion as a sort of family motto.

The thing was, with an Abberwick, those infamous words occasionally proved true.

"Situation normal," Molly muttered. She sneezed again. Her eyes watered. She sniffed loudly and yanked more tissue from the box.

Kelsey wiped her own eyes and gave Molly an apologetic smile. The perfect grin revealed the results of several thousand dollars' worth of orthodontia, which Molly had sprung for a few years earlier. Molly briefly admired her investment.

The family had not been able to afford such luxuries when she had been in her teens. The result was that Molly had two slightly crooked front teeth.

"You okay?" Kelsey asked.

"This will certainly clear my sinuses for the next six months." Molly brushed sage powder off her chair and sat down. She gave the spice dispenser device a brief glance.

The machine was composed of a series of plastic tubes and levers designed to control the release of dried and ground spice. The small motor that powered the dispenser lay in smoking ruins on the corner of the desk.

"What went wrong?" Molly asked.

Kelsey bent over the wreckage with the air of a police pathologist examining a dead body. "I think the ground sage somehow got sucked into the motor and clogged it."

"I see." There was no point getting upset over this sort of thing, and Molly knew it. Failed experiments were a way of life for Abberwicks. She leaned back in her chair and studied her sister with a mixture of affection and resignation.

Kelsey had definitely inherited the family genius and a talent for tinkering. She had been fiddling with things since she was five. From her dollhouses to her bicycles, nothing was safe. Molly still shuddered whenever she recalled the day she walked into Kelsey's room and found her little sister with a light bulb, an extension cord, and a pair of pliers. Kelsey had intended to turn her toy oven into a real, working model.

Although Kelsey had gotten the Abberwick curiosity and a flair for invention from her father, she had received her blue eyes and coppery red hair from her mother. She had also been blessed with Samantha Abberwick's fine cheekbones and delicate jaw. The orthodontia had provided the pièce de résistance. Molly wished her mother had lived to see just how lovely her youngest daughter had become.

She also wished that her absentminded father had not been so preoccupied with his endless plans and schemes that he had failed to notice Kelsey following in his footsteps.

It had been up to Molly to try to fill in for both missing

parents. She had done her best, but she knew a part of her would always fear that she had not done enough or done it right. She could only give thanks that Kelsey did not seem to mind her lack of proper parenting.

"I just need to design a filter." Kelsey studied the ruins of her spice dispenser. "That shouldn't be too difficult."

Molly glanced around the office. "First you'd better figure out a way to clean up this sage powder."

"Don't worry, I'll use the vacuum robot I installed in here last year." Kelsey reached for a screwdriver. "What did T-Rex think of Duncan Brockway's dippy idea for generating power from moonlight?"

Molly sighed. "You knew it was a dippy idea?"

"Brockway's proposal was based on wishful thinking, not good science."

"That's pretty much what Trevelyan said. Why didn't you tell me the proposal was unsound?"

"I didn't want to rain on your parade. I figured that was Trevelyan's job. It's why you pay him."

"Thanks a lot," Molly muttered. "You'd rather I look like an idiot to Harry than clue me in?"

"I'm sure he doesn't think you're an idiot. He knows that technology isn't your strong point." Kelsey looked up from the injured motor. "Hey, what's this? You're calling him Harry now? For the past month he's been T-Rex, Savage Predator. Destroyer of grant proposals."

"I'm trying to break that habit before I go out on a date with him. It could be embarrassing."

"A date." Kelsey stared at her. "You're going out on a date? With T-Rex?"

"His name is Dr. Harry Trevelyan," Molly said primly. "And he's taking me out to dinner tomorrow night."

"I don't believe this."

The phone warbled before Kelsey could recover from her shock. Molly sneezed as she reached for the receiver. "Abberwick Tea & Spice."

"Molly, dear, is that you?"

"It's me, Aunt Venicia." Molly sniffed into the tissue.

"You don't sound well. Do you have a cold?"

"I'm fine. Kelsey had a little accident with her new ground-spice dispensing device."

"No harm done, I take it?"

"My sinuses will never be the same, but other than that, everything's okay."

"Well, that's all right then." Venicia dismissed the incident with the ease of long practice. She had, after all, been married to an Abberwick for thirty years before being widowed in the accident that had killed Molly's father. "I wanted to ask you what you thought of green and gold?"

"Green and gold what?"

"For the wedding colors, dear. Aren't you listening?"

"I'm listening. Green and gold sound lovely."

"Silver might be better." Venicia paused. "But somehow I can't see green and silver together, can you?"

"I've never actually thought about it." Molly brushed sage powder off the morning mail and began to sort through the stack of envelopes and sales brochures.

Venicia launched into a detailed analysis of the virtues of pairing gold rather than silver with green. Molly listened with only a portion of her attention. She was very fond of her aunt, but it was quite possible to do two things at once when Venicia talked about the plans for her upcoming wedding.

Kelsey gave her a sympathetic grin when Molly carefully slit open an envelope.

"... I told Cutter that would be fine," Venicia said. "There's no problem, is there, dear?"

Molly realized she had missed something. "What's that, Aunt Venicia?"

"I said I told him that I was quite certain you would be able to join us for dinner on Friday night. Weren't you listening, dear?"

"Yes, of course I was." Molly exchanged a wry look with Kelsey. "I was just checking my calendar. It looks like I'm going to be busy on Friday."

"At night?" Venicia sounded startled.

"I know, it's a shock to me, too, but I've actually got a date."

"Why, dear, that's absolutely wonderful. I'm so pleased. Anyone interesting?"

"Harry Trevelyan."

"Your consultant?" Much of the enthusiasm vanished from Venicia's voice. "I thought you didn't care for Dr. Trevelyan."

"I've discovered there's more to Trevelyan than I first thought."

"Well, I suppose that any sort of date is better than nothing at all." Venicia did not sound entirely convinced. "Heaven knows that I've been quite concerned about your lack of social life for some time."

"That's the spirit, Aunt Venicia. Look on the bright side."

"Oh, I am, dear, I am," Venicia assured her. "I'm so glad to hear that you've got plans for tomorrow night. Who knows where it might lead? Why, when I first met Cutter on that cruise, I never dreamed we would fall in love."

"I'm not planning to fall in love with Harry," Molly said quickly. "We're not really each other's type."

"One never knows, dear. Opposites attract."

Molly winced. "I've never really believed in that old saying."

"Listen, I'll ask Cutter to arrange to have dinner with us some other evening. How about Saturday?"

"Saturday will be fine."

"Wonderful. Have fun tomorrow night, dear."

"I'll do that." Molly replaced the receiver with a sense of relief.

Kelsey did not look up as she unscrewed the motor housing. "What's the latest on the wedding plans?"

"Green and gold."

"What happened to blue and gold?"

"That was last week's color scheme." Molly slit open another envelope and removed an order form that had been torn out of her newest catalog. "I'll be glad when this wedding is finally over."

'I know. Aunt Venicia is kind of obsessing on it, isn't she?"

"I'm glad for her." Molly studied the list of spices that had been ordered by a customer in Arizona. "After all those years with Uncle Julius, she deserves a nice, attentive man like Cutter Latteridge."

"A nice, comfortably well-off man like Cutter Latteridge," Kelsey amended dryly. "That house on Mercer Island and that yacht of his didn't come cheap."

"There is that." Molly placed the order form in a stack on her desk. "At least we don't have to worry that he's marrying her for her money. But the important thing is that he pays attention to her. She deserves it."

"Uncle Julius wasn't so bad. He was a lot like Dad."

"Exactly." Molly reached for another envelope. "Half the time Dad forgot he even had a wife. Uncle Julius wasn't any better. Aunt Venicia told me once that in the entire thirty years of their marriage, Uncle Julius never once remembered their wedding anniversary, let alone her birthday."

Kelsey gazed deeply into the guts of the clogged motor. "Just like Dad."

Molly said nothing. Kelsey had said it all. Years of benign neglect were summed up in that simple statement. Jasper Abberwick had loved his family in his own way, but he had always loved his work more. Even the wonderful mechanical toys that he had built for his daughters years ago had been designed primarily as prototypes for the robotic devices he later developed.

Molly loved the old toys. They were stored in the basement workshop. Every six months she faithfully checked the special long-life batteries that Jasper had designed for them. At one time she'd thought that her own children would play with them someday. But lately that possibility had begun to seem more and more remote.

The office door opened. Tessa peered warily around the corner. "Everything okay in here?"

"I think we've survived another of Kelsey's experiments," Molly said.

"Great." Tessa walked into the office. There was a determined gleam in her eyes. "In that case, it's time we talked about your hot date with T-Rex."

Molly slit open another envelope. "What's to discuss?"

Kelsey put down her screwdriver. "Tessa's right. We need to talk. It's been a long time since you went out on a real date. Since you stopped seeing Gordon Brooke, in fact."

"That's not true. I had dinner with Eric Sanders just last month."

"Eric is your accountant," Tessa pointed out. "It was a working dinner. You told me the two of you spent the evening discussing your tax returns."

"So?"

Kelsey frowned. "He didn't even kiss you good night, did he?"

Molly blushed. "Of course not. He's my accountant, for heaven's sake."

"I knew it." Kelsey looked at Tessa. "She's a naive, innocent little lamb."

Tessa made a *tut-tut* sound. "We've got a lot of work ahead of us before we can risk letting her go out on a real date."

Molly eyed them both cautiously. "What are you two talking about?"

"It's a jungle out there," Tessa said. "But don't worry, Kelsey and I will give you a crash course in surviving modern dating."

Harry saw the strange black box sitting in front of Molly's door as soon as he got out of the car. Absently, he shifted the yellow roses he had brought with him to the crook of his left arm. He studied the box curiously as he went toward the front steps of the ramshackle mansion.

His first thought was that someone had tried to make a delivery earlier and had left the box in front of the door when no one had answered the bell.

His next thought was that if no one had answered the door, it could only mean that Molly was not home. *She had forgotten the date.*

Fierce disappointment gripped him. He should have called her again this afternoon to confirm, he told himself.

And then he saw the black wire. It ran from the cover of the black box to the doorknob. The top of the box would be yanked off when the door was opened.

Harry wondered if the arrangement was someone's idea of a practical joke. Perhaps a jack-in-the-box puppet on a spring would pop out when the lid was removed.

Harry climbed the steps slowly, his attention focused on the box.

*No joke.*

A tingle of awareness went through him. Something was very wrong.

There was a faint, scratching sound from the other side of the heavy door. Molly knew he was here. She was about to open the door.

Harry dropped the roses and leaped toward the box.

"Don't open the door," he shouted.

"Harry?" Molly appeared in the widening crack of the doorway. "Is that you? What's wrong?"

The wire that linked the box to the door went taut. The lid was jerked off the black box. There was a whirring sound. Harry saw a pistol mounted on a metal pedestal rise into the air.

The barrel of the gun was aimed at Molly.

*4*

**H**arry heard a soft, deadly *snick* even as he launched himself at the pistol assembly. His left hand struck the box, toppling the entire contraption just as the pistol fired.

The sensation of *wrongness* hit him in a shimmering wave at the instant his fingers made contact with the deadly looking mechanism. Harry had no time to react to the feeling. It vanished in a heartbeat.

A split second later, propelled by the momentum of his charging dive, Harry came up hard against the wall of the house. He recovered his balance automatically and watched as the pistol box clattered and banged its way down the front steps onto the drive.

Something soft unfurled from the barrel of the pistol. It fluttered limply as it hit the ground.

"What in the world is going on out here?" Molly looked down at the black box and its contents. She raised startled eyes to meet Harry's. "You do move quickly, don't you?"

"When I feel like it."

Harry straightened his jacket with a shrug and went slowly down the steps to stand over the fallen pistol assembly. A white flag had emerged from the barrel. There were letters printed on it in red. He used the toe of his shoe to spread out the strip of cloth so that he could read the words.

### BANG. YOU'RE DEAD.

"Somebody's idea of a bad joke." Harry took a slow, deep breath. He looked at Molly. "Are you all right?"

"Of course. What about you?"

"I'm fine."

"I can see that." She grinned. "You have an original method for overcoming the social awkwardness of a first date."

"As Josh recently pointed out to me, it's been so long since I've had a date, I've forgotten the usual routine." Harry glanced down at the flag pistol. "But this wasn't from me. I brought flowers."

"You did?" Molly spotted the fallen roses. She smiled in delight. "So you did. They're beautiful. How did you know yellow roses are my favorite?"

Harry followed her glance to where the bruised roses lay scattered on the drive. "Lucky guess."

He watched her hurry down the steps to collect the flowers. The roses had been a last-minute suggestion from Josh, but Harry saw no reason to mention that. He told himself he would have thought of them on his own if Josh hadn't brought up the subject. He was out of practice, but he wasn't stupid.

It struck Harry that Molly looked wonderful tonight. She had on a dashing little scarlet dress trimmed with gold buttons. The matching cropped jacket had a snappy, mock-military style. Her rambunctious hair was inadequately confined behind each ear with small gold clips. A pair of strappy black dress sandals emphasized the graceful arch of her feet. Harry realized that he had never before seen Molly in anything except business attire. It was a pleasant change of pace.

"I think most of them survived." Molly stooped to retrieve the roses.

"Forget the flowers. They're ruined."

"No, they're not. One or two are a little crushed, but that's all."

Harry decided not to argue the point. The drooping blooms spoke for themselves. He turned his attention back to the black box and its wicked-looking gun.

"Any idea who left you this?" he asked.

"No." Molly gave the gun assembly a dismissive glance as she walked back up the steps. "It looks like the handiwork of one of my sister's friends. She runs with an inventive crowd. Some of the boys are still a little immature, even though they're all starting college in the fall."

Harry recalled the fleeting but unmistakable sense of *wrongness* that had assailed him when he had reached out to knock the box onto its side. He swiftly suppressed the flash of recognition. There was nothing unusual in such a reaction, he told himself. The sight of a gun aimed at Molly was reason enough to explain the nasty feeling that had hit him at that moment.

"Your sister has friends who play jokes like this?" he asked.

"Kelsey got the family talent for invention." Molly smiled wryly. "She hangs out with a brainy bunch who have similar interests. They're all really very nice for the most part, but some of them have very strange notions of what constitutes humor. They've been known to spend weeks planning very elaborate, very clever pranks to play on each other."

Harry flexed his fingers. Some of the tension eased out of his muscles. "Sounds as if you've been through this sort of thing on previous occasions."

Molly wrinkled her nose. "If you grow up in a household like mine, you learn to take surprises in stride. Come on inside while I put these roses in water."

Harry hesitated, and then he went down on one knee to gather up the bits and pieces of the broken pistol assembly. He braced himself as he touched the fake pistol. A sense of relief went through him when he realized he felt nothing other than plastic and metal beneath his fingertips. It was okay. Just his imagination.

He frowned at the flag that hung from the barrel of the

pistol. "Are you sure this was the work of one of your sister's friends?" he asked as he got to his feet.

"What else could it be?" Molly smiled at her armful of yellow roses. "Probably a farewell gag. Kelsey is leaving town on Sunday. She's going to her new college in California to attend a special month-long summer workshop for students in the sciences."

"I see."

With the broken pistol assembly cradled in his arms, Harry followed Molly into the cavernous hall. She led the way into a bizarre kitchen.

Harry gazed around with interest. Everything was familiar but ever so slightly skewed in appearance, as if the contents of the kitchen had all been taken from the galley of the *Starship Enterprise*. The countertops and appliances were fashioned of stainless steel and plastic shaped into innovative forms. A control panel was embedded in the wall.

Molly opened a cupboard door and removed a vase. Harry carried the broken pistol assembly to a polished steel table near the window and set it down.

"Where is your sister tonight?" he asked as he poked among the remains of the black box.

"Out with friends."

"Which of her friends didn't know that she was going out this evening?"

"I have no idea." Molly turned off the water and adjusted the roses in the vase. "Could have been any number of people. Why do you ask?"

Harry picked up the pistol and turned it in his hand. "Whoever set up this contraption must have thought that she would be home this evening."

Molly frowned over a broken rose. "I suppose so." She reluctantly removed the bloom and dropped it into a strange-looking steel container. There was a soft whoosh. The damaged flower vanished from sight.

Harry took off his jacket and hung it on the back of a chair. He sat down at the table and pulled the box toward him. He glanced up and frowned at the odd apparatus that hung from the ceiling. "How do I turn on the light?"

"Red button in the center of the table."

Harry studied the small panel of buttons embedded in the steel table. He touched the red one experimentally. An even, nonglaring light struck the surface of the table. "Nice."

"Thanks." Molly stepped back to survey her flower arrangement. "Well, that takes care of the roses. They really are wonderful, Harry. I can't recall the last time anyone brought me flowers. Thank you."

Harry made a mental note to thank Josh for reminding him of the old-fashioned gesture. "You're welcome."

"If you'll excuse me, I'll get my purse. Be back in a minute."

"Take your time." Harry leaned forward to examine the spring mechanism that had been used to elevate the pistol platform.

He heard Molly leave the kitchen. Her high-heeled sandals sounded in the hall. She would be a few minutes, he decided. He unfastened his cuffs, rolled up his sleeves, and began to dismantle the platform assembly.

Molly returned a short time later. "Harry? I'm ready."

Harry did not look up from his work. He had the spring out of the box. The components of the platform assembly were spread out on the table in front of him. "I'll just be a couple of minutes here."

"Hmm," Molly said.

The artichoke and sun-dried tomato pizza Molly selected from the patented Abberwick Food Storage and Preparation Machine emerged forty minutes later. She chose a sturdy Washington State cabernet from the Abberwick Automated Wine Cellar to go with it. After some additional consideration, she ordered romaine lettuce and blue-cheese salads from the produce section of the Food Storage and Preparation Machine. The device sang softly to itself as it rinsed the fresh romaine and spun it dry.

On a whim, Molly decided to arrange the chunks of blue cheese on the lettuce leaves by hand. The decision to add the final touch with her very own fingers probably had something to do with having a man in the house, she thought.

Some primal female urge, no doubt. It would almost certainly disappear by morning, she assured herself. Such impulses never lasted long.

By the time she was ready to serve, Harry had all the various parts of the black box contraption spread out across the kitchen table. There was no room for the plates and glasses.

Molly covertly studied Harry's forbidding features as he bent over the table. He was fully engaged in the process of dissecting the pistol assembly. The image of an alchemist at work in his laboratory popped into her mind once more. She could literally feel the intensity of his concentration.

She wondered if Harry made love with the same degree of complete, all-consuming attention. The thought made her blush furiously.

Fortunately, Harry did not notice the pink in her cheeks. He was occupied with a small, battery-powered motor he had removed from the box.

Molly pressed a button. A second stainless-steel surface unsealed itself from the wall and unfolded next to the one Harry was using as a workbench. It locked itself into position.

"Well? What do you think?" Molly set the pizza and salads down on the new table.

Harry looked up at last. He blinked as though to clear his brain. Then he glanced at the pizza and salads.

"What's that?"

"Dinner," Molly announced cheerfully. "I don't know about you, but I'm starving."

Acute alarm flickered in Harry's amber eyes. "Hell." He scowled at his watch. "I've got reservations for seven-thirty."

"You *had* reservations for seven-thirty." Molly handed him a napkin. "I'm sure they gave our table to someone else sometime after eight o'clock."

Harry groaned. "I don't believe this. Sorry." He started to rise from the chair. "I'll give the restaurant a call and see if they can fit us in at eight-thirty."

"Forget it. The pizza's ready now and I'm hungry. Hope

you like artichoke and sun-dried tomatoes. I felt like experimenting tonight."

Harry gazed at the pizza with masculine appreciation. "You made this?"

"Sort of. I chose the ingredients." Molly punched a button to produce the flatware from a drawer concealed beneath the table. "The Abberwick Food Storage and Preparation Machine did all the work. Except for sprinkling the blue cheese on the salads," she added modestly. "I did that all by myself."

Harry studied the massive stainless-steel device that occupied one kitchen wall. "Amazing. One of your father's patents?"

"Yes. He tried to sell it to every single one of the major appliance manufacturers. They all told him he was crazy. They explained to him that the whole idea was to sell the consumer lots and lots of different machines to do various kitchen tasks, not one single, efficient device that would do everything and last for years."

Harry sank back down into the chair. His mouth quirked ruefully. "That's the story of a lot of interesting inventions." He picked up a wedge of pizza and took a large bite. He chewed in silence and then swallowed. "I tend to get preoccupied when I'm working on an interesting project," he said apologetically.

Molly grinned around her pizza. "I'm familiar with the syndrome."

"Because you come from a family of inventors?"

Molly shrugged. "That and because I, myself, have been known to get a tad overinvolved with a project."

"That's true, isn't it?" The hard lines of Harry's face relaxed slightly. "I've seen you get consumed by some of those grant proposals."

"I get that way about my business, too, at times."

"That makes me feel a little better about tonight," Harry said. "But I don't look forward to explaining to Josh what happened."

"Why? What's Josh got to do with our date?"

"He gave me a pithy little talk on modern dating practices. He seemed to think I had been out of the loop so long, I wouldn't know how to handle myself. Judging by this little fiasco, he may have had a point."

Molly nearly choked on a bite of pizza. She managed to swallow as the laughter bubbled up inside her. "You, too?"

One black brow rose in inquiry. "What's that mean?"

"I got the same lecture from my sister and Tessa, my assistant."

"Irritating, isn't it?" Harry took another bite of pizza. "Personally, I think Josh enjoyed holding forth. I suspect it was repayment for all the cautionary little chats I had with him while he was in high school."

"He spent a lot of time with you when he was younger?"

"He came to live with me after his father died. Josh was twelve. His mother had been killed in an accident during the setup of a carnival ride when he was a baby."

Molly put her pizza down slowly. "You raised Josh from the age of twelve?"

"I'm not sure *raised* is the correct word." Harry shrugged. "I didn't have any idea of what I was doing, but luckily for me, Josh was a great kid. He turned out all right in spite of my lack of experience."

"Mom died when my sister, Kelsey, was just a kid. Dad loved us both." Molly smiled wistfully. "He made us some incredible toys when we were younger. But he was the classic absentminded inventor."

Harry nodded in understanding. "The urge to invent can be an obsession."

"Tell me about it. Sometimes it seemed as if Dad forgot he even had a family. It got worse after Mom died. I think he used his work as an antidote for his grief."

Harry studied her with a perceptive look. "So you tried to fill in for your parents as far as Kelsey was concerned?"

Molly smiled. "I can still see her rolling her eyes whenever I gave her the cautionary lectures."

"Josh did the same thing, but he survived in spite of my

interference. He'll be starting his junior year in college this fall. He plans to go on to grad school."

"Following in your footsteps?"

"What can I say? The kid's got a brain on his shoulders."

"So does Kelsey." Molly was unable to conceal her pride. "The workshop she was invited to attend this summer is open to only the most promising high school graduates. I know she'll take to college like a duck to water."

"Josh sure did. Three-point-nine grade average last year."

Molly couldn't help it. She started to laugh.

"What's so funny?" Harry asked.

"Listen to us. We sound like a couple of middle-aged parents discussing the brilliant accomplishments of their offspring."

"I've got an excuse for sounding middle-aged," Harry said dryly. "I'm thirty-six. You're still in your twenties."

Molly made a face. "I turn thirty at the end of the month." She shook her head. "My God, where does the time go?"

Harry munched pizza in silence for a while. "Ever been married?" he finally asked.

"No. Eighteen months ago I thought maybe ... Well, it didn't work out. You?"

"I was engaged about a year and a half ago, too."

Molly stilled. "What happened?"

"She changed her mind. Married one of my cousins on the Stratton side of the family. Brandon Stratton Hughes."

"I see." Molly wasn't sure what to say to that. "I'm sorry."

"It was for the best. With the advantage of twenty-twenty hindsight, I think I can safely say that the marriage wouldn't have worked."

"Why not?"

"Olivia and I weren't well matched. She's a clinical psychologist. She was always trying to analyze me." Harry hesitated. "I don't think she liked what she found."

"I see." Molly felt the surge of unspoken communication like an undertow to his seemingly casual explanation. There was much more to the story, she thought. "I wonder what Olivia's view of your relationship was."

"I think Olivia's feelings toward me can best be summed up by the expression, 'hours of boredom broken by moments of stark terror.' "

Molly stared at him, dumbfounded. It took her a few seconds to find her voice. "Terror, huh?"

"Nothing rough. Maybe nothing very interesting. Olivia would probably call it kinky." Molly wasn't sure, but it looked like Harry was blushing.

"Hm. Kinky might not be so bad. I wouldn't know, I've never tried it." Molly strove to sound blasé.

Harry looked up, and he wasn't blushing anymore. "Is that a fact?"

Their eyes met and held.

The last wedge of pizza trembled in Molly's hand as a rush of shimmering excitement flashed through her. An awareness that was so intense it bordered on pain jolted her nerve endings. She tried to dampen the unfamiliar surge of sexual energy with sheer willpower. When that failed, she decided she had better keep talking. She cleared her throat carefully.

"So," she said.

"So what?"

Molly rallied her brain and thought quickly. "So, would this kinky stuff have anything to do with the Trevelyan Second Sight that Josh mentioned the other night?"

The amusement evaporated instantly from Harry's eyes. It was replaced by a cold, shuttered expression. "I told you, that garbage about the Trevelyan Second Sight is nothing more than an old family show gimmick."

Molly considered that. "Women have believed in female intuition for eons. Most of us simply accept it as a reality. It seems perfectly natural that some men may possess it, too. Maybe there are particularly strong veins of it in some families. Some kind of genetic thing, perhaps."

"More like some kind of bullshit."

Molly blinked. "Well, I guess that tells us where you stand on the subject."

"Sorry." Harry's fierce, ascetic features were a grim mask. "But I've been living with that crap about the Trevelyan Second Sight all of my life, and I can tell you there's not so much as a grain of truth to it."

Molly glanced at the bits and pieces of the black box that lay scattered on the table. "Are you sure? Maybe it's some sort of intuition that's making you so concerned about this silly pistol prank."

Harry glanced at the array of parts spread out on the table. "It doesn't take any special sixth sense to figure out that whoever rigged this has a lot of pent-up hostility."

"You don't know my sister's friends. They're not hostile. But like I said, some of the boys are still immature."

"Someone put a lot of time and energy into setting up the box and gun. And it was aimed at you," Harry said bluntly.

"I told you, it was probably meant to startle my sister."

"I'm not so sure of that." Harry picked up a wire spring and turned it slowly between his lean, powerful fingers. "I think whoever left the box on your step probably knew that you were the person most likely to open the door."

"That's crazy," Molly assured him. "I don't have any enemies. I told you, this is the work of one of my sister's nerdy friends. It was meant as a joke, nothing more."

Harry put down the spring. "You may have more enemies than you think."

"Give me a break. What kind of enemies would I have?"

"You've written over a hundred letters of rejection during the past month. All of them to disgruntled, disappointed inventors."

Molly was startled. "Surely you don't believe that one of them would have retaliated like this?"

"It's a possibility." Harry examined another piece of the black box mechanism. "I think the police should be notified."

"Good lord. Now you're going over the top." Molly was horrified at the prospect of involving the police. Kelsey would be mortified if her friends were questioned. "Nothing happened. It was just a tasteless prank."

"All the same, it might be a good idea to file a report." Harry broke off at the sound of the front door opening.

"That must be Kelsey." Molly sprang to her feet, relieved at the interruption. She went to stand in the arched opening that connected the kitchen to the long front hall.

"Hi, Kelsey. How was the film?"

"Molly." Kelsey's blue eyes widened in astonishment. "What are you doing home this early? What happened to the hot date with T-Rex? Don't tell me he stood you up after we went to all that trouble to find the right dress."

"T-Rex?" Harry murmured behind Molly.

Heat rose in Molly's cheeks. She gave her sister a warning scowl. "Harry is here. We decided to eat in tonight."

"Oops." Kelsey grimaced as she walked down the hall toward her sister. "Sorry about that."

"Come and meet him," Molly said.

Kelsey peered around Molly. She regarded Harry with grave curiosity. "Hi."

"Hello." Harry got to his feet. "I know I'm going to regret asking, but would you mind telling me where I picked up the nickname?"

"T-Rex?" Kelsey gave him an unabashed grin. "Molly started calling you that because of the way you tore apart all those grant proposals. And because your last name starts with the letter T. Trevelyan Rex. Get it?"

"Got it." Harry slanted Molly a speculative glance.

Molly closed her eyes and hoped that she had not actually turned the color of a ripe tomato.

"Hey, didn't mean to interrupt," Kelsey continued blithely. "I came home right after the film instead of going to Robin's house so that I could finish packing. I'm leaving for California on Sunday morning."

"So I hear," Harry said. "A summer workshop in the sciences?"

"Right." Kelsey's gaze fell on the mechanical parts scattered across the table. "What's that?"

70

"It's the remains of a very unpleasant little prank that one of your friends played on me tonight," Molly said briskly. "I suspect either Danny or Calvin. A fake gun was set to fire when I opened the door. Instead of a bullet, a flag appeared."

"Weird." Kelsey walked toward the table. She frowned at the array of parts. "But I don't think Danny or Calvin is responsible."

Harry's gaze sharpened. "What makes you so certain?"

"Well, for one thing, Danny and Calvin both outgrew this kind of stunt when they were juniors in high school." Kelsey examined the spring mechanism more closely. "And . . ."

"And?" Harry prompted.

Kelsey raised one shoulder in casual dismissal. "This isn't their style. Danny is into computers. Anything he rigged would have been based on some sort of electronic device. Calvin is into chemistry. His stunts always involved chemicals."

Harry smiled slightly. "Excellent reasoning."

Kelsey beamed. "Thanks."

"The workmanship on this thing was sloppy," Harry said. "Are any of your friends inclined to take the quick-and-dirty approach to their projects?"

"Well, Robin is a little casual when it comes to building her prototypes." Kelsey chewed thoughtfully on her lower lip. "But I can't see her setting up something like this. Lucas might have done it. He's kind of young for his age, if you know what I mean. I'll call him in the morning and see if he knows anything about this."

"I'd appreciate that," Harry said.

"Look," Molly said firmly, "I'm sure this is the end of the matter. I suggest we all forget about it."

Kelsey and Harry looked at her.

"Anyone for ice cream?" Molly asked with determined enthusiasm.

Harry glanced at his watch. "I should be going."

"Hey, don't leave on account of me." Kelsey held up both

hands and started to back out of the kitchen. "I can vanish upstairs. You'll never even know I'm there."

"That's not necessary." Harry glanced at Molly. "What with one thing or another, I seem to have ruined this evening."

"Not true," Molly assured him. She thought of all she had learned about Harry tonight and hugged the intimate information to herself. "I had a very interesting time."

Harry looked skeptical. "In that case, can I talk you into rescheduling?"

Molly didn't hesitate. "Absolutely."

"Saturday night?"

Molly started to accept and then recalled that she had other plans. "I'm having dinner with my aunt and her fiancé."

Harry accepted that. "I'll be out of town all day Sunday. I'm driving to Hidden Springs to see Josh's grandfather." He hesitated. "I don't suppose you'd like to come with me?"

Molly shook her head. "Thanks, I'd love to, but Kelsey leaves for California Sunday morning. I'm going to take her to the airport."

An unreadable expression came and went in Harry's eyes. "Hidden Springs is only an hour's drive. I can wait until you've seen Kelsey off."

"Take him up on it," Kelsey advised. "You could use a day off."

"All right." Molly smiled. "Can we go to the fair while we're in Hidden Springs? I haven't been to one in years."

"Why not?" Harry said.

"Sounds like fun," Kelsey said. "When was the last time you rode a Ferris wheel or ate cotton candy, Molly?"

"It's been years," Molly admitted.

Harry looked pained. "Please, anything but cotton candy."

Molly laughed. "Okay, okay, I'll stick to popcorn. But only if you'll promise to win me one of those big stuffed animals."

"No problem," Harry said. "As long as we play a game that's operated by one of my relatives. Without an inside connection, the probability of winning a large stuffed animal approaches infinity."

"Are those carnival games all rigged?" Kelsey asked.

"Let's just say they're not set up to favor the players," Harry said dryly.

Molly batted her lashes. "I bet you could win, regardless, Harry."

The momentary humor disappeared from his harsh face. His gaze grew disturbingly intent. "Remember the hours of boredom before you get too excited about the other stuff."

"I don't bore easily." Molly felt her pulse beat strongly in her veins. She looked into Harry's eyes and was suddenly light-headed. She said the first words that came to her. "If worse comes to worse, I can always amuse myself."

Harry's smile was slow and infinitely seductive. "I trust it won't come to that."


Saturday morning Harry stood alone in the cool, hushed darkness of the Seattle Aquarium. He frequently came here when he wanted to think.

He watched an electric eel as it dozed on the bottom of its tank. The creature fascinated Harry. He found it almost as strange and improbable as the fact that he had asked Molly to go with him to Hidden Springs.

Half an hour ago, driven by a deep restlessness that had made it difficult to concentrate on his work, he had walked down to the waterfront. He needed to think about what he had done the previous evening.

He had intended to keep his relationship with Molly separate from the complications of his family life.

The feud between the Strattons and the Trevelyans rarely broke out into open conflict for the simple reason that Harry made certain that the two clans never came into contact with each other. Harry was the only connection between the two families. Both sides had made it excruciatingly clear that they wanted the situation kept that way.

The Strattons considered the Trevelyans, with the exception of Harry, a lower form of life. They had never forgiven Sean Trevelyan for daring to marry Brittany Stratton, the family princess. The fact that Brittany had run off with Sean of her own free will did not seem to make any difference to the Strattons.

The Trevelyans took an equally dim view of the Strattons, whom they considered patronizing, effete snobs. In their considered opinion, it was the Stratton influence that had caused Harry's father to turn his back on his family.

When Harry had initially planned the affair with Molly, he had never intended to expose her to his difficult relatives. He did not understand the impulse that had made him invite her to Hidden Springs, and that worried him. He had spent a good portion of the night thinking about it.

His brain usually worked in clear, crisp, orderly patterns. The sole exceptions were his occasional *insights*. The realization that his feelings for Molly might be as inexplicable as those rare, traumatic flashes of *knowing* disturbed Harry.

A menacing shiver went through the eel. The creature's cold, emotionless gaze met Harry's through the glass barrier of the tank. Harry contemplated the primitive evolution of the eel's brain with something that could have been envy.

Nothing was complicated for the eel. There were no messy family problems, no sense of being caught between two warring worlds. No melancholy moods. *And no fear of a deep, clawing hunger for a soul-searing bond that could not even be explained, let alone consummated.*

Someone came up to stand in front of the tank. Harry turned his head and gave the newcomer one brief glance before he returned to his contemplation of the eel. He was mildly surprised to see his cousin, Brandon Stratton Hughes.

"I assume this is not a coincidence," Harry said.

"I stopped by your condo." Brandon pitched his voice very low. He looked quickly around the sparsely populated display room, obviously checking to make certain that no one could overhear him. "Your housekeeper said you had walked down here. Kind of an expensive way to kill a little time, isn't it? That ticket at the front door wasn't cheap."

"I've got an annual pass. I like to come here when I want to think."

"You would."

Harry's relationship with Brandon had never been close, but then, with the exception of Josh none of his relationships with the various members of his family could be described as close.

He and Brandon had almost nothing in common except a shared gene pool from the Stratton side of the family.

Brandon was four years younger than Harry. He had the athletic build, blue eyes, fair hair, and aristocratic good looks that had characterized the Stratton males for several generations. Brandon also had a secure position as a vice president in Stratton Properties, the family-held commercial real estate development firm.

"Well?" Harry said. "You must have wanted to talk to me very badly to make it worth paying the entrance fee to the aquarium just to find me."

"I'll get straight to the point. Has Olivia called you today?"

"No."

"What about my mother?"

"I haven't heard from Aunt Danielle today, either." Harry glanced at Brandon. "Why?"

Brandon's face tightened. "They're both a little upset."

"About what?"

Brandon drew a deep breath. "You may as well be among the first to know. I've decided to leave Stratton Properties. I'm going out on my own. I'm setting up a commercial property management firm."

Harry whistled soundlessly. "I'll bet that's been a popular decision."

"You know damn well it's going over like a lead balloon. I made the announcement last night. The whole family is in an uproar. My mother is frantic. Granddad is pissed. Uncle

Gilford has already chewed me up one side and down the other."

"I'm not surprised." Harry paused. "And Olivia?"

"Olivia thinks I'm making a big mistake." Brandon gazed glumly at the eel. "She says my decision is not based on a logical assessment of the situation. She says it's a function of my wish to rebel against a controlling grandfather and an overprotective mother."

"You've got one of each," Harry pointed out. "And the rest of the family isn't exactly laid-back, either."

"Damn it, Harry, I'm going to do this." Brandon made a fist with one hand. "I want out of the family business."

"It won't be easy."

"You managed it. You told Granddad to go to hell when he tried to force you to join Stratton Properties. You walked away from your inheritance that day. Granddad cut you out of his will, and you just turned your back on the Stratton money as if it meant nothing."

"The price he wanted me to pay was too high," Harry said softly. "Parker wanted me to pretend that I wasn't a Trevelyan."

Brandon swung around to face him. "I'm going to get out from under the family thumb, too."

"Okay."

"What's that supposed to mean?" Brandon demanded.

"What do you want me to say?"

"I don't want you to say anything," Brandon muttered. "But I want your word that you won't get involved if my mother or Olivia asks you to convince me not to leave the company."

"I won't try to stop you from leaving Stratton Properties," Harry promised. "Why should I? If you want to walk away from a cushy job at the company, that's your business. Just remember that nothing comes for free when you're dealing with Strattons. You'll pay a price."

"You mean Granddad will cut me out of the will, just as he did you?"

"Probably."

Brandon squared his shoulders. "I can live with that."

Harry heard the bold words. He also heard the underlying insecurity. "What does Olivia think of that possibility?"

"Olivia is my wife," Brandon said tightly. "She loves me. When the chips are down, she'll back me."

Harry said nothing. He was no judge of Olivia's affections. He had certainly misread her a year and a half ago, when he had convinced himself that Olivia had loved him.

# 5

"Well, Molly, did you carry out your threat to fire your so-called consultant?" Cutter Latteridge sliced into the thick, rare steak that took up half of his plate. Blood red juices ran onto the nearby baked potato.

"I've decided to give Trevelyan another chance." Molly averted her gaze from the sight of the bleeding steak. She looked at her aunt, who was sitting next to Cutter on the other side of the table. "It's not like there's a lot of choice. People with his sort of expertise are few and far between."

"Yes, I know, dear, but you did say he was being awfully difficult," Venicia reminded her. "You told me he hadn't approved a single grant proposal."

"True," Molly admitted. "But I have hopes."

"I trust you do." Venicia made a *tut-tutt* sound. "Pity to think of all that money sitting around waiting to go to a worthy cause. Jasper would have been so disappointed."

"I know." Molly smiled.

She was very fond of Venicia. Her aunt had always been part of her life. Venicia had offered comfort and support in the traumatic period following the death of Molly's mother. Years later, in the wake of the failed experiment that had taken the lives of the Abberwick brothers, Molly, Kelsey, and Venicia had grieved together and consoled each other.

78

Venicia was a slightly plump, energetic woman in her mid-fifties. Shortly after the patent royalty checks had begun arriving on a regular basis, she had discovered an abiding enthusiasm for trendy fashion. Tonight she was wearing a gold-studded, purple silk jumpsuit, huge purple and gold earrings, and several pounds of gold necklaces.

"Not much point in having a well-endowed foundation if you can't find anyone to fund," Cutter observed. His bushy gray brows bounced as he chewed vigorously on his steak.

"Jasper is probably turning over in his grave," Venicia murmured. "He and Julius were both so eager to help out other financially strapped inventors. They both spent most of their lives scrounging for cash for their projects. They wanted to make it easier for others who found themselves in their position. I wonder why it is that so many inventors are unable to handle finances."

Cutter shook his head sympathetically. "Unfortunately the same brilliant mind that can focus so keenly on invention is often not very good with the financial aspects of the work."

"How true." Venicia sighed. "Neither Jasper nor my husband could be bothered with such concerns. Jasper was worse than Julius, truth be known. He really got into deep trouble with the banks on a couple of occasions, didn't he, Molly?"

"Yes." Molly concentrated on her spicy Thai-flavored pasta. It made her uncomfortable to discuss Jasper's lamentable money habits outside the family. And although it appeared that he soon would be a member of the clan, Cutter Latteridge had not yet made the transition.

"I do believe Jasper's family would have wound up on food stamps after Samantha died if it hadn't been for Molly," Venicia told Cutter. "Poor girl had to drop out of college to go to work in order to keep a roof over their heads."

"Dad more than made up for it in the end," Molly reminded her quietly. "That patent he took out for the industrial robotic systems will provide a large, steady income for years."

79

"But the money came too late for you, my dear," Venicia said wistfully. "You had already made a success of your tea and spice shop by the time the royalties started arriving."

Molly shrugged. "Depends on your point of view. I had the satisfaction of achieving my success with my own efforts."

"An excellent attitude." Cutter gave her an approving look. "And you should be commended for not squandering the income from those patents on frivolous things. I'm sure Jasper Abberwick would be pleased to know that you've channeled so much money into his foundation."

"She's done exactly what Jasper would have wanted," Venicia said proudly. "Goodness knows she's been generous to me, and she's taken excellent care of Kelsey. There's plenty left over for the foundation."

Cutter assumed a grave expression. "Excellent cause. Never enough money for invention, sad to say. Even at the corporate level, research and development funds are always lacking. This country needs to invest much more into its inventive brains if it wants to maintain a competitive edge in the global economy."

Molly politely tuned him out, as she often did. She had nothing against Cutter. It was hard not to feel tolerant if not downright friendly toward him. He was an affable man who enjoyed playing host. He was gallant and solicitous toward Venicia. But he did have a tendency to pontificate.

Odd, how she never really minded when Harry launched into a lecture, Molly thought, amused. Harry never bored her. Admittedly, he occasionally tried her patience, but he never bored her. Even sitting in her kitchen watching him dismantle the black box that had been left at her front door had been anything but boring.

Cutter was another matter. He was a retired engineering executive who had a tendency to hold forth on whatever subject was being discussed. He considered himself an expert on everything.

Cutter was in his late fifties, a year or two older than

Venicia. Balding and blunt-featured, he had the ruddy looks and sturdy build that hinted of a childhood spent on a farm.

Molly had once asked him why he had retired at such an early age. He had given her a kindly smile and allowed as to how he'd come into some family money. In addition, he'd taken advantage of a very generous early retirement plan offered by his firm. Life was short, he'd explained. He had wanted to enjoy it while he was still relatively young and in good health.

After he and Venicia had met on the spring cruise, they had been inseparable. Their engagement had been announced a month ago.

". . . Don't you agree, Molly?" Cutter asked.

It was the note of concern in his voice that brought Molly's attention back to Cutter. She gave him an apologetic smile. "Sorry, I didn't catch that. What was your question?"

"I said," Cutter repeated patiently, "don't you think it's a little strange that your high-priced grant proposal consultant can't seem to find any worthwhile projects for you to fund?"

"I've discussed the problem with him."

"How many proposals has the foundation received?"

"About a hundred."

"And this Dr. Trevelyan hasn't approved a single one." Cutter frowned. "Odd. Very odd. My experience in the corporate world suggests that at least five or ten percent of those proposals should have been solid."

Venicia looked at him with some surprise. "Five or ten?"

Cutter hacked off another chunk of beef. "At least. I'm not saying one would want to fund all five or ten, but there should have been that many that warranted serious consideration."

"Statistics can be tricky," Molly said. For some reason she felt compelled to defend Harry's decisions. "One hundred grant proposals isn't a very large sample."

"Quite true," Cutter agreed. "Still, one does wonder what this Dr. Trevelyan is up to."

"Up to?" Molly gave him a sharp look. "What do you mean?"

"Nothing, I'm sure," Cutter said soothingly. "Nevertheless . . ."

"Nevertheless, what?" Molly demanded.

"I would advise caution, my dear," Cutter said.

"Caution?"

"You're new at this sort of thing." Cutter put down his knife and regarded her with a slightly troubled frown. "Bear in mind that there is always a great deal of money to be made in the administrative end of any charity operation. An unscrupulous person in Trevelyan's position could make himself a tidy fortune in consulting fees over a period of time."

"I don't believe Harry would use his position to con me." Molly realized that she was inexplicably incensed by what had been nothing more than a reasonable warning from a man who had seen more of the world than she had. "I'm aware that there is no shortage of embezzlers and frauds hanging around waiting to take advantage of foundations such as mine, but I can promise you that Harry Trevelyan isn't one of them."

Cutter raised his heavy brows. "The more charming they are, the more clever they are, my dear."

"Harry isn't particularly charming," Molly muttered. But he had given her very similar advice, she reminded herself.

"No offense," Cutter said gently, "but he does appear to have you eating out of the palm of his hand."

"That's nonsense," Molly said.

Venicia touched her napkin to her lips and gave Cutter a worried look. "Do you think that Dr. Trevelyan might be milking the foundation with outrageous consulting fees?"

"I'm not making any accusations," Cutter said.

Molly's fingers tightened on her fork. "I should hope not. Besides, Harry's fees aren't outrageous."

Venicia and Cutter both looked at her.

"Okay, they're on the high side," Molly admitted. "But they're within reason. Especially given his qualifications."

Cutter snorted politely and went back to his steak.

Venicia glanced at him and then turned to Molly with an uneasy expression. "I do hope you haven't gotten yourself tangled up with someone like that dreadful Gordon Brooke again, dear."

Molly winced. "Trust me, Harry Trevelyan has nothing in common with Gordon Brooke."

Cutter cleared his throat to draw Molly's and Venicia's full attention. "As I said, administrative costs are difficult to control in any organization, especially a nonprofit foundation. A trustee in Molly's position must be on her guard."

"Harry Trevelyan is not a thief or a swindler," Molly said fiercely.

Cutter sighed. "I never said he was. I'm merely suggesting that a charitable trust is very vulnerable to abuse. Anyone can call himself a consultant, after all."

Venicia nodded sagely. "Cutter is quite right. One reads about charities and foundations being defrauded all the time. You will be cautious with your Dr. Trevelyan, won't you, Molly?"

Molly stabbed her fork into a heap of pasta. She'd been forced to be cautious all of her adult life. She'd had too many responsibilities weighing on her to allow her the luxury of taking a few chances. She was nearly thirty years old, and there was finally a glimmer of excitement on the horizon. What's more, she was free to explore that glimmer.

Molly smiled blandly. "You know me, Aunt Venicia. I'm the soul of caution. I'll be careful."

Molly scrutinized Kelsey one last time as the passengers began to file on board the plane. "Are you sure you have everything you're going to need?"

Kelsey rolled her eyes. "If I've forgotten anything, you can send it down to me."

"I'm fussing, aren't I?"

"Yés, you are." Kelsey chuckled. "I'm only going to be gone for a month."

"I know." Molly gave her sister a misty smile. "But this

is a sort of trial run for me. A taste of what it's going to be like when you leave for college in the fall."

Kelsey's expression grew serious. "I've been giving that some thought. I talked to Aunt Venicia. We both think you should sell the house, Molly."

Molly stared at her in amazement. "Are you kidding?"

"No, I'm not. The mansion is too big for you to live in all by yourself."

"It's no trouble to keep up, thanks to Dad's cleaning robots. I know how to maintain them."

"That's not the point," Kelsey insisted. "The Abberwick mansion will be just too much house for you when you're there all alone. And it's filled with the past, if you know what I mean."

"I understand, Kelsey, but I don't mind that part."

"I think you will when you're rattling around in that big old house all by yourself. Promise me you'll at least consider selling it. You could get yourself a modern downtown condo."

"But it's our home. It's always been our home."

"Things will change when I leave for college."

Molly looked at the sister she had raised to womanhood and saw the future in Kelsey's intelligent eyes. "Believe me, I realize that."

Of course things would change. Molly told herself she had always known that this moment would arrive. Kelsey was about to start her own life. Her talent and brains would take her far from the crazy old ramshackle Abberwick mansion. It was the way of the world.

"Please, Molly, don't cry."

"Wouldn't think of it." Molly blinked very rapidly to clear the moisture from her eyes. "Listen, have a great time at the workshop."

"I will." Kelsey shifted her backpack and started toward the gate. She looked back once. "Promise me you'll think about selling the house, okay?"

"I'll think about it."

Molly waved good-bye until Kelsey disappeared from

view down the ramp. Then she reached for a tissue. When she realized that a single tissue wasn't going to be sufficient for the task at hand, she headed for the women's room.

It wasn't her promise to her sister that was on Molly's mind later that afternoon as she and Harry drove toward Hidden Springs. It was the one she had made to her aunt the previous night at dinner.

*I'll be careful.*

She did not know which should concern her the most, the safety of the Abberwick Foundation assets or the safety of her own heart. She had a nasty suspicion that she was falling in love with Harry Trevelyan.

Maybe it was just sexual attraction, she reassured herself.

She slanted a sidelong glance at him. His powerful, elegant hands appeared relaxed and yet in complete control as they gripped the wheel. Quiet competence radiated from him no matter what the circumstances, she thought. There was a core of strength in him that compelled respect on a very primitive level.

If this was just passion, it was heady, potentially dangerous stuff.

*I'll be careful.*

Right. She would be careful the way a mountain climber was careful when approaching Everest. Careful the way a spelunker was careful when descending into a deep cave. Careful the way an astronaut was careful when stepping out into space.

"What kind of car is this?" Molly asked curiously. "I don't think I've ever seen one quite like it."

"You haven't. It's one of a kind at the moment. It's a Sneath P2. One of a series of prototypes. Friend of mine designed and built it. It's got the aerodynamics of a racing car, the strength of a well-made European touring car, and an engine which is supposed to go for years at a time without a tune-up."

"Amazing. Why did your friend give it to you?"

"I helped him obtain the venture capital he needed to build the prototypes."

Molly gave him an inquiring glance. "I think of you as an academic type, but I suppose in your line of work you come into contact with investors all the time."

"Yes," Harry said evenly. "But unlike the Abberwick Foundation, they all want to back projects that show real potential for repaying the investment."

Molly chuckled. "Me, I just want to throw the money away."

"How did things go at the airport this morning?"

"Fine." Molly was startled by the quick change of subject. "Why do you ask?"

"It feels strange when they leave home, doesn't it? I know your sister is only going away for a month this summer, but in the fall, it will be for real. That's when you realize that things have changed forever."

Molly smiled wryly. "Okay, so I cried my eyes out in the rest room after she left. I'm all right now."

"Glad to hear it. Try to look on the bright side. No more rock music posters in their bedrooms and no more lying awake at night waiting until they finally come home. Look at me. I've been teen-free for two years now, and I'm a new man."

He understood, Molly thought. He was trying to make light of the turning point she had faced that morning, but he knew what it had been like for her. Harry had been through the same experience, accepted the same responsibilities.

"I'll take your word for it," she said. *Oh, my God. This is getting serious.*

Harry lapsed back into silence. The beautifully tuned engine of the exotic car hummed to itself. Molly settled down into the leather seat and watched the lush farmlands speed past the window. In the distance the Cascades rose toward a clear, blue sky. The future, which had seemed to be shrouded in mist a few hours ago, began to look bright once more.

The silence lengthened. Molly stirred and glanced at her watch. She realized that Harry had not said a single word for nearly twenty minutes. It wasn't the lack of conversation that had begun to bother her. It was the gathering tension she felt. It was radiating from him.

"Is something wrong?" she asked.

"No." Harry did not look away from the road. "I was just doing some thinking."

"You're not looking forward to this trip, are you?"

"Not especially."

"This may sound like a dumb question, but why are we driving all the way to Hidden Springs if you aren't anxious to see your relatives?"

"I told Josh I'd have a talk with his grandfather," Harry said. "Leon is giving him a hard time. He's leaning on Josh. Trying to convince him that he doesn't need to finish college."

"Josh's grandfather would be your uncle, right?"

"Right. My father's younger brother."

Molly thought about that. "Why didn't he take charge of his grandson after Josh's father was killed?"

"That would have been difficult. Uncle Leon was in jail at the time."

*"Jail?"* Molly turned her head to stare at him. "For heaven's sake, why?"

Harry slanted her an unreadable glance. "He was awaiting trial on charges resulting from a dispute he had with a county sheriff."

"I see." Molly digested that news. "What sort of dispute?"

"Uncle Leon was screwing the sheriff's wife. He and the lady were discovered by her husband in a motel room. The sheriff was understandably pissed."

"Oh." Molly hesitated. "I can see why the sheriff was angry, but an affair doesn't constitute grounds for arrest."

"The sheriff nailed him for auto theft, not for messing around with another man's wife."

"Auto theft?" Molly repeated weakly.

"Uncle Leon and the lady used the sheriff's car to drive to the motel."

"Good grief. That wasn't very smart."

"No, it wasn't. But then, as far as I'm concerned, Josh is the first member of that branch of the family to show any brains in three generations." Harry's hand flexed on the steering wheel. "I'll be damned if I'll let Leon pressure him into leaving college."

"Why would Leon want to do that in the first place?"

"Leon used to make his living driving race cars at county fairs. His son—my cousin Willy and Josh's father—was a motorcycle stuntman. He was killed doing a stunt. Every few years Leon gets the harebrained notion of encouraging Josh to follow in the family footsteps."

"Whew. I can see why you're concerned. Doesn't sound like a career path loaded with potential."

"It's a dead end." Harry moved his right hand to the gearshift as he prepared to turn off the highway. "Literally, in Willy's case. I'm not going to let Josh get sucked into that lifestyle."

"How will you convince your uncle to leave him alone?"

"The same way I did the last time." Harry's mouth was a grim line. "Sweet reason."

Molly did not press the matter. It was Trevelyan family business, after all. But she could not resist one last question. "What happened to Leon when he went to trial for auto theft?"

"The charges were dropped."

"He must have had a good lawyer."

"He did. I hired him myself."

The Ferris wheel came into view first. It rose majestically above the midway, a venerable, graceful, glittering contraption that still had the power to enthrall young and old alike. The engineers who designed exotic rides for the new high-tech theme parks had invented far more elaborate thrill machines over the years, but nothing would ever replace the Ferris wheel on a carnival midway.

Harry did not enjoy Ferris wheels, or any of the other rides, for that matter. He told himself that it was because he'd come from a carny family. Although his father had sold his amusement show before his son was born, Harry had spent several summer vacations traveling with his Trevelyan relatives. He had learned to set up, operate, and tear down the rides. No one who worked the midway got a kick out of the machines. It was a business, after all.

But Harry had always suspected that his personal dislike of the whirling, churning, stomach-wrenching devices went deeper in him than it did in other people involved in the world of the carnival. The real truth was that he hated the lack of control he experienced when he was trapped inside one of the small, spinning carriages.

He had struggled too long to develop a sense of self-mastery. He could not willingly surrender that control to anyone or anything else, not even for a three-minute amusement park ride.

Molly twisted in her seat to get a better view of the fairgrounds. "Where are we going?" she asked as Harry drove past the main parking lots.

"Around back to where the carnies and the fair people park their vehicles. Uncle Leon will be there somewhere."

The motley collection of trucks, vans, trailers, and motor homes stood on the far side of the fairgrounds. They were shielded from the view of the fairgoers by a fence lined with the colorful booths and tents of the midway.

Harry parked near a stand of trees and got out. A light wind blew toward him across the fairgrounds. The combined scent of grease, popcorn, and corn dogs hit him, as it always did, with a tidal wave of memory.

Molly came to stand beside him. "Something wrong?"

"No." Harry pulled his thoughts back to the present. "That smell always reminds me of the summers I spent with my Trevelyan relatives."

Molly held a wisp of hair out of her eyes and regarded him with an intently curious expression. "I'll bet you're not a big fan of popcorn and hot dogs."

"No, I'm not." He took her hand and started toward a cluster of aging trailers. "Look, this interview with Uncle Leon is not going to be pleasant. Do you think you can find something else to do until it's over?"

"No problem. I'll tour the exhibits."

"Don't get conned into buying any of the juicer-grater-slicer-dicer machines from the guys who do the demonstrations. The gadgets are all junk."

"Don't be silly," Molly said. "I'm a businesswoman, remember? I'm not likely to be taken in by someone else's sales pitch."

Harry gave her a pitying look. "Haven't you ever heard that the easiest person to sell to is a person who is in sales?"

"Hah. I don't believe it. I've never heard that particular bit of wisdom. It sounds like more of your paranoid philosophy, and I am not going to listen to it. Now, how will I find you after you've finished speaking to your uncle?"

Harry smiled faintly. "Somewhere on the midway you'll find a fortune-teller's tent. Look for a sign advertising Madam Evangeline. I'll meet you there around one o'clock."

"Got it." She touched his arm in a light, fleeting gesture, and then she walked off toward the gate.

Harry waited until she disappeared into the crowd. He still didn't understand why he had brought her with him today, but he was glad he had.

He walked through the encampment until he found the aging trailer Leon called home. It was parked near a tree. Leon's old truck stood nearby.

Harry pounded on the screen door of the trailer. "Leon, you inside?"

"Who the hell . . . ?" Leon came to the door of the trailer. He squinted against the sunlight. When he saw Harry his teeth flashed in the Trevelyan grin. "Shit. So you finally got here. You're late. Figured you'd show up yesterday."

"If I'd known you were so eager to see me again, I'd have waited a little longer."

"The hell you would have waited." Leon opened the

screen door. "When it comes to this kind of thing, you're as predictable as the sunrise. One of your bad habits, boy. Come on in."

Harry stepped into the shadowy confines of the trailer. The blinds were shut. It took a brief moment for his eyes to make the transition from the sun-drenched parking lot to the close darkness inside the metal hulk.

"Beer?" Leon asked casually from somewhere off to the left.

The cold, damp can came hurtling out of the gloom before Harry could reply. He opened his hand without thinking about it. The beer can landed firmly in his grasp. Things had a way of doing that.

"Thanks," Harry said absently.

Leon grinned. "Still fast as ever, I see. Damn shame you didn't use those talented Trevelyan hands for something a little more useful than writin' dull books."

Harry peeled back the ring on the beer can. "Reflexes have a way of going on a man as he gets older. I prefer to rely on my brains."

"That Stratton blood of yours ruined you." Leon sprawled on the battered sofa that was built into the curved rear wall of the trailer. He gestured with his beer can. "Have a seat."

Harry sank down onto the ripped vinyl bench that framed the eating nook. He glanced around without much interest.

Little had changed, either in the decor or in Leon, over the years. Trailer and owner appeared to have bonded in some indefinable manner. The stained linoleum on the floor had a counterpart in Leon's faded shirt and ancient, low-slung jeans. The torn curtains on the small windows smelled of tobacco and booze. So did Leon.

Harry decided that, on the whole, Leon was holding up better than his trailer. That was due to the sturdy Trevelyan genes, not anything resembling good health habits.

Leon was in his sixties, but he still possessed the lean build and broad shoulders that were characteristic of Trevelyan males. He was as handsome as Harry's father had been. Harry knew Leon still traded shamelessly on his looks. His uncle went through women as though they were lollipops. Willy had had the same approach to the opposite sex.

Harry was satisfied that Josh was not going to follow in their footsteps in that regard. For all his good-natured teasing about the unused box of condoms in the bathroom cupboard, Josh had more common sense and innate integrity about such matters at twenty than his father and grandfather had ever had in their entire lives. Harry had made sure of it.

Leon took a long, deep swallow of beer. "So how's the soft life in the big city?"

"Fine." Harry waited. He had learned long ago that it never paid to reveal urgency or eagerness with Leon. Leon liked to goad people until he provoked them into doing something stupid.

"Shit. I still don't know why you want to live like that," Leon mused. "Where's your Trevelyan spirit?"

"Beats me." Harry took a short sip of the beer.

"No guts, no glory, son. Haven't you ever heard that bit of wisdom?"

"I hear it every time I have a conversation with you, Uncle Leon."

"Josh tells me you're seeing some mousy little shop-keeper."

Harry did not move. "Did Josh call her mousy?"

"No, but I got the picture. Runs a tea shop, Josh said. I know the type. Prissy, uptight little business suit, right?"

"Not quite," Harry said softly.

Leon ignored him. "Hell, your pa at least had the gumption to run off with a rich man's daughter. Your ma was a real beauty, and everyone knows the Strattons have enough money to float a battleship."

"So they say."

"You're a damn fool for turning your back on all that cash, by the way."

"So I'm told."

Leon squinted at him over the beer can. "Hell, you ain't the best-lookin' Trevelyan to come down the road, but you're still a Trevelyan. Thought you could do better than a dull little shopkeeper."

"When did you develop this abiding interest in my private life?"

"Got to take an interest in it. Worried about Josh."

Harry steeled himself. "What does my private life have to do with Josh?"

"Simple." Leon grimaced. "You're a bad influence on the boy. All he talks about is goin' to college forever and a day to get some fancy science degree. Says he wants to do research, for cryin' out loud. Next thing you know, he'll be dating boring little shopkeepers, too."

"And you'd rather he got himself killed trying to make a motorcycle fly through a ball of fire?"

"Bastard." Leon flung his empty beer can against the wall of the trailer. He sat forward, his fists bunched on his knees. "I want him to be a man, like his father was. Like I am. Like your father was. I don't want him turnin' into a goddamned, overeducated wimp like you."

"How much?" Harry asked without inflection.

"What's that supposed to mean?"

"You know what it means. How much do you want in exchange for laying off Josh for the summer?"

"You think you can buy anything, don't you? That's the damned Stratton blood in you talkin'. Well, I've got news for you. This is my grandson's future we're discussin'. He's all I got left in this world. Blood of my blood, fruit of my loins. I want to see him become a man I can be proud of. You think you can put a price tag on that kind of thing?"

"No problem."

Leon's face worked furiously. "This is about family, damn you. It's not about money."

"Don't give me that crap," Harry said wearily. "We both know this isn't about Josh or his future. It's about making a deal."

"Son-of-a-bitch."

"It's okay, Uncle Leon. I'm willing to negotiate one more time. Now, how much do you want?"

Leon glowered at him for a few more seconds. Then he fell back against the couch and closed his eyes. "I need a new truck. Old one won't go another mile. Evangeline's got a whole summer of fairs lined up. Got to have reliable transportation."

Harry whistled softly. "A new truck, huh? Congratulations, Uncle Leon. You're learning to think big."

Leon slitted his eyes. "We got a deal?"

"Sure." Harry put his unfinished beer down on the table. He got to his feet. "Same deal as last time."

"Like I said, you're as reliable as the sunrise. Got to watch that, Harry. Bad habit like that'll get you into a lot of trouble."

Harry went to the door of the trailer. He looked out across the grassy parking lot. "I meant what I said, Leon. We have the exact same deal as last time."

"Yeah, yeah. I heard you."

Harry opened the screen door and went down one step. He glanced back over his shoulder. "You stop pressuring Josh to leave college, and I'll pay for your new truck."

"Like I said, we got a deal."

"Yes." Harry met his uncle's eyes. "Break your end of the bargain, Leon, and you know what happens."

"Don't threaten me, boy. You'd never go through with it. You haven't got the guts to do it, and we both know it."

Harry said nothing. He just held Leon's gaze. The sounds of the fairground receded into the distance. A great silence gripped the trailer. The shadows within seemed to thicken.

Leon appeared to shrink in on himself. "Yeah, yeah. A deal's a deal. Go on, get outa here. I got to get down to the pits. Racing starts at seven-thirty tonight."

Harry let the sagging screen door clatter shut behind him. He walked toward the fairground entrance. The smell of grease and popcorn and the aroma of the animal barns washed over him.

He suddenly wanted to find Molly.

# 6

Clutching an armful of purchases, Molly paused outside the red, gold, and turquoise striped booth. She looked up to read the words on the sign overhead.

Madam Evangeline
Learn the Secrets of the Past, Present, and Future
ADVICE ON MATTERS OF LOVE AND MONEY
Discretion Assured

Molly studied the beaded curtain that closed the entrance to the booth. She did not believe in palmistry, card readings, or crystal balls. The last thing she wanted to do was get her fortune told. She wondered if Harry intended to meet her outside or inside the booth.

She turned to scan the length of the midway, hoping to catch sight of him in the crowd. All she saw was an endless stream of people, their hands full of popcorn, candy apples, and hot dogs, wandering from booth to booth.

As Molly watched, a young man strolled past carrying a huge stuffed panda bear. He caught her eye and grinned.

"I won it for my girlfriend," he said proudly.

"Nice." Molly eyed the panda wistfully. "Was it hard to win?"

95

"Nah. You could probably win one for yourself."

"Do you really think so?"

"Sure," the young man responded very smoothly. "Why not give it a try? Only costs a quarter a toss. The booth is right across the way. See it?"

"Yes. Thanks. Maybe I'll give it a whirl."

"You won't be sorry," the young man promised. He strolled off down the midway.

Molly was about to make her way through the crowd to the coin toss game when she heard the fortune-teller's curtain snap open behind her.

"Madam Evangeline sees the past, present, and future," a throaty voice declared. "Come inside and learn your fate in love and fortune."

Molly swung around in surprise. A handsome, statuesque, middle-aged woman with silver-shot black hair stood amid the clattering beads. Fine brown eyes, a classic nose, and high cheekbones composed a face that would be striking until the woman was well into her nineties.

The fortune-teller was dressed in an ankle-length gown made of several layers of variously colored and patterned fabrics. Her long, graceful fingers were sheathed in rings. A massive necklace hung with gold and amber pendants accented an impressive bosom.

"Hello," Molly said politely. "I'm supposed to meet someone here."

The woman looked deep into Molly's eyes. "I think you have already met him."

"I beg your pardon?"

The woman inclined her head in a regal gesture. "I am Madam Evangeline. Come inside, and I will show you your future."

Molly shifted the packages in her arms. "That would be pointless. I don't believe in fortune-telling, Madam Evangeline. And, quite frankly, I wouldn't want to know my future, even if you could see it for me. Thanks, anyway. If you don't mind, I'll just wait out here."

"Please come inside," Evangeline murmured in an insistent tone. "I will not tell you anything that you do not wish to know."

Molly hesitated, her curiosity piqued. She glanced around once more to see if she could spot Harry in the crowd. There was no sign of him. She turned back to Evangeline.

"Actually, there is something you could tell me," she said.

Evangeline bowed. "I am at your service. Come inside and tell me what it is you would discover." Bells tinkled as she beckoned Molly into the tent.

Molly stepped cautiously through the dancing beads. A shadowy gloom filled the interior. The floor was covered in a midnight-blue carpet dotted with yellow stars and a moon. Yards of dark, heavy fabric cascaded down all four sides of the tent.

When her eyes adjusted to the low light, Molly was able to make out a table draped in maroon velvet. An opaque, softly glowing glass ball stood in the center. Beside it was a deck of cards. A shallow, silver bowl filled with water was placed on a nearby shelf.

"Please sit down." Evangeline gestured toward one of the two chairs that were positioned on either side of the table. "You may put your packages on the floor over there, if you wish."

"Thanks. They're getting very heavy." Molly set her burdens down and heaved a small sigh of relief. "I had no idea I'd find so many useful items in the exhibit halls."

Evangeline smiled. "Many people have had the same experience."

"I can believe it." Molly brushed her frothy, windblown hair back behind her ear. "You should have seen the crowds I had to fight in order to get this stuff. One lady actually tried to snatch my new Ace Wondermatic All-Purpose Kitchen Appliance right out of my hands."

"Amazing. Do sit down."

"All right." Molly glanced toward the beaded curtain. "But I don't want to miss my friend. He should be along at any minute."

"I guarantee that he will find you."

"If you're sure." Molly obligingly sat down and surveyed the glass ball and the deck of cards with some interest.

"Now, then, we shall begin." Evangeline cupped the glass ball in her hands. Her heavily made-up eyes met Molly's. "Tell me what it is you wish to know."

"Well, since you ask, what I'd really like to know is how this all works."

Evangeline blinked. "How it works?"

"The tricks of the trade, so to speak." Molly leaned closer. "I've heard that professional fortune-tellers are very good at guessing things about their clients' personal lives. How do you do it?"

"You want to know how I do it?" Evangeline looked scandalized.

"Exactly. Not quite my field, of course, but I'm curious. What are the clues that you use? Clothes? I expect you can tell a lot from people's clothing. But so many folks just wear name-brand jeans and sport shoes these days. What can you tell about people wearing that kind of thing?"

Evangeline's expression congealed. "I do not use tricks. I am gifted with a touch of the second sight. It runs in my family, you see."

"Hmm."

"My powers are very real. And even if I were a charlatan who used cunning to deduce facts about my clients, I would not tell you my secrets."

Molly wrinkled her nose. "I was afraid of that. Oh, well, it was worth a try."

"Look here," Evangeline muttered, "I can tell you anything you wish to know about your love life."

"I doubt it. I don't have one."

"Well, you soon will." Evangeline picked up the cards and began to lay them out, one by one on the table. "Aha. See the blue king?"

Molly glanced at the card. "What of it?"

"He represents a man you have recently met. This man is tall. He has dark hair and eyes the color of the ancient amber in my necklace. They are the eyes of a man of power. A man who will change your destiny."

Molly laughed. "I see you're acquainted with Harry Trevelyan. I'll bet you're his aunt. I believe Josh mentioned an Evangeline Trevelyan. How did you identify me, though? Did you figure out who I was when I told you that I was waiting for someone, or did Josh describe me to you?"

Evangeline gave her an exasperated glare. "I figured it out because I'm a fortune-teller. It's my business to know things like that. Now, let's get on with this, shall we?"

Molly shrugged. "What's the point? Now that I know who you are and you know who I am, I'm not going to be amazed or astounded by anything you tell me about Harry."

"What if I told you that I do not know who this Harry is?"

Molly grinned. "Come off it, you know Harry. Admit it."

"You're making this extremely difficult," Evangeline said brusquely. "Let's take it again from the top. You have recently met a tall, dark-haired man with amber eyes. This man—"

"You forgot handsome."

Evangeline looked up from her cards with a ferocious scowl. "I beg your pardon?"

"Aren't you supposed to say that I've recently met a tall, dark-haired, *handsome* man?" Molly pursed her lips. "I always thought it was tall, dark, and handsome. Yes, I'm sure that's the way it goes."

Evangeline tapped one long, crimson nail against the table. "All right, so he's not so handsome. I wouldn't be too choosy, if I were you. What are you? Thirty? Thirty-two? Time's running out, friend."

"I wasn't complaining about Harry's looks. I just said you're wrong. He is tall, dark, and extremely attractive."

Evangeline eyed Molly as if she had serious doubts about her IQ level. "You think Harry's good-looking?"

"Well, maybe not in the traditional sense," Molly admitted. "But, then, I'm not much of a traditionalist. In my family we tend to go for the unusual. Harry is definitely not the boy next door. He's one of a kind."

"You can say that again," Evangeline grumbled. "Don't know how he turned out the way he did. His father was one of the most handsome men I've ever laid eyes on, and his mother looked like a fairy-tale princess. Something obviously went haywire when the two sets of genes combined."

Beads jangled softly.

"Cut me some slack here, Aunt Evie." Harry glided into the tent. "Can't you fake it a little on the tall, dark, and handsome bit? You owe me that much, at least."

Molly spun around in her chair. relieved to see him. "Hi, Harry."

"Hello." Harry let the beaded curtain close behind him.

Evangeline's eyes gleamed with amusement as she rose from her chair. "As I was just explaining to your friend, I never falsify these things. I have my professional standards to uphold. But I will concede that handsome is as handsome does, and beauty is in the eye of the beholder, et cetera."

Harry laughed. "How are you, Aunt Evie?"

"The arthritis has been acting up again, but other than that, I can't complain. Good to see you. Josh said you were going to pay us a visit." She walked around the table, arms outstretched, bells jingling.

Harry accepted Evangeline's enveloping hug with equanimity.

Molly tried to read his face in the gloom. As usual, his expression gave no clue to his feelings. It was impossible to tell how well the interview with his uncle had gone.

Harry glanced at the stack of packages on the floor as his aunt released him. "Not hard to tell where Molly's been. I was afraid of this."

"I found some really terrific kitchen gadgets," Molly said. "Wait until you see them. One slices carrots into cute little baskets, which you can fill with olives and things for an hors d'oeuvre tray. And there's another one that makes little boats out of cucumbers."

Harry's mouth kicked up at the corner. "When was the

last time you felt an overpowering urge to make carrot baskets and cucumber boats?"

Evangeline chuckled. "Don't tease her, Harry. I'm sure she'll enjoy her gadgets."

"Not likely. She's got a kitchen full of high-tech gadgetry that puts this stuff to shame." He glanced at Molly with an indulgent expression. "I warned you not to get suckered by the sales pitches in the exhibition halls."

"Must you be so negative?" Molly retorted. "Not everyone is a con artist, you know."

Harry smiled coolly. "I'm not negative, I'm realistic."

"Sounds like the same thing to me. And for your information, I did not get taken in by fancy sales pitches," Molly said. "I examined the products and watched the demonstrations. I liked what I saw, so I bought some of the items."

"Those hucksters sell nothing but useless junk. Everyone knows that."

"Hah. Every single item is guaranteed for life," Molly informed him triumphantly.

"Is that a fact? And just how are you going to collect on the guarantees?" Harry asked. "When the fair closes, the product demonstrators will vanish. And so will the guarantees."

Molly raised her eyes toward the heavens. "You know what your problem is, Harry? You think everyone in the whole world is out to deceive and defraud."

Evangeline looked at Harry. "You two know each other fairly well, I take it?"

"I know Harry better than he thinks I do," Molly said darkly.

"We've known each other a month," Harry told his aunt. "Molly has a lot to learn."

Evangeline chuckled. "Being the gifted seer that I am, I know who she is. But why don't you introduce us properly?"

"Sorry about that," Harry said. "Evangeline, meet Molly Abberwick. Molly, this is Evangeline Trevelyan. One of my aunts. Best fortune-teller in the family."

"Nice to meet you," Molly said.

"A pleasure." Evangeline sat down at the table, picked up the cards, and reshuffled them. "Let me see, where were we?"

"You were telling her that I was tall, dark, and ugly, I believe." Harry pulled aside a heavy bit of drapery at the back of the tent. He plucked a folding chair out of the shadows.

"What I really wanted to know was how a fortune-teller makes such accurate guesses about her clients," Molly explained. "I realize that some fortunes are generic. Most people want to hear that they'll come into money or find true love. And I suppose it's always safe to say that a client is about to go on a journey since nearly everyone travels at one time or another."

Evangeline's smile twisted wryly. "Your friend has natural talent, Harry."

"What can I say?" Harry crossed the tent with the chair in one hand. "She's smart. A sucker for a sales pitch, maybe, but basically smart."

"Such flattery will get you nowhere." Molly turned back to Evangeline. "I want to know how a fortune-teller or psychic goes beyond the obvious clues. How do you personalize a fortune?"

"She's also got a streak of curiosity a mile wide." Harry dropped the folding chair lightly down next to the table, opened it, reversed it, and straddled it. He rested his arms along the back of the chair. "I'm told it runs in her family."

"Interesting," Evangeline murmured. "Well, my dear, I'm afraid I can't satisfy your curiosity in the matter of telling fortunes. What can I say? There are no secrets. It's a gift."

"Are you talking about the Trevelyan Second Sight?" Molly asked.

"No," Harry said coldly. "She isn't. Because there is no such thing."

Evangeline cocked a disapproving brow. "You should have a bit more respect for the Sight, Harry. After all, you've got more of it than anyone else in the family."

"The hell I do," Harry said.

Molly studied Evangeline intently. "If you won't tell me the tricks of the fortune-telling trade, tell me about the Trevelyan Second Sight."

"Damn," Harry muttered.

"It runs in the family," Evangeline said smoothly. "Harry won't admit he's got a full measure of it. He used to spend some of his summers with us, and I can tell you that I've seen flashes of it in him since he was about twelve. And of course there are the reflexes. He can't deny he got those, too. A genuine throwback to the first Harry Trevelyan."

"Harry told me that his ancestor lived in the early eighteen hundreds," Molly said.

"That's right." Evangeline shuffled the cards with a thoughtful air. "He was sort of an early private investigator. He used to solve crimes and find missing people."

"Did he claim to have psychic powers?" Molly asked.

"No," Evangeline admitted. "He apparently failed to understand his own talent. He wanted to deny it for some reason. But family legend records that he had the Sight. He also had excellent reflexes. We know that because there are some fascinating stories of how he saved his own life and the lives of others when he was confronted by some violent people in the course of his work."

"Fiction," Harry said. "Pure fiction."

Molly ignored him. "Did anyone else in the family become a private investigator?"

"No," Evangeline said. "No money in it. The Trevelyans took their psychic talents to the stage, instead. Mind readers, daredevils, knife throwers. That kind of thing. Every Trevelyan since the first Harry has wanted to believe that he had a touch of the Sight. Some did. Some didn't. The talent tends to skip around a lot."

Molly gave Harry an appraising look. "This Harry does have good reflexes."

"And here I thought you admired me for my brain," Harry said.

Evangeline reshuffled the cards. "In the Trevelyans, the reflexes have always been linked with the gift. The faster the hands, the keener the Second Sight, Granny Gwen always said." She scowled at Harry. "And you have more speed than anyone else in the family, Harry. It broke Granny Gwen's heart when you refused to follow in the Trevelyan tradition."

"In case you haven't guessed," Harry said to Molly, "my sainted great-grandmother, God rest her soul, had a real talent for laying guilt trips on people who didn't do what she wanted them to do. She was mightily irritated when I decided to go after a Ph.D. Granny Gwen wanted me to make a career out of throwing knives or racing cars or jumping off tall towers into little pools of water."

Evangeline gave him a reproving frown. "You're not being fair to your great-grandmother, Harry. It wasn't the fact that you wanted an education that angered and hurt her. It was your refusal to acknowledge the gift of the Sight. She was convinced that you were the first Trevelyan to be born with a complete dose of it since Harry the First."

"Sounds a bit like the Abberwick family talent for invention," Molly mused. "It skips around, too. My sister got it. I didn't."

Harry gave her an odd look. "I'm not so sure of that. Your energy was channeled into building up your business because your family needed a stable income. But I think that successful entrepreneurship is a form of inventive genius. Most people fail at it. You didn't."

Molly was so stunned by the unexpected compliment that she couldn't think of anything to say. She gazed at Harry, aware of a fierce warmth in her face. He smiled his faint, mysterious smile, and the heat descended straight into her lower body.

Evangeline glanced from one to the other with a perceptive gaze. "I think that's enough on the Trevelyan Second Sight. How did it go with the old man, Harry? I know Leon's been sniping at Josh all summer."

"Uncle Leon hasn't changed a bit," Harry said. "But he and I arrived at another one of our little understandings. He'll back off. At least for a while."

Molly heard the ice in his voice. It sent a small shiver through her, melting the sensual warmth.

Evangeline seemed blissfully unaware of the dark chill in Harry's words. She winked at Molly. "Harry has a way of dealing with Leon that none of the rest of the family can match. For some reason Leon will listen to him."

Molly smiled. "Maybe Harry does have some genuine psychic ability." She raised her hands in mock threat. "You know, the power to fog up men's minds, or whatever."

Harry gave her a disgusted look.

"Why do you say that he might actually have the Sight?" Evangeline asked with startling intensity.

Molly leaned back in her chair and shoved her hands into the pockets of her jeans. "It seems to me that Harry changed his own future. And then he changed Josh's. That's got to be a gift of some kind, don't you think? How many people do you know who alter their own destinies and the destinies of others?"

Harry stared at her.

Evangeline slanted him a sidelong glance. "You know, I hadn't thought of it quite that way. She's got a point, Harry."

"The only kind of power I exerted over my future and Josh's was the power of common sense," Harry said.

Molly grinned. "Whatever, it's a heck of a lot more impressive than mumbo jumbo."

Amazingly, Harry turned a dull shade of red.

"Well, now." Evangeline's mouth curved in a knowing smile. "Let's see about the future of your love life, Molly."

"Forget it," Molly advised.

Evangeline ignored her. She peeled a card off the top of the deck and laid it down, face up. "Aha. Here's the blue king again. He's not going to disappear, it seems. When he turns up twice in a row, one must pay attention. It means your love life is about to become very interesting."

"Coincidence. Or a very skillful job of shuffling." Molly got to her feet. "I told you, I'm not interested in having my fortune read." She swept out a hand and scooped up the cards in a single motion.

"Coward," Evangeline murmured.

"No." Harry laughed as he got to his feet. "She's smart."

"Thank you," Molly said demurely.

Evangeline spread her hands in a gesture of surrender. "Very well, I give up. If Molly doesn't want to know about her love life, that's her decision. Harry, when do you intend to start back to Seattle?"

"There's no rush." Harry glanced at his watch. "I want to say hello to Cousin Raleigh and his wife and a few of the other members of the family."

"Raleigh's handling the Ferris wheel." Evangeline idly shuffled the cards. "A word of warning. He wants to borrow money. He and Sheila have a baby on the way."

"I stand warned. Come on, Molly, I'll introduce you to some more of the family."

"All right." Molly looked at Evangeline. "I hope I'll see you again one of these days."

"Something tells me you will," Evangeline said with serene confidence.

Harry helped Molly gather up her packages. Then he paused beside the fortune-telling table. "Take care of yourself, Aunt Evie."

"I will." She smiled up at him. "You do the same. By the way, I'm going to give you a call next week. I want to talk to you about updating the video arcade. It's one of our biggest draws, and you know how quickly those darn games go out of date."

Something indefinable—resignation or perhaps even pain—came and went in Harry's gaze. It vanished immediately, leaving behind a cool, shuttered expression. Molly wanted to reach out and put her arms around him. She wanted to offer comfort, but she was not sure why.

"You know where to reach me, Aunt Evie."

Molly came to a halt beside the table. "Are you sure you won't tell me how you got the blue king to come up twice in a row, Evangeline?"

"Aunt Evie will never reveal a trade secret." Harry picked up the deck of cards and began to shuffle them with practiced grace. "I, on the other hand, have absolutely no professional ethics when it comes to this kind of thing. Here, I'll show you how to make one particular card come up over and over again."

"No, you most definitely will not." Evangeline snatched the deck back from him and put it down on the table. "Not with my cards. Off with you, Harry. You never did have any respect for the business."

"You're right, I never did," Harry agreed.

"You've ruined this deck," Evangeline grumbled as she fingered the cards. "Now I'll have to reorganize it."

Molly studied the deck. "Does that mean that the blue king is no longer on top?"

"Right," Harry said. "I shuffled it the old-fashioned way. If the blue king is on top this time, it's due to pure chance, and the odds are staggeringly against it." He reached down and flipped over the top card to demonstrate.

It was another king, but this one was not blue. It was red.

"Hell," Harry said very softly. The laconic amusement disappeared from his eyes as he looked at the colorful card.

"Oh, dear," Evangeline whispered. She stared at the red king, her attention riveted.

Molly frowned. "What's wrong? It's not the blue king. It's another card altogether."

"Yes, it is." Harry did not take his eyes off the king.

"What's the big deal about the red king?" Molly asked.

"Just a fluke," Harry said quietly.

Evangeline shook her head slowly. "There are no flukes when you deal the cards."

"All right, just for the sake of argument, let's assume that my love life may be about to improve," Molly said, trying to lighten the atmosphere. "Why so glum?"

Evangeline sighed. "This is not the blue king. It's the red king. It has nothing to do with your love life, Molly. When it's the first card in the deck it indicates something else entirely."

"What?" Molly was exasperated.

"Danger." Evangeline switched her veiled gaze to Harry. "Great danger."

Molly scowled. "I don't believe it."

"Very wise of you," Harry said. "It's superstitious nonsense."

"I wouldn't put too much credence in it, myself," Evangeline admitted with surprising honesty. She paused, then said, "If it hadn't been for the fact that it was Harry who shuffled the cards. Promise me that you'll be careful, Harry."

Molly frowned at the red king.

Harry touched her shoulder. "Relax, Molly. It's all an illusion. Smoke and mirrors. Like catching knives or reading minds. Let's go."

**108**

# 7

"**I** saw you write that check for your cousin Raleigh," Molly said as she buckled her seat belt. It was early evening, the summer sun still bright on the horizon.

"Did you?" Harry put on a pair of sunglasses that were so dark they appeared black.

"Yes, I did. You can't deny it."

Harry rested an arm along the back of the seat and turned his head to survey the chaotic parking lot traffic. "Then you know why I don't like to spend a lot of time at the carnival," he said as he eased the Sneath P2 out from under the trees where he had parked it earlier in the day. "Costs a fortune."

Molly smiled. "It was very nice of you."

"Raleigh's okay. He and Sheila aren't very good with money, but they're hard workers."

"How did things go with your uncle?"

"Let's just say we reached an understanding. With any luck it will hold until Josh graduates from college. By then Josh should be able to deal with the old man on his own."

Molly hesitated and then gave in to the compelling curiosity. "I know this is none of my business, but just how did you talk Leon into backing off?"

Harry's eyes were unreadable behind the black sunglasses,

109

but his mouth quirked in a humorless fashion. "A combination of bribery and threats."

"Bribery I can understand. But what sort of threat did you use?"

"One that has enough teeth in it to scare even Leon." Harry shifted gears with a fluid snap and accelerated toward the exit.

Molly opened her mouth to ask for further details, but the words melted away when she saw the grim set of Harry's jaw. Even the force of her Abberwick curiosity was not strong enough to overcome that *no trespassing* warning.

"I see," Molly said.

Harry did not respond. He was wholly absorbed in his driving, as though he were an integral part of the vehicle as well as its master. The black sunglasses gave him a remote, alien quality.

Molly was beginning to recognize the signs. Harry was in one of his moods. He was walking through the dark jungle of his own thoughts, contemplating something he could not or would not discuss with her.

Molly sank back into the seat and watched the rural landscape rush past the windows as the sleek, exotic sports car plunged straight toward the center of the late sun.

After a while she turned and reached behind the seat to scoop up the package of kitchen gadgets she had purchased at the fair. She settled back to read the operating instructions for the Ace Wondermatic All-Purpose Kitchen Appliance.

Seattle was bathed in the last, fading light of the June evening when Harry exited Interstate Five. He drove into the heart of the city, heading toward First Avenue. Slowly he roused himself from the brooding mood that had settled on him.

When he stopped for a red light at Stewart and Third Avenue, he glanced at Molly. He had been comfortably aware of her presence beside him for the last hour, but it suddenly struck him that she hadn't said a word since she

110

had asked him about his meeting with Leon. Then again, he had not been much of a conversationalist, himself.

*Damn.*

A much belated alarm bell sounded somewhere in Harry's brain. Women did not tolerate long silences well. He had learned that lesson from Olivia. Toward the end of the engagement she had complained increasingly about his long bouts of contemplation. The more she had berated him for them, the longer the silences had grown.

Harry wondered if he had screwed up royally this afternoon by failing to carry on a lively conversation during the drive from Hidden Springs. He tried to think of a smooth way to recover whatever ground he had lost through the extended silence.

He cleared his throat when the light changed. "It's nearly eight o'clock." He shifted gears gently. "I'll park the car in the building garage. We can walk to one of the market restaurants for dinner."

Molly turned to look at him, her gaze contemplative rather than accusing. Then she smiled slightly. "All right."

Harry breathed a sigh of relief. He couldn't tell what she was thinking, but at least she was not sulking. He was greatly cheered by the realization that Molly was not the type to hold a little silence against a man. Nevertheless, he felt compelled to apologize for his mood.

"Sorry I haven't been a great conversationalist on this trip." He turned into the alley behind his condominium building and used the remote to open the steel gate. "I was thinking."

"I know. It really bothers you, doesn't it?"

He removed his sunglasses as he drove into the garage. "What bothers me?"

"The way your family insists that you have the famous Trevelyan Second Sight."

"It's damned annoying at times." Harry parked in a numbered slot. "But bear in mind that I only get that nonsense from my Trevelyan relatives. The Strattons think it's total bunk. Which it is."

"But you don't laugh it off." Molly studied his profile as he switched off the ignition. "Whenever the subject comes up, it either angers you or it sets you to brooding."

He shoved open the car door. "If this is a roundabout way of telling me that I bored you to tears on this trip ..."

"It's not." Molly opened her own door and got out. She faced him across the Sneath's roof. "It's merely an observation. The topic of the Trevelyan psychic gifts makes you irritable. Are you going to deny it?"

"I agree it irritates me." In fact, he was getting irritated all over again at this very minute, Harry realized. He made himself shut the car door with exquisite care.

"Do you know why?"

"Because it's so much stupid nonsense." *And because sometimes I'm afraid that it's not nonsense. Sometimes I wonder if it's for real and if the knowing will drive me mad.* Harry drew a deep breath and shoved that chilling thought back into the deepest recesses of his mind.

Molly watched him from the far side of the car. "I think there's more to it than the fact that it violates your sense of academic reason and logic."

Harry's whole body tightened as though preparing for combat. He had known from the beginning that he was taking a risk with this woman.

"Such as?" he asked very casually.

Molly's vivid, intelligent face was thoughtful. "Perhaps all the talk about the Trevelyan family talent reminds you too much of a world that you feel you barely escaped. The world of fake fortune-tellers and daredevils."

Harry relaxed slightly. He rested his arms on the roof of the car. "You may have a point. But I'll let you in on a little secret."

"What's that?"

"If you think I brood whenever the topic of the Trevelyan Second Sight arises, you should see me when I have to listen to one of my Stratton relatives lecture me about how I failed to follow four generations of Stratton men into the corporate world. The real world, where real men are sharks and wolves and other assorted predators and measure their worth by the size of their investment portfolios."

She blinked in astonishment. Then she laughed softly. "How awful. I take it you haven't bothered to please either side of your family?"

"No." Harry was captivated by the amusement dancing in her green eyes. The last ghostly remnants of his latest mood evaporated. He smiled. "The Strattons don't have any more respect for the academic world than the Trevelyans do. Both families think I deliberately chose an effete, ivory-tower life devoted to meaningless academic research and study merely to annoy them. The fact that I've made money at it just irritates them even more."

"We all have our little motivations. So what if it took an overriding desire to annoy your relatives to turn you into a leading authority on the history of science?"

"On the whole, the Stratton complaints about my choice of careers aren't any worse than the Trevelyans'," Harry said. "Uncle Leon takes it a step farther, however. He worries about the genetic implications."

"The genetic implications?"

Harry smiled fleetingly. "He's convinced that my Stratton blood has unmanned me. He thinks it's turned me into a weak, prissy wimp."

"Good grief. No wonder you were feeling a bit moody on the drive home. Have you been juggling the Strattons and the Trevelyans all your life?"

"Yes." He held up a hand to forestall the inevitable question. "Don't ask me why I bother."

"I don't have to ask. None of us chooses our relatives."

Harry reached into the car to collect Molly's purchases. "I'll put these in the trunk while we get something to eat."

After dinner he would find a way to convince Molly to come back to the condo with him for the night, Harry thought as he opened the trunk. There had to be a way to manage that feat. He wanted her more tonight than he ever had. The need in him had metamorphosed into a gnawing hunger.

Perhaps if he had Molly in his bed tonight he would not lie awake thinking about the red king that he had dealt from Evangeline's deck of cards. He hated it when things like that happened.

Intent on furthering his plans for the evening, Harry whisked Molly into the elevator and tapped the lobby button.

A moment later the doors opened to reveal the building lobby. The first thing Harry saw was his ex-fiancée, Olivia. She was striding restlessly back and forth in front of the doorman's station.

"Damn," he said softly.

This situation constituted positive proof that he lacked any shred of psychic talent, he thought grimly. If he'd actually possessed a touch of the Trevelyan Second Sight, surely he would have had a premonition of trouble on the way up from the garage.

At the sight of him, Olivia came to a halt. Her fingers tightened on the strap of her expensive taupe leather shoulder bag. "Harry."

He eyed her warily. Olivia was impeccably turned out, as always. Her tendency toward perfectionism had been one of the things he had admired about her at the start of their relationship. It had implied self-control. It had implied that she was a woman who had answers.

Today she was dressed in a cream silk blouse, soft, rust-colored trousers, and a lightweight beige silk jacket. Her golden hair was drawn back into a refined twist. Her beautiful features were strained with tension. Her gray eyes were shadowed with concern.

Harry heroically resisted an urge to retreat back into the elevator. "Hello, Olivia." He tightened his grip on Molly's hand as he came to a halt in the middle of the lobby. "I'd like you to meet Molly Abberwick. Molly, this is Olivia Hughes. My cousin Brandon's wife."

"How do you do?" Molly said. She gave Olivia a polite smile.

Olivia nodded stiffly. "Hello."

"We were just on our way out to dinner, Olivia," Harry said. "Will you excuse us?"

Olivia's fine brows came together in a determined frown. "Harry, I've been waiting for you for hours. Your housekeeper left at five. She told me that she was sure you'd be home this evening."

"I am home, as you can see, but I've got plans."

Olivia spared another brief glance for Molly and then dismissed her presence. "I want to talk to you. Family business."

"Some other time, Olivia." Harry made to go around her since Olivia showed no indication of moving out of his path.

"Harry, this is very important."

Molly tugged on his arm. "Uh, Harry?"

Olivia's mouth tightened. "I really must speak with you, Harry. The matter won't wait."

Molly gently disengaged her fingers. She smiled very brightly at Harry. "This looks serious. Don't worry about me. I'll take a cab home."

"Damn it, Molly, whatever it is, it can wait. You and I are going out to dinner."

"No." Olivia's voice cracked. "Brandon's future is on the line, Harry. And it's all your fault. You're responsible for this mess. You've got to clean it up."

"Me?" Harry stared at her.

" 'Bye, Harry." Molly backed quickly toward the glass doors. "Thanks for an interesting day."

He started to go after her. Olivia put a restraining hand on his arm.

"I have got to talk to you about this situation," Olivia said urgently. "It won't keep."

"It's okay," Molly called from the glass doorway. "Really. No problem."

Harry looked from one woman to the other. He knew when he was defeated. "I'll have Chris get you a cab, Molly."

"Sure thing, Mr. Trevelyan." Chris, the evening doorman, reached for the phone.

"No need." Molly was halfway out the door. "There's one right across the street. I can see it from here."

Harry took another step toward her and stopped. His hands tightened at his sides. He did not want her to go home alone. He wanted her here with him.

"I'll call you later," he said.

"Don't worry, we'll be in touch," she assured him. "All the kitchen gadgets I bought at the fair are still in your car trunk."

She waved. The heavy glass door swung shut. Harry watched as she scurried across the intersection to the waiting cab.

Molly was gone. He could feel the darkness settle around him.

"You're in one of your moods, aren't you?" Olivia sounded vaguely petulant as Harry ushered her through his front door. "It's depression, you know. You might as well stop pretending it isn't. Denial serves no therapeutic purpose."

"I am definitely in a mood, and it is not a good one." He closed the door and went to stand at the window. The last fragment of the setting sun disappeared behind the Olympics. Night closed in on the city. The old-fashioned round globes of the Pike Place Market streetlights down below cast a golden glow.

Harry tried to spot the cab that was carrying Molly toward the weird old mansion on Capitol Hill, but it was long gone.

"Damn you, Harry, must you always be so self-absorbed? I came here to have a serious conversation with you. The least you can do is pay attention. This is all your fault in the first place."

Harry did not turn around. "I assume this is connected to the conversation I had with Brandon yesterday morning?"

There was a brief, startled pause.

"Brandon talked to you?" Olivia sounded tentative.

"Yes."

"Well? Did you make an effort to convince him not to leave Stratton Properties?"

"He's a full-grown adult. It's his future. His decision. Why should I get involved?"

"Because he would never have come up with this little scheme if it hadn't been for you," Olivia exploded softly. "Damn it, Harry, he's doing this to prove something, not because it's the best thing for our future. I've tried, but I can't get him to take a rational view of the situation."

Harry glanced at her over his shoulder. "What do you think he's trying to prove?"

"That he's as strong and independent as you are." Olivia tossed her purse down onto the sofa with an angry movement of her hand. "He's jealous of you, Harry."

"Jealous? Why the hell should he be jealous? You left me to marry him."

Olivia swung around furiously. "Must you bring that up?"

"Look, I wasn't trying to rehash the past. I was merely pointing out that if there was a competition going on between Brandon and me, he won it."

Olivia flushed. "This isn't about me, it's about stupid masculine pride. Machismo. Balls. Whatever you men call it. It's a potentially destructive urge on Brandon's part. He wants to prove to himself that he's got the same kind of guts you have. He's always secretly admired you for the way you turned your back on the Stratton money. Now he's determined to see if he can make it outside the family, too."

"So? Let him give it a whirl. Where's the harm?"

Olivia's eyes narrowed in outraged fury. "The harm is that his grandfather will punish him for following in your footsteps. We both know it. Parker will cut Brandon out of the will. Danielle is on the edge of a nervous breakdown because of this. She sacrificed a great deal for Brandon's sake, and now it's about to go up in smoke."

"I didn't know people still had nervous breakdowns,' Harry mused. "I though you psychologists had more modern terms for that condition.'

Olivia's face was tight and bleak. "This is not a joke, Harry."

"And this is not my problem."

"It most certainly is. You caused it by being a role model for Brandon."

"I didn't set out to be anyone's role model," he said very softly.

Olivia flinched. "Please, Harry, don't speak to me in that tone of voice. You know it upsets me."

Harry drew a deep breath. "I thought I was being remarkably civil under the circumstances."

"When you're in one of your moods, every word you utter sounds as though it had been dug out of a glacier."

Harry clasped his hands behind his back. "Just what do you expect me to do, Olivia?"

"Talk to Brandon. Make him see that leaving Stratton Properties is not a wise move."

"He's not likely to listen to me if he's in the middle of trying to prove something."

"The least you can do is try to talk him out of this. Harry, you've got to do something before he goes too far with his plans. Parker will never forgive him if he walks away from Stratton Properties the way you did. Danielle will be crushed. And Brandon will ultimately be sorry he made a mistake of this magnitude."

*So that was the ex-fiancée.*

Molly sat down at the kitchen table with a plate of spinach ravioli laced with Parmesan, fresh basil leaves, and olive oil. She forked up two of the ravioli and considered the stack of new grant proposals in front of her.

Surely she could find one out of this lot that would pass muster with Harry.

*Olivia was certainly pretty. No, that was putting it mildly. She was lovely.*

Molly munched ravioli and wondered what had gone wrong between Harry and Olivia.

*Hours of boredom broken by moments of stark terror.*

Olivia had not appeared terrified of Harry this evening. She had looked like a woman who had a claim on his time and attention. Molly wondered what had drawn the two together in the first place. Olivia certainly didn't look to be Harry's type. Of course, Molly reflected, her own opinion on that subject was definitely biased.

She took another bite of ravioli and turned a page. It was pointless to speculate. The bottom line was that in the end Olivia had married Harry's cousin, Brandon Stratton Hughes.

It was certainly interesting that Olivia had come to Harry for help with whatever family problem had caused her so much concern, though.

Molly pushed the haunting thoughts aside. She forced herself to concentrate on the summary page of the grant proposal that lay open on the table in front of her.

The old house hunkered down for the night with a sigh and a few creaks and groans. A distant hum from the floor above indicated that a cleaning robot was going about its duties.

After a while Molly took a break to put her dishes onto the conveyer belt that would whisk them through the patented Abberwick Dishwasher. When the machine was finished, the dishes would all be automatically stacked and stored.

Molly was concentrating on a proposal for an emission-free engine design when the cleaned dishes emerged from the machine. She did not look up as the rubber-coated mechanical arms stacked the plate neatly in the adjacent cupboard.

"Are you seriously involved with Molly Abberwick?" Olivia asked as she picked up her purse.

Harry turned away from the window. "Yes."

"You're sleeping with her?"

"That's none of your business," Harry said.

Olivia had the grace to look embarrassed. "No, I suppose

it isn't. I just wondered if there were any, uh, complications."

"Complications?"

"The sort you and I had," Olivia said brusquely.

"Ah, yes. That sort. As I recall, you said I made you nervous."

"There's no need to be sarcastic. I'm only trying to help."

Harry eyed her with some surprise. "How?"

"I've told you that I think you're suffering from posttraumatic stress disorder because of the manner in which your parents died," Olivia said quietly. "It's not an unusual reaction to serious trauma. I wish you would call Dr. Shropton. He's had a lot of experience treating the disorder. And there's medication that can help."

"I'll keep that in mind."

"You're not going to do a damn thing about it, are you?" Olivia asked in a burst of fresh anger. "You won't seek professional help. You won't discuss your dysfunctional behavior. You won't even admit you have a problem."

"Look, Olivia—"

"Let me tell you something, Harry. As a professional, I can guarantee you that your problems won't get any better if you persist in denying their very existence. They'll ruin your relationship with Molly Abberwick, just as they ruined our relationship."

"Thanks for the warning," Harry said. "But I don't think we can blame my personality defects entirely on the fact that our relationship fizzled."

"Don't you dare try to tell me that you ever loved me, Harry. Whatever you felt for me, it wasn't love."

He stilled. "Did you love me?"

"I tried," Olivia whispered valiantly. "I really did try, Harry."

"Noble of you." He knew of no way to tell her that he had tried to love her, too. She would never comprehend that it was his very attempt to do so that made her flee the engagement. *Moments of stark terror.*

"It was hopeless," Olivia said. "You're not free to love

anyone, Harry. For a while I thought perhaps we could work things out. I thought if you would only learn to communicate. If you could develop some empathy. Share your feelings. Get out of denial. But it was impossible."

"Yes, I suppose it was."

"And then the sex got . . . well, it got weird, Harry. You know it did."

Harry felt his insides grow cold. "I'm sorry." There was nothing else to say.

"I know you didn't intend to scare me, but you did. At first you were so distant, so cold in bed. I felt as if a robot were making love to me, not a man."

Harry closed his eyes.

"And then, that last time that we were together, you seemed to lose control or something. It was overwhelming." Olivia groped for words. "Terrifying, if you want the truth. I realized afterward that we had to end the engagement."

Harry vowed he would not make the same mistake with Molly.

He was well aware that women who became involved with him labeled him difficult. Over the years he had heard all the tearful accusations. He was too distant, too remote, too uncommunicative, too cold.

Until Olivia, Harry's infrequent relationships had all floundered on the rocky shoals of boredom or exasperation. But with Olivia, he had given in to a growing sense of desperation. He was in his mid-thirties. The longing for a true bond with a woman had grown so strong within him that he had succumbed to temptation. He had carefully, cautiously, opened himself ever so slightly to Olivia.

The result had been a disaster. She was right. The sex got weird.

Harry knew it was his own fault. So long as he maintained a certain emotional distance in the relationship—so long as things were limited to the physical and the intellectual—he could keep matters under control.

But there were those bleak moments when he craved something else, something he could not name. And those moments came with increasing frequency of late. More than any vampire hungering for blood, he longed for a dark consummation that he could not even comprehend.

Not only were the moments of need coming over him more often, plunging him into darker moods than any he had known in the past, they were more intense. A fear that had once been remote and easily repressed, the fear of going insane, was beginning to surface with alarming regularity. Each time it appeared it took more strength of will to crush it.

The kitchen phone rang just as Molly finished the last page of the final grant proposal. She reached across the table and picked up the receiver.

"Hello?"

"Did you get dinner?" Harry asked without preamble.

Molly smiled. "Yes, thanks. I'm perfectly capable of feeding myself."

"I know."

Molly frowned. "Are you all right? You sound weird?"

"Do me a favor and don't call me weird. Call me arrogant, pedantic, stubborn, or any of the other things you like to call me, but not weird, okay?"

"Okay. You don't sound weird. You sound weary. That's what I meant to say. Weary. What's wrong?"

"Olivia left a few minutes ago."

"Hmm."

"My cousin Brandon has decided to quit his job with the family firm. She wants me to talk him out of it."

"I see." Molly hesitated. "Can you do that?"

"I doubt it. I'm not sure I should even try. Can we reschedule dinner for tomorrow night?"

Molly hesitated.

"Please," Harry said quietly.

"Fine I'll look forward to it. Oh, by the way, Harry, I just finished going through the newest stack of grant proposals, and I think I've found some really exciting prospects. I can't wait for you to take a look at them."

"Neither can I."

"You don't sound genuinely enthusiastic."

"I will be by tomorrow night."

"Right. It's been a very long day."

"Yes. Good night, Molly." Harry paused. "Thanks for making the trip to Hidden Springs with me."

"I had a great time. I think Kelsey is right. I should get away more often. Good night, Harry."

Molly hung up the phone very slowly. She sat quietly for a while, listening to the sounds of the house. They were comfortable, familiar, soothing sounds. They were the sounds of home.

She thought about Kelsey's advice to sell the mansion. It was probably the logical thing to do. But for some reason Molly could not envision such a move.

After a time she put the last grant proposal on the pile and rose from the table. The lights in the kitchen winked off as she walked out of the room.

She climbed the curved staircase and went down the hall to her bedroom.

A short time later, she slipped into bed. She folded her arms behind her head and gazed up into the shadows for a long time. Eventually she turned on her side and fell asleep.

Her dreams were an eerie collage of red kings, knives, and unseen menace. A muted whirring sound broke into them, exacerbating the sense of threat.

It took Molly's sleep-drugged brain a few seconds to register the fact that the noise was not part of her dream. When she finally realized that something was wrong, fear sliced into her consciousness, bringing her fully awake.

Molly opened her eyes in an instant of explosive terror. A dark figure cloaked in layers of black fabric was rising from the floor beside her bed. She had a glimpse of a skeletal face, yawning holes where eyes should have been, and a clawed hand.

Molly was paralyzed. A scream got trapped in her throat.

The figure leaned over the bed. The mechanical whirring grew louder. The clawed hand lifted in a jerky fashion.

The instinct for survival unlocked Molly's frozen limbs. She shoved aside the quilt and managed to roll off the far side of the bed.

She hit the floor with a jarring thud, scrambled to her feet, and ran for the door.

The hall lights came on automatically in response to her frantic movements. Molly glanced back over her shoulder to see how close her pursuer was.

That was when she realized that the thing from under the bed had not moved to follow her. It still hovered over the rumpled sheets, clawed hand frozen in midair. The whirring sound ceased abruptly, as though a switch had been turned off.

"Oh, no," Molly whispered. "Not again."

# 8

The shrill ringing of the phone cut into a dream in which Harry was dealing from a deck of cards that contained nothing but red kings. He knew he had to find the queen or all was lost. But the damn phone kept interrupting his concentration.

He stirred and reached for the receiver with a mixture of irritation and foreboding. He glanced at the clock. It was nearly one in the morning. Calls at this hour invariably meant trouble.

"Trevelyan here." He hauled himself up against the pillows. At least he was out of the dream. *For a while.*

"Harry, it's me. Molly."

The breathless tremor in her voice had the impact of cold water on all his senses. Harry was suddenly wide awake. Every muscle in his body hardened with battle-ready tension. "What's wrong?"

"Something very strange has just happened. Remember the fake gun that someone left outside my door the other evening?"

"Hell, yes."

"Well, I think that whoever set up that prank has just played another one on me."

"Bastard," Harry whispered. He tightened his grip on the phone. "As bad as the first?"

"It was similar to the first one, but I have to admit this one was a lot more effective. I don't think I've ever been so frightened in my entire life."

"Are you all right?" Harry was already out of bed, heading across the room toward the closet.

"Yes, I'm fine. It was harmless. Just very scary." Molly hesitated. Her voice dropped to a low, apologetic mumble. "Sorry for bothering you. I don't know why I called you. I dialed your number without really thinking about it."

"It's all right." Harry cradled the phone between his shoulder and ear while he yanked open the closet door.

"I shouldn't have called at this hour."

"I said forget it. I'm on my way." Harry pulled on the first pants he found, a pair of olive-green chinos. "I'll be there as soon as I get the car out of the garage."

"Thanks." Relief was audible in Molly's voice.

"This time we notify the cops."

"Now, Harry, I don't want to do anything rash. I'm sure this is just another practical—"

"I'll see you in a few minutes." He tossed the phone into the cradle, grabbed a shirt, slid his feet into worn running shoes, and headed for the door.

He refused to think about the red king.

The streets were empty. Within ten minutes of leaving his garage, Harry drove through the massive wrought-iron gates that guarded the aging monstrosity Molly called home. The gates had been unlocked from inside the house.

He surveyed the old house as he shut off the engine. Light glowed in every window, including the peaked attic. Molly must have gone through each room and switched on every single lamp.

Whoever had pulled this stunt had definitely succeeded in scaring Molly. The perpetrator had probably not counted on the secondary effect he'd achieved, Harry thought as he loped up the front steps. The bastard had not yet realized that he'd also gotten her consultant's full attention.

He would not leave Molly here alone tonight, Harry promised himself. He didn't care how much she argued. She was coming back to his condominium until he could decide how to deal with the situation.

The front door opened just as he raised his hand to pound on it. Molly stood there, silhouetted by the hall light. She clutched the lapels of an oversized white terry-cloth bathrobe in one hand. Her hair looked as though it had been through an explosion. Her eyes were huge and shadowed.

"Harry." She stared at him for an instant as though not quite certain what to do next.

Before Harry realized her intent, she hurled herself straight into his arms and buried her face against his shoulder.

He caught her close.

She had called him. She needed him. She was right here in his arms. Where she was supposed to be.

The dark longing gathered within him, seeking that which it could not have, that which it would inevitably destroy.

Harry sucked in air. With a savage act of will he got a grip on himself and the wild emotions that threatened to sweep through him. He would not allow the hunger to gain control. There was too much at stake. He could not risk terrifying Molly. He must not lose her.

"It's all right. I'm here." Gently he set Molly away from him. It was not easy. Her arms seemed to be locked around his neck.

Reluctantly Molly raised her face to look at him. "Thank you for coming. I really appreciate it. I shouldn't have bothered you."

"Forget it." Harry searched her eyes and relaxed slightly. She was flushed, but not with fear of him.

He saw that her robe had parted, revealing an incredibly innocent-looking white nightgown trimmed with a delicately scalloped neckline. Her breasts rose gently above the scallops. Her nipples, visibly erect, were pressed against the gossamer fabric. Harry flexed his hands and listened to his blood as it roared through his veins.

Molly glanced down, blushed, and hastily secured the robe. "Come in. I'll make some tea."

Harry realized his fingers were trembling slightly. He stepped across the threshold and closed the door.

"It's every kid's worst nightmare. The monster under the bed." Molly poured tea from a white earthenware pot. The one thing she took care to prepare by hand was tea. There was something about good tea that demanded the personal touch. No machine, not even one of her father's kitchen appliances or Kelsey's gadgets, could prepare tea properly. "And I reacted just like a kid. Scared the beejeebies out of me."

"Someone got the effect he wanted." Harry surveyed the remains of the mechanical horror that he had spread out on the stainless-steel kitchen table.

Molly had watched as he dissected the creature with the finesse of a jeweler removing precious stones from a necklace. One by one Harry had taken apart the pieces of the device that had rolled out from under her bed.

Displayed in the bright kitchen light, the cheap black fabric, Halloween mask, and assorted mechanical components did not look very frightening. Molly was a little chagrined.

"I guess I overreacted," she said. "The pistol prank didn't bother me very much, but this one really got to me."

"It was meant to get to you." Harry held a gear up to the light to study it. "This thing was more of a threat than the pistol. It was right inside your house. Inside your bedroom. I think whoever is behind these incidents is deliberately trying to rev up the fear factor."

Molly shuddered. She searched Harry's grim face, trying to determine just how serious he was.

The answer was clear. He was very serious. She could feel the waves of focused energy emanating from him.

"I still can't believe that these incidents are meant to be anything more than nasty pranks, though," Molly said. She poked at the awkwardly constructed steel claw. It was composed of five metal rods thrust through holes cut in the fingers of a tattered black glove. "I wonder how he got into the house to set it up?"

"Did you check for open windows or unlocked doors?"

Molly huddled deeper into her robe. "I went through every room before you got here. There's no sign of forced entry. All the doors and windows were locked. The security system was on."

"The device was probably installed under your bed earlier today. Which leaves us with a couple of possibilities." Harry picked up the Halloween mask. "Whoever is doing this either knows you well enough to know your security code—"

"Impossible," Molly said quickly. "Kelsey and I have always been extremely careful. She wouldn't give out the code to anyone, not even a friend. And neither would I."

Harry got to his feet. "Then we're looking for someone who's good enough to bypass your household security system."

Molly looked up at him. "Good enough?"

"I guess I should say bad enough. Whoever he is, he's caused enough trouble tonight. Go upstairs and pack a bag. I'm taking you home with me."

*"Home."* She shot up out of her chair so quickly that it started to topple over backward.

"Right." Harry deftly caught the chair before it clattered to the floor. He righted it without even glancing at it. "Home to my place. You can spend the night there. In the morning we'll talk about what to do next."

Molly was torn. A part of her dreaded the prospect of spending the rest of the night by herself. But another part was reluctant to admit that things had become so serious that she had to leave her home.

"I appreciate the offer, but I don't want to put you to any trouble," she said. "I doubt if it's necessary. This was probably just another stupid prank. I can't believe that whoever set this thing would actually come back here tonight."

"Trust me." Harry urged her gently but determinedly toward the hall stairs. "It's necessary."

"Why?"

"For my peace of mind," Harry said.

"Oh." She couldn't think of an adequate rebuttal to that.

"I want to think on this for a while tonight. In the morning we'll file a report with the cops."

"Fat lot of good that's going to do. Investigating stupid practical jokes must rank right at the bottom of their list of priorities," Molly muttered.

"I know. But I want this incident on record."

He did not elaborate, but Molly knew what he was thinking. Harry wanted the prank reported because he believed that there would be more of them and that they might become increasingly dangerous.

An hour and a half later Harry stood alone in his darkened living room. He listened carefully, but there was no sound from the guest bedroom. Molly had finally gone to sleep.

He gazed out through the wall of windows that separated him from the night and considered the small gear assembly he held in his hand. It seemed to smolder with a heat only he could detect.

He prepared to concentrate. Really concentrate.

He had not wanted to do this. He had not opened himself to this kind of intense contemplation since the day Wild Willy Trevelyan had been killed in the motorcycle stunt. Harry reminded himself that he had not liked the truth that his *insights* had revealed on that occasion. He might not like whatever truth he gleaned from tonight's contemplation, either.

He certainly did not relish the sensation that he knew would accompany the exercise. He felt excruciatingly vulnerable whenever he experienced even small flashes of insight. The deeper exploration he intended to try for tonight would be far worse. He could expect to question his own sanity before it was over. He hated the fear that was waiting for him in the darkness of his own mind.

But he had to take the chance. His need for answers was stronger than his terror of going mad.

Harry plunged himself into the deepest level of thought. It was akin to sinking into a whirling void, a place at the farthest reaches of the galaxy. The trick was to avoid traveling too far into the darkness. Somewhere out there the abyss awaited him.

His concentration became so intense that he lost all sense of his surroundings. He was no longer in his own living room. He was part of the night outside the windows.

The metal burned into his palm. Something inside him screamed a silent warning, not about the mechanical gear he held, but about what was happening to his personal fortifications. He had forged those internal barriers over a period of years, working by instinct alone, not fully aware of what he was trying to accomplish.

It was not until he was well into his twenties that he had begun to comprehend that he was attempting to build a wall at the edge of the abyss.

He had done his work well, considering the fact that he had no model from which to work. Over the years he had learned to use the shallow reaches of the intense state of concentration that his mind was capable of producing. For the most part, he pretended not to see the dark depths below.

But tonight he was going to reach down into them in a search for answers.

Carefully, cautiously, he dismantled the barriers that protected him from the dangers of the abyss.

There were few things Harry feared in life, but the feeling that descended upon him now was definitely one of them. The lack of control that accompanied the complete eradication of his inner fortress was the price he had to pay to accomplish his aims.

He stood at the window, staring out into the night, and

let the vibrations of awareness flood his mind. He gave himself up to the process of *knowing*.

The darkness on the other side of the window flowed into the living room and wrapped itself around him.

Harry closed his eyes and tightened his grasp on the small gear in his hand. There was something important here. Something he needed to comprehend in order to help Molly.

He saw the abyss. And the glass bridge that spanned it. He could not see the other side. He had never been able to see it. He had never allowed himself to cross the bridge. Only rarely had he even risked stepping out onto it.

He did not know what awaited him on the far side of the abyss, but he knew with great certainty that madness lay below. He took a tentative step out onto the glass bridge. *Don't look down,* he told himself. *Just don't look down.*

"Harry?"

From out of nowhere the hunger rose within him, devastating his severely weakened defenses.

"Harry, are you all right?" Molly's voice was a whisper of sound in the distance. It reached through the endless night that surrounded him.

She was here in the living room. Right behind him.

*No. Leave. Go back to your bed. For God's sake, don't come near me. Not now.*

But the words were trapped in his mind. He could not utter them aloud.

"Is something wrong, Harry?"

*Yes. Yes. Yes.*

He could not form the words with his tongue. His body would not obey his commands. Harry staggered as he turned to face Molly.

He watched her walk toward him through the shadows and knew a savage despair. He was too far out on the glass bridge. He could not control the desperate, questing need within himself.

Balanced on the knife-thin edge of glass, Harry glimpsed the opposite shore of the abyss. He suddenly understood why he had always crushed any speculation of what might await him there. It was better not to contemplate too closely that which he could not possess.

Longing, fierce and intense, clawed his insides.

"Are you all right?" Molly came to a halt in front of him. She was cloaked in the white robe she'd brought with her. Her hair was loose and gloriously wild. Her eyes were crystal clear, fathomless pools in the moonlight.

Harry gathered himself for a Herculean effort. He finally managed to get his tongue to function. "Go back to bed."

"Good heavens, there is something wrong, isn't there?" She raised her hand to touch his face with sensitive fingertips. "Lord, you're burning up. I think you've got a fever. You should have said something earlier. I had no idea you were ill. You had no business coming to my rescue in this condition. You should be in bed."

"No," he croaked. The glass on which he was so precariously balanced shuddered beneath him. He could not retreat. He could not go forward. In another few minutes the bridge would surely shatter. "I'm okay. Leave me alone."

"Don't be silly. I can't do that." She took his free hand and turned to lead him down the hall. "I'm going to put you to bed and find a thermometer. Why didn't you tell me you weren't feeling well?"

"I'm. Not. Sick."

She paid no attention to his weak protest. She started toward his bedroom. Harry was helpless to resist the gentle tug on his hand. It drew him as surely as if she had bound him with magic.

He struggled to regain his normal, rational level of awareness. But it was too late. Molly's touch had drawn him farther out over the abyss. The hunger to discover what lay on the other side was too strong to deny.

"Here we are." Molly guided him into his bedroom. She released his hand to turn down the bed.

She had her back to him. Harry was enthralled by the nape of her neck. Never had he seen anything so lovely. He was literally entranced by the delicate curve. He took a step toward Molly, hand outstretched to touch her.

And stumbled over his own feet.

"Now I know you really are ill," Molly said as she steadied him. "Usually you move like one of those fish in the aquarium in your study."

"A fish?" Anguish flared in him. Fish were cold and emotionless creatures. Maybe Molly thought he was incapable of a normal human response. Maybe she had already seen the craziness in him.

"You know." Molly waved a hand. "You sort of glide along very slowly as if you were floating through the sea. Then, every once in a while, *flash*, you move so fast it startles me."

"Flash." Relief seared him. She was talking about the way he moved, not his mental state.

"In the whole time I've known you, I've never seen you lose your balance or stumble until tonight. Don't worry, I'm sure it's just the fever upsetting your equilibrium. You'll be fine in the morning."

Harry shook his head. He could not even begin to explain what was happening to him. He did not understand it himself. Thus far Molly seemed oblivious to the savage battle he was waging, but he knew that stage would not last long. In a few more minutes she would understand that there was something strange in him.

Molly reached out to switch on a light beside the bed.

He stood there, swaying slightly, and fought to regain his self-control. But the hunger was too strong. Molly looked more inviting than any woman had ever looked since Eve.

She was the woman who waited for him on the opposite side of the abyss.

Harry's insides were raw with the churning need.

Molly finished fussing with the bed. She turned toward him, her spectacular eyes shadowed. The concern was for him, he realized with a sense of wonder. She was not yet afraid of him. She was worried about him.

He could do nothing now to stave off disaster. He knew that in another few seconds she would begin to sense the overwhelming desire in him. She would know that it was unnatural, even though it felt completely natural to him.

She would be terrified. She would pull away from him as though he were some alien monster.

Molly would run from him as Olivia had, and because he was so very vulnerable tonight, Harry was not certain that he would survive her complete and total rejection. He would fall from the glass bridge and fall forever.

He was doomed.

"Let me help you with your shirt." Molly's hands moved lightly over his chest, seeking buttons.

Harry shuddered violently as she touched him.

"You're shivering." She paused briefly to study him more closely. "Are you cold?"

"No. Hot. Very hot." *And getting hotter.*

"I'll get you something to drink in a minute." She bent her head as she resumed the task of removing his shirt.

Her tousled hair tickled his nose. It was the most delightful sensation Harry had ever experienced. He inhaled the flowery scent of her shampoo. He took a deeper breath and drew in the underlying fragrance of her body. It was the essence of femaleness, and it riveted everything that was male in him.

She was seducing him as surely as if she had dressed in seven veils and thumped a tambourine, but she did not have a clue.

Harry groaned. An object fell to the carpet with a soft thud. He realized dimly that he had dropped the gear that he had carried from the front room. There had been something important about that gear. Something he needed to know.

But Molly had his shirt undone now, and he could no longer think about the gear. Her fingers were brushing against his bare chest. *God, such sweet, warm, soft fingers.* She was branding him with her touch.

"Molly." Her name was a plea, a prayer, and a curse. The last because he knew that his fate was sealed. He would surely lose her tonight.

"It's all right," she murmured gently. "You'll be fine. Did this fever come on quite suddenly?"

"Yes." And it was going to be the death of him.

She pursed her lips in a considering expression. "It may be food poisoning."

There was only one cure now for the fire that would soon consume him. The glass edge shivered again beneath his feet. Disaster loomed.

Molly's fingers went to his shoulders now to ease aside his shirt. Her touch warmed his bare skin to the flash point. His hands shook. The searing heat rose within him. He was harder than he had ever been in his life.

His shirt fluttered to the carpet.

Molly looked into his eyes. "You're so warm. I'd better get that glass of water."

Harry seized the chance to break the dangerous spell she had woven so unwittingly. "Yes."

"I'll get it. Sit down, Harry, before you fall down. No offense, but you look terrible."

"Yes." She hated the way he looked. It was starting. Soon she would fear him. Despair seized Harry.

He sank down on the edge of the bed and tried to pull himself together while Molly went into the adjoining bath. He lowered his head into his hands and strove to center himself.

*Get off the glass bridge. Rebuild the walls.*

Water ran in the sink.

*Faster, you fool. You'll lose her.*

But he could not retreat. It was too late.

"Here you are," Molly said softly. "Drink this, and then get straight into that bed."

Harry opened his eyes. He did not lift his head. The first thing he saw through his splayed fingers was the drawer in the bedside table. Early this morning, in an optimistic moment, he had taken the box of condoms from the bathroom and put it into the little drawer.

Molly moved to stand in front of him, blocking his view of the drawer. She thrust a glass into his fingers.

He very nearly dropped it.

"Careful," Molly said.

He managed to down the water, but it did nothing to assuage the fire. He wished it had been whiskey or brandy. Alcohol might have taken the edge off the erection that threatened to rip a hole in his pants.

"Thanks." He realized his voice sounded as if his tongue had been dragged across sandpaper.

"Maybe I should call the emergency room to get some advice."

"No. No, please. Don't call anyone."

"Okay." She knelt in front of him to untie his shoes.

Harry stared at the folds of the white robe as it eddied around her. It made him think of a bridal gown. Molly looked both sensuous and chaste. The combination was electrifying.

"I know you're the independent type." Molly tugged off one shoe. "But you may as well accept the fact that you need help tonight. You're sick, Harry."

"So they tell me."

It struck him that the reason she had not taken to her heels yet was because she still attributed his odd behavior to a bad case of food poisoning.

The sight of Molly kneeling in front of him was the most erotic vision Harry had ever had. He imagined her unzipping his pants, lifting him free with her hands, dampening his hot skin with her tongue.

"Take it easy, Harry." Molly slipped off the other shoe. "We've almost got you into bed."

"Yes." It would be his coffin by dawn. He could not survive what was bound to happen.

"You'll feel better in the morning."

"No."

"Of course you will." She paused suddenly, staring at the small leather sheath strapped to his ankle.

Harry wanted to explain the knife. He wanted to tell her that it was more than family tradition. He wanted to tell her everything. But that meant telling her the full truth about his parents and how they had died and how he'd been too late to save them. He could not even begin to tackle that subject in his present state. He wondered if the sight of the blade would turn her away from him.

Without a word, Molly unbuckled the sheath and put it on the bedside table. Then she rose, put one hand on his shoulder, and pushed him gently backward.

He fell against the pillows with all the light, airy grace of a bull elephant going over a cliff. He lay there and watched helplessly as Molly bent over him. The white robe parted slightly, revealing a bit of the scalloped neckline of her gown. He licked his dry lips and fought for words.

"Please." It was all he could say.

"What is it?" she asked. "What do you want?"

"You."

She blinked. A fiery flush crept into her cheeks. "Harry, you're ill."

"No. I'm not sick. Not the way you mean. I want you. Please."

She leaned over the bed to put her hand on his forehead. "It's the fever. You're delirious."

"No. Touch me." He flung out an arm. He managed to capture her wrist before she could remove her hand from his head. "Here." He moved her fingers to his erection. "Make love to me."

She went very still.

She would run from him now, Harry thought. This was it. The end.

"Harry?" Her eyes were green gems warmed by an inner fire.

"This is what's wrong with me," he whispered harshly. "Not food poisoning. I want you so much. So damned much."

"Oh, Harry."

She was about to panic. Harry was sure of it. In another instant she would flee. He could do nothing to stop her.

"Don't go," he whispered.

Her fingers closed tentatively over the bulge in his pants.

**138**

Harry thought he would go up in flames. Then she straightened slowly. Her eyes never left his face. This was it, he realized bleakly. She had finally seen the weirdness in him. She would leave him here alone in the darkness.

The white robe fell to the carpet. It was followed by the white nightgown.

Harry drank in the sight of Molly's nude body. The vision threatened to swamp all his senses. Moonlight gleamed softly on the curves of her small, high breasts and the lush flare of her thighs. The dark triangle of hair that shielded her secrets mesmerized him.

She came to him.

*She came to him.*

For a split second Harry did not understand. He had been so certain she would run.

"Molly?" he gasped.

She settled slowly on him like soft, warm tropical rain. She brushed her mouth gently, tentatively across his. He could feel her breasts pressed against his chest.

She was making love to him.

The last remnants of his control vanished. Harry broke into a headlong run across the glass bridge, heedless now of the threat that lay below. All he cared about was reaching the opposite shore of the abyss.

He wrapped Molly in his arms, turned her, and crushed her into the bedding. He heard her soft, startled cry, and then she was clinging to him, clutching wildly at his shoulders. He felt her nails on his back.

He reached down between her legs, thrust his fingers through the soft hair and found her hot and wet and ready for him. He vaguely recalled the condom in the drawer beside the bed. He groped for the knob of the drawer. He could not seem to get hold of it.

Clumsy. So impossibly clumsy. Not like him. "Damn."

"I'll get it." Molly sounded breathless as she reached out to open the drawer for him.

He fumbled around inside. Found the box. Found the packet.

*Foreplay.* The voice inside his head was very insistent. Women liked foreplay. Lots of foreplay.

"What's wrong?" Molly sounded frantic, but eager. Definitely eager. Not terrified.

"Foreplay," Harry muttered. "Supposed to be foreplay."

"We can do it later, can't we? Make it afterplay." She yanked at his zipper. "Harry, I can't wait. I've never felt like this."

He sucked in his breath as she jerked open his pants. But no damage was done. His hand shook so violently he could not unroll the condom. Molly had to help him.

He watched her frown intently over the task. Her sweet awkwardness was electrifyingly erotic. Each tug, each touch, each delicate fumble translated into a caress that threatened to make him explode.

Then he was finally, achingly ready, and she was waiting for him, reaching for him. She wanted him.

The wonder of it stole his breath. She wanted *him*, weirdness and all.

Molly lifted herself, opening for him, inviting him into her warmth. The hot, moist, womanly scent of her body took him on a journey to the heart of creation.

Harry covered her mouth with fierce urgency. Her lips parted for him. He drove himself into her body, pushing past the resistance of her delicate muscles. She was tight. Unbelievably tight. Then he was inside, and she was holding him so snugly that he could not tell where his body ended and hers began.

He moved within her, sinking deeper and deeper into her welcoming heat. Her legs closed around him. He felt her nails score his shoulders.

Molly screamed softly, a passionate cry of release that Harry knew he would never forget as long as he lived. It was the most beautiful song in the world.

But there was little time to savor the erotic notes. The tiny tremors of her climax tugged at him, demanding that he follow her into the vortex.

He could not have resisted even had he wanted to try. And resisting Molly's sweet summons was the last thing he wished to do.

Harry raced off the far end of the glass bridge and landed on the opposite shore of the abyss.

He was safe. Molly was there with him.

# 9

This was what came of taking chances.

Molly opened her eyes to a wall of morning light. It poured through the windows, flooding the bedroom.

So that's what making love with Dr. Harry Stratton Trevelyan felt like.

She smiled. Then she grinned. There was nothing quite so deeply fulfilling for an Abberwick as having her curiosity satisfied.

Molly suppressed an exuberant giggle with some difficulty. She had certainly never had her curiosity satisfied the way it had been last night. Her whole body seemed to be purring this morning.

She stretched, propped herself on one elbow, and regarded Harry as he slept beside her. The intimate sight sent a shiver of excitement through her. He was spectacular. A magnificent male beast. Of course he wasn't handsome. Handsome did not even begin to describe him. Handsome was a ridiculously weak, soft, trivial word for such an outstanding specimen of manhood. He was wonderful. He was the most fascinating man on earth.

Even sprawled facedown amid the rumpled sheets, Harry retained an aura of masculine grace. The muscles of his shoulders and back were sleekly contoured with unmistakable strength. His alchemist's hands looked powerful against the white linens. The harsh, exotic lines of his face were etched with the potential for passion and relentless will, even though his brilliant eyes were temporarily veiled behind closed lashes.

Molly laughed silently at her own extravagantly romantic flight of fancy. She was obviously falling in love. Probably already there. So what? she thought. She had waited long enough for the right man to come along, long enough to take a chance.

The responsibilities that had been a part of her for years suddenly seemed weightless. She had never felt more free in her life.

She reflected on the revelations the night had brought. She now knew for certain that Harry's capacity for passion and his seemingly inexhaustible, implacable will were tempered by a startling vulnerability.

She would never forget the look in his eyes last night when he had pleaded with her to make love to him. He obviously had not realized the depth of her feelings, or he would have known that there was no need to beg. He would have to be insensate not to know it now.

She recalled the stoic lack of hope that she had seen in him during those first fragile moments. The bleakness in his gaze had baffled her. It still did. It was as though he had offered himself to her with the expectation of being rejected.

A man like Harry did not willingly make himself vulnerable. He had been in a very strange mood, even for him, last night.

She thought about the damp sweat that had glistened on his forehead and the strained lines of his face. The intense heat of his body had alarmed her initially. When she had found him standing alone in the darkness she had been convinced he was ill. Yet he had denied it. Then he had proven just how healthy he was by making love to her with driving vitality.

Odd. Very odd.

Molly considered the situation. Granted, her experience

in these matters was somewhat limited, but common sense told her that, whatever had been wrong with Harry last night, he had not been suffering from food poisoning.

The precise instant when he had surged into her for the first time would be engraved on her memory forever. It seemed to her that it had been far more than a simple act of passion. It was as if he had bound himself to her in that moment.

The experience had exhausted both of them. They had fallen asleep immediately after their bodies had trembled and shuddered together in the climax.

Then again, perhaps her imagination had just gone off the deep end, Molly thought. That was a very likely possibility under the circumstances.

Unable to lay quietly in bed when she was feeling so energized, Molly pushed aside the covers. She was careful not to awaken Harry as she got to her feet.

The first step made her draw a sudden breath. She winced slightly at the subtle tug of muscles that had been strained by unaccustomed nocturnal activity. She recovered quickly and padded barefoot across the gray carpet.

Midway to the bathroom, she paused to collect her nightgown and robe, which lay in her path. Then she went into the white-tiled bath.

She hung her robe and gown on a hook, turned on the water in the glass-framed shower, and stepped beneath the hot spray. It felt wonderful. But, then, she had a hunch everything would feel terrific today. She was in a fabulously good mood.

She was lathering herself with a huge bar of plain, unscented soap when the glass shower door opened without warning. Steam billowed out into the room.

Molly turned quickly, blinking water out of her eyes. Harry loomed in the opening. Misty tendrils of vapor swirled around him. He stared at her with an intensity that made her blush from head to toe. Instinctively she lowered her hands to cover the dark thatch of hair at the apex of her thighs. It was an ancient, utterly pointless gesture. Harry had seen everything there was to see of her last night

He certainly did not suffer from a similar false modesty Molly noted with interest. He had come straight from the bed without bothering to don a robe. His body was heavy with arousal. His amber eyes were starkly, sensually aware.

But something about him was vastly different this morning, Molly realized. Then she saw that his gaze no longer held the desperate vulnerability that had been so evident last night. He looked at her now with ferocious attention, as if amazed to find her in his shower.

She managed a tremulous smile. "Hi. You look as though you've just seen a ghost or something."

"Not a ghost." Harry stepped into the shower and closer the door. "You."

"Who were you expecting?"

"No one." His voice was low and husky. He grasped her slick shoulders and pulled her gently, deliberately against his rock-hard erection. "I thought it had all been a dream."

Molly drew a quick, steadying breath as he pressed against her. Then she grinned. "I hope you're not going to tell me that you thought I was just a wet dream?"

"Not just an ordinary wet dream," he whispered against her throat. "A really, really good wet dream. Better than any wet dream I've ever had in my life."

She trembled in his arms. "Oh, well, that's different, I suppose."

"Yes, it is. You're different." He bent his head and took her mouth with a slow thoroughness that had not been a part of last night's feverish lovemaking.

Molly shivered beneath the warm water. Her body responded immediately, just as it had during the night. She wrapped her arms around his neck and returned the kiss with hot urgency.

Harry laughed softly against her mouth. "Not so fast. What with all the excitement last night, we forgot something important."

"What was that?"

"Foreplay."

"Oh, that. To tell you the truth, I don't think it was necessary. I didn't miss a thing."

"Maybe it's not strictly necessary." Harry slid one hand down her back, tracing the line of her spine. Then he cupped her buttocks and squeezed gently. "But I think it's going to be a lot of fun."

Molly felt her knees weaken. She sighed and leaned into his strength, glorying in the hard lines of his body. This was not the time to ask him about his strange mood last night. He was no longer vulnerable. The barriers of his self-control were firmly back in place. He would not welcome her questions, no matter how subtle.

She felt his long fingers dip lower, gliding straight into the dark cleft that divided her soap-slick derriere.

*"Harry."*

"Like I said. A lot of fun."

A long time later Molly opened the refrigerator door and surveyed the contents. After due deliberation she selected a carton of eggs, milk, and some butter. She set all of the items on one long granite countertop while she rummaged through various cupboards in search of syrup. There was a bottle of pure Canadian maple on a shelf near the refrigerator.

She discovered a heavy, unsliced loaf of fresh sourdough bread securely wrapped in a plastic bag. Further research turned up several frying pans in various sizes. Uncertain of which would be best for her intended purpose, she set out three of them. Next, she began a search for a suitable bowl.

When she was through, she stepped back to survey the array of items she had set out on the counter. Now, all she needed was a cookbook.

It was oddly pleasant to putter around Harry's kitchen. There was a satisfying intimacy implicit in the process of making breakfast for the two of them, even without the aid of the Abberwick Food Storage and Preparation Machine.

Perhaps during the meal there would be an opportunity

to ask Harry the questions that were uppermost in her mind this morning. She wanted to know what he had been thinking last night when she had found him standing in front of the window staring out into the night.

To her surprise, she found several cookbooks in a corner cupboard. She wondered if Harry had collected them or if his housekeeper, Ginny, kept them on hand. After due consideration, Molly selected one subtitled *Simple Steps to Gourmet Delights*. She flipped the pages to the index.

She looked up from her task when she heard Harry's footsteps in the hall. "I hope you like French toast," she called. "I haven't done much cooking without the Abberwick Food Storage and Preparation Machine, but I think I can cope."

There was no response. She sensed that something had changed yet again in Harry's mood before he appeared.

He came to a halt in the doorway. One glance told her that this was not the time to ask him intimate questions about the vulnerability she had seen in him last night. Her playful shower companion had disappeared. In his place was the grimly serious man she had seen so often during the past month.

His hair was still damp. He was dressed in a pair of khaki trousers and a black cotton shirt. His eyes were hooded and thoughtful. One of his hands was clenched tightly at his side.

Molly closed the cookbook very slowly. "Harry, what's wrong?"

"I think I know him."

"What on earth are you talking about?"

He held out his clenched hand and opened his fingers to reveal the gear assembly he held. "I think I know whoever was responsible for making this."

"That's impossible."

"No." He walked to the counter and set the gear down on it. He studied the mechanism the way a hawk studies a mouse. "I started to realize it last night. But it was vague and distorted. And then you came into the front room. I got sidetracked."

Molly raised her brows. "That's one way of putting it."

He ignored her weak humor. His attention was riveted on the gear. "A few minutes ago I found it on the carpet as I was getting dressed. I must have dropped it last night."

"So?"

"So it all came flooding back to me the minute I picked it up." He raised his eyes to meet hers. There was cold speculation in his gleaming gaze. "Only this time the feeling wasn't mushy or unclear. It was clean and sharp."

"I don't understand. What's all this about mushy feelings?"

"Forget it." Harry scowled, as if he'd said more than he'd intended. "Just an expression. What I meant was that I—"

Molly held up one hand. "Hold on here. Harry, are we talking about your infamous Trevelyan Second Sight?"

"Don't get silly on me now, Molly. You're too smart for that kind of nonsense. Let's just say that things clicked in my head a couple of minutes ago when I took a second look at this gear."

"Aha. One of your insights, then?"

"Something like that," he allowed coolly. "I would have figured it out last night, but my thinking got a little fuzzy due to very understandable reasons."

"What reasons?" she demanded.

He looked briefly amused. "You seduced me."

"Oh, that." She blushed. "I thought you meant something else. All right. So it clicked. What was it?"

"I realized something I should have understood immediately. I know the man who made this gear assembly." Harry frowned. "Or, at least I know his work. It's almost the same thing."

"You're losing me, Harry."

"Remember how your sister took one look at the fake pistol device and announced that at least two of her friends were innocent?"

"She said it wasn't their style."

"Exactly." Harry sat down on a counter stool. "There's a certain style to this kind of thing. The fake pistol and that damned hobgoblin that was put under your bed were not off-the-shelf items. The devices were individually built and tailored to their particular tasks."

Molly eyed the gear. "I think I'm beginning to see where this is going."

"It defies the laws of probability to believe that two different people would have designed precisely the same gear assemblies, using the same jury-rigged motor and battery design and the same sloppy elevation mechanisms."

"All right, so it was probably the same person who built both the gun and the goblin," Molly said. "We already assumed as much. What makes you think you know him?"

"I've seen these sloppy designs somewhere else."

Molly stared at him. "You're sure?"

Harry smiled slightly. "That's what I'm trying to tell you. I know this person's work. Now all I have to do is figure out where I've seen this particular style of crude engineering design."

"How do you intend to research the problem?"

"That's easy," Harry said. "I'll start by going back through all one hundred of those grant proposals I told you to reject."

The implications of what he was saying hit Molly so hard that she had to grasp the edge of the counter for support. "Oh, my God. You don't think it's one of those inventors, after all, do you?"

"Yes," Harry said. "That's exactly what I think. It looks like one of the people whose grant proposals we turned down has decided to take some revenge."

Molly sighed heavily. "My father's foundation has caused me nothing but trouble. I wish he had thought of something else to do with his money."

"Well," Harry said slowly, "there are two schools of thought on that subject."

"There are?"

"One, as you just suggested, is that the Abberwick Foundation is a headache."

"Uh-huh." Molly raised her brows. "What's the other point of view?"

"The other side of the issue is that I would never have met you if your father hadn't appointed you sole trustee of the foundation."

"Hmm." Molly cheered at that observation. "There is that."

"Yes." Harry's eyes gleamed with sensual memories. "There is that." He glanced at the cluttered counter. "What are you doing here?"

"I'm going to make us some breakfast. French toast, to be exact." Molly selected a large knife from a drawer and prepared to attack the loaf of sourdough.

"When was the last time you cooked without the aid of the Abberwick Food Storage and Preparation Machine?"

Molly frowned in thought as she began to saw through the end of the loaf. "I think I was eighteen or nineteen. Why?"

"Maybe you'd better let me give you a hand."

"Nonsense. Any fool can make French toast." At that moment the wide-toothed bread knife hit a rough spot in the sourdough. Molly bore down with grim determination.

Too much determination. And at a bad angle. The acrylic bread board suddenly skidded across the granite countertop. Molly yelped in surprise. Instinctively she yanked the knife out of the loaf. It came free with unexpected speed and flew out of her hand. She stared in dismay as it soared and wheeled in the air and then plunged down toward the granite, point first. She wondered how much a fine-quality bread knife cost.

With a deceptively easy motion that was almost too fast for the eye to follow, Harry reached across the counter and caught the knife by the hilt just before it struck the unforgiving granite. He smiled. "I'll slice the bread for you."

"Thanks. I'd appreciate that."

"And there you have it," Molly said as she concluded her tale two hours later. "The adventures of Molly Abberwick and the mysterious hobgoblin."

"You spent the night with T-Rex?" Tessa paused in the

act of replacing a glass canister full of smoky Lapsang Sou-
chong tea on the shelf. "I don't believe it."

Molly gave her a repressive glare. "He was kind enough
to let me stay at his place after I was nearly scared out of
my wits by that stupid goblin prank."

"Kind? He doesn't look like the kindly type to me." Tessa
narrowed her eyes. "And why do I have this feeling that
you did not sleep on the couch?"

"Now, Tessa, you know I don't believe in discussing my
personal life."

"That's because you haven't had a personal life to discuss
for ages," Tessa retorted. "What's going on here? Are you
and Trevelyan having an affair?"

"I'd hardly call it that."

"Damn. You are having an affair." Tessa looked at her
with worried eyes. "Do you think that's smart? You said
yourself that the two of you have absolutely nothing in common. You said he's stubborn and difficult and arrogant. You
said—"

"I'll be in my office if anyone needs me." Molly strode
through the opening and slammed the door behind her.

She dropped into her desk chair. The door promptly
opened again, and Tessa stuck her head around the corner.
"All right, forget the juicy personal stuff. I'll worm the truth
out of you later. What's Trevelyan going to do about that
goblin thing that someone put under your bed?"

"I'm not sure. He seems to think he recognizes the guy's
work. He says it's sloppy. He's sure that he can identify the
same style of design in one of the grant proposals."

Tessa's eyes widened. "He thinks that whoever is behind
this is one of the inventors you rejected?"

"Uh-huh."

"Shouldn't you be talking to the police?"

"We will, as soon as Harry gets a lead on a likely suspect.
At this point all we've got are a couple of nasty pranks and
an unlimited pool of possible perpetrators."

"I see what you mean. No one's been hurt. There's no
evidence of forced entry. So far they're just pranks."

"Right. I'm afraid that if we go to the cops now they'll think one of Kelsey's friends is responsible, just as I did. Lord only knows where that assumption would take the police. Assuming they have time to investigate such a minor event in the first place."

Tessa looked troubled. "What are you going to do?"

"There's nothing I can do at the moment. We'll have to wait and see if Harry can come up with anything useful. In the meantime, I've got a business to run. Let's get to work."

Gordon Brooke strode into Abberwick Tea & Spice at five minutes before noon. Molly was in the process of measuring out a half pound of Keemun tea for a customer. She stifled a groan of dismay.

Gordon had a file folder tucked under one arm. Stylish as always, he was clad in a pair of loose-fitting, multipleated stone-colored trousers and an open-throated coffee-colored shirt with wide, billowing sleeves. A rakish embroidered vest completed the ensemble. He would have looked at home sitting in a sidewalk café in Paris or Rome.

Molly made a show of being very busy with a flurry of new customers who wandered into the shop at that moment. Tessa did the same. Gordon lounged against a display of gift-boxed spice sets and waited. Molly hoped that he would become bored and leave before the rush of customers did, but her luck was out. Gordon did not budge.

Tessa exchanged a commiserating glance with Molly as the crowd gradually dwindled.

When the customer base was down to two, both of whom were still browsing the shelves, Molly reluctantly turned to Gordon. He gave her his most endearing grin, the one that put a dimple in his cheeks.

"Got something to show you, Molly." He held up the folder he had brought with him.

Molly eyed the folder with deep suspicion. "What?"

Gordon straightened and started forward. "Let's go into your office."

He disappeared inside before Molly could think of a polite excuse. She trailed slowly after him. Tessa rolled her eyes.

When Molly reached the door of her office, she saw that Gordon had already made himself at home. He was sitting in the chair behind her desk. He had the folder open in front of him.

"I want you to see my projections for the next three years, Molly."

"Gordon, if this is about a loan, you're wasting your time. We went through this three months ago."

"Just take a look at these numbers. That's all I'm asking. They're solid as a rock. The only thing I need to make it come together is a little infusion of cash."

"I told you, I'm not going to finance your expansion plans, Gordon."

He looked up from the papers he had spread out on her desk. "Think of it as an investment, because that's exactly what it is. A hell of a better investment than some zany invention cooked up by a crackpot inventor, for God's sake."

Molly planted her hands on the desk. "I will say this one more time, and that's it. I am not interested in making you a loan."

Without any warning, the warm, persuasive charm on Gordon's face disappeared. "Goddamn it, Molly, you've got to listen to me."

Startled by the outburst, Molly took a quick step back. "What do you think you're doing?"

Frustration and rage flashed in his eyes. "I've got too much riding on this. Do you think I'm going to let all of my plans go down the tubes just because you're harboring a grudge?"

"I'm not harboring any grudges."

"The hell you aren't." Gordon surged to his feet. "You're still pissed because of what happened between us."

"Are you nuts? That was eighteen months ago. Believe it or not, I've had better things to do in the meantime than nurse a broken heart or carry a grudge."

"Then stop letting your emotions get in the way of good business," Gordon shot back. "Don't you understand what's at stake here?"

"Sure. Your reexpansion plans. Do you think I care about financing a half-dozen Gordon Brooke Espresso Bars? I've got my own business to worry about."

"This isn't about expansion for the sake of expansion. This is life and death."

Molly's mouth fell open. "Life and death?"

"No joke, Molly. I'm sitting on the brink of bankruptcy." Gordon's hands clenched into fists. "I have to have fresh money, or Gordon Brooke Espresso is going to go under. All of it. Everything I've worked for will come crashing down around my ears."

Molly closed her eyes briefly. "I'm so sorry, Gordon. I didn't realize things were that precarious."

"You can save me." He started around the desk with renewed determination. "I need you, honey. For old times' sake, say you'll help me."

She bit her lip. "Please, don't make this a personal thing. You said it was business. And as a businesswoman, I don't want any part of it. I'm into tea and spices, not coffee."

He took a step toward her. "Molly, what happened between us is old news. You and I can start over. We'll be partners this time. We've got so much in common."

Molly felt the hair stir softly on the nape of her neck. She knew without turning around that the door to her office had just opened. She also knew who had entered.

"Am I interrupting anything important here?" Harry asked with a dangerous chill in his voice.

Molly whirled around, relieved to see him. She gave him an overly bright smile. "Not at all."

Gordon's expression turned thunderous. "I'm trying to have a business conversation with Molly."

"Too bad. I've got an appointment with her, myself." Harry glanced at his watch. "For lunch. You'll have to excuse us "

Gordon's jaw resembled a concrete reinforcing bar. "I don't think I've met you."

Molly leaped into the awkward silence that fell between the men. "That's right, you two don't know each other. Gordon, this is Dr. Harry Trevelyan. He's a noted authority on the history of science. He's consulting for the Abberwick Foundation. Harry, this is Gordon Brooke of Gordon Brooke Espresso. You've probably had some of his coffee."

Harry said nothing.

Gordon scowled. "You're the guy who's helping Molly select funding projects for the foundation?"

"Yes." Harry looked at Molly. "Ready?"

"Let me get my purse." Molly hurried around the corner of her desk.

Gordon put out a hand to catch hold of her arm. "Damn it, Molly, this is important. Let me finish what I've started here."

"Some other time." Molly ducked his outstretched fingers. She pulled her purse out of a drawer. "Harry's right. He and I have an appointment to discuss some foundation business."

"Yeah, I'll bet you do." Gordon gave Harry a fulminating look. "I know all about you so-called foundation consultants."

Harry cocked a brow. "You do?"

"Sure. You latch onto people like Molly who handle the funds for a foundation or a charity. You convince them that they need you in order to get the job done, and then you milk the operation for all the fees and associated costs you can get. It's nothing more than a legal scam."

Molly was shocked. "Gordon, stop it. I don't want to hear another word."

"It's the truth. Guys like Trevelyan here are the reason so many charities wind up with such high administrative and management costs and so little cash for their projects."

Molly gripped the strap of her purse. "Please leave, Gordon. Now."

"Hell." Gordon's eyes slitted in sudden comprehension.

"He's screwing you, isn't he? I should have guessed." He gathered up his papers and crammed them into the folder. "He'll bleed your precious foundation dry, Molly. And then he'll dump you. Don't say you weren't warned."

Gordon stormed toward the door. Harry stepped politely out of his path.

# 10

It had been a very near thing, Harry thought later as he waited in line at the sidewalk window of a waterfront café. A chill went through him whenever he thought about the events of the night. He felt as if he'd been standing in the path of an onrushing train and had somehow, inexplicably, managed to escape certain disaster.

He still did not comprehend his good fortune, but he was profoundly relieved to know that he had not scared the living daylights out of Molly. In fact, she seemed virtually unruffled by his behavior during the night.

Perhaps a little too unruffled. Harry frowned. She acted as if she hadn't noticed anything strange or even slightly out of the ordinary during last night's lovemaking.

Memories of her passionate, exquisitely feminine response to him returned in a heated rush. She had come to him, made love to him, taken him deep inside her warm, tight, fiercely welcoming body. He had actually *felt* the joyous delight in her, frothy as fine champagne. It was as though she had been waiting for him all of her life.

And for the first time in his life, he had known true sexual satisfaction. Last night the relentless hunger, the craving for an incomprehensible consummation that had been growing so strong during the past few years had been assuaged, temporarily, at least. He would never forget the experience. It was far more profound than any physical release he had ever known.

But as glorious as it had been, there was no getting around the fact that Molly's reaction still baffled him. He was sure that she had been exposed to a full onslaught of that part of him he had fought to conceal even from himself. Yet she hadn't seemed fazed by it. Olivia had caught only the merest glimpse and had been convinced that he was more than a little crazy.

He had been lucky, Harry told himself. Very, very lucky. Molly had attributed his behavior to a fever. Or perhaps she had simply been too shaken by the malicious prank that had been played on her earlier in the evening to be aware of the weirdness in him. Whatever the reason, he had not terrified her the way he had Olivia. But he had certainly scared the hell out of himself.

The whole thing had been too damn close. He would make certain that he did not take such risks a second time. From now on he would be careful.

From now on he would be in control whenever he made love to Molly.

Harry paid for two cups of chowder. He picked up the cardboard tray and walked across the pier to where Molly was sitting at an umbrella-shaded table.

He was braced for the sight of her, but the euphoric thrill that he had experienced this morning, when he had discovered that she had not left him, struck again. He realized with some chagrin that he was getting hard just looking at her. He could only hope that his pants concealed his uncontrollable physical reaction. He wondered if he would be forced to take deep breaths every time he saw her, or if he would gradually grow accustomed to the sudden clench of excitement in his gut.

Molly's attention was on the gulls that soared and swooped like miniature fighter planes in pursuit of stray french fries and bits of fried fish. The soft breeze played with her hair the way an electric beater played with egg whites.

Wistfully, Harry studied the graceful line of the nape of Molly's neck. The deep hunger throbbed within him. He could almost feel her warm, silken skin. More hot images of the night drifted through his head. It was only about the thousandth time that day that they had interfered with his concentration. His hands tightened on the tray. Fortunately he had a lot of concentration.

Harry put the tray of chowder down on the table. "Lunch is served. Red for you and white for me. Did I get it right?"

Molly held a tendril of tawny hair out of her eyes and surveyed the two cups of chowder. "Right. How can you stand that thick, white, pasty stuff, anyway?"

"Just one more point on which we differ," Harry said equably as he sat down. It would probably be a good idea to remind himself more frequently of how little they had in common, he thought. It would help restore a certain crucial distance. "I like New England–style clam chowder. You prefer the red kind which amounts to nothing more than some clams and potatoes floating around in tomato juice."

"A matter of opinion," she said loftily. "Any luck with the grant proposals?"

"No. It's going to take time to find what I'm looking for. If I have to go through all of the proposals it could take several days. The sort of details I'm after aren't obvious. They're subtle."

Molly tapped her plastic spoon impatiently against the rim of her chowder cup. "Days?"

He looked up from his chowder. "You'll stay with me until we nail the bastard."

"I will?"

"Do you really want to go back to that big old spooky house by yourself every night and stay there all alone? Wondering what the son-of-a-bitch's next little trick will be?"

"It's not spooky." Molly closed her eyes and shuddered. "But, you're right. I'm not sure I want to stay there alone at the moment." Then she eyed him through her lashes. "I could stay with my aunt."

"And draw the prankster's attention to her house?"

A shocked expression lit Molly's eyes. "Oh, my God. I can't do that."

"You'll be safe at my condo. The doormen are on duty twenty-four hours a day. They won't let anyone into the building who isn't supposed to be there."

"If you're sure," she said hesitantly.

"I'm sure."

"Well, maybe just until we identify the prankster," she clarified.

"Right. Until we know who's behind this." It was settled. She would stay with him. Harry suppressed a rush of pleasure. "I'll start looking for our rejected inventor immediately."

"You really think you can pick his work out of that pile of grant proposals?"

"Given time, yes."

Molly shook her head. "Amazing. It'll take hours of work."

"I know you're not the patient type," Harry said quietly.

"But you are?"

He shrugged. "It usually pays off."

"Just another little example of how different we are?" she asked smoothly. "Like our different tastes in clam chowder?"

"Out of curiosity, which type of chowder does Gordon Brooke prefer?" Harry asked before he could stop himself. "Red or white?"

"Gordon?" Molly wrinkled her nose. "Red, I think."

"Naturally."

"Why do you say that?"

"It strikes me that you and Brooke have a lot in common."

"Not really," she said much too swiftly.

"You're both entrepreneurs." Harry knew for certain now that he was on to something important. "You both sell similar products to a similar market base. Seems like you two would have a lot to talk about."

"Like what?"

"Business problems," Harry suggested. "Taxes. City government regulations on small businesses. That sort of thing."

"Okay, so we have some business problems in common. Big deal."

"You're both single," Harry pointed out.

"So?"

"So, I sensed a certain informality between the two of you," Harry said dryly.

"What is this? The Trevelyan Inquisition? All right, Gordon and I have known each other for a couple of years. We don't have so much in common, however, that I intend to loan him fifty grand from the Abberwick Foundation."

*Damn,* Harry thought. *So that's what this is all about. The sucker is trying to use her.* He ripped open a tiny packet of pepper. "Fifty thousand?"

"Uh-huh." Molly concentrated on her chowder.

"That's a lot of money."

"Gordon needs cash. He got overextended. He says he's in financial trouble. He's already had to close two of his espresso bars."

"Talk about raw nerve." Harry dumped the pepper onto his chowder and tossed the empty packet aside in disgust. "He actually tried to convince you that his business plans qualify as an invention worthy of the backing of the Abberwick Foundation?"

"Something like that." Molly's brows drew together in a small frown. "He's been after me for several weeks now, but he didn't tell me that he was actually on the brink of bankruptcy until today."

"He probably saved the sob story for the last-ditch effort."

Molly's fingers tightened on the handle of her spoon. "He must be desperate to confess that he's in danger of losing his business. I know him well enough to realize what that admission cost his pride."

Harry did not like the note of sympathy that had crept into her voice. "Just how well do you know him?"

"As you said, Gordon and I have some business interests in common."

"And you both like the same kind of chowder."

Molly glowered. "And his shop is right across the steps from mine. What of it?"

"That well, huh?"

"Sheesh, all right, already. I surrender. A year and a half ago Gordon and I were involved for a while. I'm sure you've guessed as much. Now, are you satisfied?"

"You can't blame me for being a little curious," Harry said.

"The heck I can't."

"It's only natural under the circumstances. You grilled me a bit on the subject of my ex-fiancée, if you will recall."

Molly blushed. "I guess that's true. Okay, now we're even."

"Not quite," Harry murmured. "What happened between you and Brooke? Why did you two stop seeing each other?"

Molly lifted one shoulder in an elaborately casual shrug. "You know how it is. A year and a half ago I was very busy with the legal and investment work required to set up my father's foundation. I was also running my own business. And there was Kelsey to worry about. She was still in high school. What with one thing and another, there wasn't much time left over for a personal life. Gordon and I just drifted apart. It's over."

"How did it end? With a bang or a whimper?"

Molly gave him a frosty look. "We're not talking about the end of the universe as we know it. We're talking about a casual dating relationship that sort of petered out."

"Petered out? An interesting expression, given the topic."

The frost in her eyes turned to ice. "You're being difficult, Trevelyan."

"So how did it end?"

"Good grief, you're the most persistent man I've ever met."

"Part of my charm," Harry said humbly.

"Is it?" A glint appeared in Molly's eyes. "If you must know, it ended with a hiss."

Harry paused, his spoon halfway to his mouth. "A hiss?"

Molly's smile was grim. "The sort of hissing shriek an espresso machine makes when the steam is forced through the ground coffee."

"I see. That kind of hiss."

"Exactly."

Harry considered the matter for a short time and then decided to push for the rest of the story. "Would you mind explaining the hiss?"

Molly sighed. "Gordon and I had been dating for nearly two months. I thought things were going rather well. As you noted, we had a lot to talk about. But one day I walked into his shop shortly before closing time. The place was empty. The young woman who was usually on duty behind the counter was not around, but . . ."

"But?"

"But I thought I heard the sound of an espresso machine. The noise was coming from the storage room at the back of the shop."

"Ah," Harry said. "I believe I begin to perceive the ending of this tale."

"It certainly doesn't take ESP to do that," Molly muttered.

Harry stilled. He searched her face but saw no sign that she had intended any veiled references to last night. He relaxed slightly. "Go on."

"To make a short story even shorter, I went into the storage room expecting to find Gordon testing out a new espresso machine. But he was testing out his counter assistant, instead. The two of them were going at it on top of a pile of sacks full of Gordon Brooke's Special Espresso Roast Costa Rican Blend."

"I can understand how an encounter like that would have left an indelible impression."

"Enough to put one off espresso for life," Molly assured him.

"And the hissing sound?"

Molly grimaced. "That was Gordon. He sounded just like one of his machines."

"You didn't, uh, recognize the noise?" Harry asked carefully.

"Our relationship had, thankfully, not progressed to that stage."

"You weren't sleeping with him?"

"No." Molly smiled wryly. "Now, are you satisfied?"

"Almost," Harry said.

Molly glowered. "You're impossible. Do you have to pursue every little detail?"

"I like to collect odd scraps of information."

"This isn't exactly an interesting footnote in the history of science. Why do you want so much information on Gordon?"

"I figure it's to my benefit to learn as much as I can about him."

She regarded him with deep suspicion. "Why?"

Harry watched a dozen gulls dive toward the same french fry. The bird that got to it first seized the morsel and climbed swiftly skyward to escape the competition. "I like to plan ahead. When did you and Gordon first start dating?"

Molly was silent for a moment. Harry sensed that she was choosing her words with great care. He wondered why the subject of Gordon Brooke required such extreme caution.

"We met about two years ago. I told you, we started going out together about eighteen months ago," Molly said finally.

"That would have been about six months after your father died?"

"Yes."

"About the time you took the first legal steps to establish the Abberwick Foundation?"

"Uh-huh." Molly studiously spooned up more chowder.

Harry whistled softly. "So it took Brooke that long to figure out that you were in control of a five-hundred-thousand-dollar-a-year foundation? He must be a little slow. No wonder he's on the verge of bankruptcy."

"That's it." Molly slammed her spoon down onto the table. "I knew you'd say something like that. I just *knew* it."

"What did I say?"

"Don't you dare try that innocent expression with me, Dr. Trevelyan. You know perfectly well that you just implied that Gordon tried to use me eighteen months ago."

"Now, Molly—"

"You virtually accused him of having his eye on the Abberwick Foundation assets, not me. The implication is that I was too naive and too gullible to realize it until I saw him going at it with his assistant."

"I'm sorry," Harry said.

"Hah. I don't believe that for one single minute. You think I'm soft in the head when it comes to financial matters, don't you?"

"Not in the least," Harry said, surprised by her conclusion.

"Yes, you do. You no doubt gained that unfortunate impression because I seem too eager to make grants to the various inventors who have applied for them."

"I think you've got a soft spot for inventors, yes. But that's another issue."

"You bet it is." Molly aimed her spoon at him as though it were a ray gun. "Bear in mind, Dr. Trevelyan, that I did not make Abberwick Tea & Spice a successful business enterprise by being stupid about money."

"True," he conceded.

"Nor am I naive and gullible when it comes to investments. The fact that I got my father's foundation up and running is proof of that."

"Absolutely."

"So maybe I am a little softhearted when it comes to inventors. What of it? It's a family trait. Abberwicks have spent generations looking for funding for their inventions. It's only natural that I would feel for others who are in the same position my father and uncle were in for most of their lives."

"I understand. I apologize."

Molly abruptly collapsed against the back of her chair with a disgruntled expression. "Why should you be sorry? It's the truth. Gordon did try to use me to get money for his damned espresso bars. I hoped you wouldn't find out. It's embarrassing."

"I doubt if it was any more embarrassing than discovering that my ex-fiancée was in love with my cousin," Harry said.

Molly looked briefly nonplussed. Then her mouth kicked up at one corner. "You've got a point. I'll bet that was a little rough, wasn't it?"

"It didn't do a lot for my ego, but I survived."

Molly's hair bounced in the wind as she leaned forward and folded her arms on the table. "Maybe you and I have more in common than we first thought."

Harry gazed into her shatteringly clear eyes and felt the desperate hunger rise within him. He fought savagely to squelch it. He could not take any more risks. He had gotten lucky last night because Molly had believed him to be ill. He must not lose his control again. At least not until he was absolutely, positively certain that she would not fear the strangeness in him.

"Maybe we do," Harry agreed.

"Eighteen months ago Gordon wanted cash to expand," Molly said quietly. "When he didn't get it from me, he talked a bank into making him a loan. He opened five new locations within three months. He moved too quickly. Now things have started to implode. He needs more money to stay afloat, and the bank won't give him another dime."

"So he's come to you."

"Uh-huh."

"But this time," Harry said carefully, "you know what he's after."

"Yes."

Harry looked out across Elliott Bay. "Ever wish things had worked out differently between you and Brooke?"

"I think I can state with great certainty that Gordon and I would not have lasted very long as a couple."

Harry glanced at her and saw the fresh mischief in her eyes. "Why not?"

"I hate to sound picky, but going to bed with a man who makes noises like an espresso machine during intimate moments is out of the question. I have my standards."

Relief poured through Harry. "I'll try not to hiss at the wrong time."

Harry studied the drawings attached to the grant proposal that was spread out on his desk. The sketch was for a device that would supposedly collect energy from the sun and use it to power an automobile. Harry had nixed the grant on the grounds that the inventor's theories and technological ability were both equally mundane. The proposal embodied no original thinking. Nor did it exhibit the level of mechanical engineering expertise required to carry it out.

But whoever had set up the fake gun and the hobgoblin was not a truly original thinker, Harry reminded himself. Clever but not original. There was a vast difference.

The disgruntled inventor had used ordinary ideas and well-worn technology to create his malicious devices. Technically speaking, whoever had submitted the solar-powered automobile proposal could have been the creator of the pranks. But there was something that did not quite fit. Something did not feel right.

Harry set the proposal aside and turned to the next one on the pile. He had worked his way through nearly half of the hundred documents stacked on his desk. He intended to keep going until he found the one he was searching for. It was here, somewhere. He was convinced of it.

Molly, seated at the glass table next to the aquarium, looked up from her small computer. "Any luck?"

"No." Harry scanned the cover page of the next proposal. "But I'll find it. I'm a patient man."

Molly made a face. "I do not want to hear that patience is a virtue."

"I'll skip the lectures tonight. I've got better things to do."

"Thanks." Her expression sobered. She regarded him with

a shadowed look. "This is really going above and beyond the call of duty, Harry. No one's paying you to find this guy."

"Forget it," Harry said. "That bastard is here somewhere, and I'm going to dig him out." He turned the page of the proposal and concentrated on the drawing of a wind-driven generator.

Molly returned to her computer.

A companionable silence settled on the study. Harry realized absently that he was starting to take such silences for granted. He no longer worried about offending Molly when he sank into his thoughts. She always seemed to have plenty to do herself. She did not have to be entertained. Nor did she pester him with questions about his moods.

The buzz of the lobby intercom jarred Harry out of his concentration a few minutes later. He glanced at his watch. It was nearly ten o'clock.

"We've got a visitor," he said.

"Who in the world would drop by for a visit at this hour?"

"Family."

"Ah, yes. Of course."

Harry got to his feet and went across the room to the intercom panel. He punched the button. "This is Trevelyan."

"You have a visitor, Mr. Trevelyan," Chris, the doorman, announced. "Mrs. Danielle Hughes is here to see you."

Harry closed his eyes in brief resignation. "Send her up, Chris."

"Sure thing, Mr. Trevelyan."

Harry released the intercom button. "My Aunt Danielle. Brandon's mother."

"Ah."

He turned to Molly and saw empathy in the jeweled depths of her gaze. It was an odd sensation to know that she somehow understood his feelings at that moment. He was not entirely sure that he comprehended them himself. It was always like this when he dealt with his family.

Molly started to close the top of her computer. "You'll probably want to talk to your aunt alone in here. I'll go out into the living room."

"No, stay where you are. No sense allowing Danielle to disrupt your work as well as mine. I'll introduce you to her, and then I'll talk to her in the front room."

"Whatever you want. I take it this is going to be an unpleasant conversation?"

"Let's just say I think I know what Danielle wants." Harry walked toward the door. "Experience tells me that the sooner I give it to her, the sooner I'll be able to get back to work."

"Good luck."

The doorbell chimed. Harry went to answer the imperious summons. Danielle was standing in the outer hall. Her handsome, patrician features were set in an expression of steely determination. The anxiety in her eyes was real. Harry knew her well enough to realize that in this mood, she would not be easily deterred.

Although his mother and Danielle had been sisters, there was little more than a superficial resemblance between the two women as far as Harry was concerned. Both had been beautiful in their youth, and their fine bone structure had accepted age well. But Harry remembered his mother as a happy, energetic woman whose eyes had sparkled with an exuberant love of life and an easy, affectionate spirit.

Harry could not recall ever having seen Danielle in a genuinely cheerful mood. She could be coolly pleasant and gracious when the occasion demanded, but that seemed to be her limit. The shadows of her miserable marriage to Dean Hughes still clung to her, even though Dean had had the decency to get himself killed in a car accident several years earlier.

"Harry, I must talk to you about Brandon." Danielle swept into the condominium. She came to an abrupt halt and looked straight down her nose at Molly, who was standing in the doorway of the study. "Who's this?"

"Hello," Molly said politely.

"I didn't realize you had company, Harry." Danielle glanced at him as if she expected him to dismiss Molly the way he would have dismissed a servant.

"This is Molly Abberwick. Molly, my aunt, Danielle Hughes."

"Danielle Stratton Hughes," Danielle corrected coldly.

"How do you do?" Molly murmured.

"You must be Harry's new little friend," Danielle said. "Olivia mentioned that she had met you."

"Harry's little friend?" Molly pursed her lips. Amusement danced in her eyes. "Somehow I never thought of myself as any man's *little friend.* What a concept."

It did not take the Trevelyan Second Sight to know trouble when it was about to explode in his face, Harry thought. "Ms. Abberwick is a client, Danielle."

Molly looked more amused than ever. "A little friend and a client."

Danielle made a show of looking at the diamond-framed watch she wore. "It's rather late to be doing business, isn't it?"

"Depends on the business," Molly said.

Danielle lifted her chin. "If you will excuse us, I have family matters to discuss with my nephew."

"You bet. No problem." Molly backed into the study. "Take your time. I won't bother you at all. You won't even know I'm in here."

She winked at Harry just before she closed the study door.

Danielle gave the closed door a disdainful look as she went past it into the living room. "Really, Harry, you're not going to tell me that woman is a client of yours."

"You didn't come here to discuss my relationship with Molly."

"Don't be rude." Danielle settled onto the sofa. "I'm in no mood for it. I've got problems enough on my hands."

Harry went to stand at the window. He looked out into the night. "What do you want, Danielle?"

"You've spoken with Brandon?"

"Yes. And with Olivia."

"Then you know about Brandon's ridiculous scheme to go into business on his own?"

Harry glanced briefly at her over his shoulder. "Yes."

"You've got to talk him out of it, Harry."

"Why should I? Brandon's smart, and he's willing to work hard. Let him follow his dream."

"That's impossible, and you know it," Danielle said tightly. "My father will never allow him to go out on his own. Especially since you refused to join the company. Brandon has to stay with Stratton Properties. You know that as well as I do."

"It's the money, isn't it? You're afraid Parker will cut Brandon out of the will if he leaves the company."

"That's exactly what he'll do, and we both know it. You know how Father feels about the firm."

"Parker's feelings aren't as important as Brandon's in this instance," Harry said. "He wants to try his wings. Let him go, Danielle. If you don't, he'll only resent you for not having any faith in him."

"Don't you dare lecture me on how to deal with my son. You've done enough damage already."

"Me?" Harry swung around to confront her. "What the hell have I done?"

"You know perfectly well that you're the one who put the idea of leaving Stratton Properties into Brandon's head."

"Olivia tried to tell me that. Damn it, Danielle, this is not my fault."

"Brandon was perfectly content to stay with Stratton Properties until you came along. After you walked away from your Stratton inheritance, I realized that Brandon actually envied your streak of foolish independence. It got worse after he married Olivia. Now he's convinced himself that he must go out on his own."

Harry slowly massaged the back of his neck. "You think Brandon is leaving the company in order to prove something? Maybe he just wants to start his own business. What would be so unusual about that? He's a Stratton. Business is in his blood."

"He's jealous of you, don't you understand?" Danielle stood up abruptly. "God knows why, but he is. He wants to prove to himself and to Olivia that he's as strong and self-reliant as you are. In the process he's going to ruin his life."

"I think that's overstating the situation."

"No, it's not," Danielle said. "It's the truth. If Brandon doesn't stay with Stratton Properties, my father will disinherit him. I know he will."

"You can't be sure Parker will go that far."

"I am sure of it," Danielle retorted. "He disinherited Brittany when she ran off with Sean Trevelyan, didn't he? And he disinherited you, too, when you refused to join the company. He swore you'd never see a dime of the Stratton money. He means it, Harry."

"I don't doubt it, but the circumstances are a little different."

"I wish I could believe that, but I can't risk it. You must do something. Just because you don't want the Stratton money, that doesn't give you the right to influence Brandon. I will not stand by and see my son deprived of his inheritance because of you. Do you understand me, Harry?"

"Even if I admit, for the sake of this idiotic discussion, that I am guilty of inadvertently persuading Brandon to leave Stratton Properties, what the hell do you expect me to do about it now?"

"Talk him out of it." Danielle turned on her expensively shod heel and went down the hall.

Harry closed his eyes in weary resignation as Danielle went through the door and shut it behind her.

After a moment he heard the study door open quietly. He looked across the room to where Molly stood watching him.

"I couldn't help overhearing." Molly propped one shoulder against the jamb. "Your aunt's voice carries."

"Tell me about it." Harry massaged the back of his neck. "I'm sorry you had to sit through that."

"Did your grandfather really offer to reinstate you in his will if you joined the family firm?"

"Yes."

"And you turned him down, of course."

"Parker Stratton uses money to control people. It's as

natural for him as breathing." Harry went into the kitchen to find the bottle that he kept in a cupboard next to the refrigerator. "Can I interest you in a little medicinal brandy?"

"Sure." Molly unpropped herself from the jamb and came forward. "What happens now? Will you try to talk Brandon out of leaving the family firm?"

"No." Harry splashed brandy into two glasses. "I'll talk to Parker. See if I can convince him to let Brandon go out on his own without reprisals."

Molly accepted the brandy snifter. "Do you think that's possible?"

"Maybe." Harry smiled humorlessly. "With a little luck, I think I can convince Parker to do the right thing."

Molly's eyes were very green as she regarded him over the rim of the brandy glass. "The way you convinced your uncle Leon to lay off Josh?"

"Something like that, yes."

"Correct me if I'm wrong, but I get the impression that everyone on both sides of your family seems to think it's your job to solve all of their problems."

"Not all. Just some of them."

Molly was silent for a while. "How did you get into this situation, Harry?"

He did not pretend to misunderstand the question. "Damned if I know."

"Harry, this is me, Molly, remember? You can't brush me off with that kind of answer. I'm too smart."

He smiled reluctantly. "Granted. And you've got the Abberwick curiosity. I mustn't forget that."

"Look, if you don't want to tell me why you put up with scenes like the one you just went through with your aunt, that's fine. It's your business. And it is a family matter. I have no right to pry."

"It's not that I don't want to explain the situation." Harry contemplated his brandy. "I'm just not sure of the answer. No one's ever asked me that particular question before."

"Leave it to an Abberwick," Molly said lightly. "We're inquisitive by nature."

Harry thought about it for a good thirty seconds before he made his decision. He looked up from the brandy and found Molly watching him with calm perception and something that might have been sympathy.

"I got into this mess because I had some damn fool notion of ending the feud between the Strattons and the Trevelyans," Harry said eventually.

"Ah." Complete understanding lit Molly's eyes. "Of course."

"The only thing my parents wanted from either side of the family was peace. It was the one thing no one would give them."

"And as the one who has blood from both sides flowing in his veins, you decided to try to build a bridge between the Strattons and the Trevelyans."

Harry swirled the brandy in his glass. "That was the general idea."

"It was to be your tribute to the memory of your parents, wasn't it?"

"Something like that." He wasn't surprised that she understood it all, in one single gulp. What startled him was the odd sense of relief he experienced now that he had confided his quixotic dream to her.

"You're committed to ending the feud just as I'm committed to my father's foundation."

"Yes," Harry said. "But just between you and me, I think you're going to be a lot more successful with the Abberwick Foundation than I'm going to be with ending the Trevelyan-Stratton feud."

"Really?"

"After all these years, both sides of my family look at me and still see the past, not the future. Each wants me to make a choice between the two families, and neither will be satisfied until I do."

"And you won't do that."

**174**

"I'm half Stratton and half Trevelyan. How can I choose?"

"I notice that the feud doesn't stop anyone on either side of your family from using you," Molly said dryly. "It's weird, isn't it, Harry?"

"What is?"

"That even though you're the family outcast, in a way you've managed to become the head of both clans?"

"I'm not the head of the families," Harry said. "I'm just the fool who got stuck in the middle. There's a big difference."

# 11

$\mathcal{M}$olly could not stand the ravishing torment any longer. She was so buffeted by the endless waves of pleasure that she could hardly catch her breath. Harry's stunningly intimate touch left her shivering with need. He made love to her with an enthralling thoroughness. His powerful, elegant hands were gentle and sure and utterly relentless. He coaxed the climax from her as if he were mining liquid diamonds. His long fingers glistened in the moonlight.

"*Harry*. Oh, my God, Harry. Please. No. I can't . . . I can't . . ."

"Jump," he whispered against her skin. "I'll catch you."

The delicious tension exploded inside her. She clenched her fists in his dark hair and surrendered with a wordless gasp of wonder. He held himself back, waiting until she was trembling in the heart of the storm before he pushed deeply into her body. Molly trembled at the impact.

She wrapped Harry close and clung to him as he shuddered heavily in the throes of his own release.

It wasn't until he sprawled on top of her, the skin of his shoulders damp with perspiration and the elemental scent of sex thick in the air, that Molly realized the truth.

It had been good. Better than good. It had been a fantastic, deliciously erotic, incredibly sensual experience. But something had been different this time.

Something had been missing.

She lay awake for a long while afterward. Granted, she did not have a great deal of experience, which made logical comparisons difficult. But last night her body had been tuned to Harry's in some way she could not explain. Tonight everything within her, each nerve and muscle, had tried to recapture the experience. She had come close, but it had not been the same.

The sense of resonance was missing.

Last night Harry had opened a locked door and invited her into a secret chamber. Tonight that door had remained firmly closed. Molly knew she would not be fully satisfied until he unlocked it again.

She awoke alone in the big bed. For a few drowsy seconds it seemed entirely normal to have the bed to herself. Then she opened her eyes and saw the unfamiliar expanse of night sky outside the wall of windows. Her first clear thought was that there was too much darkness. Then she remembered that she was in Harry's bed, and she should not be alone. Harry should have been there with her.

She stirred and peered at the clock. The illuminated numbers informed her that it was nearly three in the morning. It didn't take ESP to figure out that Harry had left the bed to go back to the stack of proposals in his study.

Molly folded her hands behind her head and contemplated what she had learned about Harry. A pattern was emerging.

He had come to Seattle within a year after the deaths of his parents. She had no doubt but that he had told himself he wanted to make peace between the families in honor of his mother and father. But Molly suspected there was more to the story than that. Perhaps more than even Harry himself knew.

He'd had every right to turn to the Strattons and the Trevelyans after he'd found himself completely alone in the world. They were his blood kin. They had accepted him, but Molly was learning that the acceptance had come at a high price. Everyone wanted something from Harry.

Molly sat up abruptly and threw aside the covers. She got out of bed, tugged on her robe, and padded, barefoot, down the hall to Harry's study.

A shaft of light was visible through the half-opened door. Molly walked quietly into the room.

She knew that she had not made a sound on her way down the hall, but Harry must have heard her approach. He was seated behind his desk, watching the door, waiting for her. He was wearing a dark gray terry-cloth robe. The pattern of intensely contrasted light and shadow from the halogen lamp etched his stark features. His midnight dark hair was tousled from the pillow. His amber eyes glowed with the anticipation of a raptor that is just about to sink talons into prey.

Molly knew at once what had happened. "You found the proposal you were looking for?"

"About three minutes ago. Take a look."

Molly crossed the room to the desk and glanced at the papers spread out in front of Harry. "I remember that one." She craned her head to read the cover page. *"Proposal for the Construction of a Device to Measure Paranormal Brain Waves,* by Wharton Kendall. I liked it, but you vetoed it the same way you did all the others."

"Paranormal brain waves? Give me a break." Harry shot her a disgusted look. "Kendall is the kind of inventor who gives other inventors a bad name. A classic crackpot. No solid scientific training. No formal technical background. No originality or true insight. And to top it off, he's into this damn paranormal garbage. I should have remembered this guy right off."

"Hmm." Molly tapped one finger absently on the desk. "What makes you think Kendall's the person who played those nasty pranks on me?"

Harry turned the proposal document around so that she could see one of the diagrams more clearly. "Take a look at his design for the gearing mechanism that he planned to use on his crazy brain wave gadget."

Molly studied the drawing of an elaborate machine composed of myriad wires and an electronic panel mounted on a movable platform. "So?"

"Phony, pseudoscientific aspects of the project aside, the design is inelegant, unoriginal, and uninspired. Exactly like the designs of the fake gun and the goblin contraptions. The whole device has a jury-rigged look, just as those machines did. And this gear assembly," he pointed to a small section of the drawing, "is our smoking gun. Kendall's our man, all right."

"I'm amazed that you remembered such small details, Harry. This was one of the first proposals I showed you and, as I recall, you glanced at it for all of ten seconds."

"That was nine seconds more than it deserved." Harry's mouth quirked wryly. "But that was early on in our association, and I was still trying to play the polite consultant. I hadn't yet realized that you and I were going to go toe-to-toe over each and every off-the-wall grant proposal the foundation received."

"You mean, before I realized how stubborn and picky you were going to be?"

"Something like that." Harry lounged back in his chair and surveyed her with a thoughtful expression. "The question now is, what do we do about Kendall? I don't have any hard evidence here. Certainly not enough to take to the police."

Molly searched his face curiously. "Are we talking about a conclusion reached on the basis of your famous intuition?"

"We are talking about one of my insights, which, in turn, was produced by years of experience and trained observation," Harry said coolly.

"Have you ever noticed that you get downright snappish whenever there's a reference to intuition or psychic stuff?"

"I have no patience with that kind of nonsense."

Molly smiled. "You have patience for just about everything else."

"Every man has his limits."

"I see. Well, even if you did have convincing proof that Kendall had pulled those stunts, we're not dealing with attempted murder or even real mayhem here. I doubt that the cops could do much except issue a warning."

"Something I can do myself," Harry said very softly.

Molly was instantly alarmed. "Now, Harry—"

He picked up the drawing and examined it intently. "I wonder if Kendall is still at this address. I don't recognize the name of the town."

"I don't like that look in your eye."

Harry's head came up so swiftly that Molly was startled into taking a step back.

He pinned her with a fierce gaze. "What look?"

"Take it easy." Molly spread her hands. "It was just an expression."

"Sorry." Harry was silent for a moment. "My ex-fiancée used to make similar comments about my expressions. She said I made her nervous."

"Do I look nervous?"

Harry studied her closely. "No."

"Bear in mind at all times, Harry, that I am not your ex-fiancée."

He blinked slowly and then he smiled. "Don't worry. I won't ever confuse you with Olivia."

This time the amber in his eyes was so warm Molly could almost feel the heat. She cleared her throat and pulled her attention back to the matter at hand. "Now, then, what I meant to say was, I am not sure I approve of your plans to confront Wharton Kendall. What, exactly, do you intend to do?"

"Pay a personal call on him to discuss the little matter of nasty pranks."

Molly pursed her lips. "He'll probably deny everything."

"I don't plan to give him the chance to deny anything. I'm going to convince him that I have proof that he's the one behind the pranks and that if he tries anything else, I'll go to the cops."

"In other words, you're going to try to put a scare into him?"

"Yes."

Molly contemplated that. "Think you can do it?"

Harry looked up from the drawing. All of the warmth had drained out of his gaze. "Yes."

Molly was suddenly aware of a distinct chill in the room. Instinctively she raised a hand to pull the lapels of her robe more closely together. "I'll go with you."

"No, you will not." Harry went back to studying the drawing.

Molly stopped clutching her robe. She planted her hands on the desk and narrowed her eyes. "You are not a lone crusader, Dr. Trevelyan. You are working for the Abberwick Foundation. That means you take orders from me. I will accompany you when you visit Wharton Kendall. Is that clearly understood?"

Harry glanced up once more from Kendall's drawing. He gave her a long, thorough assessment, and then his mouth twitched at the corner. "Understood."

"Good." Molly straightened.

"There's just one small problem."

"What's that?"

"Finding Kendall may take some time." Harry indicated the cover page of the proposal. "There's no phone number. He gives his address as a post office box in a place called Icy Crest."

"Where's that?"

"I don't know. First we have to find the town, and then we have to find Kendall. It's going to take at least a full day to track him down and talk to him once we've located him. You probably don't want to be out of town on a work day. I know how important your business is to you."

"Oh, no," Molly said swiftly. "You're not getting rid of me that easily. I can arrange to leave Tessa in charge for a day."

"You're sure?"

"Absolutely, positively certain, Dr. Trevelyan."

181

"Have I ever told you that I don't like to be called Dr. Trevelyan?" Harry asked conversationally.

"No." Molly grinned. "I figured out weeks ago that it irritates the heck out of you."

Icy Crest proved to be little more than a blip on the map. It was located deep in the Cascade Mountains, at the end of a narrow, twisting, two-lane road. It was several miles from Interstate 90, which linked eastern and western Washington.

Molly studied the scruffy little town through the windshield of Harry's sleek car and wondered why she was suddenly consumed by a deep sense of unease.

The tiny mountain hamlet possessed the usual accoutrements of small rural villages everywhere, namely a single gas station, a dreary-looking grocery called *Pete's*, a café, and a tavern. A small sign in the dirty window of the grocery store declared that the post office was located inside.

A handful of men clad in worn denims, boots, and billed caps lounged in front of the store. Molly noticed that all of the caps bore the colorful logos of various farm equipment manufacturing companies. Malevolent eyes watched as Harry parked the car and switched off the ignition.

"Something tells me this may not be as simple as it sounded," Molly said.

Harry surveyed the men hanging around in front of the store. "What gives you that impression?"

"I'm not sure. I think it's the hats." Molly nibbled on her lower lip. "I don't know, Harry. I don't like this."

"It's a little late for second thoughts. You were the one who insisted on coming along."

"I'm aware of that. Usually I enjoy small towns. But there's something about this one—" She broke off, unable to put her qualms into words.

"What about it?"

She slanted him a quick, sidelong glance. "What would you say if I told you that I had an unpleasant feeling about this place?"

"I'd say that's an eminently reasonable feeling to have under the circumstances. We're here to see a man who's been trying to scare you to death, remember. Why would you feel enthusiastic about coming face-to-face with him?" Harry opened the door and got out.

Molly followed quickly. Harry was right. Given the situation, there was nothing odd about her troubled mood. She smiled tentatively at the cluster of men watching her. None of them smiled back.

Harry looked straight at the small crowd gathered in front of the store and inclined his head slightly. To Molly's surprise, one or two of the men gave him a stiff response. The others shifted their booted feet and found something else besides Molly to engage their attention.

Harry took Molly's hand and walked into the grocery store.

Molly took in the shelves of dusty canned goods, packages of toilet paper, and assorted household necessities. Neon beer signs hung in the windows. A soft drink machine hummed to itself in the corner.

Harry released Molly's hand, slipped some change out of his pocket, and crossed the room to the pop machine. He dropped the coins into the slot and punched in his selections. Machinery whirred. Cans clanked.

A massive figure appeared in the doorway behind the front counter. Molly caught a glimpse of a vast, hairy stomach draped over the waistband of a pair of old, sagging jeans. She quickly averted her eyes from the sight.

"Can I help ya?" The voice was unexpectedly high and nasal for such a large man. There was a distinct lack of welcome in it.

Harry picked up the soft drink cans that had rolled into the tray. "Are you Pete?"

"Yeah."

"I'm Harry. This is Molly."

Pete squinted at Molly. She smiled brightly. He gave her a grudging nod and snapped his gum. Then he turned back to Harry.

"Somethin' you wanted, Harry?"

"We're looking for a man named Wharton Kendall. We understand he lives here in Icy Crest."

Pete chewed gum and squinted in thought. "Used to." There was an air of challenge in the statement, as if he dared Harry to ask for more details.

Molly was acutely aware of the tension in the air. It was probably nothing more than the natural reluctance of a small town resident to provide information to a stranger, but it was uncomfortable.

Harry seemed oblivious to the atmosphere. He popped the top on one of the cans and took a long swallow. Then he looked at the big man behind the counter. "How long has Kendall been gone?"

"Not long. Coupla days."

"Did he live nearby?"

Pete's broad face set in lines of mulish resistance. It was apparent that he did not intend to answer any further questions.

Harry just looked at him for a long time. The silence thickened. Molly had an urge to run out of the store. She stood her ground only because she could not leave Harry alone.

The strain of the extended silence finally broke Pete's resolve to say nothing further on the subject of Wharton Kendall.

"Rented a cabin from Shorty for a while." Pete went back to work on his chewing gum.

Harry took another swallow of his soft drink and continued to study the big man with cold, unblinking eyes. "Any idea where Kendall went?"

Pete stirred restlessly beneath Harry's gaze. His obvious discomfort reminded Molly of the reactions of the men out in front of the store.

"Shorty told me the crazy son-of-a-bitch was headed for California. No loss. Guy was weird, y'know? Kendall a friend of yours?"

"No." Harry did not elaborate "Who's Shorty?"

"Runs the tavern next door."

"Thanks."

"Sure. Right." Pete scratched the large portion of his stomach that was not covered by his shirt.

Harry handed the unopened soft drink can to Molly. 'Let's go see Shorty."

"I can't believe you pulled that off," Molly said half an hour later as Harry halted the Sneath in the drive of an aging cabin.

"Pulled what off?" Harry rested his arms on the wheel and examined the cabin with close attention.

"The way you convinced Pete and Shorty to give us the information we wanted. You have an interesting effect on people, Harry. Have you ever noticed?"

He glanced at her in mild surprise. "What makes you think Pete and Shorty weren't happy to give us the information about Kendall?"

"Hah. Don't give me that. You know perfectly well you somehow intimidated Pete, and you bamboozled Shorty." She held up the key in her hand and dangled it in front of him. "So we're interested in renting a cabin, are we?"

"It was as good a line as any." Harry opened his door and got out.

"You're as smooth as silk when you want to be, Harry." Molly scrambled out of the car and walked around the front of it to join him. "Do they teach the fine art of concocting outrageous stories in graduate school?"

"As it happens, I got that talent from the Trevelyan side of the family."

"You do know what Shorty thinks, don't you?"

"I can take a wild guess." Harry took the key from her fingers and started toward the front door of the cabin.

"I'll just bet you can, since you're the one who put the idea into his head." Molly hurried after him. "He thinks we're looking for a secluded cabin far from the city in order to conduct an illicit weekend affair."

"Yes."

"Somehow," Molly said very deliberately, "Shorty got the impression that one or both of us is married."

"Well, it wouldn't be an illicit affair if we were both free, now, would it?" Harry fitted the key into the lock of the cabin door.

"I'm not sure I like having my reputation trashed just for the sake of a peek inside Wharton Kendall's cabin."

"Relax." Harry pushed open the cabin door. "If Shorty ever sobers up long enough to talk to Pete, he'll realize that we were more interested in checking out Kendall than we were in using this place as a love nest."

"That should confuse him no end."

"It won't matter," Harry said. "By then, we'll be long gone."

"I know, but—" Molly stopped talking abruptly, her attention captured by the interior of the cabin. "Good grief. I'd say *what a dump*, but I think someone else has already used that line."

From the eroded rug in front of the hearth to the layered stains on the linoleum floor of the kitchen, the cabin was a disaster. The smell of old cooking grease and rotting garbage permeated the air.

Harry surveyed the scene. "Looks like Kendall cleared out quickly."

"This," Molly declared, "is not just evidence of a hasty departure. A mess like this is weeks, even months in the making. This is the work of a born slob."

Harry smiled briefly. "I told you Kendall was a sloppy thinker."

"It shows." Molly walked cautiously through the clutter. "I wonder where he did his work?"

"Must have been right here in the living room. Unless he converted the bedroom into a workshop. I'll take a look." Harry crossed to the short hall and glanced around the corner of the bedroom door.

"See anything in there?" Molly called.

"Just a broken-down bed that only a truly desperate couple forced to conduct their illicit love affair here in Icy Crest would find romantic."

"That lets us out." Molly went to peer over his shoulder. "We're not desperate, and we're not illicit."

The bedroom was no cleaner than the living room and kitchen. Tattered curtains hung limply over the single grimy window. The mattress had the uniform gray patina and unpleasant stains that only long years of hard use could provide. The closet doors stood open. The interior was empty except for a broken shoelace and a sock on the floor.

"He's definitely gone," Harry said. "I wonder why?"

Molly shrugged. "Shorty said that Kendall told him he was going back to California. Maybe that was the simple truth."

"Maybe." Harry looked unconvinced. "Or maybe he's back in Seattle planning another prank."

"Maybe he'd had enough of revenge," Molly suggested, feeling quite optimistic now that it was obvious Kendall was gone.

"Possible." Harry moved into the center of the room. He went down on one knee to look under the bed. "Or maybe he realized he'd pushed his luck a little too far. Any way you cut it, there are a lot of maybes."

Molly watched as Harry rose and went into the bathroom. "What are you looking for?"

"I'm not sure. I'll know it when I see it."

"It looks like Kendall took all of his possessions."

"Yes." Harry walked out of the bathroom and headed for the front room. "But he packed in a hurry. And he was sloppy, remember?"

"So?"

"So, it's possible he overlooked something in his haste to get out of Icy Crest." Harry began systematically to open and close the kitchen cupboard doors.

"Such as?"

"An address. The phone number of someone he knows in California. Whatever. Anything that will give me a lead."

Molly's uneasy mood had begun to lift, but Harry's words

sent it plunging once more. "But he's gone. It's over. He can't continue his stupid revenge scheme from California."

"Something tells me it would be good policy to know exactly where he is. I don't like the idea that he's drifting around out there in the ether. I want to get a handle on him."

"I think you're being overly cautious here," Molly said.

"It's my nature. I do things methodically and logically, remember?"

"Yeah, sure."

Molly gingerly raised a couch cushion to see what evil lurked underneath it. When she discovered the decomposing remains of several crushed potato chips, she eased the cushion back into place. She cautiously continued the search, but all she discovered was further evidence that Wharton Kendall had subsisted on junk food.

In an effort to demonstrate that she, too, could be systematic and orderly, she knelt on the couch and peered down into the darkness behind it. She was surprised to see a notebook wedged between the wall and the back of the couch.

"Aha," she said.

Harry glanced at her from the other side of the small room, where he was going through a desk. "Aha, what?"

"I see something." Molly scrambled off the couch and tried to shove the massive relic away from the wall. It didn't budge. "This sucker is heavy."

"Hang on, I'll give you a hand with that." Harry crossed the room and took a firm grip on one arm of the couch. He shoved it away from the wall as easily as though it were made of cardboard.

Molly sidled into the opening and plucked the notebook off the floor. "It's probably nothing at all. But my father used to keep his notes in three-ring binders like this."

Harry stood behind her and watched as she flipped open the notebook. He frowned at the crude drawings inside. "Looks like more of his wild designs for paranormal instrumentation. The guy is really out there on the fringe. And

188

you were ready to give him ten grand to finance his loony project."

"That is very unfair. You know perfectly well that I did not argue with you when you turned down his proposal. I was still at the point in our association where I was trying to show due respect for your technical expertise."

"That stage didn't last long," Harry said absently. "Wait, turn the page back."

Molly obediently flipped back to the previous sheet of paper. She studied the sketch that had caught his eye. "Well?"

"Don't you recognize it?"

"No. Should I? It looks like a box with a jumble of mechanical stuff inside."

"It's the box that housed the fake gun assembly," Harry said with soft certainty. "This is it. This is our proof that Kendall was behind the pranks."

Half an hour later Molly experienced a quiet surge of relief as the unfriendly town of Icy Crest vanished behind a curve in the road. She adjusted her seat belt, settled back, and picked up Wharton Kendall's notebook. She began to turn the pages with casual interest.

"Do you still think it's necessary to track Kendall down?" she asked as she studied one of the sketches.

"Definitely. I want him to know that we're on to him and that we've got enough evidence to call in the police, if necessary." Harry accelerated smoothly out of a tight curve. "But the more I think about it, the more I'm convinced that you're right. It's going to be tough to convince the cops to get involved in this."

"There's been no real violence, and he's apparently left the state. I can't see anyone getting too worked up about Kendall except you and me."

"With any luck, Kendall has abandoned his revenge in favor of trying to find some fresh funding in California."

"Think he'll convince someone down there to back him?"

"We're talking about California." Harry glanced in his

rearview mirror. He frowned slightly and then returned his attention to the road. "No shortage of nuts down there who will be more than willing to finance one of his flaky paranormal inventions."

"I suppose you're right." Molly heaved a small sigh. "Well, since the dynamic duo of Abberwick and Trevelyan seems to have solved the mystery of the malicious pranks I guess I'll be able to move back home."

"I've got plenty of room."

"Yes, I know, but if I stay at your place much longer I will cross that invisible line that separates houseguest from roommate."

"Feel free to cross it."

"I can't stay with you indefinitely," she said gently.

"Why not?"

She gave him an exasperated look. "Because I can't, that's why not. Our arrangement was that I would stay with you until we located Kendall."

"Which we have not yet done."

"Harry, I have a home of my own."

"I don't see—" Harry broke off abruptly.

"What's wrong?" Molly asked without glancing up from the notebook.

"Nothing. Why?"

"I don't know. I just had a feeling that something was bothering you." She turned another page and paused to examine a sketch of what appeared to be a helmet with wires attached to it. "This is interesting. Harry, maybe we shouldn't have been so quick to dismiss Kendall's research."

"What research? There's no research behind his crackpot ideas. Just fantasy." Harry eased his foot down on the pedal. The car picked up speed.

Molly closed the notebook with a snap. "What is it? What's wrong?"

"Some fool in a blue Ford is coming up behind us too fast for this road."

Molly turned in the seat and glanced through the rear window. She saw a late-model blue car emerge from the last curve. It was moving swiftly. Too swiftly for the winding road. The Ford's tinted windows made it impossible to see the driver's face.

"Looks like the impatient type. Better let him pass, Harry."

"There's no passing lane and nothing but a series of curves for the next ten miles."

"You could pull over to the side." A sense of urgency gripped Molly as the Ford drew closer. "Do it, Harry. The guy may be drunk."

Harry did not argue. He started to downshift.

The Ford leaped ahead, moving out to pass.

"He's going to go around us," Molly said, relieved at this evidence of the Ford's obvious intentions.

The Ford was abreast of them now. It made no move to shoot past them. Instead, as Molly watched in horror, it edged closer to the front fender of Harry's sleek sports car. She suddenly realized that the driver of the Ford intended to force them off the road.

There was no place to go. A sharp, tree-studded incline waited on the other side of the all-too-fragile guard rail.

*"Harry."*

"Hang on," Harry said softly.

Molly held her breath. Some part of her knew that they could not possibly escape the Ford now. It was too close. And the next wicked curve loomed ahead. Close. Much too close. She waited for the impact.

What happened next was a blur to Molly. Braced for the crash, she was unprepared for the sudden, violent deceleration of the sports car as Harry braked abruptly. Molly heard the tires scream in protest. The Sneath went into a slide.

She was dimly aware of the blue Ford flashing past as it overshot its target. It swerved frantically as the driver fought to recover control before he entered the next curve.

And then it was gone.

Molly waited for the sliding Sneath to crash through the guard rail.

# 12

Harry ended the controlled slide and brought the Sneath to a clean stop in the right-hand lane. He automatically checked the rearview mirror to make certain there was no one coming out of the curve behind him. Then he surveyed Molly. She was safe within the cocoon of her seat belt and shoulder harness. Her face was strained, but she appeared astonishingly calm.

"Are you all right?" Even to his own ears his voice sounded as rough as a lava field. He couldn't help it. The impact of the realization that Molly could have been killed would take a while to wear off. Maybe a lifetime.

"I'm fine, thanks to you." She turned her head to look at him. Her eyes were enormous. "That was an incredible piece of driving. I thought we were going over the side."

"Good car."

Molly shook her head. "Good driver. Anyone else would have lost control. Josh was right. You do have terrific reflexes."

Harry dredged up a smile that he knew very probably resembled the skeletal grin of a Halloween mask. "We all have our little talents."

"Your little talent just saved both our lives," she said with great depth of feeling. "If I weren't so terrified of unfasten-

192

ing my seat belt while we're sitting in the middle of this road, I'd give you a big, wet, squishy kiss."

"I'll take you up on that later." Harry checked the mirror once more and then put the engine in gear.

He could have caught up with the blue Ford, he thought with fleeting regret. He would have liked very much to do just that. And if he had been alone, he would have done it. There was little doubt but that he had a distinct advantage on a road full of curves such as this one. His reflexes and the handling characteristics of the Sneath guaranteed it. But it would have been a risky chase, and he was not about to put Molly in further danger.

"Do you think we should report that car to the highway patrol?" Molly asked after a minute.

Harry shrugged. "Sure. But I doubt that anything will come of it. Near misses aren't uncommon. Especially on back roads like this."

"We can describe the car. It was a late-model blue Ford."

"Yes, but there were no plates."

"No license plates?" Molly stared at him. "I guess that in all the excitement I didn't even notice. I hate to ask, but do you think it was a deliberate attempt to run us off the road? Or do you think the driver was under the influence, and we happened to be in the wrong place at the wrong time?"

"I don't know," Harry said honestly. "But I don't like co-incidences."

"The guy was probably drunk."

"Maybe."

Molly slanted him an assessing look. "You're not thinking what I think you're thinking, are you?"

"That the driver of the Ford was Wharton Kendall?"

She sighed. "I knew it. You're thinking the same thing. It's highly unlikely, isn't it? I mean, Kendall is supposed to be in California by now."

"That's where he's supposed to be. But there seems to be a general consensus that the bastard is nuttier than a fruitcake. Who knows where he is."

"Why would he sneak around Icy Crest waiting to see if

**198**

someone came looking for him? It doesn't make sense. He moved out of Shorty's cabin. Where would he sleep?"

"In his car."

"Where would he eat?"

"He could have a supply of junk food stashed in the trunk of the Ford."

"How would he know when and where to watch for us?"

Harry thought about that one for a couple of seconds. "He could have hidden in the woods in order to keep an eye on the cabin. Waited to see if anyone came looking for evidence. Or someone in Icy Crest might have done the legwork for him. Maybe good old Pete or Shorty or one of the men standing around out in front of the grocery store called Kendall and let him know someone was in town looking for him."

Molly looked thoughtful. "That implies he had a phone available."

"Cellular car phones aren't exactly a novelty these days."

She made a face. "You have an answer for everything, don't you? The thing is, the good folk of Icy Crest all seemed to dismiss Kendall as a weird kook. I don't think they liked him very much."

"Even weird kooks have money. Someone in town might have been willing to take his cash in exchange for providing information."

Molly frowned. "Wharton Kendall doesn't have a lot of money. If he did, he wouldn't have had to apply for funding from the Abberwick Foundation."

"I don't think it would take more than fifty bucks to tempt any of those men who were hanging around Pete's store. Hell, Pete himself would probably turn in his own mother for twenty-five dollars and a shirt that was a couple of sizes larger."

"You could be right. Damn. This mess is getting more and more complicated, isn't it? Things could go on like this for a very long time." Molly became very quiet.

Harry understood quiet. He was accustomed to sinking into his own personal pools of deep silence for hours on end. He had been around Molly long enough to know that she was quite capable of occupying herself with her own thoughts. But the remote expression on her face now made him uneasy. There was an important issue he wanted settled before they reached Seattle.

"Molly?"

"Hmm?"

Harry flexed his hands on the wheel. He had to handle this carefully. "This incident today settles one matter. You're definitely going to stay with me until we get this thing sorted out."

She looked slightly startled. "How did you know that I was thinking about moving back into my own house?"

"Because I can read your mind," he shot back, irritated by her stubbornness.

"Read my mind?" She flashed him one of her brilliant, laughing smiles. "Ah, yes, the infamous Trevelyan Second Sight."

"It was a joke, Molly."

"I know." Her smile vanished. She touched his arm briefly. "I was just teasing you."

He opted for the logical, well-reasoned approach. It was what he did best. "You would feel safer, and I would worry a whole lot less, if you stayed with me until I've located Kendall."

"That could take a while. And what happens if you can't find him? What if he's just vanished?"

The implications of the question took Harry's breath away. It ignited a fantasy that had been smoldering deep inside him. What if Molly came to live with him for good?

He would eventually find Kendall, of course. The man was too sloppy and too disorganized to disappear without a trace. Harry would locate him and take steps to make certain that he never bothered Molly again.

But what if Molly did not move out?

"Would that be a problem?" he asked softly.

She crossed her arms beneath her breasts and focused intently on the road. "As I was saying before we were so rudely interrupted by the blue Ford, I can't stay with you indefinitely."

"Why not?"

"You have to ask me that? Harry, at the beginning of our relationship, you're the one who took great pains to point out to me just how many things we do *not* have in common."

"You added a couple of things to the list," he reminded her. "Something about tomatoes. Look, maybe we both overestimated the number of areas of disagreement. We seem to be able to deal with the ones that do arise."

She turned her head quickly to look at him. Harry could feel the intense curiosity and the sensual awareness emanating from her. He struggled to find the logical, reasoned words that would convince her that moving in with him for good was the right decision. But his excellent brain failed him in his hour of need. He could not pressure her. He could only ask.

*Ask. Plead. Hope.* That was not his way. He knew better than to risk asking others for what he needed. What the hell was happening to him?

A shock of recognition went through him. What he was experiencing now as he waited for Molly's answer was all too familiar. It was akin to what he had felt the other night when he had been caught up in the vortex of intense concentration and she had come to him dressed in bridal white. He was vulnerable in a way he did not understand. It was a terrifying sensation.

"Staying with you for a few days is one thing," Molly said gently. "Staying indefinitely means we're living together."

*Yes, it does,* he thought. *You'd be in my bed every night. You'd be sitting across from me at the breakfast table every morning.*

"Well . . ."

"Just until we find Wharton Kendall and deal with him," he said.

She tensed. Then she gave him another brief, searching glance. "All right. If you're sure this is what you want."

*It's what I need,* he thought, still numbed by the shock of realization. "It's the only logical way to go," he said aloud. "Right. Logical."

The following morning Harry got off the elevator on the thirty-first floor of the downtown high-rise office tower. The massive, gleaming brass letters on the wall across from the bank of elevators spelled out the name of the company that had made the Strattons a family of movers and shakers in Seattle.

STRATTON PROPERTIES, INC.
COMMERCIAL REAL ESTATE
AND PROPERTY DEVELOPMENT

Harry turned to the right and went down the plushly carpeted corridor to the reception desk. An attractive, neatly suited woman in her twenties looked up with a smile of immediate recognition. Harry did not appear in the offices of Stratton Properties very often, but the staff knew him on sight. His visits tended to be memorable.

"Good morning, Mr. Trevelyan. What can I do for you today?"

"Good morning, Verna. Would you please tell my grandfather that I want to see him for a few minutes?"

"Certainly." Verna pressed the intercom button on her desk. "Mr. Stratton?"

"What is it, Verna?" Parker Stratton's voice was gravelly with age, but it had lost none of its authority.

"Mr. Trevelyan is here to see you."

There was a brief pause. Then Parker's voice came back through the intercom in a low growl. "Tell him I'm busy. Give him an appointment for next week."

Harry nodded pleasantly to the receptionist and started past her desk. "Thanks, Verna. Hold all his calls until I leave."

"But, Mr. Trevelyan," Verna called anxiously. "Mr. Stratton says he's busy at the moment."

"He can't be busy. He's officially retired." Harry went around the corner, past the tasteful display of art glass that occupied one wall. He opened the door of Parker's office without bothering to knock.

Parker was seated behind his desk. He had a gold pen in one gnarled hand. He still had a finger on the intercom button. He glowered at Harry. "You've got the manners of a damned Trevelyan."

"I am a Trevelyan." Harry closed the door and took a chair. "Unfortunately for you, I'm also a Stratton."

"I assume you didn't barge into my office to discuss genealogy. What do you want?"

"I'm here to talk about Brandon's plans to go into business for himself."

"Damn it to hell." Parker tossed aside the gold pen. "I knew sooner or later you'd interfere in this fiasco. Did Danielle go crying to you? Or was it Olivia?"

"I've talked to both of them. I've also talked to Brandon."

"What the hell is it with you, Harry? Why do you always have to get involved in family stuff like this?"

"Beats me. Maybe it's because I am family." Harry stretched his legs out in front of him and contemplated his grandfather.

A few years ago at the age of seventy, Parker had reluctantly turned over the day-to-day operation of Stratton Properties to his son, Gilford. Nothing short of an act of God, however, could keep Parker from going into his office every day. Stratton Properties was his life.

Parker had lived and breathed business from the cradle, and the diet had served him well. He used a cane when his arthritic knee bothered him, but other than that, he was in excellent health. He looked at least ten years younger than his chronological age, thanks to his fine Stratton bone structure. His doctor had told him that he had the heart and lungs of a man twenty years younger.

Stratton Properties was a part of Parker, as necessary to him as the very air he breathed. The day he died, he would be seated behind his desk.

"I'll get right to the point," Harry said. "I think you should give Brandon his chance. Tell him you're behind him. Tell him there will be no reprisals."

Parker aimed a finger at him. "You stay out of this, by God. As far as I'm concerned, you're the reason he's taken this damn fool notion into his head in the first place."

Harry held up both hands, palms out. "Scout's honor, I never once encouraged him to try his hand at commercial property management. He came up with the idea all on his own."

"The hell he did. He saw how you walked away from your Stratton heritage, and he's decided to show everyone else in the family that he's just as goddamned stubborn and independent as you are."

"I think you're giving me entirely too much credit," Harry said.

"I'm not giving you any credit." Parker's eyes turned fierce. "I'm giving you the full blame for this stupid situation. If you hadn't come along, Brandon would never have thought about leaving the firm."

"You can't be sure of that."

"I am sure of it, damn it," Parker insisted. "You've been a bad influence on him."

"He wants to spread his wings a little. Why not let him do it?"

Parker's hand clenched into a bunched fist. "He won't survive a year out there on his own."

"You don't know that for certain. After all, he's got Stratton blood in his veins. Your blood. Who knows what he can do?"

"You've got Stratton blood in your veins, too." Parker's eyes narrowed. "But it wasn't enough to turn you into a businessman."

"We both know that I wasn't cut out for the corporate world," Harry said mildly.

"You mean you weren't cut out to face the real world. You prefer to hide in your damned ivory tower. You'd have been a vice president today if you'd joined the company when you first came to Seattle."

"Not likely," Harry said. "You and Gilford would have fired me within three months. I would never have fit in around here."

"Because you lack the discipline to fit in," Parker retorted. "That's your problem, Harry. You're too damned arrogant and bullheaded. It's your father's fault. He deliberately turned you against your heritage. It was his way of thumbing his nose at all things Stratton. It was his final revenge against me, that's what it was."

"I think we've covered this territory fairly thoroughly in the past."

Parker's jaw was rigid. For a moment it looked as though he was prepared to continue the old argument. Then he lounged back in his chair. "What's this I hear about you having a new lady friend?"

Harry raised his brows. "Word gets around. Her name is Molly Abberwick."

"Danielle says she appears to have moved in with you."

"She has. For a while."

Parker scowled. "You know I don't approve of that kind of thing."

"I know." Harry steepled his fingers. "Let's get back to the subject of Brandon."

"There's nothing to discuss. Don't expect me to encourage him in this idiotic scheme to go into business for himself. He has a duty to his family."

"Danielle is afraid that you'll disinherit Brandon if he goes off on his own."

"I will," Parker said immediately. "Told him as much the other day."

"Skip the threats. Give him your blessing, Parker."

"Why the devil should I?"

"Because he's going to go off on his own, anyway, and because it would be a lot less nerve-wracking for Danielle if you tell her it's okay by you."

"Why should I make it any easier for anyone?"

Harry waited a heartbeat or two until he knew he had Parker's full attention. "You owe Danielle this much."

"I owe her? Are you crazy? I've given my daughter everything. Given everyone in the family too damn much. That's half the problem around here. They're all spoiled." Parker beetled his brows. "What do I owe her?"

"She helped you save your precious company after your oldest daughter ran off with my father," Harry said evenly. "She did what my mother was supposed to do for you. She married Dean Hughes. Because of her you got the infusion of cash you needed so badly at the time. And you got the Hughes connections. They were worth even more than the money, weren't they?"

Parker stared at him, openmouthed, for a few seconds. Then his teeth snapped together. "How dare you imply that I forced Danielle into that marriage! As if I could. This isn't the Middle Ages."

"It might as well be, as far as you're concerned. You're still trying to run people's lives as if you were some feudal lord."

"I have a right to run a few things around here. I built this company. If it wasn't for me there would be no Stratton Properties, Inc."

"You had a little help along the way," Harry said softly. "Specifically from your daughter Danielle. She stepped into the breach when my mother ran off with my father. You owe her, Parker."

"I don't owe her a damn thing."

"You owe her big time, and you know it. She endured a hellish marriage for the sake of the family business. If it hadn't been for her, Stratton Properties would have gone under thirty-five years ago. It's payback time."

"What's this sudden concern with whether or not your aunt had a happy marriage? Most people don't have happy marriages, you know."

"My parents did," Harry said softly.

Parker flushed with rage. "Sean Trevelyan stole my little Brittany from her family. He seduced her, by God. He came like a thief in the night. He took her away from her home and her heritage and everything that was rightfully hers."

"And he kept her happy."

"He never gave her what she should have had, what she deserved."

Harry met his eyes. "If you want to see what would have happened to my mother if she had been married to Dean Hughes for a few years, take a look at Danielle."

"How dare you!" Parker roared. "At least she would still be alive."

Harry felt as if all the air had suddenly been sucked out of the room. *He was too late. They were both dead. And now he was going to die, too. He would never reach the surface in time. Too late. Too late.*

Emotion howled like a cold north wind across his soul. For a moment the barriers that protected him from the abyss wavered and threatened to dissolve. Harry could see straight through them to the endless darkness, and it beckoned with a terrible seductiveness. It would be so easy just to let himself fall into the depths and be lost forever.

And then an image of Molly appeared. She smiled at him from the opposite side of the abyss. Reality solidified around him.

Harry looked at Parker. "Like I said, you owe Aunt Danielle. Give her the one thing she really wants. The one thing that only you can give her."

"What's that?"

"Peace of mind about Brandon's future. Brandon doesn't need it, but she does. Danielle hasn't had much peace of mind in her life. She's been too busy trying to please you."

Parker's hands bunched into fists on the arms of his chair. "Who the hell appointed you avenging angel in this family?"

"Damned if I know." Harry opened the door.

"You can be a real SOB, Harry, you know that?"

Harry looked back over his shoulder, met and held his grandfather's eyes. "Runs in the family. Both sides."

He went out the door and closed it quietly.

He was not particularly surprised to find his uncle, Gilford

Stratton, waiting for him in front of the art glass display. Harry smiled bleakly. This was not going to be one of his lucky days.

Gilford was forty-nine, the youngest of Parker's three off-spring. With his aristocratic bones, fair hair, and hazel eyes, he was as handsome as the rest of the Strattons. Fifteen years ago he had married Constance Heeley, the daughter of a prominent Northwest shipping family. They had two children.

Luckily for the Strattons, Gilford had inherited more than just the family looks. He had also inherited the Stratton business talents. Stratton Properties was thriving under his administration.

"What are you up to now, Harry?" Gilford watched him with cool caution. Then understanding blazed in his eyes. "Damn it, you've upset Parker again, haven't you?"

"It doesn't take much. You know as well as I do that Parker gets annoyed at the very sight of me. But don't worry, he'll survive our latest discussion."

Gilford took a menacing step forward. "You talked to him about Brandon's stupid plan to leave the company, didn't you?"

"Yes."

"Stay out of this. You know how the old man feels about anyone in the family leaving the firm."

"I know," Harry said.

"I'm warning you, Harry, don't get involved in this. Let Parker handle it."

"His refusal to let Brandon go gracefully is tearing Danielle apart."

Gilford's expression tightened. "I know. I'm sorry about it, but that's the way it goes. It's not your problem. For once, try not to meddle in family business." He turned on his heel and strode off down the corridor to his corner office.

Harry watched him go, and then he made his way back through the reception area to the bank of elevators. The good news was that Molly was coming home for lunch.

\*     \*     \*

Molly folded her hands on top of her desk and regarded the sober, serious countenances of her aunt and Cutter Latteridge. She knew they both meant well, but their concern was irritating, nonetheless.

"Don't worry about me, Aunt Venicia. I'll be fine at Harry's place."

"But, dear, if you don't feel comfortable staying in your own home, you can stay with me." Venicia, dressed in a flowing orange and fuchsia dress, was as bright as any of the tropical fish in Harry's aquarium. But her eyes were troubled. "I really don't know if you should be moving in with Harry Trevelyan like this. You hardly know him."

"Believe me, I'm getting to know him better every day," Molly said.

Venicia straightened her shoulders with a determined air. She slanted a quick glance at Cutter and then frowned at Molly. "Dear, Cutter and I have discussed your Dr. Trevelyan, and we feel there is something not quite right about this whole situation."

"Not quite right?" Molly repeated.

Cutter cleared his throat meaningfully. "I know this isn't any of my business. I'm not exactly a member of the family yet." He paused to reach out and lightly touch Venicia's hand. "But I feel as if I'm almost one of the clan, and I must speak up here."

"Cutter, please," Molly said. "Don't worry."

"I can't help it, my dear." Cutter assumed the pontificating air he did so well. "I'm extremely concerned about this entire matter. If odd things have been happening to you lately, and if you're sure that the pranks are not the work of one of your sister's friends, I urge you to let the police handle the situation."

"As a matter of fact, Harry talked to the police yesterday," Molly said. "There's not much they can do, especially if Wharton Kendall has left for California."

"But surely they can do something about that car that tried to run you off the road," Venicia said.

"They couldn't do anything except make a note of it and

promise to keep an eye out for a blue Ford driven in a dangerous manner," Molly explained. "Harry and I can't even be certain there's a connection between the attempt to sideswipe us and Wharton Kendall. Personally, the more I think about it, the more I doubt that there is. We were probably just the near victims of a drunk driver."

Cutter gave her a considering look. "Why do you believe there's no connection?"

"Because until now, Kendall's idea of revenge has been to scare me with childish pranks," Molly said. "He certainly hasn't tried to hurt me."

Cutter's eyes narrowed. "If this Wharton Kendall fellow is responsible for the incidents, he's obviously a sick man, my dear. His insane rage may escalate. He could be very dangerous. Your aunt is right. You probably ought to move in with her until this is all over."

"I'll be safe at Harry's," Molly insisted. She did not want to point out that if Kendall was pursuing her, the last thing she wanted to do was put Venicia in jeopardy.

Venicia sighed. "My dear, I hate to sound old-fashioned, but you really must think about how this looks. People will wonder what Dr. Trevelyan's intentions are."

Molly rolled her eyes. "Aunt Venicia, please. We're not living in the last century."

Cutter looked grim. "I think we can guess Trevelyan's intentions."

Molly scowled at him. "What's that supposed to mean?"

"It means," Cutter said, "that there may be more to this than meets the eye. I realize that you are attracted to the man, my dear, but you must keep a level head. You are responsible for a great deal of money."

Molly unclasped her hands and braced them against the edge of her desk. "Are you still concerned that Harry may be interested in me only because he intends to skim a fortune in consulting fees off the foundation assets?"

"Don't be angry, dear," Venicia said quickly. "Cutter and I are both worried about this unusual relationship that seems to have sprung up between you and Dr. Trevelyan."

"I hate to say this," Cutter added ominously, "but it has struck me that your Dr. Trevelyan may be taking advantage of this Wharton Kendall situation."

"That's outrageous," Molly said.

"Is it?" Cutter looked unconvinced. "It appears to me that he's drawing you deeper and deeper into his web. Trevelyan has convinced you that you need his protection in addition to his expertise. You've become emotionally involved, my dear."

"For the last time," Molly said through her teeth, "I know what I'm doing."

Cutter shook his head. "Anyone who is the trustee for a well-endowed foundation must question such a personal relationship with someone who stands to profit from that foundation. No, my dear, the way I see it, you've got two distinct threats to worry about. The possibility that an unstable inventor is out for revenge, and the equally unwelcome prospect of working with an unscrupulous consultant."

Molly realized she was seething. "If Harry was so interested in getting his hands on a fortune, he wouldn't have walked away from the Stratton money."

Cutter studied her with a sympathetic expression. "He didn't exactly walk away from it, my dear. According to my sources, he and his grandfather, Parker Stratton, quarreled bitterly. Harry refused to go to work for the firm. Stratton cut him off from the family money. And there's something more. Something you may not know."

"What's that?" Molly demanded.

Cutter hesitated. "I hate to say this, but I have heard a rumor to the effect that Harry Trevelyan may not be a well man, mentally speaking."

*"What? Where on earth did you hear that?"*

Cutter sighed. "An acquaintance of mine once worked for Stratton Properties. He knows people there. Apparently Trevelyan's fiancée broke off her engagement to him when she discovered that he had some sort of psychiatric disorder. She's a psychologist, I understand, so she understood the implications."

Molly leaped to her feet. "That is absolutely, positively untrue. Harry is not crazy."

"Please, Molly," Venicia soothed. "You must be rational about this."

Molly glowered at her. "Just what do you suggest I do?"

Venicia smiled reassuringly. "Actually, I have an idea, Molly."

"What's that?"

"You could turn the trusteeship of the foundation over to me," Venicia said. "I know it's been a trial to you from the start. Let me handle things for you. If I took over, you would be able to step out of the picture entirely."

Molly stared at her. "Turn the foundation over to you?"

"It's a thought," Cutter said slowly. "Wharton Kendall would soon realize that you no longer hold the purse strings. The knowledge might cool his obsession with revenge. And Dr. Trevelyan would no longer be a risk, either."

"He's not a risk," Molly whispered.

"Look at it this way," Cutter said gently. "If his romantic interest in you is genuine, he won't care if you're no longer in charge of the foundation."

"You'll discover soon enough if his intentions are honorable," Venicia put in helpfully.

Molly shook her head. "Aunt Venicia, you don't want the task of running the foundation, believe me. It's a constant headache."

"Well, no, I don't want the job," Venicia said honestly. "But I'm willing to undertake the responsibility. It's the least I can do. Cutter could assist me. He's got a strong background in engineering. He could sort through the proposals and make selection decisions."

"I must admit, I would find the work interesting," Cutter said thoughtfully. "Keep the old brain sharp."

"We're both retired," Venicia reminded Molly. "We have the time for charity work."

"Give the matter some consideration, Molly." Cutter rose to his feet and took Venicia's hand. "Turning the reins of the foundation over to your aunt might solve all of your problems. Now, you must excuse us. Venicia and I have an appointment with our travel agent. Got a honeymoon to plan, you know."

"That reminds me," Venicia said. "You won't forget that you promised to come with me when I shop for my wedding gown, Molly?"

"I won't forget," Molly said.

Venicia and Cutter turned toward the office door. They halted abruptly when they saw that it was open. Harry lounged there, one shoulder against the jamb.

"Don't let me get in the way," he said softly.

Cutter bristled. "We don't intend to." He conducted Venicia through the doorway.

A moment later the front door of the shop closed behind them.

Molly swallowed. "I didn't hear you come in."

"Why is it," Harry asked, "that every time I walk into your office lately I find someone trying to convince you that I'm a threat to the Abberwick Foundation assets? First Gordon Brooke and now your aunt and her fiancé."

"I'm sorry you overheard that. Venicia and Cutter are concerned, that's all. It's the Wharton Kendall thing."

"It sounded like more than that," Harry said. "I thought I heard something about honorable intentions."

Molly blushed. "Aunt Venicia and Cutter are a little old-fashioned."

"What a coincidence." Harry's eyes were unreadable. "I just came from a meeting with someone else who takes an old-fashioned view of two people living together without benefit of a marriage license."

Molly gave him a very bright smile. "Luckily for us, we're both modern thinkers."

# 13

"He goes by the name of Wharton Kendall," Harry said into the phone. He paced the floor of his study as he talked to Fergus Rice. "I want you to find out where he is now and where he might have been yesterday, if possible."

"I'll do my best. Fax me what you've got from that grant proposal you said he wrote and anything else that looks interesting."

"I will."

There was a pause accompanied by soft clicking sounds on the other end of the line. Harry knew that Fergus was making notes on his computer.

Fergus Rice was a private investigator. One of the best. Harry had used his services occasionally in the past when he had needed practical information to supplement his own scholarly deductions in the course of an investigation into scientific fraud.

Harry was an expert when it came to studying the academic and technical evidence, but he was not a trained investigator in the old-fashioned, gumshoe sense of the word. He could have learned the craft, but he preferred not to spend his time in the mundane task of checking addresses and phone numbers. He paid other people to do that for him when necessary and billed the client for the expense.

"Is that it?" Fergus asked when he'd finished his notes.

"For now. If I come up with more, I'll let you know. Put a rush on this, will you, Fergus? The man's getting flakier by the day. The first two practical jokes were not lethal, but if that was Kendall in the blue Ford yesterday, he's definitely become dangerous."

"I'll get right on it."

Harry tossed the phone down into the cradle and went to stand in front of the large saltwater aquarium. He contemplated the angel fish as they cruised the miniature reef and wondered how many more people were going to get in line to convince Molly that she should not put her trust in him.

He had a reputation for being able to identify swindlers and charlatans of the most sophisticated kind, Harry thought. Large corporations and the government sought out his services when scientific fraud was suspected. He had written a book on the history of scientific hoaxes and another volume on the perils of scientific and academic illusions.

It seemed to him that his entire life had been devoted to the study of deception. His Trevelyan birthright had given him the skills to detect hustlers, liars, and cheats. His Stratton blood had provided him with sound business instincts. His academic training had endowed him with the knowledge and insight that enabled him to spot high-tech flimflammers.

Always he had been on the side of truth. Always he had been the one to expose the deceivers. Always he had taken the righteous stance and pointed the finger at those who sought to deceive.

Now people were telling Molly that he was very probably trying to deceive and defraud her. And he had no way to prove his innocence.

So far she seemed to trust him. How many times would she have to hear him accused of sleeping with her in order to get his hands on the Abberwick Foundation assets before she began to put some credence in the notion, he wondered.

He also wondered how many times she could listen to someone label him crazy before she began to believe it.

There was a soft sound from the hall.

"Brooding again?" Molly asked cheerfully from the doorway.

Harry turned swiftly to face her. "I didn't hear you come home."

"I arrived just as Ginny was leaving." Molly crossed the study to put her arms around his neck.

He folded her close and bent his head to kiss her. It felt good to have her here at the end of a long day, he thought. It felt right. He did not want to think about what might happen if she listened to the accusations and warnings.

Molly leaned her head back and searched his face with her gem-green eyes. "Want to talk about dinner?"

He smiled slightly. "What did you have in mind?"

"I think we should go out this evening. You're in one of your morose phases. Probably the full moon. Dinner out might help you shake off the mood."

"All right." A shiver of unease went through him. He wondered if his periodic bouts of solemn contemplation were starting to bother her. The possibility darkened his already bleak frame of mind. He struggled to strike an upbeat note. "You choose the restaurant."

"Why don't we go across the street to that new place featuring Pacific Rim cuisine?" She paused as one of the two phones on the desk burbled. "Oops. Private line. Must be family." Her hands dropped away from his neck.

"Damn." Harry eyed the phone with misgivings. For a few seconds he actually thought about ignoring the call. He did not want to deal with any more family problems today. Then he reached for the receiver.

"This is Harry."

"Harry, it's me, Josh."

The urgency in Josh's voice fueled Harry's gathering gloom as nothing else could have done. "What's wrong?"

"Grandpa is in the hospital here in Hidden Springs. He crashed his new truck an hour ago."

Harry closed his eyes briefly. "How bad?"

"Bad. The doctor warned us that the next few hours are critical." There was a desperate, disbelieving note in Josh's voice. "He said Grandpa might not make it through the night."

Harry glanced at his watch. "I'll be there as soon as I can. Don't give up the ship. Leon is one tough old bird."

"He's not really that old. He's not even seventy, you know. Lots of people live a lot longer."

"Take it easy, Josh."

Josh paused. When he spoke again, his voice was very subdued. "There was a fire at the scene, Harry. Just like there was when Dad was killed."

"I'm on my way, kid."

"Thanks."

Harry put down the phone. He looked at Molly. "I'm sorry. I've got to drive to Hidden Springs tonight. Leon managed to smash up his new truck. And, being Leon, he managed to make a spectacular mess of the situation."

"I'll go with you," Molly said.

Harry was startled at his reaction to her quiet offer. He was so accustomed to dealing with Trevelyan and Stratton family crises on his own that he did not immediately recognize the sense of relief that he felt.

Molly stood near the window of the hospital room and listened to the beeps, pings, and clicks of the machines that kept Leon Trevelyan from slipping through death's trapdoor. Leon was not aware of her presence. His attention was equally divided between his pain and Harry.

Harry was alone at Leon's bedside. A variety of Trevelyans, including Josh and Evangeline, hovered in the waiting room down the hall. The nurse had refused to allow them all into Leon's room at the same time.

Molly had seen the way the entire family had turned toward Harry when he had walked into the hospital a short while ago. It was as if they expected him to take charge. And in some subtle but unmistakable manner, he had done just that.

He had first conferred quietly with the doctor. Then he had announced that he wanted to talk to Leon for a few minutes. Molly had started to take a seat near Josh, but Harry had looked at her, and she had known that he wanted her to accompany him into the room.

"Well, Leon, you nearly did it this time, didn't you?" Harry said quietly.

"Shit. Who sent for you, Harry?" Leon's voice rasped in his throat. "I don't need you here."

"Believe me, there are a number of other places I'd rather be."

"Me, too." Leon paused as if to gather energy. "Where's Josh?"

"Out in the waiting room."

"Send him back in here, damn it."

"I will in a few minutes. We need to talk first."

"Why?"

"I spoke to the cops," Harry said. "They told me that you wrapped the truck around a tree. It was raining. Driving too fast in unsafe conditions, according to the report."

"Son-of-a-bitch," Leon muttered. "I'm dyin', and you want to give me another one of your damned safety lectures."

Molly saw Harry's jaw tighten, but his expression did not alter. It remained implacable. She knew then that he had a very specific goal, and he would do whatever he had to do in order to achieve it.

"Not a lecture," Harry said. "I want to make a deal with you. Don't get me wrong. I think you'll probably make it through this. God knows you've made it this far."

"The old Trevelyan reflexes," Leon whispered hoarsely.

"Right. The old Trevelyan reflexes. But just in case you don't come through this time, there's something you should know."

Leon opened one eye and squinted up at Harry. "What's that?"

"Don't expect me to polish your hero image with Josh after you're gone. Not unless you and I reach an understanding here."

"Christ, he's my grandson. He's all I've got left."

"I know. But I'll tell him everything, Leon, if you don't agree to my terms."

"Goddamned blackmailer. That's what you are."

"You and I have been blackmailing each other for years, Leon."

"Bullshit." Leon sucked in air. "It was a rigged game. You always held the winning hand."

"One more deal, Leon. One more deal, and you can die a hero in Josh's eyes. Of course, he'd rather have you live, but that's up to you."

"Jesus H. Christ. What d'ya want from me?"

Harry rested his arms on the raised bed rail and clasped his hands loosely together. He looked down into his uncle's haggard features. From where she stood Molly could see his eyes. They were as hard as polished amber, but she could have sworn she saw pain burning beneath the surface. He did not like what he was doing, but he was going to see it through. Josh was his first priority.

"I'm going to send Josh back in here in a few minutes. When I do, I want you to set him free of the past."

"What's that supposed to mean?"

"It means I want you to tell him that times have changed. The days of wild living and stupid risk taking are gone forever. Tell him that his father would never have wanted him to follow in his footsteps. Tell him that you don't want him to do it, either. Tell him that you want him to continue on the new road that he's chosen. That you're proud of him. Give him your blessing, Leon."

"Christ, Harry. You want me to tell him it's okay to become like you? You want me to encourage him to turn his back on his heritage?"

"I want you to tell him," Harry said with relentless determination, "that you've been wrong all these years. That you realize now that it's time for the next generation of Trevelyan men to evolve. It's time for them to rely on their brains instead of their guts and their reflexes."

"Why should I do that?" Leon hissed. "You've already convinced him to finish college. Isn't that enough for you?"

"It's not enough for him. He loves you, Leon. He wants your approval. He needs to hear you tell him that you don't think he's a failure as a man just because he's chosen a path that will lead him away from fast cars and hard living."

"Josh doesn't give a damn about me." Leon's voice was strained with bitterness. "You've been his hero for years. Ever since you took him away from his family."

"You're wrong. You're his grandfather, and nothing can ever change that. He needs something from you that I can't give him, Leon. He needs to know you approve of the future he wants to pursue. It will make things a hell of a lot easier for him."

"Five will get you ten I know what the terms of this deal are."

Harry shrugged. "Same as always. If you do this for Josh, I won't tell him about Willy."

"Shit. I knew that was coming."

Leon's face contorted with anguish. He drew another rasping breath. "How do I know I can trust you?"

Harry was silent for a moment. "Have I ever lied to you, Uncle Leon?"

Leon's answer was lost in a wracking cough. When he recovered, he gazed blearily up at Harry. "You win, you SOB. Send him in, and then get outa here. I'll do this in my own way."

"Sure." Harry straightened.

For a few seconds he continued to gaze down at Leon. A wave of intense sadness went through Molly. She knew there was something else Harry wanted to say. Something that would not have been a threat or a form of coercion. Something that might have constituted a gesture of peace, an offer to end what was obviously an old war.

But in that brief moment, Molly also knew that Harry did not know how to claim the truce he wanted. He had asked Leon to set Josh free of the past, but Harry could not ask for a gift of equal value for himself.

Without a word, he turned away from the bed. Molly met

his eyes in the shadows. She held out her hand. He took it, his fingers closing fiercely around hers.

Together, they left the room.

"It was weird." Josh picked up the hospital cafeteria tray and carried it toward a small table. "It was as though Grandpa was trying to say good-bye. He was different than I've ever seen him. Not so tough. Much older, if you know what I mean."

"He's been through a lot tonight." Molly sat down and took the plastic cups off the tray. "It's probably given him a great deal to think about."

"Yeah."

Molly was well aware that it was Harry, not the near-fatal truck accident, that had been responsible for whatever philosophical change had come over Leon. Harry had said nothing to her about the scene she had witnessed in Leon's room, but she knew without being told that he did not want Josh to know what had occurred.

It was nearly midnight. She had invited Josh to join her in the cafeteria after he had left his grandfather's side a few minutes earlier.

Harry was occupied with the hospital paperwork and the insurance forms. Everyone seemed to assume that it was his job to take care of those things. The other Trevelyans talked quietly to each other in the waiting room while they took turns maintaining the bedside vigil.

"Cheer up, Josh. Your grandfather has made it this far." Molly sipped the excruciatingly bad tea she had bought at the counter. She hated tea made from a tea bag. It never compared to the freshly brewed product. "The doctor said his condition has stabilized. I'd say his odds of making it until morning are getting better all the time."

"But he talked as if he expected to die. Said he wanted to tell me some things that have been on his mind." Josh stirred his coffee with a plastic stick. "He told me that he'd been wrong all these years when he tried to get me into racing."

"Did he?" Molly kept her voice neutral.

"He said the Trevelyan men have always lived by their guts and their reflexes, but that a lot of 'em didn't live very long. He said the world has changed. It's brains that count now. He said I've got more than my father and he had put together, and I shouldn't waste them."

Molly nodded. "Your grandfather obviously wants a different future for you than the one he and your father made for themselves."

"Yeah." Josh hesitated. "I've always planned on finishing college and going for my doctorate. I've wanted to do the kind of work Harry does since I was thirteen. But Grandpa always said a man has to prove himself by looking death in the face and spitting in its eye. He said a man has to live on the edge or he'll go soft. He's always said that Harry was a gutless wonder."

"Hmm."

Josh looked up from his coffee. "He said things like that about Harry even after he found out what happened when Harry's folks were murdered."

Molly put down her cup and stared at Josh. "What, exactly, did happen?"

Josh was chagrined. "I take it Harry hasn't told you the full story?"

"No."

"I shouldn't have said anything. Everyone on both sides of the family knows the basic facts. But Harry never talks about it."

Molly shuddered. "I can understand that. But you can't leave me hanging like this. What happened?"

Josh gazed into his coffee as if it were an oracle glass. "The only reason I know the whole story is because one night when I was fourteen, I heard Harry call out in his sleep. I thought something terrible had happened. I went tearing down the hall to his room. He was sitting on the edge of his bed, staring out the window. He looked as though he had just awakened from a nightmare."

"Go on."

'I wasn't sure that he even saw me. I asked him what was wrong." Josh's hand tightened on the cup.

"What did he say?"

"Nothing for a long, long while. It spooked me, if you want to know the truth. I'd never seen him like that. He always seemed strong. So centered. Controlled. But that night I had the strangest feeling that he was pulling himself together. It was like he was picking up various bits and pieces of himself and regluing them back into place, if you know what I mean."

Molly recalled the night she had found Harry staring out the window, Kendall's gear in his hand. She remembered the shockingly vulnerable look in his eyes, so alien for him. "I think I do."

"After a while he started to speak. For some reason, maybe because I'd found him just after he'd awakened from the dream, he talked to me in a way he never had before. I'll never forget it. He sat there on the bed, staring out into the night, and he told me exactly what had happened the day Uncle Sean and Aunt Brittany were killed."

Dread welled up inside Molly. "Harry was there?"

"My aunt and uncle had a dive shop on one of the smaller islands in Hawaii."

"Yes, I know."

"That day they took the afternoon off to go diving. They decided to explore an underwater lava flow cave that they had discovered a few weeks earlier. They were checking out the entrance when they were surprised and killed by two men who had followed them down."

"Dear God," Molly whispered. "But why did the men murder them?"

"Uncle Sean and Aunt Brittany were in the wrong place at the wrong time. There had been an armored car robbery three days earlier in Honolulu. The killers had hidden a fortune in negotiable securities in the cave. I guess the plan was to wait for the search to cool down before they brought the haul back to the surface. In the meantime, they were keeping an eye on the cave. They were posing as tourists. They had rented a boat and dive gear."

"And when they saw Harry's parents diving in the vicinity of the cave, they assumed that they were cops or other thieves who had somehow stumbled onto the hiding place?"

"Apparently." Josh rubbed the back of his neck in a weary gesture that was strangely reminiscent of Harry. "They followed Harry's folks underwater, found them inside the cave, and shot them in the back with spear guns. Uncle Sean and Aunt Brittany never had a chance."

Molly closed her eyes. "How ghastly."

"Yes." Josh paused. "Harry arrived on the scene a few minutes after his folks had been killed."

"Oh, no."

"He had just arrived on the island for a visit. He'd gone straight to the shop and was told that his folks had taken the afternoon off to go diving near the old lava flow. Harry decided to surprise them. He took a boat and some dive gear and went to find them."

Molly could hardly breathe. "He could have been killed, himself."

"Yes. But as it turned out, it was the two armored car robbers who died."

"How?"

Josh raised his eyes to meet hers. "Harry killed them."

"What?" Molly was stunned. "Are you certain?"

"Yes," Josh said. "I'm certain. The night of the nightmare, he told me that when he found his parents' boat and saw the other boat anchored nearby, he knew something was very wrong. He got into his dive gear, took a spear gun, and went down to find out what was happening. The killers were just exiting the cave. Apparently they hoped the sharks would take care of the evidence. Harry said . . ."

"What did he say?" Molly prompted gently.

Josh frowned, as though groping for words. "He said it seemed as if the whole sea had turned red. He said he felt as though he were swimming through an ocean of blood.

rie told me that he knew what had happened even before he discovered his parents' bodies."

Molly's stomach churned. "I can't even imagine how terrible it must have been."

"He ran straight into the killers. But unlike Uncle Sean, he was prepared. He knew something was wrong. There was a fight. But Harry is fast. Very fast."

"Harry killed those two men?"

"Yes. He nearly died, himself, in the process. I gather one of the murderers cut his air hose during the struggle. Harry brought his parents' bodies to the surface before the sharks came, but it was too late. They were both dead."

Molly blinked back tears. "Dear heaven."

"I don't think Harry has ever forgiven himself," Josh said. "I think that's why he tends to brood sometimes, you know? Olivia told him that he's got posttraumatic stress disorder or something."

"I don't understand. It was a terrible tragedy. But why would Harry blame himself?"

"I think he blames himself for being too late to save his folks." Josh swallowed the last of his coffee. "The night that I found him sitting on the edge of his bed, he told me that if he'd been just a few minutes earlier, he could have saved his parents' lives. He kept saying that he had been too late."

At five-thirty that morning, Harry opened his eyes to see a doctor standing in the doorway of the hospital waiting room.

"Wake up." Harry gently eased Molly's head off his shoulder. "We've got a visitor." He took one look at the doctor's face and knew at once that Leon was going to live. He was surprised by the force of the wave of relief that went through him. The old bastard was as tough as nails.

Molly opened her eyes and glanced at the doctor. "Something's happened?"

The doctor surveyed Harry and Molly and the weary crowd of half-dozing Trevelyans. He smiled. "Good news. I'm happy to tell you that Mr. Trevelyan's condition has been upgraded to satisfactory. He's out of the woods. I think it's safe to say he'll live to pay off that new truck he cracked up last night."

A weak but heartfelt cheer went up. Josh looked at Harry and grinned.

Evangeline heaved a sigh of relief. "I knew Leon wouldn't go out that easily."

"He always claimed he had nine lives, like a cat." Raleigh grinned weakly. "But by my reckoning, he's used up at least eight."

"You can say that again," Raleigh's pregnant wife murmured wearily. "Some day the old coot is going to take one chance too many."

"But not today, apparently," Harry said quietly.

The doctor looked at him. "He's asking for you."

Harry got to his feet and stretched. Molly stood up beside him. She gave him a questioning glance. He shook his head. "It's okay. I'll go see what he wants. Then we can get some breakfast in the cafeteria and head back to Seattle."

She nodded. "I'll wait here."

Harry went down the hall to Leon's room. Sunlight filtered in through the window. A nurse was just leaving Leon's bedside. She smiled as she went past him.

Harry waited until she was gone. Then he went to the bed.

"Congratulations," he said to Leon. "I had a hunch you'd pull through."

Leon turned his head on the pillow and glared at him. "Yeah? Wish I'd been as certain. If I'd been sure I wasn't going to kick the bucket this time, I wouldn't have let you push me around last night. You took advantage of my weakened condition."

"A deal's a deal."

"Yeah, yeah. You got what you wanted." Leon paused. "How's Josh?"

"Fine. He told everyone what you said to him last night. About how it's time for the Trevelyan men to start using their heads instead of other portions of their anatomies."

"Make him happy, d'ya think?"

"Yes. You took a load off his shoulders." Harry fixed his

uncle with a meaningful look. "You gave him something I couldn't give to him. Something he'll have for the rest of his life."

"What's that?"

"The knowledge that you're proud of him and that his father would have been proud of him, too. He no longer feels that he's being a traitor to the Trevelyan heritage."

"Yeah, well, maybe you were right. Maybe it's time for a new heritage, y'know?"

Harry smiled. "What's this? Don't tell me that a little brush with death has given you a new philosophy of life?"

"Nah. It just made me a little more practical. I've never made much money in the racing game, and as for Willy, well, we both know what happened to him. Be good if Josh tries something different."

"You surprise me, Leon. I don't know what to say, except thanks."

Leon squinted up at him. "Now that you mention it, there is something else you can do to show your undyin' gratitude."

"What's that?"

"I'm gonna need a new truck."

Molly glanced at Harry as she buckled her seat belt. She was amused. "Leon wants you to buy him another truck?"

"Leon has never been one to let a golden opportunity slide past without making a grab for it." Harry eased the Sneath out of the hospital parking lot.

He drove out onto the main road with a sense of satisfaction. It was seven-thirty. They would be back in Seattle in an hour. Molly would be at her shop in plenty of time to open it for the day.

"Your uncle is a real piece of work." Molly hesitated. "I couldn't help but notice that you definitely play hardball with him."

"If that's a polite way of saying that I put the screws to him last night when he thought he might die, I plead guilty.

From past experience, I've learned that there is no other way to deal with Leon."

Molly was silent for a few minutes. Harry wondered what she was thinking. It occurred to him that she might not approve of the way he handled his relatives.

"I know it's none of my business," Molly said after a while. "But would you mind telling me what it is that you hold over Leon? Is he really afraid that you'll tarnish his image in Josh's eyes?"

"Yes."

"What makes him think you could do that, assuming you would do it?"

Harry flexed his hands on the wheel. She had a right to know, he thought. Maybe that was the real reason he had asked her to accompany him into Leon's room last night. Maybe he wanted to tell her the truth.

"Leon and I share a secret. He and I are the only two people in the world who know that Josh's father died because the mechanic in charge of his motorcycle failed to give the engine a thorough going over the night before Willy did his last stunt. There was something wrong with the fuel lines. Something that the mechanic would have caught if he had done his job properly."

Molly turned slightly in the seat. "Who was Willy's mechanic?"

"Leon."

"I had a feeling you were going to say that. What went wrong? Why didn't Leon check out the engine?"

"Because he was too busy screwing the sheriff's wife in a motel room."

Molly looked stricken. "I remember your telling me something about Leon being in jail the day Willy was killed."

"He was. The sheriff made his arrest around ten that morning. Willy died at one o'clock that afternoon."

"How did you figure out that Leon hadn't done his job as a mechanic?"

Harry concentrated on the road. "Because I examined the wreckage after the accident. When I went over the remains of the engine, I knew that something had gone wrong in the fuel lines."

She gave him a searching glance. "You just knew?"

"I spent a lot of time with the bits and pieces that were left over after the explosion," Harry said carefully.

"You got one of your insights?"

"You could say that."

"Is that what happened the day your parents were murdered?" she asked softly. "When you found their boat and the one the killers had used, did you know that something terrible had happened? Is that why you went down with a spear gun?"

Harry reminded himself to breathe. "Josh talked to you?"

"Yes."

He gripped the wheel so tightly he wondered that it did not crack. "If I'd been just a few minutes earlier—"

"No," she interrupted very calmly. "You had nothing to do with their deaths. You are not responsible for what happened, Harry. Life is full of *what ifs*, but they are meaningless questions. You're a man who has devoted himself to scholarly study and reasoned thinking, you must know how futile it is to ponder the *what ifs*. The answers change nothing."

Harry could not think of any response to that.

"You're also a man who is very much in control of most things in his world," Molly continued. "But some things are out of your control, Harry. You must accept that simple fact or you will drive yourself crazy."

"I sometimes wonder about that possibility." It was the first time he had ever admitted his deepest fear aloud, Harry realized. Doing so made the threat all the more real.

"Don't be ridiculous." Molly smiled slightly. "I was speaking metaphorically. The very fact that you can even wonder if you're going crazy means you very likely aren't crazy. Real nuts don't question their own nuttiness. They think they're the only normal ones. That's why they're nuts."

"That's an interesting way of viewing the current state of the art of clinical psychology," he said dryly.

Molly touched his shoulder. "Remember what you wrote in *Illusions of Certainty?* 'Absolute certainty is the greatest of all illusions.' "

"I remember. What the hell does that have to do with this?"

"Total control is an illusion, Harry. The biggest one of all. You aren't responsible for everything and everyone. You're only human."

# 14

Harry went straight to his study the moment they walked in the front door. Molly, thinking fondly of a hot shower and a bracing cup of tea, trailed after him, yawning. She was learning the patterns of his life, and it had become obvious in the past few days that this particular routine was an indelible one.

She lounged in the doorway of his private sanctum, arms folded, and watched as Harry methodically played back the calls that had come in on his private line.

There were three messages on Harry's answering machine. Molly knew they had all come in sometime during the night. She was not particularly surprised to learn that all three were from Strattons.

> *Harry? It's Brandon. Where the hell are you? Call as soon as you get in. I need to talk to you.*

The machine whirred and clicked.

> *This is your Aunt Danielle, Harry. Call me immediately.*

More clicks from the answering machine.

*Harry, this is Gilford. If you're screening your calls, pick up the phone now. If you're not there, call me as soon as you get this message. Where the hell are you? It's seven-thirty in the morning.*

The answering machine pinged to indicate the end of the messages. Harry hit the rewind button. He glanced at his watch and then reached for a pen and a pad of paper.

"Want some advice?" Molly asked softly.

Harry did not look up from the notes he was making, but one black brow rose in inquiry. "What's that?"

"You've dealt with enough family problems in the past few hours. Give it a break."

His mouth curved humorlessly. "Different family."

"No, all the same family. Yours. Harry, you've had a long night with very little sleep. Take a shower. Have a cup of coffee. You can answer those calls later. Much later." Molly paused. "Like maybe this afternoon or tomorrow. Next week might be a good time."

He slowly put down the pen and looked at her. "What's that supposed to mean?"

"It means that you have a right to put yourself first once in a while." She held out her hand. "Come on. Let's go take a shower."

She saw the hesitation in his face, and then, to her intense relief, he took her hand and allowed himself to be led down the hall.

At five o'clock that afternoon, Molly flipped the sign in the shop window so that it read CLOSED and groaned aloud. "I've had it, Tessa. I'm going to stop by my place to check on things and pick up some fresh clothes. Then I'm heading straight back to Harry's. I'm looking forward to putting my feet up and having a nice glass of chilled chardonnay."

"Is that a fact?" Tessa repainted her mouth with heavy brown lipstick.

"I'm getting too old for short nights followed by full work days. I don't know how you do it."

"It's the music." Tessa dropped the lipstick into a huge leather bag as she came around the counter. "It gives me energy. How much longer are you going to stay with T-Rex?"

"I don't know." Molly watched a gaggle of tourists climb the broad steps toward First Avenue. "To tell you the truth, I'm starting to worry a little about the situation. I feel as though I'm living in limbo."

"I'm starting to worry about your situation, too. I understand why you don't want to stay at your own place, but maybe you should move in with your aunt. I don't like this business of you living with Trevelyan. It's not you."

Molly glanced at her, astonished. "What the heck is this? You've been after me for months to get a love life."

"Is that what you've got? A love life?" Tessa's vividly outlined eyes held an old-fashioned expression that was disconcertingly at odds with her nose ring, neon hair, and clashing arm chains. "Or are we talking just a sex life here?"

The question had a strange effect on Molly. She felt as though she had suddenly stepped out into space. Her insides fluttered wildly in the weightless environment. "I wish I knew."

"Damn. I was afraid of this."

"Tessa, it's after five. Begone."

"Look, if you want to talk—"

"I don't. But thanks, anyway."

Tessa hesitated. "Sure. Whatever you say, boss. I'm here if you need me."

"I know. Thanks."

Tessa opened the front door. "Hey, I almost forgot."

"About what?"

"A friend of mine in the band wants to talk to you. She's working on a really strange gadget. I told her about your foundation, and she got excited. She could use the money to help finance her project."

Molly was momentarily distracted from her own problems. "Your friend is an inventor?"

"Yeah. Her name is Heloise Stickley. Plays bass guitar in

the band. But her main interest is alternate levels of consciousness."

"How nice," Molly said. "What are alternate levels of consciousness?"

"Beats me. She's got some kind of theory about people who can sense things that the rest of us can't. You know, like colors that go beyond the normal spectrum. Stuff like that. She's working on a machine that detects special brain waves or something."

Molly winced. "Uh, maybe you'd better not encourage her to apply for funding to the Abberwick Foundation. Harry is a little biased against inventors who work in the field of paranormal studies. To be perfectly blunt, he thinks it's all garbage."

"You don't need T-Rex's permission for every single project, do you?"

"Well, no. But I'm paying big bucks for his advice. It would be stupid not to follow it."

"Just talk to Heloise, okay? There's no harm in that, is there?"

"No, of course not." Molly smiled wryly. "You could sell ice in Alaska during the winter, Tessa. Tell Heloise that I'll be glad to talk to her."

"Great." Tessa grinned as she went through the door. "See you tomorrow."

Molly waited until the door had closed again. Then she walked through the shop one last time, going through her evening ritual. She straightened canisters of tea. Checked the special orders file. Pulled the shades in the front windows.

When all was in order, she let herself out the front door and secured it firmly. The steps in front of the shop were still cluttered with people, but the crowd was thinning rapidly. The fountains sparkled in the late afternoon sun.

Molly walked up toward First Avenue, heading toward the nearest bus stop. Gordon Brooke stepped out of the front door of his coffee bar as she went past.

"Molly." He gave her an ingratiating smile. "On your way home?"

"Yes." She paused briefly. "Did you have a good day?"

"Fair. Look, I wanted to apologize for my behavior in your office the other day. I didn't mean to embarrass you in front of Trevelyan."

"Forget it."

Gordon sighed. "I didn't handle that scene very well, but I am genuinely concerned. You seem to be getting serious about him."

"Don't worry about me, Gordon."

"That's just it, I do worry about you." He shoved one hand into the pocket of his fashionable bronze-colored trousers. "If nothing else, we're old friends. I don't want to see you get in over your head with a guy like Trevelyan. He's not really your type."

"Amazing how everyone seems to have an opinion on the subject. You'll have to excuse me, Gordon. I've got a bus to catch."

Molly hurried up the remainder of the steps, crossed the street, and caught a crowded bus to Capitol Hill. There was one empty seat in the middle of the bus, but it was next to a bag lady who had stacked all of her worldly possessions on it. This being Seattle, none of the standing passengers stooped to the incivility of requesting that the woman move her things.

The bus made its way past the eclectic collection of bookstores, cafés, body-piercing parlors, and leather clothing shops that gave the Capitol Hill district its colorful identity. When it lumbered into the old residential district beyond, Molly got off.

She walked along the quiet, tree-lined streets to the Abberwick mansion. The sight of the sprawling old house beyond the iron gates filled her with an unexpected rush of affection. Kelsey was wrong, she thought. She could not sell the mansion. It was home.

The massive front gates swung open when she keyed in the code. She walked up the drive, noting that everything seemed to be in order so far as the gardens were concerned. The perpetual sprinkling system that her father had designed had obviously been working without a hitch.

She went up the steps and let herself into the hall. For a moment she stood there in the shadows, allowing memories to coalesce around her. There were ghosts in this house, but they were part of the family, part of her. She could not abandon them.

After a moment Molly looked down. The wooden floor gleamed. The polishing robot had been at work. She walked into the front parlor. The bookcases had all been recently dusted by the dusting machine.

She left the parlor and went up the massive staircase to the second floor. There, she turned and went down the hall to her bedroom.

No, she definitely would not put the house on the market, Molly thought as she took fresh clothes out of the closet and stuffed them into a patented Abberwick Nonwrinkling Suitcase. The crazy old mansion would never sell, anyway, except possibly to a developer who would tear it down to make room for condominiums or apartments. Only someone who valued the unique and the bizarre would love it the way she did.

She could live here by herself, Molly decided. Granted, the house was technically too big for one person, but her father's endless household inventions would take care of most of the work involved in maintaining the mansion.

*What it really needed was a family. A very special sort of family, one with an extraordinary father whose brilliant eyes were the color of ancient amber.*

The thought came out of nowhere. Molly stood very still in the center of the bedroom, clutching the red jacket she had just taken off a hanger.

An image of two dark-haired, amber-eyed children materialized in the gloom. The pair, a boy and a girl, were laughing with gleeful anticipation. She sensed that they were eager to run downstairs to her father's old workshop. They wanted to play with the automated toys that Jasper Abberwick had invented years ago for Molly and Kelsey.

For a few seconds Molly could not breathe. *Harry's children.*

The vision faded, but the emotions it had generated inside Molly did not.

After a while she adjusted the cleverly engineered clothes-folding mechanism inside the suitcase and shut the lid. She made a quick tour of the remainder of the rooms on the second floor to make certain that all was in order. Then she went downstairs.

She left the suitcase in the hall while she toured the rooms on the first floor. Nothing was amiss. The only thing left to do was to make her way down to the basement to check the machinery that powered the household robots.

She went down the steps into the windowless rooms below the house. The bright overhead lights winked on in the workshop when she opened the door. Across the room she saw the glowing lights on the control panel that regulated all the various mechanical and electrical systems in the house.

Molly heard the faint creak just as she stepped into the workshop.

Two thoughts struck her simultaneously. One was rational, intellectual, and based on common sense. It held that such creaks and groans were to be expected in an old house.

The second thought was irrational and intuitive. It emanated straight from the most primitive part of her mind, the region charged with the tasks of survival. It told her with grave certainty that she was not alone in the mansion. She was being stalked.

Someone had been hiding in one of the basement storage rooms while she methodically toured the upstairs rooms.

A floorboard groaned.

Panic seized Molly. She glanced back toward the stairs and knew a searing helplessness. She would have to go past a long line of storage rooms in order to escape. Someone waited in one of those rooms.

Even as she contemplated her chances, a door opened at

the end of the hall. A man materialized in the shadows. His face was covered with a ski mask. He raised his hand. Molly saw the gun in his fist.

She chose the only option open to her. She dashed through the workshop doorway, whirled around, and slammed the old wooden door closed. She threw the bolt.

Muffled footsteps thudded down the hall. They came to a halt on the other side of the door. The antique glass knob rattled under Molly's hand. Instinctively she jerked her fingers away from it.

Belatedly she realized that it was not smart to stand directly in front of the door. The intruder could easily shoot through the aging wood.

She took several more steps back from the door until she reached the center of the workshop. A heavy, jarring crash shook the door. It rattled on its hinges. The gunman intended to force his way into the workshop. It was only a matter of time before he achieved his goal.

Molly turned in a slow, desperate circle, feeling like a trapped animal. There was no escape from the workshop. The brick walls of the basement loomed around her, confining her in a space that was no larger than the upstairs parlor. There was no place to hide.

Her gaze fell on the brooding, shrouded shapes that lined one wall of the room. The image of two black-haired children with intelligent amber eyes popped into her head again.

*The children wanted to play with the glittering, flashing, mechanical toys that Jasper Abberwick had built for his daughters.*

There was another thud. The door shuddered and groaned as if it had taken a mortal wound. Molly knew now that the intruder meant to kill her. She felt the menace in her bones. She had to act or else she would die right here in the basement of her own home.

*Harry. Harry, I need you.*

The silent scream for help shrieked through her head. There was no point calling out. No one would hear her.

*The amber-eyed children wanted to play.*

Molly gathered herself and hurried across the room to the nearest tarp-covered form. She yanked the canvas aside to reveal the huge, lumbering toy she had once named the Creature from the Purple Lagoon. It was as tall as she was, with a great, gaping, toothy mouth and a long tail. When she had been eight years old she had thrilled to the knowledge that she could control such a grand beast.

Molly steadied the monster on its wonderfully hideous feet and punched a button on the control panel. Her faithful, semiannual attention to the special long-life batteries was rewarded.

Red lights flashed in the creature's eyes. With a hiss of fake steam, the monster cranked slowly into motion. It started forward on its huge, claw-footed legs. The thick tail shifted from side to side.

The door trembled beneath another blow.

Molly jerked the canvas shroud off another one of the mechanical toys. This one was a spaceship. Two large dolls dressed in bizarre costumes manned the ray guns. Molly punched a button. The ship hummed to life. Strobes pulsed around the outer edge. The imitation weapons beamed green rays into the shadows.

There was another jarring crash of noise from the door. Molly uncovered more toys. One by one she powered up the robots, monsters, and vehicles of her small army.

She was working on a miniature glider, a prototype of the machine that had killed/her father and her uncle, when she heard the door give way with a splintering crack.

She hit the master switch on the panel that controlled all of the household electricity.

The workshop was instantly plunged into a stygian darkness just as the man in the ski mask came through the door. Molly's mechanical defenders chugged, roared, and hummed through the inky blackness, filling it with a nerve-shattering barrage of flashing lights and whirring, clanking noises.

The toys surged willy-nilly around the room, charging blindly into each other, the walls, and anything that got in their path. Molly ducked down behind a workbench and held her breath.

It was a scene out of a special effects nightmare.

The cavelike darkness was pierced with wildly pulsing strobes. A cacophony of roars, hisses, and grunts created a deafening howl.

"What the hell?" The hoarse shout of surprise from the gunman held a note of raw terror.

Thunder boomed in the lightless chamber. Molly crouched closer to the floor, aware that the intruder had just fired his gun.

"Goddamn it," the intruder yelled.

This time there was pain in the rasping cry. Molly knew the man had collided with one of the war machines in the darkness.

Molly heard the clang of metal on metal and realized that the gunman had swung out blindly in an attempt to ward off another automated attacker. She heard one of the large toys crash to the floor. Its pulsing lights continued to flash in a crazed rhythm that periodically spotlighted its churning claws.

The spaceship turned its ray guns toward the doorway. Green beams lit the darkness as the toy opened fire. Molly glimpsed the strange, jerky movement of the gunman as he was caught in the path of the strobes. She realized that he was struggling frantically to escape.

He tripped over a dinosaur's swishing tail. Screaming in rage and fear, he regained his feet and plunged blindly ahead.

A scattered burst of green beams from the spaceship's armament revealed the doorway. The intruder ran through it into the dark hall. The erratic strobes swung in another direction, and Molly lost sight of the gunman. The toys were creating too much of a racket to enable her to hear the sound of footsteps on the stairs, but a moment later Molly thought she felt impact vibrations from the wooden floor over her head. The intruder was running down the front hall.

Molly waited for a long time behind the milling ranks of

her toy defenders. Eventually she made her way by feel to the master control panel. She switched on the household lights with trembling fingers and reached for the phone.

Her first call was to 911. The second was to Harry.

As it turned out, the second call was not necessary. Harry came through the front door of the mansion five minutes later.

"It was that crazy bastard, Kendall." Harry prowled back and forth in front of the wall of windows. He felt as restless and trapped as a lion in a cage. "Had to be him. So much for the theory that he went to California. Damn that son-of-a-bitch. He's really gone over the edge. We've got to find him."

Molly, coiled in a chair, her feet tucked under her, sipped chardonnay. "Harry, stop pacing. You're making me dizzy."

He ignored her. "I keep thinking there's something else I should do."

"You've given the cops everything we've got, and you've called your private investigator, Fergus Rice. What else can you do? Try to relax."

"Relax?" Harry swung around to confront her. "How the hell am I supposed to do that?"

"You could start by doing what I'm doing." She held her wine glass aloft. "Pour yourself a drink. We both need to unwind."

Harry knew she was right. He was almost vibrating with a sense of helpless rage.

*Kendall had almost killed her this afternoon.* The knowledge churned in his guts. He was in a foul mood, and he knew it. The truth was, he had been sinking into this state slowly but inexorably for several hours. He had been seething with a sense of terrible urgency since shortly after five that afternoon.

The undefined sensation of doom had descended on him with the force of a tidal wave. He had been working in his study, waiting for the sound of Molly's key in the front door lock, when it had hit him. He had suddenly needed to know where she was. Needed to know that she was safe.

He had called her shop, but there had been no answer. It had occurred to him that she had gone to the mansion for fresh clothes. He had started to dial the number.

But for some reason, he had felt an overpowering urge to get the car out of the garage and drive to Capitol Hill. He had fought the illogical need as long as he could before he had finally given in to it.

The open front gate had given the first verifiable proof that there was a basis for his alarm. He had heard the sirens in the distance just as he raced through the front door of the mansion.

There had been no sign of Molly. It was the thundering din in the basement that had drawn him downstairs. His first thought was that some of Jasper Abberwick's machines had run amuck.

As long as he lived, Harry knew he would never forget the sight of Molly surrounded by a herd of bizarre mechanical toys. He had taken one look at her stricken face and known, without her having to explain, that she had very nearly died in that workshop.

He had also known that he would have been too late to save her.

Harry came to a halt in front of Molly. He leaned down and gripped the arms of the chair, forcing her to look up at him. "From this moment until Wharton Kendall is in custody, you are not to go anywhere alone. Is that clear?"

"Harry, I know you're a little upset over what happened, but there's no need to overreact."

"I will walk you to work in the mornings. I will pick you up for lunch. I will meet you after work and escort you back here. Understood?"

"I promise I won't go home alone again," she temporized.

He leaned closer. "You won't go anywhere alone."

She bit her lip. "Harry, you'll drive me crazy if you try to make me a prisoner."

"Don't use the word lightly. You don't know what crazy is."

"And you do?"

"Some people," he said very deliberately, "have implied that I may have a nodding acquaintance with the condition."

"But I thought we settled that issue. You're not crazy." She studied him with sudden comprehension. "Ah. You're referring to Olivia, aren't you?"

"She is a professional," he said through set teeth.

"Maybe. But I wouldn't worry about her diagnosis, if I were you."

"Easy for you to say," Harry muttered. "I can certainly testify to the fact that I went a little nuts this afternoon when I realized you weren't home on time and that I had no idea where you were."

Her eyes widened. "Now that is interesting, isn't it?"

"No, it's crazy-making, not interesting. I don't want to go through that again. Ever. And that is why you are not to go anywhere by yourself until Kendall is caught."

She pursed her lips, her eyes thoughtful. "When did you first realize that I was in trouble?"

He was suddenly wary. "I realized you were late around five-thirty."

"That would have been about the time that I wished you were with me. I remember thinking your name very, very clearly."

"Molly, for God's sake, don't try to tell me that you believe there was some extrasensory perception involved here."

"Maybe it was your intuition at work again," she suggested ingenuously.

He released the arms of her chair and straightened abruptly. "Are you serious?"

"Let's look at this rationally."

"Now, that would certainly be a novel approach."

She paid no attention to his sarcasm. "Tell me, how did you know that I'd gone home to pick up some clothes?"

"Hell." Harry resumed his pacing. "Not from any paranormal powers, I can promise you that. It was a perfectly logical deduction under the circumstances."

"Hmm."

"Don't say that."

She gave him a quizzical look. "Don't say what?"

"Don't say *hmm* in that tone of voice."

"Okay. But, Harry, in all seriousness, I'm starting to wonder if there is something to this paranormal stuff."

"For the last time, I do not have any psychic powers. Even those in the family who believe in the Trevelyan Second Sight don't believe it takes the form of the kind of mental telepathy that allows two people to communicate without words. Not even the original Harry Trevelyan believed he could do that."

"Hmm."

Harry glared at her.

"Sorry," Molly said. "I was just thinking. We're back to intuition, I suppose."

"Insight," he said grimly. "Reasoned, logical insight occasionally gives the illusion of being something more than what it actually is."

"So it was reason and logic that enabled you to deduce that I was in trouble at the mansion?"

"For all the good it did." Harry shut his eyes and let the stark truth roll through him. "I was too late to make a difference. Too damn late. If you hadn't had that inspiration to hide in your father's workshop and use those old toys to defend yourself, I would have found you—" He broke off, unable to put the rest into words.

"Yes. It was a useful inspiration, wasn't it?" Molly took another sip of wine. A faraway expression lit her eyes.

"What the hell gave you the idea to use the mechanical toys the way you did?" Harry asked. "Or was it just a case of necessity being the mother of invention?"

"What would you say if I told you that I got the idea to use the toys from a couple of children?"

He scowled briefly. "What children? Are you telling me

there were some children involved in this? You didn't say anything about them to the police."

"There was no point," Molly said, oddly wistful. "The children haven't been born yet."

Harry stared at her. She'd been through a lot today, he reminded himself. She was probably suffering from some sort of delayed shock. "Molly, we'd better get you into bed. You need rest."

She smiled. "Harry, have you ever thought about having kids?"

He came to a halt in front of the window. His imagination projected a clear, unmistakable picture of her rounded and ripe with child. His child. An intense longing welled up within him. He took a deep breath. "I think that wine is getting to you. It's probably because of the stress. Come on. I'll help you undress. You need a good night's sleep."

"Hmm."

# 15

'Too late."

The hoarse, desperate words were barely audible, but they woke Molly from a dream of huge, marauding mechanical toys. Adrenaline surged through her. She opened her eyes and looked at Harry, who was asleep on the bed beside her.

A broad shaft of moonlight slanted into the room through the wall of windows. The icy light bathed him in silver. There was a damp sheen of sweat on his bare shoulders.

"Too late," he muttered into the pillow. He shifted restlessly. "Can't breathe. Can't *breathe*."

"Harry, wake up."

"Can't breathe. Too late."

Molly touched him gently. It was as though she had plugged him into a light socket. Harry came awake with shocking suddenness, rolled to the edge of the bed, and got to his feet in one smooth motion. He whirled to look down at her.

In the cold moonlight she could not make out the curious amber color of his eyes, but she had no problem seeing the haunted expression in them. She sat up slowly against the pillows and pulled the sheet to her throat.

"You were dreaming," she whispered.

"Yes." He blinked a few times as though to clear away

the ghosts. A shudder went through him. He took a deep breath and seemed to steady himself. "Sorry."

"A nightmare?"

He ran a hand through his hair. "I haven't had one like that in a long time. Years. I'd almost forgotten how bad they were."

Molly pushed aside the covers and stood. She padded quickly around the end of the wide bed and went to him. Wrapping her arms around his waist, she leaned against him, offering the only comfort she had to give.

"It's all right, Harry. It's over."

He stood rigidly in her embrace for a long moment, and then, with a husky, wordless groan, he put his arms around her and held her as though she were the only woman on earth. For a few minutes they stood there quietly in the moonlight.

"It was because of me, wasn't it?" Molly finally dared to suggest. "The incident this afternoon triggered your dream. You feel guilty because you got to me after Kendall had already gone."

"I got to you too late." Harry's voice was uncompromisingly harsh. "You could have been killed."

"The way your parents were?"

Harry went absolutely still. "Yes."

"What happened to me today brought back all the old memories, didn't it?"

"Probably."

"And some old dreams."

"I guess so." He sounded weary all the way to his soul.

"You can't save everyone, Harry. Not even all the people you care about. Life doesn't give us that option. I learned that the hard way, myself. Let it go."

"I don't think I can. Not completely. Not ever."

"Then share it with me." Molly braced herself. "Tell me what it was really like that day your parents were murdered."

"You don't want to hear about it."

Molly was not certain she had the right to pry further,

but something within her drove her to push on, even though it was obvious her questions would not be welcome. "You said that you were too late to save your folks that day."

"Too goddamned late." Without warning, rage and pain poured from him in a torrent. It was as if somewhere inside him a dam had burst. "Just as I was too late today. Too late. Always too damned late."

Molly hugged him fiercely. "You went down with a spear gun that day your parents died."

"Christ. Did Josh tell you that part, too?"

"Yes." Molly lifted her head to search his face. His eyes glittered. "You were almost killed, yourself, weren't you?"

"They saw me as they emerged from the cave." The words sounded as if they emanated from somewhere near the outer rings of Hades, the region of unbearable cold. "I knew then what had happened. They came straight toward me. I killed the first man with the spear gun. The other one was on me before I could reload. His shot missed. But he had a knife. Took it from a sheath he wore on his ankle. Sliced through my air hose."

"Oh, God, Harry." She tightened her hold on him.

"I had a knife, too. Dad had given it to me. I killed the bastard with it. But I was out of air. Took a tank off one of the dead men. Used it to swim on down to the cave. But I was too late. They were both dead."

Stark silence fell.

Molly cradled Harry's face between her palms. She sensed that the tale was unfinished, although she did not know what remained to be told. She only knew that he had to tell her everything.

Molly probed cautiously, feeling her way as carefully as though she walked through a minefield. "You said you knew as soon as you arrived on the scene that there was danger. That something terrible had happened?"

Harry gazed past her into the night outside the window. "I saw the second boat anchored next to theirs. I reached out to touch the hull. Everything was wrong. So goddamned wrong."

"I understand."

"I found them. Brought them back to the surface. I couldn't seem to breathe, even though I had a half-full tank of air." Harry rubbed his eyes with one hand. "And the water was a strange shade of red. A trick of the late afternoon light, I think. But it looked like blood."

"It must have been unbearable."

"Yes."

"No wonder you still dream about it. Harry, you couldn't save your parents' lives that day. But you must never forget that your father saved yours."

He pulled his attention away from the night and looked down at her with a scowl of confusion. "What?"

"Your father taught you how to use a knife, didn't he? He gave you the one you wear. The one you used that day."

"He taught me everything he knew. It's the only reason that I survived that fight."

"The skills your father gave you saved your life that day, just as the mechanical toys my father made for me saved my life this afternoon."

Harry was silent for a moment. "Yes."

"Sometimes it's good to remember things like that, Harry. We're all connected to each other. Sometimes we save others. Sometimes they save us. That's the way life is. None of us can do all of the saving, all of the time."

Harry said nothing. But he did not pull away from her embrace.

"Your father fulfilled his responsibility to you by teaching you the things you needed to know in order to survive in that terrible moment."

"Molly, I don't know what you're trying to do here, but if this is your idea of a little amateur psychology, forget it." His mouth twisted bitterly. "Olivia already gave it her best shot, and she's an expert."

"What did Olivia say?"

Harry shrugged. "She talked a lot about the destructiveness of guilt. Said there was medication for posttraumatic stress disorder. I told her that I wasn't interested in rewriting history with a feel-good pill."

Molly gave him a small shake. "What I'm telling you isn't therapy, it's truth. You're the one who's supposed to be the expert when it comes to sorting out reality from illusion. Well, look at this piece of truth I'm giving you, and tell me honestly if you think it's a lie."

"And just what is this truth you want me to see?"

She refused to be intimidated by the anger that was pulsing through him. She knew intuitively that it was good for him to release the emotion. He had kept too many things bottled up inside for too long.

"Listen to me, Harry. Your father saved your life that day, and that is exactly the way he would have wanted it. He was your father, and you were his son. He took care of you that day. It was his right as a father. Your mother would have felt the same way. That's the way it's supposed to be. You repaid the gift by passing it along."

Harry's jaw tightened. "I don't understand."

"What if it had been Josh instead of you who went down that day? What if he had been the one to encounter those two murderers?"

Harry stared at her with unblinking eyes and said nothing. He did not have to say anything. Molly knew exactly what he was thinking. Harry had raised Josh. He had a father's instincts toward him.

"I agree that a man like you would never be content to rewrite history in order to make himself feel better," Molly continued gently. "That's not the way out. You make things right by balancing the scales. It's not therapy, it's a karma thing."

"I don't believe this. Karma? Don't tell me that you're into that kind of mystical nonsense."

"All right, you're a man of science, think of it in technical terms. Apply Newton's Laws of Motion. For every action there is an equal reaction. Your father saved your life, and you responded by doing the same for Josh."

"What does Josh have to do with this?" Harry asked tensely. "I've never saved his life."

"Yes, you have. You saved him from the legacy of the past. It was a legacy that could easily have gotten him killed or left him washed up and embittered like his grandfather. You gave him a future filled with promise. That was a priceless gift, Harry."

"All I did was make sure he got an education."

"No, you gave him much more than that. You gave him a stable environment. You were a true father to him. You wrestled that old devil, Leon, for his soul, and you won."

Harry leaned his damp forehead against hers in a gesture of unutterable exhaustion. "This is a strange conversation to be having in the middle of the night."

"Josh isn't the only one you've saved," Molly said steadily. "From what I can see, you've made a habit of saving Strattons and Trevelyans during the past few years."

He stilled. "Now what are you talking about?"

"Well, as an example, you've made it possible for Brandon to go out on his own without risking his inheritance."

"Brandon won't thank me for it."

"Maybe not, but that's his problem. I know you've also helped your cousin Raleigh and his wife. I suspect that you had something to do with making it possible for Evangeline to buy Smoke & Mirrors Amusement Company. I have a hunch the list is endless."

"Things like that are different."

"No, they're not. They're important because they help people." She smiled up at him. "And you know what? You did save my life today, although it was indirectly."

His face hardened. "Don't joke about it, Molly."

"This is no joke." She held his eyes with her own, willing him to see the truth. "I told you that I got an inspiration for using my old toys to save myself from Kendall."

"You said you got the idea from a couple of kids."

"The children were yours, Harry."

"Mine?" Harry was thunderstruck. "I thought I was the crazy one here."

"They were your children. I saw them very clearly. A boy and a girl. They had your eyes."

Harry gripped her shoulders, his eyes fierce in the moonlight. "Are you telling me that you had a vision or something?"

Molly smiled tremulously. "Well, maybe it was just wishful thinking."

"Wishful thinking," he repeated blankly.

"I have a very good imagination. It runs in the family. Along with the streak of curiosity."

"Molly—"

She touched his lips with one fingertip. "I think it's time you thought about having kids of your own. You'd make a really fantastic father. You have an aptitude for the job."

His mouth opened. No words came out. He closed it again. Then he wrapped one arm around her neck, bent his head, and kissed her with such seething hunger that Molly went limp in the face of it. Her head fell back against his shoulder.

She was stunned by the wave of sharp, searing need that rolled over her and through her. It left her weak and breathless. And filled with anticipation.

Harry was kissing her now the way he had that first night. She felt like a flower caught in a hurricane. She trembled beneath the impact of the storm and sensed the darkness at its heart. She heard Harry groan. She felt his hands close around her waist. The moonlit room spun around her. Her senses were tumbled into chaos.

The next thing she knew, she was lying flat on her back across the bed. Her legs were splayed wide. The skirt of her nightgown was hiked up to her waist. Harry came down on top of her.

Molly was intensely aware both of her own softness and of the crushing weight of Harry's body. He was fully, heavily aroused. She felt the unyielding hardness of him pressing against her inner thigh.

She gasped for breath when he briefly freed her mouth to kiss her throat. She fought to recover her senses, which were in complete disarray. She was swamped by sensation. Frantically she tried to sort out her impressions. There was something in this that was not coming from her.

She was aware of a deep, raging hunger. A desperate craving that was unlike anything she had ever known. She was in danger of being consumed by an explosive, demanding need that had been tethered too long. The need was fueled by sexual desire, but desire was only a part of the volatile brew.

Harry's hands moved on her body, touching her everywhere. His teeth rasped against her nipple. The urgency in him nearly overwhelmed her.

This wasn't sex, Molly thought, dazed. This was . . . something else. Something more.

The dark storm howled, creating a dangerous vortex. Molly knew that she was in danger of being sucked into the spinning whirlpool of unleashed hunger.

*Harry's hunger.*

A shock of recognition lanced through Molly. In a blinding flash of certainty, she understood that what she was experiencing was emanating from Harry. The emotions that tore through her, the searing need, the intolerable aloneness, the desperation, it was all coming from him.

And it resonated with something deep inside her.

Molly reacted instinctively. She clung to him, knowing that she could satisfy the clawing need in him, aware that she needed him to satisfy her own newly discovered hunger. "I'm here."

*"No."* Harry abruptly heaved himself upward as though he would break the current of contact that sizzled between them. He stared down at her, his hands caging her, his face a mask of torment. "Damn it, I never meant to do this. I swore I would not risk it again. I can't."

And suddenly Molly knew that if she was afraid of what was happening, her fear was nothing compared to his own. The knowledge was strangely reassuring.

"It's all right," she whispered. "You're not alone." She sank her fingertips into the perspiration-slick skin of his powerful shoulders and pulled him back down on top of her. She cradled him between her thighs and covered his hard, alchemist's face with hot, fervent kisses.

Harry shuddered in surrender. "Molly." His mouth closed over hers.

She opened herself for him. She sensed that Harry had been struggling with the dark hunger for years. He had chained the driving need with the force of his self-control. But that formidable willpower had been breached tonight. *Just as it had the first time they had made love,* Molly realized. Now she knew what it was that had been different.

"Together," she whispered. "We do this together.' She lifted herself, curling her legs around him.

"Molly. God, Molly." Harry reached down between their damp bodies, centered himself. He entered her with a long, shuddering sigh.

He filled her completely, stretching her to the limit. He began to move with deep, powerful, surging strokes. The rhythm was flawless. It was as if he could read her body, understood it, knew what was required to satisfy it. He was tuned to her, just as she was tuned to him.

Molly's climax was upon her with such suddenness that she could not even cry out. She simply gave herself up to it. It went through her in shock waves.

She was vaguely aware of Harry's harsh shout of satisfaction as he shook in the throes of his own release.

He collapsed heavily on top of her. Satisfaction radiated from him. It was a satisfaction that went beyond the physical.

Molly understood his satiated sensation because it reverberated through her.

Wholeness.

Completion.

Consummation.

*Hours of boredom broken by moments of stark terror.*

The words beat relentlessly through Harry's head until they finally succeeded in waking him. He opened his eyes reluctantly. He was obsessive on the subject of truth, but at that moment he would have traded his soul for a fistful of lies that he could tell himself.

His worst nightmare had come true. Molly had seen the darkness in him. All of it. She had stood beside him, held his hand, and looked down into the abyss.

Olivia's words came back to haunt him.

*And then the sex got ... well, it got weird, Harry. ...*

But Olivia had never even gotten close to the real truth. She had experienced nothing more than a small hint of the reality that Molly had faced. For Olivia, that pale shadow of the true darkness had been more than enough to scare the daylights out of her.

Tonight, Harry knew that he had exposed Molly to the entire production. A shroud of despair settled over him. He had lost everything.

Molly stirred. Harry turned his head on the pillow and made himself look into her moonlit face. He would face the rejection in her. He would confront the full weight of his loss. And know that he had only himself to blame.

Molly smiled with drowsy, dreamy warmth. "So, have you given any more thought to the idea of having kids?"

Harry felt as if the world had fallen away beneath his feet. All of his fine reflexes turned to mush. He could only stare at her, amazed, bewildered, hardly daring to hope. It took him a while to find his tongue.

"Kids?" he finally got out.

"I really think you ought to consider the subject."

"Kids."

"Yes. With me."

"With you?"

She gave him an expectant look. "Probably best not to wait too long. Neither of us is getting any younger."

"Kids. With you." He could not seem to collect his thoughts.

She touched his cheek with gentle, questing fingers. Her eyes were luminous. "I know I'm not exactly your idea of the perfect wife. I remember the list very clearly."

His mouth was dry. He had to swallow. "What list?"

"The list of all the reasons why we aren't well suited. *I say tomayto, you say tomahto.*"

He shook his head, dazed. "Tomatoes were on your list, not mine."

"Were they? Yes, I guess they were, come to think of it. Your list had other stuff on it, didn't it? Boring stuff. Temperamentally different, you said. No interests in common outside of our mutual concern with the grant proposals. Just two ships passing in the night, you said."

"No." Harry levered himself up on one elbow and leaned over her. He curved a hand around her bare thigh, savoring the sleek feel of her. "I never said anything about ships passing in the night. I'd remember."

She reached up to curl a strand of his hair around one fingertip. "Maybe it was something about the fact that I didn't have a Ph.D. to hang on the wall next to yours."

"No. I never said anything about your not having a Ph.D., either."

"You're sure?"

"I'm certain."

"Absolutely, positively certain?"

"Yes," Harry muttered. "Absolutely, positively. Molly, before we got off on this tangent, you said something about kids."

"It was a subtle hint."

He drew a deep, steadying breath. "Are you asking me to marry you?"

"That's what I like about a well-educated man. If he contemplates the obvious long enough, he finally gets a clue." Molly smiled. "Will you marry me, Harry?"

He fought for the words. "What about . . ."

"What about what?"

He clamped his teeth together. "What about the hours of boredom broken by moments of stark terror?"

"What about 'em? So far I haven't encountered any boring parts yet."

"What about the other?" he made himself ask. "Molly I

swear to God, I don't understand what happened when we made love earlier. I don't want to understand it. I just know that sometimes, if I'm caught off guard, I get . . . too intense or something."

"You know what I think? I think there's something to that business about the Trevelyan Second Sight."

He closed his eyes in despair. "You can't be serious."

"Harry, an intelligent person must remain open to all possibilities. I believe a noted authority on the history of science once wrote that it is a dangerous illusion to believe that one can always distinguish the possible from the impossible."

"I wrote that."

"As I said, a noted authority. I happen to agree with you. I come from a long line of flaky inventors who flourished because they refused to be bound by the illusion of certainty. I think we have to consider the possibility that you've got a trace of some kind of paranormal sixth sense."

"No."

She ignored him. "It's possible that when some heavy-duty emotion, such as sexual desire, kicks in, the elevated intensity of your feelings adds energy to your extrasensory abilities."

"Molly . . ."

"In those moments of heightened sensitivity, perhaps it becomes possible for some unusual things to happen. Maybe some of your innermost thoughts can spill over into the mind of whoever happens to be, uh, intimately connected to you."

"That's crazy. Utterly without scientific basis."

"Just a logical explanation for something that cannot otherwise be explained. Now, will you stop muttering and give me an answer to my question?"

Harry took a serious grip on a universe that seemed to be spinning out of control around him. He pulled her down on top of him. Spearing his fingers through her wonderful, unruly hair, he wrapped his hand around the back of her head and held her still for a deep kiss.

His answer was in that kiss, but just in case she had not understood, Harry said the words aloud. "I'll marry you."

# 16

⚭

"You're going to marry Harry Trevelyan?" Venicia kicked aside the lace-trimmed train of the billowing, white wedding gown. She turned away from her image in the mirror to stare at Molly in stunned amazement. "You can't possibly be serious."

Molly, seated in a small chair, flapped her hand in a small, hushing gesture. "I am. Very serious."

She was aware that the saleswoman behind the counter was eavesdropping. Another customer politely averted her head, but it was obvious that she, too, was all ears.

The boutique, which specialized in bridal gowns and dresses for members of the wedding party, was not very large. Venicia's exclamation of dismay had not gone unnoticed.

"But my dear, you said yourself, you and Trevelyan have absolutely nothing in common," Venicia continued, oblivious to Molly's unsubtle signal for silence. "You said he agreed with you."

"I think he's decided we have more in common than he first thought." Molly studied the lines of the wedding gown with a critical eye. "Are you sure you want to fuss with that long train?"

"What? Oh, the train. I've always wanted to wear a gown

with a train." Venicia brightened briefly as she shook out
the satin skirts. "I feel like a different woman in this gown.
Lord knows, I couldn't even afford a new dress when your
uncle and I were married. This time around, I'm going to
do it right. Cutter insists."

"Good for you." Molly had a sudden inspiration. "You
know something? I think I'll do the same thing."

"What on earth are you talking about?"

"I'm going to pull out all the stops for my wedding, too.
Fancy gown, catered reception, the works. I can afford it,
and it would be good for Harry."

"Good for Harry?" Venicia's delight in her own plans
vanished once more. "I was afraid this would happen. Cutter
has been very worried, also. We both feared you were becoming too involved with Trevelyan."

"I'm involved, all right."

"Molly, please listen to me. I'm well acquainted with the
effects of romantic chemistry these days. Cutter is an extremely romantic man, after all. But you're old enough to
understand that there's a difference between a flash-in-the-
pan passion and true love."

"Sure."

"You want what Cutter and I have." Venicia's eyes misted
briefly. "True affection and commitment."

"Of course."

"Dear, I really don't think you'll find that sort of thing
with Trevelyan. He's not your type at all. You must take a
more realistic view of your relationship with him."

"I am taking a realistic view of it." Far more realistic than
anyone could possibly guess, Molly thought wistfully.

Realistic meant understanding that Harry was different.

Realistic meant accepting that he had a long way to go
before he would allow himself to admit that he was in love,
assuming he ever could admit it. He had an abhorrence of
that which could not be explained logically. There was no
denying that Harry had too much to untangle within himself
before he could deal with such an illogical emotion as love.

Realistic meant accepting that Harry was a man at war with his own nature.

Last night in the crucible of the passion that had flared between them, Molly had finally comprehended the deepest truth about Harry. It was not that he was haunted by his parents' deaths, as Olivia had assumed.

Although he would no doubt suffer from occasional nightmares for the rest of his life, Molly sensed that Harry had found ways to deal with the terrible memories. The proof of his resilience lay in the core of willpower and inner strength that had enabled him to live a productive life.

The trauma of that episode had not stopped him from carving out a notable career, nor had it kept him from being a good father figure to Josh. Harry coped with his exacting work and his equally exacting families quite well. He had told Molly that the nightmares had become increasingly rare in the past few years.

No. Although he would never completely escape the lingering sense of guilt he experienced whenever he thought about the way his parents had died, Molly knew that Harry could deal with it. That was not his real problem.

Harry's real problem was that he was being slowly split asunder by the powerful forces of his own nature. It had all become so painfully clear last night.

For a man of learning and logic, a modern-day Renaissance man who prided himself on his intellectual prowess and his self-mastery, there could be no more threatening concept than the idea that he might possess a paranormal sixth sense. A sense that could not be explained or comprehended was anathema.

Harry could not even bring himself to believe in the possibility of paranormal abilities, let alone accept the fact that he might actually be endowed with some.

Realistic meant being patient while Harry struggled to unite the two sharply divided elements within himself. His talent for rationalizing the situation was astounding, Molly thought wryly. With true Trevelyan sleight of hand, he had pulled off the very neat trick of occasionally tapping his sixth sense without admitting to himself that he even possessed it. Insight, he called it.

*Insight, my big toe,* Molly thought. Whatever Harry's sixth sense was, it was a lot more than reasoned insight. And on some level he knew that. That was what was tearing him apart.

Oh, yes, she was being excruciatingly, painfully, realistic about her relationship with Harry.

Realistic meant accepting that his talent, whatever it was, might very well prevent him from ever experiencing the emotion of love in the same way that normal people experienced it.

Molly was absolutely certain that they shared a bond, and she was sure that Harry realized it. The deep hunger in him was undeniable, as was the satisfaction they found together. But she could not even begin to guess how Harry interpreted the nature of that bond.

She would have given a great deal to have a slightly more unrealistic view of the situation, Molly thought. She was, after all, about to marry a man who had never even told her that he loved her.

Of course, she hadn't told him that she loved him, either.

Venicia seemed unaware of Molly's distracted air. "The thing is," she continued forcefully, "you're not exactly a poor woman, Molly. I hate to say this, dear, but a lady in your situation must seriously question a man's interest in her before she commits herself to marriage. Surely you learned that lesson from your experience with Gordon Brooke."

"You're not living below the poverty line, either, Venicia. But you don't seem concerned about Cutter's interest in you."

"That's different, and you know it. Cutter is quite comfortably well off in his own right. You've seen the yacht and the house on Mercer Island. He has an established background."

"So does Harry."

"I know he's a member of the Stratton family, but you

heard Cutter explain that he's not in line for any of the money."

"Harry doesn't want the Stratton money. He's got enough of his own."

"You mean from his books and consulting fees? Dear, that sort of income would hardly make him wealthy. He writes academic tomes, not best-sellers that get made into films. I'm sure the consulting business pays quite handsomely by most people's standards, but it can't possibly compete with your own income. You are a very wealthy woman, Molly."

"Only when you consider the assets of the Abberwick Foundation."

"One can hardly ignore them. You control those assets, my dear. And that's just my point. It was bad enough when Cutter and I were concerned that Trevelyan was planning to skim off exorbitant fees for his consulting services. Now we've got to wonder if he's marrying you in order to get his hands on the foundation income."

"Set your mind at ease," Molly said. "Harry was not exactly pushing for marriage. As a matter of fact, technically speaking, he never even asked me to marry him."

Venicia looked dumbfounded. "He didn't?"

"I'm the one who proposed to him," Molly explained. "And it wasn't easy. I had to drag the appropriate response out of him."

Harry might possess an unusual talent for seeing beneath the surface, Molly thought, but he was blind as a bat in some ways.

"I don't believe this. You're going to marry him?" Tessa's expression was every bit as astonished as Venicia's had been. "I thought this was supposed to be just an affair or something."

"Things change." Molly opened the copy of the *Post-Intelligencer* that was lying on her desk and surveyed the ad for Abberwick Tea & Spice. "This looks great. Terrific placement. Right next to an article on the health benefits of tea drinking."

Tessa glanced at the ad. "My friend at the newspaper told me that the article was planned for today's issue. I got the ad department to cooperate."

"Nice going. Remind me to give you a raise one of these days."

"Will do. Look, are you sure you know what you're doing here, boss?"

"Well, maybe a raise would be overkill. How about a nice letter of commendation for your file?"

"I'm not talking about my raise," Tessa said. "I'm talking about your marriage plans. Your aunt and her fiancé are worried about Trevelyan's intentions. I heard them talking to you the other day."

"They think he's after the assets of the Abberwick Foundation." Molly frowned. "Actually, I think it was Cutter who put the idea into my aunt's head."

"I hate to be the one to say this, Molly, but it's not exactly a paranoid thought. In fact, it's a realistic possibility. The only reason you even met Trevelyan in the first place was because of the foundation."

"I'm the one who found him, remember? He didn't come looking for me."

"Yes, but he certainly moved fast enough after you introduced yourself, didn't he? Molly, let's get real. I know you're a successful businesswoman, and you've done a terrific job raising your kid sister. I realize that you had the full financial responsibility of your family after your mother died."

"So?"

"So, while I'll admit that you've had some experience with harsh reality, you haven't had a lot of experience with the male of the species. Molly, what do you know about this guy?"

"Enough."

"Bull. You knew a lot more about Gordon Brooke, and look how that ended."

"I seriously doubt that I'll ever walk into a room and

find Harry boffing a counter assistant on a pile of coffee bean sacks."

Tessa threw up her hands. "Can you be sure of that?"

Molly smiled. "Absolutely, positively."

"But *how* can you be sure?"

Molly considered the matter briefly. She could think of no way to describe the bond she sensed existed between herself and Harry. There was no way to explain that if anything ever happened to sever that bond, she would be aware of it immediately. Things would not get to the counter assistant boffing stage without her sensing well in advance that something had gone dreadfully wrong in the relationship.

But even without that intuitive knowledge, Molly knew that she had logic and reason on her side. Harry's relationships with his difficult relatives proved that he had a history of making commitments and sticking by them, even when he wasn't given much encouragement. And she intended to give him plenty of encouragement.

"Harry's the loyal type," Molly said simply.

Tessa's nose ring quivered as she drew a deep, resigned breath. "Have you told Kelsey?"

"No. She's very busy at that summer workshop. I don't want to distract her. I'll give her the news when she comes home." Molly smiled. "You and Kelsey can both be bridesmaids."

"Don't tell me you're planning a traditional wedding?"

"With all the trimmings," Molly assured her.


Harry wandered slowly through the darkened corridors of the Seattle Aquarium. His attention shifted from one illuminated display tank to the next. Cold, emotionless eyes gazed out at him as though aware of his presence.

A chill moved through him. He could almost feel the creatures on the other side of the glass assessing him. He knew that as far as a fish was concerned, he fell into one of two categories. He was either food or a threat.

The world was simple when one possessed a simple brain governed by simple imperatives, Harry thought. Decisions were easy. Choices were limited. Complex emotions were nonexistent.

One didn't need complicated, disturbing emotions when one was trapped forever in the dark abyss. Only the simple ones were required. Anger. Fear. Hunger. There was no room for hope.

Harry paused in front of a large tank occupied by several cold-eyed denizens. He drew a deep breath, allowing the memories of last night to flood him with warmth.

Molly wanted him. She was not afraid of the darkness in him. She had asked him to marry her. She wanted to have babies with him.

Harry let the knowledge sink into his soul. Flames flickered in the darkness.

He gazed into the display tank for a while longer, and then he turned and walked out of the shadowed passages of the aquarium.

Outside Molly waited for him in the bright sunlight.

He stopped at the entrance and gazed at her with a sense of wonder. She leaned against the pier railing, her honey-colored hair dancing around her vibrant face. She smiled with welcome when she spotted him amid the crowd of joggers, tourists, and lunch-bound office workers.

Harry watched, bemused, as she waved and hurried toward him with the eagerness of a lover. Not just a lover, he thought. His future wife.

"Here I am, Harry."

An indefinable sensation washed through him. As it receded, it left behind traces of raw vulnerability. But for some reason the knowledge did not terrify him the way it would have done a few days ago.

"I'm starved," Molly said breathlessly as she reached him.

"Me, too." He took her arm and walked her toward an outdoor café.

"Something wrong?" she asked.

"I'm not sure."

"What's that supposed to mean?" She gave him a look of anxious inquiry. "Harry? What is it?"

"Probably nothing."

"Uh-oh. You've had another one of your insights, haven't you?"

"Maybe. I'll tell you the details after we get our clams and chips."

Harry realized that he was no longer amazed by her perception. Somewhere along the line he had come to accept the fact that she would almost always recognize his various moods. She would know when he was merely feeling in a contemplative or reflective frame of mind and when he was seriously concerned.

Not even his parents had understood him as well as Molly did. No one had ever understood him so well. It was an unsettling thought.

Ten minutes later they sat down at a small, round table that was protected from the sidewalk traffic by a low, decorative barrier.

Harry drizzled malted vinegar over his fried clams and considered where to begin. "I've been going through Kendall's notebook."

"Find anything interesting?"

"Nothing more than what we already discovered. I've gone through every page of the book. There isn't any other reference to his plans to terrorize you other than those sketches of the machines he used to set up his damn pranks."

"No notes about his desire for revenge?"

"Nothing like that. The brief descriptions of the pistol assembly and the goblin were all very businesslike."

Molly paused in the act of stuffing a french fry into her mouth. "Businesslike?"

"You know what I mean." Harry moved his hand in a vague gesture. "It's as if the plans for those gadgets were nothing more than just designs for ordinary, routine projects."

"Hmm." Molly munched thoughtfully. "No passion in them, is that it?"

Harry considered her succinct description. She had put

her finger on what was bothering him. "Maybe that's it. You'd think a man bent on vengeance would display more emotion toward the project. An inventor's sketches are unique to the individual. They convey a great deal to the trained eye."

Molly nodded. "I've seen the differences in my sister's drawings when she's really excited about a project. Lots of strong, positive lines. There's an eagerness and enthusiasm in them."

"Exactly. I was once asked to examine some notebook sketches made by a man who planned to blow up a research lab because he believed the company had stolen his ideas. He had made some drawings of an explosive device he planned to mail anonymously to the research facility."

"And?"

Harry ate another clam. "And there was something in those sketches that was not in his other work. An intensity, an outrage. You could almost feel the anger radiating off the page."

"Insight or intuition?"

He scowled. "Neither. It was similar to interpreting someone's handwriting. You could see the rage and the craziness in it."

"You could see it, but I'll bet very few other people could. What happened to the crazed inventor?"

"He got caught trying to mail the explosive device," Harry said absently.

Molly smiled. "He got caught because you deduced what he was about to do from his sketches and the cops staked him out, right?"

Harry shrugged. "I was asked to give my opinion on the drawings. I told the cops that it was a safe bet the guy intended to kill someone with his device. I also told them that, judging from the skilled details of the sketches, the device would probably work."

"My, you do lead an exciting life, Harry."

"Actually, it was a rather placid existence until you came into it."

Molly grinned. "I don't believe that for a minute."

"To be blunt," Harry said deliberately, "I can do without some of the added excitement you've brought into my life. Unfortunately, I don't foresee it fading until they catch Kendall."

"They'll catch him," Molly predicted. "You heard the detective who talked to us yesterday. They'll track him down now that they know he's truly dangerous. Want to talk about our wedding plans?"

Harry nearly choked on a fried clam. It was the first time she had mentioned the subject of marriage since she had proposed last night. He grabbed his iced tea and took a deep swallow.

Molly frowned in concern. "Are you all right?"

"Yes." He took another slug of tea and set the cup down with great precision. He cleared his throat. "I was thinking of something simple. Vegas, maybe."

"I was thinking of something large and magnificent," Molly said.

Harry eyed her warily. "Do you have a lot of friends to invite?"

"Yes. And then there's all those Strattons and Trevelyans."

Harry raised his brows. "Are you kidding? The Strattons and Trevelyans won't sit in the same room together long enough for a preacher to say the magic words."

"Hmm."

"Forget the fancy wedding. It'll have to be a courthouse marriage or Vegas. Take your pick." Harry paused. "If you're still serious about this, that is."

"Oh, I'm very serious about it," Molly assured him.

Harry's stomach unclenched. He downed the rest of his fried clams with a curious sense of relief.

Molly sat alone in the front room of Harry's condominium the following evening and listened to the silence. It was an unnatural sort of silence. A silence fraught with meaning and portent.

Olivia was in Harry's study. She had been in there alone with him for nearly twenty minutes. The door of the study was firmly closed.

Molly had immediately excused herself when Olivia had made it clear that she wished to speak to Harry alone. Harry had not appeared pleased at the prospect of a private interview with his ex-fiancée, but he had accepted the situation with his usual stoicism.

Molly watched the late summer twilight give way to night and thought about Olivia and Harry. It was difficult to see what Harry had thought he'd had in common with his ex-fiancée other than a Ph.D. It was odd that a man who had a talent for insight had made such a mistake in his personal life. He did appear to have a gift for shooting himself in the foot every time he tried to apply his intellectual abilities to matters of emotion.

Molly glanced at the clock. Another five minutes had passed. She went back to the book she had been trying to read.

The study door opened. Molly put one arm on the back of the couch and turned her head to see Olivia walking toward her. There was no sign of Harry.

"Finished?" Molly asked politely.

"Yes. It was family business."

Molly nodded. "Harry gets a lot of that."

Olivia frowned. "I beg your pardon?"

"Never mind. Inside joke."

Olivia glanced back at the study door with a look of irritation. "Harry's in one of his moods."

"He's probably just thinking. Can I make you a cup of tea?"

"No, thank you. Harry got a business call just as I was getting ready to leave. He's still on the phone."

Molly started to rise. "I'll see you out."

"That won't be necessary." Olivia's smile was cool. "I know my way around here."

"I'm sure you do."

"He tells me that the two of you are going to be married."

"That's right." Molly gave Olivia her most winning smile. "I'm planning a big wedding, by the way."

"Are you?"

"Everyone from both sides of his family will be invited, of course."

"That should be interesting." Olivia hesitated. "I'd like to ask you a personal question, if you don't mind."

"Okay. I can't guarantee an answer, though."

"Are you sure you know what you're doing?"

"Yes, thank you."

Olivia's mouth tightened. She glanced again at the closed study door. "I probably shouldn't tell you this, but in my professional opinion, Harry has some serious problems. He ought to be in therapy."

"Harry is different, I'll give you that. But I don't think a shrink will do him any good."

"I'm sorry, but I know him a great deal better than you do, and I think it's a mistake for him to marry. Any marriage that Harry enters into is bound to fail."

"Are you nuts?"

Olivia gave her a cold stare. "You do realize that I am a clinical psychologist, don't you?"

"Harry told me. I have a great deal of respect for your professional expertise, Olivia, but I don't think you understand Harry very well. He's quite unique."

"He's dysfunctional, not unique," Olivia snapped. "He's very likely suffering from posttraumatic stress disorder and periodic bouts of depression. To be quite honest, he's an excellent candidate for medication."

"A candidate for medication?" Molly wrinkled her nose. "I don't think he's interested in running for that office."

"I'm not joking, Molly. This is a serious matter. I cannot advise you to marry a man with Harry's problems."

"Relax, you're off the hook. I'm not asking for your advice."

Olivia glared at her in obvious frustration. "Look, I'll be frank. You and Harry haven't known each other very long. Your relationship is still in its early phase. I think you should know that sooner or later Harry will demonstrate some clinically significant abnormalities in his sexual relationship with you."

Molly held up a hand. "Hold it right there. I'm not one of your patients. I have no intention of discussing my sex life with you."

"I'm trying to save you from making a terrible mistake."

"You don't have to worry about saving me from Harry."

Olivia narrowed her eyes. "You do realize he's not in line for any of the Stratton fortune, don't you? He quarreled with his grandfather. He won't see a dime."

"Money has nothing to do with this. Good night, Olivia."

"You're either very stupid or very foolish."

Molly grinned. "You mean I have a choice?"

Olivia swung around on her heel and went swiftly down the hall toward the front door. She let herself out without a word of farewell. The door slammed shut behind her.

Molly saw Harry lounging, arms folded, in the entrance of his study. He gazed thoughtfully after Olivia for a long moment. Then he met Molly's eyes.

"Clinically significant abnormalities?" he repeated slowly.

"You heard that, did you?"

"Only the last part. Did she give you her complete diagnosis?"

"Yes, but I wouldn't put too much stock in her theories if I were you. She is one weird shrink. That's why she probably became a shrink in the first place. She was looking for answers to her own problems."

His mouth curved slightly. "I see."

"Which is not to say that I don't believe that one can't get a great deal of help from a good therapist," Molly continued with scrupulous honesty. "But one does need to select one's therapist with great care."

"Care."

"Right. There's all that business with transference and countertransference, you see. One has to find a therapist whose own hang-ups don't get in the way of treating the patient's."

"You sound like an expert."

"I consulted a therapist for a while after my mother died," Molly said. "As a matter of fact, I consulted half a dozen of the little suckers before I found one I could talk to. I went to her a few times. She helped me work through some stuff."

"What kind of stuff?"

Molly hesitated, reflecting back on those difficult days and the dreadful fear she had faced at the age of twenty. "A feeling of being overwhelmed by the responsibilities I knew I had to handle. Some anger at being stuck with those responsibilities. My therapist was good. I only saw her a handful of times because I couldn't afford her for long. But I got a lot out of our little chats."

Harry smiled fleetingly. "I guess that makes you an expert, all right."

Molly eyed him thoughtfully. "It doesn't require expertise, just plain old common sense, to figure out that Olivia is not qualified to diagnose you. She's got her own problems, and they're connected to you."

Acute interest burned in Harry's eyes. "What kind of problems?"

"Isn't it obvious?"

"Not to me."

"The two of you have a history. At the very least, I'd say she feels guilty about having ended the engagement. She's probably rationalized her actions by telling you and herself that you've got psychological problems that make it impossible for you to have a healthy relationship."

"You don't think she might be right?"

"Heck, no." Molly smiled. "You're different, Harry. Definitely one of a kind. But you're going to make a terrific husband and father."

Harry was silent for a moment. "Maybe you have a thing for clinically significant abnormalities," he suggested.

"Maybe I do. Who was that on the phone?"

"Fergus Rice, the private investigator I hired to keep tabs on Kendall."

"Did he discover something?" Molly asked.

"Two hours ago Wharton Kendall drove a blue Ford over a cliff somewhere along Highway One in Oregon. He was apparently heading for California. Kendall was killed in the crash."

It took a few seconds for the significance of that simple statement to sink in. When it did, Molly leaped off the sofa and raced across the room to Harry.

"It's over," she whispered as she threw herself into his arms.

Harry's arms tightened around her. "That's what Rice said."

# 17

"All right, that's it. I've had it." Molly sat straight up in bed and turned to glower at Harry. "Enough is enough. What's wrong? Why aren't you asleep?"

Harry slanted her a surprised glance from beneath his lashes. The sheet was crushed to his waist. His arms were folded behind his head. The expression on his savage features was one of intent concentration.

"I'm thinking," he said.

"Your thinking is giving me a severe case of insomnia."

"Sorry. I didn't realize I was keeping you awake."

"How am I supposed to sleep when you're lying there staring at the ceiling?"

"Why should it bother you if I stare at the ceiling?" he asked with what appeared to be genuine curiosity.

"Darned if I know, but it does. It's as if you're humming in my brain or something. It's keeping me awake."

"I can't help it. When I think, I think."

"Nope. This definitely isn't the sort of humming I hear when you're just thinking. I can sleep through that. This humming is more like a seriously-concerned-that-we-may-have-a-very-big-problem-on-our-hands kind of humming."

His eyes narrowed. "What the hell is this stuff about me humming in your head?"

She shrugged. "I can't explain it. It's just sort of a sensation I've been getting lately. Don't you feel it?"

"No." Harry seized the edge of the sheet and started to shove it aside. "Look, if I'm keeping you awake, I'll go into the front room."

"No, you won't." Molly caught him by his bare shoulder and pulled him down onto the pillow. "Stay right where you are."

He relaxed against the pillow without protest, one brow raised in polite inquiry.

Molly punched her own pillow a few times and adjusted it against the headboard behind her. "Now, then, tell me what the problem is."

He hesitated for only a couple of seconds before he seemed to come to a decision. "It's Kendall's notebook."

"You're still worrying about that? But I thought we had decided that our problems are over now that Kendall is dead."

"There's something wrong with that notebook." Harry levered himself up to a sitting position beside her and arranged his own pillow behind his back. "I just wish I could put my finger on it."

"You said that you didn't think the drawings of the gun and goblin mechanisms conveyed a sense of extreme rage."

"Yes, but that's not what's bothering me now."

Molly studied him in the shadows. "What, exactly, is bothering you?"

"It's the way the intruder went after you the other day in your house. There was something about the way he did it that doesn't fit with the designs in Kendall's notebook."

Molly shivered. "It all seemed very efficient to me."

"That's just it," Harry said softly. "It was efficient. Straightforward. Simple. Not very creative. Or personal."

"I guess that depends on your definition of creativity. And I can assure you that I took the attempt very personally." Molly blinked as realization struck her. "Uh-oh. I think I see where you're going with this." ·

Harry drummed the long, lean fingers of his right hand

absently against the sheet beside him. "If a man such as Kendall was bent on murder, he would be inclined to use a gadget of his own design to kill his victim."

"Harry, maybe you're carrying your deductive insights a little too far here."

"He used gadgets to try to terrorize you," Harry said, oblivious to the interruption. "It's logical that he would have come up with something in the same vein if he went so far as to try to murder you."

"Uh, Harry . . ."

"A mechanism that he had designed and built, himself. A device of his own invention, one that would have given him satisfaction when it worked properly. The same logic applies to his use of a car to try to run us off the road. It doesn't fit."

Molly reached out to touch his arm. "Now, hold on here. The blue Ford belonged to Kendall. You said your investigator, Mr. Rice, verified that it was registered to him."

"Yes."

"So it's only logical to assume that it was Kendall at the wheel the other day when that same Ford tried to run us off the road."

"Someone else could have used Kendall's car to try to kill us."

"But no one else has any reason to kill us."

"So far as we know." Harry looked out into the darkness beyond the windows. "I've been lying here wondering if someone else is involved in this."

Molly pulled the bedclothes up to her throat. "All right, let's assume for the moment that there is another person involved. What's his or her motive? We decided Kendall was out for revenge because I turned down his grant proposal."

"It was a logical assumption." Harry pushed aside the covers and got out of bed. "But what if there was another person with another motive?"

Molly watched him as he started to pace the room in front of the bank of windows. She could feel the intensity pooling within him as he focused on the problem at hand. Harry was nude except for a pair of white briefs that hugged his strongly muscled flanks. There was an eerie, spectral quality about him as he moved in and out of the moonlight.

"What other person?" she asked gently. "And what other motive could there possibly be? I've turned down approximately a hundred grant proposals. I suppose we could be dealing with more than one disgruntled grant applicant. But it seems a little unlikely that we'd have two homicidal inventors in the batch."

"Who knows?" Harry paced through a shaft of cold, silver light and on into the deep shadow at the far end of the room.

"It would also imply," Molly continued, thinking through the obvious logic, "that at some point Kendall and this other mystery inventor worked together on their little terrorist project."

"Or it could mean that someone else knew about Kendall's desire for revenge and used it as camouflage for himself."

"Good lord." Molly drew up her knees and wrapped her arms around them. "Are you saying that another, more vicious individual who actually wants to kill me knew that Kendall was angry? And set him up to take the rap once I was dead?"

"There's a certain logic to it." Harry reached the bookcase, turned, and retraced his path toward the opposite end of the room. The force of his concentration was so powerful that it seemed to charge the atmosphere around him.

"I don't know," Molly said doubtfully. "It's awfully far-fetched. Chances are that, with Kendall dead, the whole thing really is finished, just as Fergus Rice said."

Harry came to a halt in front of the windows. "It doesn't feel finished, Molly."

She smiled slightly. "Then you'll have to do something about it, won't you? If you don't, neither of us will ever get any sleep."

He looked at her, his eyes bleak. "It's beginning to look that way."

"Any ideas?"

"It might help if I could examine something else that belonged to Kendall," Harry said slowly. "It might give me a fix on whether or not I'm right about his preference for inventing his own weapons."

"It occurs to me that, if there is someone else involved in this mess, Kendall's recent demise might not have been an accident."

"Hell." Icy moonlight turned Harry's face to stone. "You're right. I've been concentrating so much on the possibility that there are two people involved that I didn't consider all the implications. If Kendall had a partner, or if he was being used as a fall guy by someone else, that second person might have gotten rid of him because he had become a liability."

"This is getting very complicated, not to mention nasty."

Harry swung away from the window. "I need to get a look at that blue Ford. Rice can find out where it was taken after the crash."

"It's after one in the morning. Fergus Rice will be sound asleep. He won't be able to do anything at this hour." Molly yawned. "Why don't you come back to bed?"

"I'm in no mood to sleep."

She gave him a smugly angelic smile. "In that case, perhaps we could discuss a few of your significant clinical abnormalities."

Harry, who was halfway across the room, en route to the telephone, spun around. There was a strange glitter in his eyes. "What did you say?"

"Don't you like it when I talk dirty?"

"Molly . . ."

"Come back to bed, Harry." She patted the sheet beside her. "There's absolutely nothing you can do until after breakfast. If you can't sleep, we'll find some way to fill the time."

He hesitated. Then the taut lines of his face relaxed slightly. He walked to the side of the bed and looked down at her with a thoughtful expression that was belied by the extraordinarily brilliant gleam in his eyes.

"Significant clinical abnormalities?" he murmured.

"What can I say? I'm a sucker for 'em. Yes, sir, give me those hours of boredom followed by moments of stark terror, and I'm a happy camper."

Harry's teeth flashed in a lethally sexy grin. He put one knee on the bed and leaned down, trapping her between his arms. "I eat happy campers for bedtime snacks."

"Can't wait." She put her arms around his neck and pulled him down on top of her.

He came to her in a rush of sensual, startlingly playful energy. He seized hold of her and rolled over and over with her until the sheets were tangled and Molly was laughing helplessly.

He finally brought the tumbling game to a halt near the foot of the bed and braced himself on his elbows above her.

Flushed and breathless, Molly looked up and saw the uninhibited joy in him.

"There is nothing quite like the taste of a happy camper," Harry murmured. His eyes gleamed in the shadows as he slid slowly down the length of her body. He settled himself between her legs.

Molly felt his teeth on the inside of her thigh. She gasped and dug her fingers into his shoulders. He parted her gently with his fingers.

"Harry?"

And then she felt his mouth on her in an unbearably intimate kiss.

The world came apart.

Molly shut the refrigerator door and set the box of fresh raspberries down on the counter next to the sink. "You know, Harry, I've been thinking. This condo of yours is nice enough and the view is terrific, but it's not very functional."

"Functional?" Harry echoed absently. He held the kitchen phone in one hand as he prepared to punch in Fergus Rice's phone number.

"You know, efficient. I miss my housekeeping machines. The dusting robots, the dishwasher, and the kitchen clean-up devices. The Abberwick Food Storage and Preparation Machine. Honestly, I don't know how you get along with these old-fashioned appliances. They're straight out of the Dark Ages."

"I've got a housekeeper, remember?" Harry listened impatiently as the phone rang on the other end of the line.

"Yes, I know, but still, it all seems so primitive."

Harry scowled as the phone rang for the third time. "Put that knife down."

"I was just going to slice some English muffins to go with the raspberries."

"I'll slice the muffins when I get off the phone."

"Sheesh. Are you always this grumpy in the morning?"

"Only when I see you with a knife in your hand." The phone continued to ring.

Molly set the knife aside and propped her elbows on the counter. "How do you feel about moving into my house after we're married?"

"The Abberwick mansion?" Harry glanced at the clock. It was nearly eight. Fergus usually went into his office early. "You want to stay in that crazy old house?"

"It's a great place for kids. They'd have Kelsey's and my old toys to play with. And you'd have plenty of room for your books. You could have one whole wing for your offices and library. The kids would be underfoot all the time, of course, but I think you'd like that."

Harry stopped listening to the phone, his full attention suddenly riveted on Molly. "Kids?"

"Sure. How many do you want? I know we're going to have at least two."

"Uh—" Harry broke off at the sound of Fergus's voice. "Rice here."

"Fergus, it's Harry."

"For crying out loud, Harry, it's two minutes to eight. I just walked in the door. Haven't even had my second cup of coffee."

"I'm calling about the Kendall situation."

"What situation? I thought the accident down in Oregon took care of the problem. The man's dead, Harry."

"I know. But I want to examine his car. Where did the authorities take it?"

"It'll probably be hauled off to a wrecking yard sometime today. Something wrong?"

"I don't know. Have the authorities finished the acci-dent investigation?"

"Sure. Finished it yesterday. It was all very straightfor-ward. Nothing of a suspicious nature. The Ford was totaled, though. That kind of thing can happen to a car when it goes straight over a sheer cliff."

"Can you arrange for me to get a look at it?"

"I don't see why not." Fergus paused to make some notes. "I'll contact the owner of the wrecking yard this morning and set it up."

"Thanks, Fergus. Call me as soon as you've cleared it. I'll fly down to Portland and rent a car to drive to the coast."

"Right."

Harry replaced the receiver and looked at Molly. "He's going to arrange for me to examine the Ford."

"What do you think you'll be able to tell by looking at it?"

"I don't know." Harry watched Molly rinse the raspber-ries. "Maybe nothing."

She gave him a knowing look. "Or maybe something?"

"Rice says the authorities have already completed their investigation, but since they had no reason to suspect that Kendall was killed, they could have overlooked something."

"Such as?"

"I don't know. Sabotaged brakes. Evidence of an encoun-ter with another car."

Molly nibbled thoughtfully on her lower lip. "You think maybe someone sideswiped Kendall?"

"The idea has a familiar ring to it, doesn't it?" The lobby intercom buzzed, breaking into Harry's chain of thought. "Who the hell could that be at this hour?"

"I'll give you two guesses." Molly gently piled the fragile raspberries into a bowl.

"Two guesses?"

"It's either a Stratton or a Trevelyan. Take your pick."

Harry raised his brows as he depressed the intercom button. "Yes?"

"Mr. Trevelyan, this is George downstairs in the lobby. There is a Mr. Hughes here to see you."

Harry groaned. "At this hour?"

"Yes, sir."

"Tell him this is important," Brandon said in the background. There was a hard, determined edge to his voice. "Tell him it's a family matter."

"Send him up, George," Harry said. He released the intercom button.

"Want me to get lost?" Molly asked.

"No." Harry thought about his conversation with Olivia the previous evening. "Stay right where you are."

A few minutes later the front doorbell chimed discreetly. Harry reluctantly went to answer it. He was not feeling enthusiastic about the prospect of dealing with any of his relatives this morning. He had other things on his mind.

He opened the door. Brandon, dressed in a lightweight sweater and slacks, stood glowering in the hall.

"Good morning," Harry said mildly.

Brandon strode into the hall without a greeting. His expression was thunderous.

"Want a cup of coffee?" Harry asked as he closed the door.

Brandon ignored the polite inquiry. He swung around to confront Harry. "Olivia came here to see you last night."

"Yes."

"Damn it, I told her I didn't want her getting involved in this. I told my mother the same thing. Why the hell won't they stay out of it?"

"Probably because they're worried about you."

"I don't need anyone worrying about me. I can handle this thing just fine all by myself." Brandon stalked into the front room. He came to an abrupt halt when he saw Molly behind the kitchen counter. "Who are you? A new housekeeper?"

"No," Molly said. "I'm Harry's fiancée."

"His fiancée?" Brandon stared at her. "Olivia said something about Harry getting engaged to the trustee of the Abberwick Foundation. I didn't believe it."

"This is Molly Abberwick," Harry said, annoyed by the expression of amazement on Brandon's face. "Molly, this is my cousin Brandon Hughes. Aunt Danielle's son. Olivia's husband."

Molly nodded. "How do you do, Brandon? We're just about to eat. Have you had breakfast?"

"Yes. Thanks." Brandon's eyes narrowed. He glanced speculatively at Harry. "So this engagement is for real?"

"It's real, all right." Harry took his seat at the counter.

"Sort of sudden, isn't it?" Brandon asked.

"Time is relative." Molly gave Brandon a smile that was sweeter than the sugar she was spooning lightly over the berries. "Harry and I feel we know each other well enough to commit to marriage. Don't we, Harry?"

"Yes," Harry said. "Why don't you sit down, Brandon?"

"I'd rather talk to you in your study."

"Too bad. I'd rather eat breakfast." Harry glanced at the bowl of raspberries Molly had set in front of him. "Give me those muffins and the knife."

Wordlessly, Molly handed him the requested items. Harry went to work slicing the muffins.

"If you won't have coffee, how about some tea, Brandon?" Molly asked. "I'm making a pot for myself."

"No, thanks. Look, Harry, this is a personal matter." Brandon shot a quick look at Molly. "Family business."

"From now on," Harry said softly, "Molly is family. My family. Anything you want to say to me can be said in front of her."

Brandon's mouth compressed into a thin line. "The two of you are engaged, not married."

"Same thing as far as I'm concerned." Harry handed the

278

neatly sliced muffins across the counter to Molly. "Talk if you want to talk. Otherwise, you can leave. I've got a busy day ahead."

Brandon took a step closer and lowered his voice. "Harry, let's be realistic here. Given your track record, I don't think you should be counting chickens until they're hatched."

"What the hell is that supposed to mean?" Harry asked.

"You want me to spell it out?"

"Yes."

"You know damn well what I'm trying to say." Brandon glanced uneasily at Molly, who smiled brightly in return. He turned back to Harry. "Look, this is a little awkward. Let's go into your study."

"No."

Brandon lost his temper. "I can hardly be expected to discuss sensitive matters in front of a stranger."

"I told you, Molly's not a stranger. She's going to be my wife."

Brandon reddened. "Not according to Olivia. She thinks this engagement isn't any more likely to survive than your other one did. And she should know."

"Think so?"

"She knows people, Harry. It's her job, remember?" Brandon had the grace to give Molly an apologetic look. "My wife is a clinical psychologist. One of the best in the city."

"Yes, I know," Molly said demurely. "We've met. She was kind enough to give me some free advice."

Brandon turned back to Harry. "I'm sure Molly is very discreet, and I have absolutely nothing against her. But until you actually get yourself married, I'm not prepared to discuss my business in front of an outsider."

Harry reached the end of his patience. He came up off the stool in a movement that caused Brandon to take a hurried step back.

"You came here to talk," Harry said very softly. "Say what you want to say or leave."

"All right, if that's the way you're going to be," Brandon said stiffly, "I'll come back later."

"I may not be here later," Harry said. "I've got plans for the day."

"You're doing this deliberately, aren't you? You're trying to make this as difficult for me as possible. What do you want me to do? Grovel to you just because you convinced Granddad to let me go out on my own?"

"Why don't you ask Olivia? She seems to think she's an authority on my motives." Harry sat down again and picked up his spoon.

"Whoa. Time out." Molly formed a referee's T with her hands. "I vote we call a truce here." She put a cup and saucer on the counter. "Here, have some coffee, Brandon. Gordon Brooke's finest. It's his Dark Seattle Roast."

Harry looked up from his raspberries. He was irritated. "I didn't know we were drinking a Gordon Brooke blend."

"Not me. You. Personally, I never touch the stuff. And don't look at me that way. Your housekeeper bought it."

"Remind me to have Ginny buy another brand." Harry went back to his raspberries. "Either sit down or leave, Brandon. I don't like having you hover while I eat."

Brandon fumed for a minute longer, and then he subsided onto a stool. He picked up the coffee cup Molly had given him and took a long swallow. When he was finished he set the cup down with a soft crash. "Okay, let's talk."

"I'm listening."

"I'm here because I want to discuss the financing of my new plans. Granddad has agreed to let me leave the company without any repercussions, which is a great relief to Mother and Olivia, but he won't help me."

"Hold it right there," Harry said. "I'm not a bank. I talked to Parker for you, but that's as far as I can go."

"That's not true. You know people, Harry." Brandon fiddled with his coffee cup. "I'm aware that you arranged financing for one of your Trevelyan relatives when she decided to buy that carnival amusement company."

"That was different."

"Yeah? How was it different? Don't your Stratton relatives count?"

"My Stratton relatives are all rich."

"Not all of them," Brandon said meaningfully. "When I leave Stratton Properties, I'm going to be on my own."

"Olivia charges her patients as much as a good tax attorney charges her clients. You won't starve."

"It's true, we'll have Olivia's income to live on until I establish myself," Brandon said. "But she can't afford to capitalize an operation the size of the one I'm planning. You know that as well as I do."

"So?" Harry could feel Molly watching him from the other side of the counter.

"So the banks won't touch me unless Stratton Properties is involved in the loan. Even if I could talk Granddad or Uncle Gilford into backing me, I'd rather not," Brandon said. "You know that if they're involved, they'll try to take over."

"True."

Brandon frowned. "I think I know why you never joined Stratton Properties."

"My interests lie in other areas."

"Tell me something. Did you know that when you came to live here in Seattle, the whole family was convinced that you were out to take your Stratton relatives for whatever you could get?"

Harry set his spoon down with great care. "That was evident from the start."

"Granddad said it was the Trevelyan blood in you. He said you would try to con us Strattons out of what you figured was your rightful inheritance. He said he wouldn't give you a dime unless you proved that you were a true Stratton."

"Which meant joining the company," Harry finished wearily. "Brandon, this is old history. What do you want from me?"

Brandon straightened his shoulders. "You've got some contacts with venture capitalists because of the technical consulting work you've done. I want you to introduce me to some of the money people. I'm not asking you to go out on a limb for me. I just want the introductions. I'll take it from there."

Harry looked at Molly. She gave him a wry, understanding smile but said nothing. He turned to Brandon. "I'll see what I can do."

Relief flared in Brandon's eyes. "Thanks." He got to his feet. "You won't regret this, Harry. Like I said, I'll make my presentations to the investors and take my chances. Just put me in touch with people who are interested in making sound investments."

"On one condition," Harry temporized.

"What's that?"

"Give me your word of honor that you'll do your best to stop Olivia from handing out her professional opinions of my psychological profile to all and sundry. It's getting to be annoying."

Brandon was plainly startled. He started to scowl, and then a spark of reluctant amusement lit his gaze. "I'll try, but it might not be easy."

"I know." Harry caught Molly's eye. "But I'd appreciate it if you could convince her to keep her diagnoses to herself. Just tell her some people don't mind hours of boredom broken by moments of stark terror."

Brandon looked mildly baffled. But he shrugged it off and turned to leave. Then he stopped and smiled at Molly. "Thanks for the coffee."

"You bet," she said. "Oh, by the way, Brandon, Harry and I are planning a big wedding. Everyone in both families will be invited. We'll expect you and Olivia, of course."

"Olivia and I will attend," Brandon said slowly. "But I wouldn't count on any of the others from the Stratton side of the family unless you can guarantee that none of the Trevelyans will be there."

"Everyone will be there," Molly repeated coolly.

Brandon glanced at Harry. Harry said nothing. He knew as well as Brandon did that there was no hope of getting all of the Strattons and Trevelyans to attend the wedding. Sooner or later, Molly would have to face that simple fact of life.

"Right, well, I'd better get going," Brandon said hastily. He headed toward the door, his step a good deal lighter than it had been when he entered earlier.

# 18

"**H**ow the hell can you be certain that Trevelyan's not marrying you in order to get his hands on the foundation assets?" Gordon grumbled as he scooped up the papers he had spread out on the counter. "That's all I want to know. How can you be so damned sure?"

Molly regarded Gordon with an acute sense of irritation. It was shortly after five. Tessa was in the storage room, finishing some labels for a mail order shipment. Harry would be here any moment. It was time to close the shop and go home.

Home.

It struck her that she was home when she was with Harry. She wondered if he felt the same way when he was with her. She hoped he did. He needed a sense of home more than any man she had ever known.

Gordon had appeared at the door of Abberwick Tea & Spice just as Molly was turning the CLOSED sign in the window. He had stuck one foot in the door and made another pitch for financing. Molly had allowed him to ramble on about his new expansion plans as she tidied the shop for the night. When he had finished his arguments in favor of using Abberwick funds to promote Gordon Brooke Espresso Bars, she had politely refused. Again.

Gordon had turned quite red in the face. He seemed unable to accept either her unwillingness to finance him or her engagement to Harry. The two seemed to be linked together in Gordon's mind, and for some reason it was the latter that apparently annoyed him the most.

"I just don't get it, Molly." Gordon dumped the papers into a leather file. "Why are you so sure you can trust him?"

"It's none of your business, is it?"

Gordon contrived to appear hurt. "We've known each other a long time. It's only natural that I'm concerned about you."

"Let's be honest here." Molly leaned against the spice counter and regarded Gordon with an impatience she did not bother to conceal. "What you're really asking me is how do I know that Harry is not another you, isn't it? How do I know I won't discover the hard way that he has a taste for pretty counter assistants?"

Gordon flushed. "Don't twist my words."

"I don't owe you any explanations," she continued. "But the truth is, I'm absolutely, positively certain that Harry is not another Gordon Brooke. How do I know this? I think it has something to do with the way he hums."

Gordon ignored that. "It's not a joke, damn it. I'm just trying to keep you from making a big mistake. One that could cost you a fortune."

"I doubt if it will cost me as much as financing several new Gordon Brooke Espresso Bars."

"The espresso bars would be an investment," Gordon insisted. "That's a whole different matter. This is your future I'm concerned about. Molly, you control a lot of money through the Abberwick Foundation. Chances are the assets will continue to grow through the years. How can you be sure that you'll be able to keep it out of Trevelyan's hands? You've made him your technical consultant, for Christ's sake."

"So?"

"So he'll be making all the important decisions."

"No, he won't. I will be making the important decisions."

Molly was thoroughly irritated now. "Why does everyone assume that I'm a complete idiot when it comes to the Abberwick Foundation? What makes you think that I'm going to turn control of the assets over to Harry or anyone else?"

Gordon waved his hands in a soothing gesture. "Take it easy. Calm down. I was just trying to point out the facts."

"The heck you were. You're trying to undermine my relationship with my fiancé. I'm not going to listen to another word."

"Okay, okay. If that's the way you're going to be about it, fine. But don't blame me when you wake up some morning and discover the assets of the Abberwick Foundation have vanished sometime during the night."

"Out. Now."

"I'm leaving." Gordon clutched his file of papers and started to back toward the door. "But if you had an ounce of common sense, you'd—" He broke off abruptly as he collided heavily with Harry, who had just opened the door. "Ooph."

Harry didn't flinch under the impact, but Molly noticed that Gordon bounced a little.

Gordon recovered and swung around to see who was standing behind him. "What the hell are you doing here, Trevelyan?"

"I'm engaged to Molly, remember?" Harry said.

"You could have knocked," Gordon muttered.

"The door was unlocked."

"Gordon was just leaving." Molly gave Gordon a steely look. "Isn't that right?"

"Yeah, yeah, I'm on my way," Gordon grumbled.

"Don't let me stop you." Harry moved politely out of the doorway.

Tessa emerged from the storage room. "The labels are done, Molly. I'm off."

Molly stilled. She glanced at Tessa, and then she looked at Gordon.

"Gordon?" she said softly.

"What?" He turned to scowl at her from the doorway.

"Want some advice?"

He looked distinctly wary. "What sort of advice?"

Molly tapped one finger on the counter, thinking swiftly. "You put out a good product. I don't care for coffee, but I know that yours is some of the best in the city."

"So?"

"You got into trouble with your espresso bars because you expanded too rapidly," Molly said. "If you're serious about salvaging your business, you're going to have to pay closer attention to the basics of running your operation. You need professional advice regarding marketing techniques, packaging, and advertising."

"Yeah?" Gordon glared, half-defiant, half-intrigued. "Where do you suggest I get that advice?"

"From Tessa," Molly said.

A startled hush fell on the shop.

Tessa reacted first. "What are you talking about, Molly? Are you saying I should give Gordon the benefit of everything I've learned working for you?"

"Only if he's willing to pay for it," Molly murmured.

Tessa was incensed. "You actually want me to help the competition? You want me to show him how to beef up his advertising program? Redesign his packaging? Tell him how to handle suppliers? What would that make me?"

"A consultant," Harry said.

Tessa blinked. Then she met Gordon's eyes across the room.

"A consultant." Tessa savored the word.

"I couldn't afford much in the way of consulting fees," Gordon warned.

"That's okay," Tessa said smoothly. "I'll take a percentage of the profits."

"There aren't any at the moment," Gordon said.

Tessa glanced at Molly and then smiled. "There will be."

Gordon hesitated. "You want to go have a latte and talk about it?"

"Sure," Tessa said. "What have I got to lose?" She

grabbed her oversized backpack and followed him out of the shop.

Harry raised one brow as the door closed behind the pair. "Should I be concerned about this sudden show of compassion for Brooke?"

Molly was surprised by the question. "I didn't do that for Gordon's sake. I did it for Tessa."

"I see."

"Tessa has a feel for sales and marketing," Molly said. "She's a natural, but she'll never fit in with corporate America. I've been worrying about her future. She can't work as my assistant forever. She needs to find a specialized niche where she can develop her talents. It occurred to me that Gordon Brooke Espresso Bars may be a good place to start."

Harry's eyes gleamed. "Know what I think?"

"What?"

"I think that, in addition to the Abberwick curiosity, you also got the family urge to tinker. It just so happens that you do your tinkering with people rather than inanimate objects."

"Never mind Tessa and Gordon. Any news from your investigator?"

The wry humor vanished from Harry's gaze. "Rice phoned twenty minutes ago. He finally located the car and made arrangements with the owner of the wrecking yard. I'm going to take a look at Kendall's Ford in the morning."

"You're going to fly to Portland tomorrow morning?"

"First thing."

"I'll go with you," Molly said.

"What about your shop?"

"Tessa can handle things here tomorrow. She can bring in one of the other women in the band if she needs help."

Harry gave her a considering look. Then he nodded once. "All right. Maybe it would be better if you came with me."

Molly was pleased. "You think I might be able to give you some helpful advice?"

"Not exactly," Harry said. "I think that if Kendall really

was murdered by someone who was trying to cover his tracks, I'd rather have you where I can keep an eye on you."

Molly made a face. She collected her shoulder bag and started toward the front door. "Always nice to feel wanted."

At ten o'clock the following morning Harry stood with Molly amid the carcasses of a herd of dead automobiles. A formidable steel fence topped with frothy coils of barbed wire surrounded the remains of the deceased vehicles. The sign at the entrance of the metal graveyard bore the name Maltrose Wrecking.

It was a suitable day for viewing the departed. A leaden sky promised rain at any moment. A brisk sea breeze snapped at the sleeves of Harry's shirt. It had already whipped Molly's hair into a fluffy froth. She had to hold the stuff out of her eyes with one hand.

The owner of the junkyard, one Chuck Maltrose, stood next to Harry. He was a big man who looked as if he had once played football and lifted weights. His glory days appeared to have ended at some point in the distant past, however. Much of the muscle had turned to fat over the years.

"This the one you wanted to see?" Chuck glanced at Harry.

Harry eyed the remains of the blue Ford and then glanced at the notes he had made during Fergus Rice's last phone call. "This is it."

"Take your time," Chuck said. "You're welcome to look all you want for your fifty bucks."

"Thanks."

"Let me know when you're finished. I'll be in my office."

"Right." Harry did not glance at Chuck as the bulky man trundled off toward the aging trailer that served as an office. He could not take his attention off the Ford.

He had not even touched the car, but already he could tell that there was something not quite right about it. Despite its crumpled condition, the Ford should have felt familiar. Only a few days ago it had been used in an attempt to force his

Sneath P2 over a cliff. Admittedly, he'd only seen it in a series of disjointed snapshots, first in his rearview mirror and then as it flashed past the Sneath. He'd had his hands full with the task of keeping his vehicle from jumping the guard rail. But still . . .

"What is it, Harry?" Molly asked.

He glanced at her. "I don't know yet. Maybe nothing except the obvious,"

She hugged herself. "It's a mess, isn't it? We're looking at a car that went over a cliff. A man died in that Ford. It gives me chills just to look at it."

Harry said nothing. The knowledge that Wharton Kendall had died in the car was not what was making him so uneasy. Something else was niggling at him. The wrongness emanated from the car in subtle waves.

And he wasn't even in one of his moods of intense concentration.

It occurred to Harry that the part of his brain that was good at what he preferred to call *reasoned insight* had become unaccountably more sensitive lately. Ever since he had started making love to Molly, to be precise.

The realization dumbfounded him. He stared at the blue Ford and wondered what was happening to him. His imagination was running wild, that was the problem. Or maybe it was much worse, much more ominous than that.

The old dread unfurled deep inside. Maybe he really would go crazy one of these days.

"Harry?" Molly touched his arm. "Are you okay?"

"Of course I'm okay. Why shouldn't I be?" Harry willed the old fear back into its hiding place. He summoned up Molly's reassuring advice on the subject. *The very fact that you can even wonder if you're going crazy means you aren't crazy.* He took a savage grip on his self-control. "I'm trying to think."

"Sorry."

Harry deliberately turned away from the concern he saw in her eyes. He would apologize later for his short temper. He would also put off worrying about the possibility of being fitted for a straitjacket until some later time. He had been postponing that particular concern for years. It could wait a little longer.

He made himself take a careful look at the ruined Ford. The guts of the dead beast were exposed to view. The hood had been ripped off in the crash. The doors hung open at odd angles, as though the bones inside the metal skin had been broken. The windows were empty of glass. They reminded Harry of sightless eyes.

He walked slowly around the Ford.

"What are you going to do?" Molly asked.

Harry rolled up his sleeves. "Just look things over."

"Everything was smashed when the car went over the cliff. How will you know if any damage you discover today was done before the accident?"

Harry leaned over the fender and studied the dented valve cover. "I'm not sure I'll be able to tell a damned thing. I just want to take a close look."

"Sort of get a feel for the situation?" Molly suggested innocently.

Harry ignored her. Very cautiously he allowed himself to concentrate as he leaned farther over the crumpled fender.

The sense of wrongness eddied around him, lapping gently at his senses. But it was not coming from inside the engine compartment. He stepped back from the fender. He tried to be subtle as he took a deep breath, but he could feel Molly watching him very intently.

Something was definitely not right.

After a few seconds, when he was sure he had himself firmly under control, he got into the driver's seat. He surveyed the damage to the interior. The steering wheel was gone. The glass cover on the instrument panel was a spider's web of tiny cracks. He bent down to examine the brake pedal.

Again the wrongness assailed him. But it was not as strong inside the car as it had been when he had been standing near the front fender.

"Something wrong with the brakes?" Molly asked expectantly.

"I don't think so." Harry wrapped himself in the armor of his willpower and gingerly touched the brake pedal. Experimentally he depressed it.

. . . and simultaneously sharpened his concentration.

It was so damn tricky. This matter of trying to think with this degree of utter clarity was so useful and yet so dangerous.

"What is it?" Molly asked. "What do you feel?"

"I don't *feel* anything," Harry muttered. "The brakes are all right."

"Are you sure?"

"As sure as I can be under the circumstances." He was almost positive that no one had cut the brake lines. There was still plenty of resistance in the system.

"I guess discovering something as dramatic as severed brake lines would have been a little too obvious."

Harry glanced sharply at her. "You sound disappointed."

She shrugged. "I've seen my share of old movies."

"That kind of sabotage only works well on film," Harry said absently. "It's too unpredictable in real life. The problem is that the person who cuts the lines has no way of knowing for certain just when the last of the fluid will bleed out."

"You mean there would be no way to time it so that the brakes would fail on the right curve?"

"Exactly." Harry thought about it. "It's a very uncertain way to kill. And our man, assuming there is someone other than Kendall involved in this, prefers more straightforward, predictable methods."

"What makes you say that?"

"Think about it, Molly. The guy tried to run us off a road, and he attempted to kill you with a gun."

"I see what you mean." Her brow furrowed delicately. "He takes the blunt approach."

"Only when it comes to the actual murder attempt," Harry said slowly. "He's certainly been extremely subtle when it comes to setting his scene and choosing his fall guy. In fact, he's a lot better at that end of the business than he is at closing the deal."

"What do you think that means?"

Harry looked at her as his mind tore into the problem. "It may mean that whoever's behind this has had a lot more experience with setting the stage than he's had with murder. Killing people may be new to him."

Molly shivered visibly. "But why would he have had more experience with establishing his camouflage?"

"Maybe," Harry said, "because that's all he's had to do until now in order to accomplish his objectives. When it comes to the backdrop of his operation, he thinks like a con man with a lot of experience."

"A con man?"

"It's possible that he's got a background in fraud or embezzlement or some other nonlethal crime."

"So he's clever with that part but not so skilled when it comes to murder." Molly closed her eyes briefly. "Thank God."

"Yes."

"Well, now that we know this definitely wasn't an accident, it would be very interesting to discover exactly how Kendall's car was sabotaged," Molly said thoughtfully.

"We don't know for certain that it wasn't an accident. We're making an assumption."

"Your assumptions are more in the nature of inspired guesses, Harry. You know it and I know it."

Harry heard something click and realized it was the sound of his back teeth coming together. He was irritated by Molly's certainty that Kendall had been murdered. He knew that she was picking up on his own sense of the situation and that she trusted his instincts.

The knowledge that Molly had developed such unquestioning faith in his insights worried him. It was as though her belief in his abilities rendered those abilities even more suspect. It made it seem all the more probable that there really was something abnormal involved.

Harry got out of the car and cautiously put a hand on the front fender. The wrongness hit him again, more insistent this time. He bent down to take a closer look at the crushed metal.

The impact of the crash had scraped and scarred the blue paint all the way to bare metal in places. Harry moved his fingers along the huge gouges that had been left in the fender. He stopped abruptly when his fingertips touched a deep dent near an empty hole that had once been occupied by a headlight. He stilled.

Molly hurried over to where he stood. "What did you find?"

"Blue paint."

"What's so strange about blue paint? The Ford is painted blue."

"I'm aware of that." He fingered a small fragment of paint. Something about it bothered him.

Harry took a deep breath and centered himself mentally as best he could. Slowly, carefully, he allowed himself to consider the flecks of blue enamel in all their tiny, varied aspects.

He tried to assign only a limited portion of his concentration to the task. He did not want to lose control. *Let the information seep in,* he cautioned himself. *Just a little bit at a time. Think about it. Look for the inconsistencies.*

Harry took a cautious step out onto the glass bridge.

The wind off the sea sharpened suddenly, whipping at his clothing, threatening to topple him into the abyss.

He fought to keep his balance. If he lost control, he would fall into the deepest, coldest canyon at the bottom of the darkest part of the sea.

"Harry?" Molly's voice was soft, gentle, questioning. Concerned.

The glass shuddered beneath his feet. He lifted his fascinated gaze from the endless darkness beneath him and looked toward the opposite side of the chasm.

Molly waited there. She held out her arms.

He regained his balance and started toward her. Each step was steadier, more certain.

He was wide open to sensation and awareness. The world around him was a thousand times more vivid than it had been a moment ago. The overcast sky was no longer a uniform gray. Instead it was a hundred variegated shades of light and shadow. Molly's smile was brighter than any sun, and her eyes were green jewels.

The paint beneath his fingers screamed at him.

Harry sucked in his breath.

"Take it easy, Harry. I'm here."

He lurched the last few steps across the glass bridge. Reached for Molly with desperate hands. She came into his arms, warm and comforting and alive. He was not alone out here in the darkness.

Harry closed his eyes and held Molly with all the strength that was in him.

The world steadied swiftly, returning to its natural shades and intensities. The force of the sea wind lessened. The bridge and the abyss beneath it vanished.

Harry opened his eyes. Molly peered anxiously up at him from within the circle of his arms.

"Are you okay?" she asked gently.

"Yes." He focused on her concerned expression as he fought for breath. "Yes, I'm okay."

"You look terrible."

"I'm all right."

"You were burning up a minute ago." She put a hand on his forehead. "You feel a little cooler now. I wonder if men have hot flashes."

Harry gave a choked groan, caught between old fear and fresh laughter. His mixed emotions warned him that he was not yet back in full control.

She studied him closely. "What did you see there on the fender?"

"I told you, blue paint." Harry crouched beside the front wheel. "But not from this car."

"What?" Molly's mouth fell open. She hunkered down beside him. "Blue paint from another car?"

"I think so." He looked at her. "Blue on blue. The differences in the two colors is so slight that the investigating officers would never have noticed it. But there is a difference."

"So there was another car involved."

"Yes." Harry rose to his feet. "What's really interesting is that it was probably from the same blue Ford that tried to force us off the road. Because this is not the same car that we encountered outside of Icy Crest."

"Oh, my God. Two blue Fords."

"I told you, this guy is very good at setting up the scenery for his little plays. He's had plenty of experience in that department."

"This isn't just one of your logical insights, is it?" Deep curiosity burned in Molly's eyes. "You can actually *feel* that there's something wrong with that streak of blue paint on the fender, can't you?"

"I can *see* the small differences in it. I've trained myself to observe tiny details. It's one of the reasons I'm good at what I do."

"Don't play games with me," Molly said quietly. "Or yourself. You knew something was wrong with this car the instant you took a close look at it. Why not admit it?"

Under normal circumstances, he would have reacted to her insistent prodding with cool sarcasm or a show of irritation. But even though he was feeling more or less back in control, he was still raw around the edges.

The result was that Molly's questioning ignited the dark fear in him. He fought the dread with the only weapon he had, a firestorm of rage.

"Damn it, what the hell do you want me to say?" The anger, fed by the fear, beat in his veins. "That I really do think I've got some kind of sixth sense? I might as well announce to the world that I'm crazy."

"You are not crazy. I've told you that."

"What are you? Some kind of authority?"

Molly did not flinch beneath the storm. "Harry, if you do have some sort of paranormal ability, you'd better acknowledge it and deal with it. It's a part of you, whatever it is."

"You're the one who's nuts if you think I'm going to go around claiming that I've got extrasensory perception. People who believe they've got paranormal powers end up on serious medication." Harry closed his eyes. Visions of psychiatric asylums danced in his fevered brain. "Or worse."

"You don't have to admit the truth to anyone except yourself." Molly smiled bleakly. "And to me, of course. You can't hide it from me."

"There's nothing to admit."

"Listen to me, Harry. I've got a feeling that if you don't accept the reality of your abilities, whatever it is, you'll never figure out how to control them. You can't repress them forever."

"I can't repress what doesn't exist."

"You're a man who deals in truth. Admit the truth to yourself. Think of this sixth sense, or whatever it is, the same way you do your excellent reflexes. Just a natural, inborn ability. A talent."

"Natural? You call that paranormal crap natural? Molly, you're starting to sound nuttier than Olivia thinks I am."

"That's not fair to Olivia. She doesn't think you're nuts. She believes that you're suffering from posttraumatic stress disorder and maybe some periodic depression."

"Trust me, she thinks I'm ready for the psycho ward."

"But, Harry—"

He took a step toward her, his hands clenched at his sides. The wind picked up once more. The sky darkened. "I swear to God, Molly, I don't want to hear another word about this psychic stuff. Do you understand me? Not another damned word."

She put her hand on his shoulder. "Listen to me."

"We will not discuss this matter again," Harry said through his teeth. Her fingers were warm. He could feel them through the fabric of his shirt. The anger seeped slowly out of him, leaving a great weariness.

"Hey, am I interruptin' something here or what?" Chuck Maltrose heaved into Harry's field of vision.

Harry drew a deep, steadying breath and switched his attention to the owner of the wrecking yard. "We were discussing a private matter."

"Sure. No problem." Maltrose held up one hand, palm out. "I'm not one to get into the middle of a private squabble. Just wondered if you were finished with your look-see."

"I believe Harry's finished here, Mr. Maltrose," Molly said crisply.

Harry watched her give Maltrose one of her brilliant smiles.

Chuck Maltrose was not so sanguine. He shot Harry a covert, wary look.

Harry wondered if the crazy stuff actually showed in his eyes, or if Maltrose was merely reacting to the remnants of anger that were undoubtedly still evident. He just needed a few more seconds to pull himself together, Harry thought. He would be fine in a minute.

Fortunately Molly took immediate charge of Chuck Maltrose. Harry listened as she chatted with him about the impending storm. By the time they had concluded that the rain would hit fairly soon, Harry had himself back under control.

"So now we know there's another blue Ford out there somewhere," Molly said as she slid into the passenger seat of the rental car. "What do we do next, Sherlock?"

"I'll stop at a pay phone and put in a call to Fergus Rice." Harry turned the key in the ignition. "He can notify the cops."

"There must be a zillion blue Fords."

"Yes, but with any luck, there won't be that many with a dented right front fender."

"Still, it seems like a long shot." Molly flopped back against the seat. "This thing just doesn't make sense any more. The motive doesn't seem logical."

"I've been thinking about that. There may be another

motive." Harry frowned as he pulled out onto the road. "One we haven't considered."

"There are only so many motives in the world. Revenge, passion, and greed sum up almost the entire list."

"So far we've been concentrating on revenge," Harry noted.

"I find it hard to believe that I'm the target of two disgruntled inventors," Molly said flatly. "One, maybe. But two? And we can forget about passion. My life simply has not been that exciting until recently."

"That leaves us with greed."

Molly wrinkled her nose. "Killing me isn't a real good way of getting the foundation to finance someone's grant proposal."

Harry stared at the road ahead as it all started to come together in a rush of crystal clear perfection. The theory assumed form and substance with such speed that he could only marvel at how he had overlooked the obvious for so long.

"Last night," he said carefully, "when I walked into your shop, you were assuring Brooke that you wouldn't be idiotic enough to turn control of the foundation assets over to anyone else."

"Darn right."

"Molly, what does happen to those assets if you're out of the picture?"

"Huh?"

"You heard me. If something happened to you, would Kelsey become the trustee of the Abberwick Foundation?"

"Not until she's twenty-eight. I drew up the papers that way because I didn't want her to get stuck with the burden of running the foundation until she'd had a chance to finish school and get started on a career."

"Who becomes the trustee if you're gone?"

"Aunt Venicia."

Harry whistled soundlessly. "I should have seen it from the beginning."

"What on earth are you talking about? Surely you aren't

about to accuse Aunt Venicia of plotting to murder me? That's ludicrous. She could care less about running the foundation."

"Not her. The man she's going to marry."

Molly stared at him, stunned. "Oh, my God. Cutter Latteridge."

# 19

∞

**M**olly panicked. "Stop the car. I have to get to a phone. I've got to warn Aunt Venicia."

"Take it easy," Harry said. "Venicia is safe enough for the moment. Cutter isn't married to her yet. If he harms her now, she's useless to him. He needs her alive until after the wedding."

"That's true, isn't it? He doesn't stand a chance of getting his hands on the foundation until after the marriage." Molly closed her eyes in a silent prayer of gratitude. "Thank heavens Aunt Venicia insisted on a big wedding that takes weeks to plan."

"Yes."

"But what are we going to do?"

"Nothing for the moment." Harry's elegant hands flexed on the wheel. "We haven't got a dime's worth of proof that Latteridge is behind this. We need background information on him. If he's an expert, he'll have a history. I'll get Fergus on it immediately."

Molly began to calm down. As soon as she was thinking clearly again, the questions descended in a flood. "This is wild. How on earth could Cutter have planned and carried out such a bizarre scenario?"

"Whoever he is, he's set up elaborate schemes before.

This isn't the work of an amateur. He knows how to take care of the details." Harry's expression became very intent. "At least when it comes to the window dressing part. He's not so good at murder."

"For which we can thank our lucky stars."

"All right," Harry continued, "we're dealing with a professional con artist. As I said, he's probably got a record of some kind. We'll find it and use it to focus the attention of the authorities on him."

Molly considered. "He knew about the Abberwick Foundation. Only someone who is familiar with the world of inventors and invention would have been aware of my father and the fact that he had made arrangements to establish the foundation."

"True. He could have met your father or your uncle at one time."

"I doubt it."

"Why?" Harry asked. "I certainly knew about your father's work long before I met you. A lot of people involved in the commercial application of robotic devices were aware of Jasper Abberwick."

"I suppose so," Molly agreed.

The storm that had been threatening for the past few hours finally struck. Rain splashed on the windshield. Harry switched on the wiper blades.

The drive toward Portland continued in silence for several miles. Molly glanced at Harry from time to time, aware that he had fallen into one of his thoughtful moods. She knew that he was examining the problem of Cutter Latteridge from every possible angle. She could almost feel his razor-sharp intellect dissecting the situation.

"When, precisely, did Latteridge first appear on the scene?" Harry finally asked.

"I told you, Aunt Venicia met him on a cruise that she took in the spring. Why?"

"I'm trying to figure out the timing," Harry said. He lapsed back into silence.

A few miles later he spoke again. "I think I've got enough to give Rice. I'm going to find a phone."

A short while later a gas station loomed in the mist. Harry slowed the car and eased it off the road and into a parking area. He shut off the engine and opened the door.

"I'll be right back." He got out, shut the door, and loped through the rain to the limited shelter of the phone booth.

Molly watched him through the rain-washed windows. From time to time ghostly ripples, an unfamiliar awareness of danger, went through her. At first she did not understand. She knew that she was scared and extremely worried about Venicia's safety, but this other sensation felt as though it emanated from outside herself.

It wasn't until she saw Harry replace the receiver and start back toward the car that she realized she was picking up a distant echo of *his* own awareness of the danger they faced.

It was not unlike the sensation she experienced more and more often when she was in bed with Harry. Alien, yet familiar.

Harry broke into her disturbing thoughts when he opened the car door and got in behind the wheel. "It's pouring out there." He ran his fingers through his damp hair to get rid of the moisture. He scowled when he saw Molly's face. "What's wrong?"

Molly cleared her throat. If he had felt anything at all during the past few minutes, he was not about to acknowledge it. "Nothing." She managed a weak smile. "I'm just a little anxious, that's all."

"Not surprising under the circumstances." Harry turned in the seat, his expression intent. "I talked to Rice. Told him to start looking into Cutter Latteridge's background. With any luck he'll have some preliminary information for us by the time we get back to Seattle."

"But what are we going to do about Aunt Venicia? We can't allow her to continue to date a murderer."

"If you try to warn her about Latteridge, you'll put both

her and yourself in extreme danger." Harry reached across the seat to squeeze her hand. "Let me handle it, Molly."

"You always seem to end up in this role."

He released her fingers and put the car in gear. "What role?"

"Playing the hero. It hardly seems fair. Someday someone ought to save you."

He gave her an odd glance as he drove out of the parking lot. "I'm no hero."

"Yes, you are. Trust me, I know one when I see one."

The green light on Harry's answering machine was blinking frantically when he walked into his study late that afternoon. There were three messages.

"Your private line," Molly observed. "Must be family calls."

"With any luck one of them will be from Fergus Rice." Harry punched the playback button. "I told him to use the private number."

The first call was from Josh. He sounded upbeat.

> *Harry? It's Josh. Thought you'd like to know that the hospital discharged Grandpa this morning. He's on crutches, but he swears he'll be back in the racing pit tomorrow night.*

The second call was from Danielle.

> *Harry, this is your aunt. I understand you're going to give Brandon a list of venture capitalists. He says he's determined to go outside the family for financing. I don't think it's wise for him to do that. Please give me a call. I want to discuss this with you.*

"I knew Aunt Danielle would start acting like a nervous hen when her only chick tried to leave the nest," Harry said. Molly glanced at him. "What will you do?"

Harry scrawled Danielle's name on a pad of paper. "Talk to her. Persuade her to lay off Brandon." He waited for the next voice, hoping it would be Fergus Rice with information. It was.

*Harry, it's Rice. Give me a call as soon as you get in. I've got some news that I think will interest you.*

Harry reached for the phone and punched in the number. Fergus answered on the first ring.

"It's Harry. What have you got?"

"The good news is that I got lucky right off the bat, thanks to your guesswork. I started by checking a couple of charitable foundations which operate along the same lines as the Abberwick Foundation. You know, the kind that make grants for scientific and technical work."

"What did you find?"

"It looks like Cutter Latteridge is an alias for a con man named Clarence Laxton. He's had a half-dozen different names during the past five years. He specializes in scamming foundations. Been pretty successful at it from what I can tell, but he got caught by investigators a year ago."

"Any jail time?"

"No. He literally vanished hours before the authorities moved in. When they got to his office, it had been cleaned out. There was no trace. He covered his tracks very well. You'll be interested to know that until now there's been no indication that he's ever resorted to violence."

"I think the violence is new for him," Harry said. "His original goal may have been to work himself into a position of trust."

"In other words, he would have eventually offered his consulting services to Molly?"

"Exactly. Maybe he figured he could persuade her to turn the day-to-day running of the foundation over to him. After all, he was about to become a member of the family, and he had a working knowledge of engineering technology."

"He probably thought that he could drain the assets and then disappear," Fergus agreed. "But when she hired you, he panicked and concocted another plan. One that required him to get rid of Molly altogether."

"He used Wharton Kendall, a rejected inventor, as a stalking horse."

"Makes sense," Fergus said. "This guy has a reputation for doing his research. He would have known who you were and that you were a potential threat to him."

"So what's the bad news?" Harry asked.

"I'm not sure if it's good or bad. Sort of depends on your point of view," Fergus said. "It looks like Latteridge left the country this afternoon."

Harry felt everything inside him go very still. "You're sure?"

"As sure as I can be under the circumstances. A man answering Latteridge's description was on the two-thirty flight to London. He had a passport, luggage—the works."

"The passport was in Latteridge's name?"

"According to my sources. I've talked to my friends in the police department. The problem is, we don't even have proof of fraud, let alone murder or attempted murder."

Harry put his hand over the receiver to speak to Molly. "Latteridge got on an international flight at SeaTac earlier today."

Molly's eyes widened. "He's gone?"

"Looks like it." Harry heard Fergus say something on the other end of the line. "What's that?"

"I said, it looks like this thing is over, Harry."

"That's what you said when you told me Wharton Kendall had gone over a cliff."

"This times it feels real," Fergus said. "You know these guys. Once the con goes sour, they pull a vanishing act."

"True."

Molly frowned. "I wonder if Aunt Venicia knows he's gone. I'd better call her right away."

Harry shook his head. "We'll go see her in person. This isn't the kind of news you deliver over the phone."

Molly sighed. "You're right,"

"Harry?" Fergus sounded confused. "Are you still there?"

"I'm here. I wonder what made Latteridge suspect that someone was getting close."

"I don't know," Fergus said. "Maybe your sudden trip down to Oregon worried him. He would have kept very close tabs on your movements. And he does have a history of getting out of the picture just in time to avoid the authorities."

"A good con man always knows when to cut his losses."

"Exactly," Fergus said. "You want some more of the details?"

Harry picked up a pen. "Let me have everything you've got."

Giving the bad news to Venicia was one of the hardest things Molly had ever done. She was grateful for Harry's solid, steadying presence. He stood beside her in Venicia's newly redecorated mauve-and-green living room while Molly explained that Cutter Latteridge was never coming back.

Venicia's initial reaction of irate disbelief gradually crumpled, first into stunned shock and then into tears. Molly began to cry, too. When she got too choked up to continue, Harry calmly and gently filled in the details.

"But he was a man of comfortable means," Venicia protested as she dabbed her eyes with a tissue. "The house on Mercer Island . . ."

"He took possession of the house with an elaborate scam," Harry explained. "The banks and the realtors are scrambling to put all the pieces together, but it looks like he established a phony line of credit with an East Coast bank and used it to con the real estate agency and the escrow company."

"And the yacht?"

"Same story," Harry said. "The yacht broker is till trying to sort out the mess."

"I don't know what to say." Venicia sniffed sadly. "He was such a gentleman."

"His good manners and charming ways were part of his stock-in-trade," Harry said.

Venicia looked at Molly with woebegone eyes. "I've been nothing but an old fool, haven't I?"

"Wrong on both counts." Molly hugged her tightly. "You aren't old, and you definitely aren't a fool. Cutter or Clarence or whatever his name is conned all of us, Aunt Venicia."

"He's conned a lot of other people, too," Harry said. "He's an expert."

"An expert at hurting people." Venicia stiffened. "What if he returns? You say he's dangerous."

Molly looked at Harry.

"It's not likely that he'll come back to Seattle any time soon, if ever," Harry said. "At heart he's a con artist, not a killer. Fraud is his thing. He needs anonymity to pursue his business. His main goal now will be to bury his Cutter Latteridge identity so that he can go back to work on a new scam somewhere as far from here as possible."

Venicia shrank back into the enfolding cushions of her designer chair. "Now I know why he had begun to pressure me to move the date of the wedding forward. He said he couldn't wait to marry me."

"He was starting to get nervous because of my presence in the picture," Harry said. "He probably sensed that the con was in danger of blowing up in his face."

"I'm supposed to go for one more fitting on my gown," Venicia whispered. "It's so lovely. And it cost a fortune." She reached for a fresh tissue. Then she paused and looked at Molly. "I've just had a thought."

"What's that?" Molly asked.

Venicia smiled with the natural resiliency of a woman who had been married to an inventor for thirty years. "We'll tell the boutique to fit the gown to you, dear."

* * *

Ten days later Molly was in the process of measuring out a tiny smidgeon of saffron when she heard the shop bell jingle. She glanced toward the door and saw a young woman dressed in a studded leather belt, black vest, and jeans hovering anxiously in the doorway. The woman had short, spiky hair that had been tinted dead black. Her bare arms were decorated with a variety of tattoos. She wore little round glasses on her nose.

"Are you Molly Abberwick?"

"Yes, I am." Molly smiled. "Can I help you?"

"I'm Heloise Stickley." Heloise glanced at Tessa, who was just returning from the storage room with a sack of green peppercorns. "Hi, Tessa."

"Heloise. You made it." Tessa looked at Molly with an air of determination. "Molly, this is my friend, the inventor. You know, the one who plays bass guitar for Ruby Sweat?"

Molly got a sinking sensation in her stomach. "The one who wants to apply to the Abberwick Foundation for grant money?"

"You got it." Tessa beamed at Heloise. "Did you bring your sketches and notes?"

Heloise nodded. She cast another nervous glance at Molly. "I promise I won't take up much of your time, Ms. Abberwick."

"This is about some sort of device designed to measure paranormal brain waves, isn't it?" Molly said slowly.

Heloise came forward eagerly. "I'm on to something here, Ms. Abberwick. I'd really appreciate it if you'd give me a few minutes to explain my theories. No one else will even listen to me."

Molly sighed. "Come with me."

She led the way into her office. Heloise followed, her face aglow with enthusiasm and excitement.

A three o'clock the following afternoon it dawned on Harry that something in his environment was not functioning in a normal manner. He slowly surfaced from the deep pile of notes he was making for his paper on François Arago's work in light and optics. It took him a moment to figure out what was bothering him. Then it hit him.

The private line phone had not rung all day.

Because he had intended to devote himself to the paper on Arago, he had set the answering machine on his business line to take messages. He had turned off the ringer so that he would not be bothered by incoming calls.

But he had not turned off the private line. Everyone in the family knew that when he was at home, he was available.

There had not been a single call on his private line all day. An unusual turn of events. Harry could not remember the last occasion when he had gone an entire day without a phone call from someone in one or the other of his extended clans.

It was not as if everything had quieted down. On the Stratton side, Danielle was still fretting over Brandon's decision to seek funding from a venture capitalist. Parker was fuming about Brandon's intentions and demanding to have input into the decision-making process. For his part, Brandon was trying to get his grandfather off his back.

Gilford was annoyed because he blamed Harry for having upset Parker. Olivia was dropping dark hints that Harry and Molly should seek couples counseling before they got married. Yesterday she had called to give him the names of two more psychologists.

On the Trevelyan side, Evangeline had begun a campaign to convince Harry to help her find financing for a new thrill ride. Josh had been calling in regular reports of Leon's progress. Raleigh had let it be known that he was out of money again and the baby was due at any moment.

No question about it, Harry thought, the private line phone should have rung sometime during the day. He leaned back in his chair, steepled his fingers, and contemplated the unnaturally silent telephone.

His gaze settled on the phone cord that was discreetly draped over the side of the desk. He followed it with his eye to the point where it disappeared behind a reading chair.

After a moment he got to his feet and walked to the chair.

He looked behind it and saw that the phone cord was lying on the floor. Someone had disconnected it from the telephone jack on the wall.

Harry was very certain that he had not accidentally unplugged the phone. He was equally sure that Ginny would not have made such a mistake while cleaning.

It did not take long to narrow the range of possibilities.

Harry reconnected the phone cord to the wall jack. Then he went back to his desk, picked up the receiver, and dialed the number of his business line.

He waited for his own prerecorded message to come on the line. He was not unduly surprised when he heard Molly's voice instead of his own.

> *You have reached the office of Dr. Harry Stratton Trevelyan. If you are calling on a business matter, please stay on the line and leave a message after the beep. If you are a member of his family on either the Stratton or the Trevelyan side, and you are calling this number because you cannot get through on his private line, please dial the following number immediately. You will receive extremely urgent and vital information which will directly impact your life.*

Harry listened to the phone number that Molly rattled off at the end of the message. He recognized it at once. It belonged to the Abberwick Tea & Spice Company.

Molly had found a way to reroute all of his family calls to her shop.

Harry stood quietly for a long time, phone in hand, and wondered what the hell was going on. Life with the daughter of a genius inventor was definitely not going to be dull.

The phone on the desk in Molly's office warbled loudly. She ignored the insistent summons while she finished ringing up a sale. The customer was a writer who lived near Seattle.

She came in regularly to buy great quantities of the special blend of tea that Molly had created for her.

"Thanks, Ann." Molly handed over the packet of tea. "See you next month."

Ann smiled. "I'll be back. Can't sit down in front of the word processor without a pot of my special blend."

Tessa leaned through the doorway of the office. "Phone for you, Molly."

"Thanks, Tessa."

Molly hurried into her office and took the receiver from Tessa's hand. "This is Molly Abberwick. How can I help you?"

There was a short, charged silence on the other end of the line.

"Molly?" Olivia's voice reverberated with outrage. "What on earth do you think you're doing? Where's Harry?"

"Harry is busy at the moment."

"Put him on the line. I want to speak with him. This is a family matter."

"Sorry. Harry is not available."

Molly perched on the edge of her desk and idly swung one leg. This was the fourth family call that she had taken since she had unplugged Harry's private line and inserted her own message into the answering machine attached to his business line.

She knew that he had intended to turn off the business line that morning in order to work. But he never turned off the private line. She had, therefore, disconnected it so that any Stratton or Trevelyan seeking to get through to Harry would be forced to try his business line. Whereupon said caller would get her message and call her, instead.

Word was spreading quickly through the Stratton and Trevelyan clans. Thus far she had dealt with Brandon, Evangeline, and Danielle.

"This is ridiculous," Olivia snapped. "What's going on?"

"I'll tell you exactly what I have told the others who called. I'm giving the Strattons and Trevelyans a small sample of the power I shall wield once Harry is married to me."

*"Power?"*

"Precisely." Molly smiled into the phone. "As his wife I shall be in a unique position to limit access to Harry."

"Is this some sort of stupid joke?"

"I promise you, I am very, very serious," Molly assured her. "Today I merely made it difficult to reach Harry by phone. But if my demands are not met, there will be worse to come. I can and will make it virtually impossible to gain access to Harry."

"Are you out of your mind?"

"What an odd question from someone in your line of work. No, I am not out of my mind, but I am determined to get what I want. Be warned, if the Strattons and Trevelyans fail to comply with my demands, I shall find ways to make it extremely difficult for anyone on either side of his family to get to Harry."

"I don't understand." Olivia was clearly nonplussed now. "This makes no sense at all."

"I shall present my demands to representatives of the Stratton and Trevelyan clans tomorrow at noon. I guarantee that everything will make perfect sense then."

"Harry is going to hear about this," Olivia threatened.

"Not if you and the others want to continue to have reasonably free access to him, he won't," Molly warned sweetly. "As I was saying, I shall present my demands tomorrow. High noon at the vegetarian restaurant around the corner from my shop. Be there or face the consequences."

Molly hung up the phone before Olivia could suggest she get professional psychiatric help.

# 20

The Strattons were the first to arrive.

Molly stood at the head of the long table in the alcove of the trendy vegetarian restaurant and watched as Danielle, regal in her disapproval, led the contingent.

"This is an absolute outrage," Danielle declared.

"Good afternoon, Mrs. Hughes." Molly inclined her head. "I'm glad you could make it."

"You were impossibly rude on the phone, Miss Abberwick," Danielle informed her. "As far as I'm concerned, you issued a threat."

"You were right," Molly said. "It was a threat."

She deduced that the two men following Danielle were Parker and his son, Gilford. Their ages and signature bone structure identified them as clearly as a fingerprint. Both men radiated icy anger. Olivia and Brandon brought up the rear. Each wore an expression of great caution.

"Good afternoon." Molly waved the newcomers to the chairs that lined the left-hand side of the table. "Please be seated."

Parker's silvered brows came together in a straight line above his patrician nose. "We know who you are. I'm Parker Stratton."

"Yes." Molly smiled. "We spoke on the phone this morn

ing. You wanted to know what the hell I was up to. I believe."

"Now, you listen to me, young woman," Parker snapped, "I have better things to do with my time than play stupid games. I don't know what you're trying to pull here, but if it's money you're after, you can damn well—"

"It's not about money, Granddad," Brandon said quietly. He watched Molly with speculative eyes. "Whatever this is all about, it's not about cash. Ms. Abberwick has plenty of that at her disposal."

Olivia went to one of the chairs on the left side of the table. "I'll tell you what this is all about. It's about power and control. Isn't that right, Molly? You think you can exert both over the rest of us because of your position as Harry's fiancée."

Molly gripped the back of her chair. She kept her smile fixed determinedly in place. "Have a seat, Olivia. You can psychoanalyze me later to your heart's content. But please don't send me a bill."

"No one controls a Stratton, by God," Gilford said evenly. "Ms. Abberwick, I'm a busy man. I'm here today only because you made it clear that there is some sort of family crisis. You've got exactly five minutes to convince me of that."

Molly looked at him. "Have a seat, Mr. Stratton. I will explain everything." She glanced toward the door as the next group of people arrived.

Danielle opened her mouth to speak and then closed it abruptly as her gaze fell on the newcomers who hovered in the doorway. She stared as if she could not believe her eyes. "My God. How dare they intrude like this."

"What the devil?" Parker swung around to see what had alarmed Danielle. His eyes widened with fury. "Christ Almighty. What are *they* doing here?"

Molly looked at the cluster of Trevelyans who had arrived. She saw at once that she'd managed to get a fairly good turnout. Josh had been no problem, of course. He had agreed to come without hesitation. But she was secretly relieved to see Leon, who was still on crutches, and Raleigh and Evangeline with him.

Evangeline, as statuesque and commanding in a skirted suit as she had been in her colorful fortune-teller's grab, swept through the room full of Strattons. Then she glowered at Molly.

"You didn't say anything about them being here."

"There's a lot I haven't had a chance to explain yet, Evangeline." Molly indicated the chairs on the right-hand side of the table. "But everything will soon become clear. Please sit down."

Parker looked as if he were about to explode. He made for the door. "I'll be damned if I'll sit across the table from that lot of thieving Trevelyans."

Leon's face twisted with fury. He lifted one crutch and swung it across the doorway, effectively barring Parker's escape. "You're not going anywhere, you old son-of-a-bitch. If us thieving Trevelyans have to sit through this, so do you goddamned prissy, high-toned Strattons."

"Prissy?" Parker beetled his brows at Leon. "Just who are you calling prissy, you bastard?"

"Enough." Molly banged a spoon against the glass in front of her. "You will all sit down right now. I don't particularly care whether or not you eat the lunch I have ordered and paid for, but you will sit and you will listen to me. Or else none of you will ever have ready access to Harry again."

The roomful of Strattons and Trevelyans turned on her, momentarily united in their fury.

"I fail to see why you think that you hold some sort of club over the rest of us," Danielle said. "Harry is a Stratton. He's a blood relative. You can't keep us from contacting him whenever we wish."

"Oh, yes, I can," Molly retorted. "I proved as much yesterday when I disconnected his private line. That was nothing, I assure you. The possibilities are virtually limitless when it comes to cutting you off from Harry. Now sit down. All of you."

They sat. Grudgingly, reluctantly, refusing to make eye

contact with the people who sat across from them, both groups sat down at the table.

Molly alone remained standing. She surveyed the irate faces turned toward her. Only Josh looked at her with a trace of amused anticipation in his expression. She took a deep breath. "Thank you."

"Get on with it," Leon muttered.

"Very well." Molly tightened her grip on the back of her chair. "I shall come straight to the point. I have two demands. If they are both met, I shall allow contact with Harry to resume. I cannot promise you that I will not occasionally limit that contact if I feel it has become abusive, but I will not make it impossible for you to reach Harry as I did during the past twenty-four hours."

Parker scowled. "What makes you think that access to Harry is so damned important to any of us?"

"The fact that you're all here makes me think that." Molly released her hold on the chair and began to walk slowly around the long table. "Harry is important to both the Strattons and the Trevelyans. Vitally important. You have all found ways to use him, have you not?"

Olivia eyed her. "What is that supposed to mean?"

Molly clasped her hands behind her back. "Let us return to those forgotten days of yesteryear when Harry first arrived here in Seattle. That would have been about seven years ago, I believe. He had lost his parents less than a year before that. He had no brothers or sisters. He was not married. In effect, he was alone in the world. He came here in search of his blood kin."

"Wrong," Gilford said. "He came here because he got a grant to do research in the history of science at the UW."

Molly glanced at him. "The type of grant which Harry received did not stipulate where he should do his research. He had a choice of several prestigious universities. He came here because he had roots here. The Stratton side of his family has lived in Seattle for three generations. The Trevelyans have made Washington their home base for years."

Olivia drummed her polished fingers on the table. "Harry

once told me that he stayed on here after he completed his grant work because he liked Seattle. He said that he had developed a good network of academic contacts in the local colleges and universities. He said it was a good place for him to establish himself professionally."

"He could have done that anywhere." Molly shook her head. "No, he stayed in the area because by the time he had finished his grant, he had found a place for himself in both the Stratton and Trevelyan families."

Parker bridled. "He made it damned clear he wanted no part of his Stratton heritage."

"That's not true," Molly said quietly. "The only thing he didn't want was the Stratton money."

"It's the same thing," Parker grumbled.

"No, Mr. Stratton, it's not. At least, not to Harry." Molly made her way around the end of the table and started up the Stratton side of the room.

Gilford frowned. "When Harry told us that he refused to join the company, he as much as told us that he considered himself more Trevelyan than Stratton."

"He *is* more Trevelyan than Stratton," Evangeline announced triumphantly.

"Damn right," Raleigh put in helpfully. "Got the reflexes. And Granny Gwen always said she thought he had the Sight."

Olivia grimaced. "For God's sake, could we please keep this conversation in the realm of reality? Harry has a disorder, not paranormal abilities."

Evangeline deigned to fix her with a freezing glare. "Just because you don't believe in such things doesn't mean they don't exist."

"I certainly don't believe in that psychic nonsense," Olivia shot back. "No reasonably well-educated person does believe in it, and that includes Harry, himself."

"Now see here—" Leon began.

"That's enough on that topic," Molly interrupted forcefully. "Whether or not Harry has paranormal abilities has nothing to do with this discussion. Harry is in Seattle be cause he wants to be involved with both his Stratton and Trevelyan relatives. He wants what his parents longed for and never got—an end to the feud."

Leon shot Parker a scathing look. "The Strattons started it."

Parker gave a muffled squawk. "Why you washed up, no-good, sneaky bastard—"

Molly paused to bang on Josh's water glass with a fork. "I'm not finished here."

The Strattons and Trevelyans turned disgruntled faces toward her once more.

"Thank you," Molly said. "Now then, as I was saying. In an effort to find a place for himself in the bosom of his family, Harry has allowed all of you to take serious advantage of him."

Danielle stiffened in her chair. "Are you implying that we use Harry?"

Molly smiled approvingly at her. "Yes, Mrs. Hughes, that is exactly what I'm implying."

Danielle stared at her, open-mouthed, and then she turned red. "That's an outrageous insult, Ms. Abberwick. And I for one object."

Evangeline was equally annoyed. "What's all this about us using Harry?"

"That is precisely what all of you do," Molly said quietly.

"He's a Trevelyan," Evangeline sputtered. "He has a certain responsibility to his family."

Gilford glowered at Evangeline across the table. "His mother was my sister, and don't you forget it. That makes him a Stratton. His responsibility is to his Stratton relatives, not to you freeloading Trevelyans."

Leon climbed to his feet with a roar. "Why you lousy little two-bit wimp. Harry doesn't owe you a damn thing."

"Sit down, Leon. Now." Molly paused to regain everyone's attention. "Listen to me, all of you. I've lived with Harry long enough to hear the kind of messages that come in on his private line. Two or three a day sometimes."

"So?" Gilford challenged.

"So, he's told me about some of your demands, and I've overheard many of you whining to him about various and assorted problems."

"Whining?" Gilford looked scandalized by the accusation.

"Yes, whining," Molly repeated. "All of you who contact Harry seem to have one thing in common."

A hush fell on the room.

Olivia toyed with a spoon. "I suppose you're going to tell us what that one thing is?"

"Yes," Molly said. "I am. The one thing both Strattons and Trevelyans have in common is that whenever you talk to Harry, you all want something from him."

Stunned silence greeted that simple observation. The unnatural hush was immediately followed by an uproar that made conversation impossible. For several minutes Molly could hear nothing above the thundering din of objections, exclamations, and defensive responses.

Josh was the only one who did not leap to his feet or yell in protest. He lounged in his seat with that cool masculine grace that characterized the Trevelyan men and gave Molly a slight, knowing smile. She winked at him.

Eventually, when she deemed the initial explosion over, she raised her hands to regain control of the room.

"People, people, take your seats," she said loudly. "Sit down, all of you, or I'm going to walk out of here right now."

There were a few more angry protests before the Strattons and Trevelyans reluctantly subsided back into their chairs.

"Now, then," Molly said calmly, "for those of you who doubt my interpretation of events, let me list just a small sampling of the many ways in which you all try to use Harry. Shall we begin on the Trevelyan side?"

"Why not?" Parker fumed. "Bunch of lazy, shiftless cons and carnies. That's all they are. They'd take advantage of their own grandmothers."

Leon started to get to his feet. "Why, you—"

"Down, Leon," Molly said quickly. "As I was saying, we shall begin on the Trevelyan side of the family. Evangeline, who did you go to four years ago when you wanted help putting together a financing package for Smoke & Mirrors Amusement Company?"

Evangeline's face tightened in astonishment. "That was business."

"Business which you could not have conducted if you hadn't had help from Harry." Molly held up a finger. "Now, just to keep things even, we shall go to the Stratton side of the family. Brandon, who did you approach when you wanted assistance in setting up your new property management firm?"

Brandon blinked. "That's different. I just needed some names of venture capitalists."

"Names which Harry supplied." Molly held up another finger. "Back to the Trevelyans. Leon, who bought your new truck for you?"

Leon's dark eyes glittered with anger. "That's between me and Harry, damn it."

"Precisely. Harry bought it for you." Molly held up another finger and looked toward the Stratton side of the table. "Gilford, who did you go to when you wanted help convincing Parker that it would be a good idea to expand Stratton Properties into commercial development on the Eastside?"

Gilford looked shocked. "How did you find out about that? That's proprietary information."

"Harry mentioned it," Molly said dryly.

Danielle bristled. "I shall have to speak to Harry about maintaining family confidences."

"Too late, I'm afraid," Molly murmured. "Like it or not, Harry now considers me one of the family. That means the rest of you will have to do the same."

That brought another wave of charged silence. The Strattons and Trevelyans glared at each other and then at Molly.

"Now, then," Molly continued briskly, "since we're talking about confidential Stratton information, perhaps this is as good a time as any to remind you, Mrs. Hughes, of just how much you've relied on Harry during the past few years."

"Me?" Danielle's expression was one of deep indignation. "I'm his aunt. I have every right to discuss certain problems with my nephew."

"Problems which you want him to resolve for you," Molly said. "I'm sure you recall how you went to Harry when you became anxious about Brandon going out on his own?"

"There's no need to bring that up now." Danielle cast a quick, uneasy glance at her father, Parker.

"Fine." Molly turned toward Raleigh. "Maybe we should talk about how useful you find Harry when money runs short?"

Raleigh winced. "I get your point."

"I think we all do," Parker said in a tone of weary resignation. "It's clear where this is going. Ms. Abberwick, you seem to feel that Harry has been imposed upon by both sides of his family."

"It's a little more complicated than that," Molly said carefully. "I believe that he has *allowed* himself to be imposed upon because deep down he wants a connection with both sides of his family, and this was the only way you would allow him to be a part of your lives."

"That's not true," Danielle said. "Naturally we wanted Harry to take his rightful role within the family."

Molly turned to confront her. "Did you? That's not the way it came across to Harry. All his life the Strattons and Trevelyans have tried to make him choose sides in the war between the families."

Olivia grimaced. "That's putting it rather strongly."

Molly ignored her. "You're all guilty of trying to make him declare himself either a Stratton or a Trevelyan. When he refused to deny either side of his heritage, you tried to punish him for it."

Parker narrowed his eyes. "That's your view of the situation, Ms. Abberwick. There's another side to Harry that you don't seem to know about. He's not exactly Mr. Nice Guy when he wants to force one of us to do what he thinks we ought to do."

"You can say that again," Leon muttered. "Harry plays hardball, and that's a fact."

Gilford gave Molly a wry look. "My father and Leon are both right, Ms. Abberwick. Harry doesn't hesitate to resort to blackmail, arm-twisting, or outright threats when he deems it necessary."

Molly smiled complacently. "I don't doubt it. He gets that from both sides of his family, I'm afraid."

Evangeline was irritated. "What's that supposed to mean?"

"It means," Molly said coolly, "that Harry can be just as hard as you force him to be. He's half Stratton and half Trevelyan, after all. The thing is, none of you truly understand him."

Olivia waved one hand in a disgusted, supercilious gesture. "That's an inane thing to say, Molly. I assure you, I understand Harry very well."

"No," Molly said simply. "You don't. You can't."

"I happen to be a professional," Olivia reminded her.

"That's your problem," Molly said. "No offense, Olivia, but you're a prisoner of your own professional training. It forces you to view the behavior of other people from a certain theoretical perspective."

"That perspective happens to be grounded in years of solid scientific research and study," Olivia retorted.

"You've tried to analyze Harry using conventional techniques," Molly said. "But they won't work on him. I don't intend to go into the subject now, but you can believe me when I say that Harry's different."

Olivia gave a ladylike snort. "That ridiculous statement only goes to show how sadly uninformed and willfully naive you are. You have no experience in the field of clinical psychology, Molly. Your opinions are nothing more than examples of wishful thinking."

"Speaking of wishful thinking," Brandon said dryly, "I wish you would get off the subject of Harry's psychological problems, Olivia. I more or less promised the guy that I'd try to keep you from analyzing him at every opportunity."

Olivia flushed. "What are you talking about?"

"It annoys him," Brandon explained. "And I can't say I blame him. You know something? Molly's right. Harry has done me a major favor. The least I can do is keep you off his back. Whatever else you can say about Harry, he's smart. If he wants professional help, let him get it outside the family, okay?"

Olivia was clearly taken aback. She started to say something and then lapsed into silence.

Brandon looked at Molly. "I think we all understand what you're trying to say here. I, for one, have to agree that, from your point of view, it probably does look as if we've all tried to use Harry in one way or another."

"And tried to force him to choose sides in a war he never started," Molly concluded.

"You can say that again," Josh muttered. "I lived with him for years, remember? I know what it's been like for him. Everyone is always after him. Always trying to get him to turn his back on one side of the family or the other. Molly's right. Everyone here has been more than happy to use him when it was convenient."

Danielle lifted her chin imperiously. "I disagree completely. No one has used Harry. He has responsibilities in the family, and he's carried them out from time to time. That's all there is to it."

"Whatever the truth of the matter," Gilford said, "it's obvious that Molly has a different take on the situation. And like it or not, she's the one who's going to be married to Harry. I think she's made her point. None of us wants to have to go through her to get to Harry. As his wife, she's going to have a lot of control over the situation. If she decides to protect him from the rest of us, she's going to be able to do it."

Evangeline gave Molly an assessing look. "What do you want from us?"

"As I told you when you first sat down," Molly said, "I have two demands."

Josh's mouth curved with anticipation. "What are they?"

"First," Molly said, "in honor of his forthcoming marriage, I want a bachelor party for Harry. A real bachelor party. One that will be attended by every able-bodied male on both sides of the family. No excuses will be accepted. Josh and Brandon will organize it."

Everyone seated at the table gaped. Josh and Brandon exchanged wary looks.

"Second," Molly continued, "I want everyone on both sides of Harry's family to attend the wedding. Anyone who is not there will find it extremely difficult to get to Harry at any time during the next fifty or sixty years."

"Good God," Parker muttered.

Molly looked at the stunned faces of Harry's family. 'Do I make myself perfectly clear?"

Josh grinned. "Absolutely."

She frowned at him. "One more thing. There will be no naked women jumping out of cakes at Harry's bachelor party. Understood?"

"Yes, ma'am," Josh said. "No naked women in the cakes. Got it."

Molly glanced toward the door where a waiter carrying a large tray had appeared. "Well, that's that. Let's eat. And no food fights allowed."

That night Harry woke up at midnight. He came awake gradually, not with a start. He lay quietly for a few seconds, wondering what had roused him from sleep. He could not put his finger on it. Nothing felt wrong. There had been no nightmares. No strange sounds in the dark.

Then suddenly, inexplicably, he knew that Molly was wide awake beside him. He gathered her close. With a soft little murmur, she snuggled deeper into his arms. He slid one leg between her thighs.

"What's wrong?" he whispered on a yawn.

"Nothing."

"You sure?" He nuzzled the curve of her shoulder. The scent of her warmed him, delighted him, thrilled him. A certain part of him was abruptly wide awake.

"I'm sure. I was just lying here, thinking."

"Humming." He nibbled her earlobe.

"What?"

"You were humming." He slid the sleeve of her night-gown downward to free one delicate breast. She felt so good beneath his hands. Soft. Warm. Exciting. "I heard you."

She ignored that. "Harry, what are you doing?"

"What does it look like I'm doing?" He bent his head to kiss one nipple. It firmed at the touch of his tongue.

"Harry?" She stroked his shoulders.

"Yes?" He flattened his hand on her stomach.

"How does the first of the month sound? That's two weeks from now."

"What happens on the first of the month?" He tangled his fingers in the hair at the apex of her thighs, probing for the warmth and gathering dew he knew he would find there.

Molly sucked in her breath. "Our wedding. Kelsey will be back from her summer workshop by then. I . . . Harry." Her hands clenched in his hair. She twisted, lifting herself against his questing hand.

Satisfaction coursed through Harry. Her response to him seemed to grow stronger, more familiar, more intimate in some indefinable manner each time he made love to her. It was like playing an instrument, he thought. The more they practiced together, the better the music got.

"The first of the month sounds fine," Harry whispered.

"You'll be finished with your paper by then?" She was breathless now.

"Yes." He settled between her silken thighs and entered her slowly. "The sooner the better, as far as I'm concerned."

He did not even bother to fight the urge to sink himself, all of himself, completely into her. This opening of his senses brought such powerful, intense pleasure to both of them.

It was as though he had lived in a shuttered room all of his life until he had met Molly. Now, when he was with her like this, the windows were fully open at last, and he could see the true colors of the world.

* * *

A long time later Harry drifted contentedly on the verge of sleep, allowing himself to luxuriate in the deep satisfaction that had come in the aftermath of the lovemaking.

Part of him was dimly aware of the moonlight on the bed, the feel of Molly cuddled against him, and a gentle sensation that had no name.

He considered the sensation with idle curiosity. It was a sort of muted singing, he thought. No, make that a *feeling*. Almost a presence somewhere in his mind.

Molly was humming again.

It wasn't an unpleasant sensation, he decided. In fact it had a certain comforting quality.

"Don't worry about it," Molly murmured sleepily. "You get used to it."

Harry stirred. "Get used to what?"

But Molly did not answer. She was already fast asleep.

# 21

Olivia sipped thoughtfully at the cup of specially blended Assam tea Molly had just finished making. She glanced around the front room of Harry's condominium, which was littered with several packing cartons full of books. "Do you know where they've taken him?"

"No." Molly poured tea for herself and sat back on the sofa. She curled one jean-clad leg under herself and gave Olivia a wry smile. "Maybe it's better that way. I warned Josh about naked women bursting out of cakes, but that still leaves a lot of entertainment possibilities that I'd rather not contemplate too closely."

"Bachelor parties do have a certain reputation."

Molly made a face. "Don't remind me. Talk about an archaic tradition. Must be a leftover from the Medieval days when the male members of the wedding party got the groom drunk and then pushed him into bed with the bride."

Olivia gave her a keen look. "So why did you insist that the Stratton and Trevelyan men throw a party for Harry?"

"I think you can guess the answer to that."

Olivia met her eyes. "Yes. It doesn't take a degree in psychology to figure out that you want Harry to feel that his family cares enough about him to call a truce for his sake."

"It's the one thing he wants from them. The only thing he's ever asked of them."

"And you made certain he got it. I have to admit, I'm amazed. I didn't think there was any force on the face of the planet that could persuade the Strattons and the Trevelyans to put aside the feud even for a short time."

"The Strattons and the Trevelyans aren't so tough. You just have to know how to deal with them."

Olivia studied her with sudden understanding. "You really do love Harry, don't you?"

"Yes."

"Has he—" Olivia broke off and looked away for a brief moment. "I'm sorry, this is a very personal question. You would be within your rights to tell me to mind my own business, but I can't resist asking. Has he told you that he loves you?"

"Not in so many words," Molly admitted.

She was not altogether certain why Olivia had shown up at the door ten minutes ago. It was nearly nine o'clock. An hour earlier Josh had dragged Harry off to the parking garage on the pretext of showing him a brand-new Ferrari that he claimed was lodged in one of the stalls. There was more than enough Trevelyan blood in Harry to make him take a serious interest in that particular lure.

What Harry had not known when he agreed to go downstairs to view the mythical car was that he was about to be abducted in a stretch limousine that Brandon had hired for the evening.

Molly had had a few anxious moments, but the fact that Harry and Josh had not returned to the condominium meant that the plot had been successfully carried out. Pleased at the promising start to her scheme, she had finished the dinner dishes and was about to curl up with a book when Olivia had arrived.

As far as Molly could tell, Olivia simply wanted to talk.

"Doesn't it worry you that he hasn't told you that he loves you?" Olivia asked.

"He'll get around to it." At least Molly hoped Harry

would eventually get around to figuring out that what he felt for her was love. "Harry does things in his own time and in his own way. He's different."

"You keep saying that."

"It's true." Molly smiled over the rim of her teacup. "I come from a long line of people who were all a little different. I know 'em when I see 'em."

"Yes, but Harry's differences, as you call them, go rather deep."

"Olivia, do you mind if I ask you a personal question?"

Olivia looked briefly uneasy. "What is it?"

"What did you see in Harry in the first place? It's obvious that the two of you were a bad match."

Olivia sighed. "You may not believe this, but I honestly thought at the beginning that we were a very good match. I met Harry at a small reception in his honor after he gave a talk on the contributions of eighteenth-century Enlightenment thinkers to the development of psychology."

"You figured you had something in common?"

"Well, yes." Olivia frowned. "Harry is very well respected in the academic world. He's intelligent. Well educated. He seemed well-grounded emotionally. At least he did at first."

"Ah, yes. His infamous self-control." Molly grinned. "When did you discover that it conceals a seething cauldron of dangerous passions and dark desires?"

Olivia went blank. "I beg your pardon?"

"Never mind. I'm just teasing you. When did you decide that the two of you were not cut out for each other?"

Olivia shifted slightly in her chair. "Are you sure you want to go into this?"

"Absolutely. I'm dying of curiosity."

"To be honest," Olivia said, "it became clear very quickly that Harry had a serious emotional disorder which had to be dealt with therapeutically before he would be able to form a healthy, normal relationship with a woman."

"Hmm."

"I tried," Olivia said, grimly earnest. "Lord knows I tried. He wouldn't talk to me. He refused counseling or therapy.

I told him there was medication now that could help him. He wouldn't even speak to a doctor about it. And then . . ."

"Then, what?"

"Well, he began to make me nervous, if you want to know the truth."

"Why?"

Olivia gazed out into the night. "I had the feeling that he wanted something from me, something I could not even begin to give to him. I didn't know what it was that he seemed to need. I just knew I couldn't supply it."

"What did you want from him?" Molly asked.

Olivia shot her a swift, searching glance. "A healthy, well-balanced, mutually satisfying relationship, of course. A marriage based on respect and trust and compatibility."

"And you didn't think you could find that with Harry?"

"It was impossible. Harry . . ." Olivia struggled for the right words. "Harry seemed so restrained at first. But toward the end of our engagement he became stranger. He started to *overwhelm* me."

"Overwhelm you?"

"It's difficult to explain. I never really understood it, myself. I had never encountered his particular symptoms in my clinical practice, and I had never studied such a syndrome when I was in school. I'm sure his odd behavior is the result of a posttraumatic stress disorder, but it was not clear what was going on. I became very frightened. I knew that I had to get out of the relationship."

"And Brandon was there, waiting to rescue you?"

Anger flashed in Olivia's eyes. "He didn't rescue me. I rescued myself."

"Sorry."

"Brandon and I had come to know each other during the weeks I was engaged to Harry. I admit that there was a strong attraction between us from the start. We both knew it and tried to ignore it. But Brandon realized that I was becoming increasingly anxious about Harry's bouts of depression and his . . . his intensity."

"You talked to Brandon about Harry's behavior?"

Olivia nodded. "I could talk to Brandon in a way that I could never talk to Harry. It was such a relief."

Molly leaned forward. "Olivia, it's all right. Don't torture yourself any longer with guilt."

"I don't feel any guilt in the matter," Olivia flared. Tears glittered suddenly in her eyes. "Guilt is a paralyzing, destructive emotion. I have no reason to feel guilty."

"No reason at all," Molly soothed. "You and Harry were never meant to be a couple. Trust me on this. I'm absolutely, positively certain of it."

"What makes you say that?" Olivia demanded.

"Harry connects emotionally in ways that you will never be able to explain with any fancy psychological theory. You will never truly understand him. As I keep telling you, he's different."

Olivia's teacup rattled in its saucer. "I tried to help him."

"I know."

"I did everything I could to get him into therapy." Olivia grabbed her purse, reached inside, and snatched a tissue. She blotted her eyes. "Oh, God, you can't possibly understand. It was like watching my father all over again."

"Oh, dear," Molly whispered.

Olivia did not appear to have heard her. She dabbed at more tears. "My father suffered from bouts of depression. They got worse as time went on. Mother tried to get him to see a doctor. So did I. But he refused. One day he went into the woods with a gun. He never came back."

Molly put down her teacup and rose from the sofa in a single movement. She went to Olivia and hugged her tightly. Olivia did not resist the offer. Instead, she turned her face into Molly's shoulder and began to sob.

Molly patted her gently. "Olivia, you're an expert. Surely you don't need me to tell you that you weren't responsible for your father's suicide."

"No. Lord knows, I've had enough therapy in the course of my training to deal with that." Olivia's tears began to subside.

"And you probably don't need me to remind you that

Harry is not your father. You don't have to worry about saving him. He's not your problem."

Olivia sniffed once or twice and then raised her head. She managed a tremulous smile. "You know something? I think you missed your calling. You should have studied psychology."

"Thanks. But I prefer the tea and spice business."

"Maybe it's your lack of formal training that makes it easier for you to see the situation more clearly," Olivia mused as she dropped the damp tissue into her purse. "All I know is that you feel you failed with Harry, and your feelings about that are complicated because you were personally involved with him. I can only imagine what a mess it must have been."

"A mess?"

"Sure. There you were, engaged to a man you were beginning to view as a patient, rather than as a lover. A man whose problems reminded you of your father's problems." Molly waved a hand. "At the same time you were falling in love with another man who happened to be related to your patient-fiancé. To top it all off, your patient was growing increasingly weird, and he refused to go into therapy. No wonder you freaked and broke off the engagement. It was the only intelligent, sensible thing to do."

There was a short, sharp pause.

"We do not generally use the term *freaked* in clinical psychology," Olivia murmured. "But maybe it's apt in this particular instance."

Molly blinked. "Was that a little joke I just heard? A bit of psychiatric humor? Olivia, you surprise me."

Olivia smiled wanly. "I've got a really good one about how many shrinks it takes to change a lightbulb."

Molly started to laugh. "I can't wait to hear it."

Olivia's smile finally reached her eyes. "Maybe you're right. Maybe it's time to let go of the guilt I feel toward Harry. I think he's in good hands."

\* \* \*

Parker surveyed the noisy, crowded tavern with a scowl of acute disdain. A country-western band filled the room with a wailing tale of bad love and good liquor. The lead singer was dressed in a skintight silver lamé jumpsuit. None of the men who lounged at the bar had bothered to remove his hat. In the far corner a rowdy group had gathered around a pool table. It was obvious that money was on the line.

"Who the hell chose this place?" Parker demanded.

"We did." Josh glanced at Brandon for backup.

"Thought it would be neutral territory," Brandon said with somewhat forced enthusiasm. He signaled to a woman dressed in rhinestone cowboy garb. "Have a beer, Grand-dad."

"I drink whiskey," Parker grumbled.

"Matter of fact, so do I." Leon leered at the waitress as she approached the table. "Nice boots, honey."

Raleigh groaned. "Jeez, Uncle Leon. Don't make an ass out of yourself, okay?"

"Like my boots, mister?" The waitress glanced down at the red sequined cowboy boots that matched her hat.

Leon grinned. "Yeah."

"You can have 'em if you want 'em. By the end of the evening my feet are dyin' in these things."

"I could take care of that little problem for you, darlin'." Leon waggled his brows.

"No, thanks." The woman gave him a laconic smile. "I've got someone else who likes to massage my aching feet."

"How big is he?" Leon asked with calculating interest.

"It's a she," the waitress murmured. "And she's five foot eleven, rides a Harley, and wears a lot of leather and metal. Plays the drums in a band called Ruby Sweat. Ever hear of it?"

"Uh, no," Leon admitted. "Probably not my kind of music."

"Probably not. Somehow, I doubt that you and my friend would get along," the waitress said.

Leon winced. "Figures. Go out with a bunch of Strattons and what do you expect?"

Parker glowered at him. "Try not to make an even bigger fool of yourself than you already are, Trevelyan. I've got a reputation in this town."

Leon squinted. "A reputation for what? Flower arranging?"

"Give it a break, Grandpa," Josh hissed.

Unperturbed, the waitress tapped her pen firmly against her little pad of paper in order to get the attention of everyone at the table. "May I take your orders?"

"A beer for me," Josh said hastily.

"Same for me," Brandon said. "And maybe some nachos."

Parker scowled. "If beer is all that's available, I suppose I'll have the same."

Raleigh followed suit. "Me, too."

Gilford frowned in consideration. "Do you have a selection from the local microbreweries, by any chance?"

"Yes, sir, we've got one local brand," the waitress assured him. "Skid Road."

Gilford looked pained. "I don't believe I've ever heard of that one."

"It's from a small brewery that just opened in Pioneer Square," the waitress said.

"All right. I'll try it."

The waitress glanced expectantly at Harry, who sat at the head of the table. "What about you?"

"Skid Road sounds fine," Harry said.

"Make 'em all Skid Roads," Gilford ordered.

"You bet. I'll be right back." The waitress dropped her little pad into the pocket of her short red cowboy skirt and moved off into the crowd.

Leon watched her with a wistful expression. "Cowgirls ain't what they used to be."

"Shut up, you old coot," Parker ordered. "Haven't you heard of sexual harassment?"

Leon feigned astonishment. "Why, no, I haven't. Where do I go to get me some?"

Josh heaved a long-suffering sigh and looked at Harry. "Are we having fun yet?"

Harry considered the men who were seated at the table. The small crowd was composed of virtually every one of his nearest male relatives who was twenty-one or older. It was the first time he had ever seen them all together in one room.

"I assume this bachelor party was Molly's doing?" he said into the silence that had descended on the table.

"Whatever gave you that idea?" Gilford muttered.

"Just a wild guess," Harry said. Out of the corner of his eye he saw the waitress returning with a tray of Skid Roads. He wondered how soon they could all call a halt to this farce and go home.

Raleigh frowned. "Now, Harry, I know what you're thinkin', and it wasn't like that. We all wanted to give you a send-off. Isn't that right, Uncle Leon?"

Leon cocked one brow. "Sure." He leaned back as the waitress set a bottle of beer down on the table in front of him. "Hell, I'm always willin' to party."

Parker picked up his beer. "Would you mind answering one question for me, Harry?"

"What's that?" Harry asked.

"I've got no objections to the idea of you getting married. It's your business. But why in hell do you want to go and marry a bossy little piece like that Molly Abberwick? Son, take it from me, she's going to make your life a living hell."

"You can say that again." Leon shook his head. "I'll tell you something, that lady's got balls."

Harry looked at him. "No balls."

"Huh?" Leon blinked in confusion.

"She's got guts, but no balls." Harry took a swallow of beer. "There's a small but significant difference. Maybe you're not particular, Uncle Leon, but when it comes to things like this, I prefer accuracy."

There was a moment of stunned silence around the table. Everyone stared at Harry. And then Brandon's mouth twitched. A moment later he exploded in laughter. Josh joined in with a howl of amusement. Gilford started to grin.

"Son-of-a-bitch," Leon muttered. Then he started to chuckle.

Parker and Raleigh traded strange looks.

Harry was the only one who noticed the three burly men in denim and leather who sauntered into the tavern at that moment. They appeared no different than many of the other tavern patrons, but something about them sent a stab of unease through him.

The newcomers surveyed the room with expressions of drunken anticipation.

"Damn." Harry set down his beer. "I think it's time to leave."

Raleigh glanced at him. "What's wrong?"

"Nothing. Yet." Harry started to reach for his wallet. He saw the newcomers start toward the Stratton-Trevelyan table.

With an instinct for trouble that had served him well over the years, Leon looked up expectantly. He grinned when he saw the three men bearing down on the table. "Well, well, well."

Parker frowned. "What's going on here?"

"With any luck, the evening is about to liven up," Leon assured him happily.

The three men reached the table. The one in the lead sported a couple of days' growth of beard and a greasy ponytail. He hooked his broad thumbs into a wide leather belt.

"Say, now, this wouldn't be the bunch of sweet-cakes that belongs in that fancy limo parked out front, would it?"

"Who you callin' a sweet-cake?" Leon asked pleasantly.

"Now, see here," Parker said. "This is a private party."

A second man grinned, displaying darkened teeth. "Too bad. We wanna have some fun, too."

Leon gave him a toothy smile. "Not at our table."

"Don't see why not," the first man replied. He swept out

a long, hairy arm, caught hold of the edge of the table, and turned it on its side.

Bottles and glasses went flying. Chairs scraped. The Strattons and Trevelyans scrambled to their feet. A shout went up at the nearby tables.

"Son-of-a-bitch." Leon waved one crutch with enthusiasm.

"Oh, shit," Raleigh said. "This is gonna be one fun bachelor party, ain't it?"

Harry seized his beer bottle before it hit the floor. He held it the way he would have held a knife. He caught Josh's eye. "Front door," he ordered. "Now."

"Right." Josh glanced at the makeshift weapon Harry held and grabbed his own bottle. He started to back toward the door.

Gilford looked outraged. An expression of surprise crossed Parker's face. Harry shoved both of them toward the front door.

He didn't see who threw the first punch, but he saw Leon swing a crutch in response. The man with the oily ponytail doubled over with a choked gasp.

In the end it didn't matter who started the fray. The result was entirely predictable by all the known laws of science. The tavern erupted into a free-for-all. Screams, shouts, and curses rang out. The band turned up the volume in a desperate attempt to drown out the crowd.

Intent on getting his relatives to the safety of the limo, Harry moved quickly. He ducked the swinging fist of one of the denim-clad men and came up under the blow to plant a solid punch into a bulging stomach.

The man staggered backward. An expression of astonishment lit his beefy face. Before he could recover, Harry grabbed Parker by the shoulder and launched him in the general direction of the door.

His grandfather, however, was concentrating on other matters.

"No-good hooligan." Parker swung a bottle of Skid Road at one of the three men who had initiated the scene. The bottle shattered on the man's shoulder, eliciting a growl of outrage.

Harry hauled Parker out of harm's way.

Josh and Brandon looked at Harry for direction.

"Josh, take charge of Raleigh," Harry ordered. "Brandon, get Gilford and Parker out of here. I'll handle Leon."

"Right." Brandon took hold of Parker and started toward the door.

Josh seized Raleigh's arm. "Let's get outa here, cuz. Party's over."

"Ah, shoot. The fun was just startin'," Raleigh complained. But he allowed himself to be dragged toward the door.

Harry grasped Leon's collar just as his uncle was winding up for another swing of his crutch.

"What the hell?" Leon scowled at him. "Leggo. I've got business to attend to."

"This is my party," Harry said as he hustled Leon toward the door. "And I'm ready to leave."

"You never were any fun, boy," Leon said as Harry hauled him out into the night. "That's your whole problem in life. You don't know how to enjoy yourself."

Harry ignored him. He did a quick head count as everyone piled into the waiting limousine. There was a brief, awkward moment when Leon's crutch got caught on the door frame, but Harry got the door closed just as the fight spilled out into the parking lot.

"Looks like we're all here." Harry caught the limo driver's eyes in the rearview mirror. "Let's go."

The driver already had the engine running. "My pleasure, sir."

The big car's tires kicked up a storm of gravel as the limousine roared out of the tavern parking lot. Somewhere in the distance sirens wailed, but the limousine was safely on its way.

For a few minutes no one said a thing. The subdued lights in the plush passenger compartment revealed a selection of interesting expressions as everyone looked at everyone else.

Then Leon chuckled and held up several bottles of Skid Road that he had somehow managed to liberate on the way out the door. "Anyone want another round?"

"Hell, yes," Raleigh said. "Give me one of those, Uncle Leon. I need it."

"Personally, I could use something stronger," Parker muttered.

Josh grinned and began to rummage around in the limousine's tiny bar. "I do believe there is a bottle of whiskey here, Mr. Stratton. Yep, here we are." He held up a bottle.

"Thank God." Parker watched Josh pour the whiskey. "I haven't been in a situation like that since I was in the Marines."

Leon looked at him with sudden interest. "You were in the Marines?"

"Yes, I was." Parker took the whiskey from Josh.

"Well, I'll be damned. So was I." Leon stuck out his hand.

Parker hesitated, and then he shook Leon's hand.

Harry was aware of a curious new mood settling on the small crowd in the back of the limousine. He was not certain what it was, but it felt good.

Brandon looked at the others. "Gentlemen, I do believe that this is what my wife, the noted shrink, would call a male bonding experience."

"Don't know what that means," Leon said cheerfully, "but I'll drink to it."

The sound of a key scraping haphazardly in the front door lock roused Molly. Harry was home at last. She sat up on the sofa where she had fallen asleep reading and glanced at her watch. She was surprised to see that it was nearly one o'clock in the morning.

Relief poured through her. The bachelor party must have been reasonably successful to have lasted this long.

She yawned, got to her feet, and went down the hall to greet her husband-to-be. The scratching sound came again. Harry was apparently having a problem unlocking his own front door.

"I do hope you're not soused, Harry," she said as she opened the door. "A little male bonding is one thing, but if those Stratton and Trevelyan relatives of yours got you rip-roaring drunk, I'm going to be very annoyed."

She broke off in horror when she saw who stood at the door.

"I assure you, I'm not drunk, my dear," Cutter Latteridge said. He gave her his most charming smile and showed her the gun in his hand. The barrel was oddly shaped. "And I won't be staying long. There's just one or two things I want to take care of before I start another project."

"Cutter." Molly was too stunned to move. "How did you get in here?"

"Actually, the name is Clarence, but you can call me Cutter." He motioned with the gun. "And to answer your question, I got in through the garage. Garage security is always so lax, isn't it?"

Molly took a step back. Cutter walked into the hall and closed the door behind himself.

"They said you had disappeared," Molly whispered. "They said it wasn't your style to come back after the con went sour."

"Generally speaking, they're right." Cutter heaved a sigh of regret. "I'm not fond of the physical stuff. Entirely too messy. I prefer to make my living with my wits. But in this instance, I feel that I must make an exception."

"You mean another exception, don't you? You killed Wharton Kendall."

"He became unreliable," Cutter said. "There was simply too much money at stake, I suppose. He felt he had a right to more of it than I planned to give him for his services. Amazing how greedy some people can be, isn't it?"

"You'll never get your hands on the Abberwick Foundation assets now," Molly pointed out desperately. "Why take the risk of coming back to Seattle?"

"Because Trevelyan won't give it up." Cutter's face suffused with sudden fury. "He's like a goddamned bloodhound. He's got his investigator rummaging around in my past, looking for evidence, trying to find patterns. And we all have patterns. Sooner or later he'll track me down. I can't have that."

Molly had not realized that Harry had kept Fergus Rice on the case, but the news did not surprise her. "You can't stop Harry."

"I must," Cutter said. "If I don't get rid of him, I won't have any peace for the rest of my life."

Fear seized Molly's insides. "What are you going to do?"

"I'm going to dispense with both you and Trevelyan in one neat, tidy package."

"You can't get away with this. Everyone will realize who murdered us."

"I don't think so." Cutter smiled coldly. "I've spent quite some time planning this project. And I've waited for just the right moment."

"What are you talking about?"

"It will appear that Harry Trevelyan, psychologically disturbed man that he is, went over the edge. He came home drunk and depressed after his bachelor's party. Shot his fiancée, whom he mistakenly believed had resumed her affair with her old boyfriend, Gordon Brooke, and then turned the gun on himself. Happens all the time, eh?"

"You're the crazy one if you think this will work."

"It will work, my dear. I'm very good with details." Cutter glanced at his watch. "We may as well sit down. There's nothing we can do until Trevelyan returns home, after all, and I understand that bachelor parties can go on for some time."

Molly knew she would never have a chance to scream aloud. Cutter stood too close, his gun at the ready. He could knock her unconscious or kill her before she could utter a sound.

She recalled the day that Cutter had trapped her in her father's basement workshop. Harry had arrived on the scene within minutes after Cutter had left the house.

He would never admit it, but Molly knew that Harry had come to the Abberwick mansion that day because he had sensed that she was in danger. She had called to him and he had come. Admittedly, he'd arrived a little late, but he had come.

Molly looked into Cutter's cold eyes and saw death. In desperation, she screamed a silent warning into the night.

*Harry.*

*Danger. Death.*

*Be careful. Be careful. Be careful.*

Harry opened the door of the limousine as soon as it pulled into the loading zone in front of his condominium building.

Leon gave him a reproachful look. "You sure you want to go home this early? Night's young, boy."

"It's one-thirty in the morning, and I'm not accustomed to this kind of excitement." Harry got out of the car and looked at his relatives through the open door. "I've had about all the partying I can stand for one night. But I want you all to know that I had a hell of a time."

"Hey, we oughta do this more often," Raleigh said.

"I'm not so sure about that." Brandon grinned ruefully. "I think I'm about ready to call it a night, too."

"Me, too," Gilford said.

Parker snorted. "These youngsters don't have the stamina we did in our heyday, do they, Leon?"

"What d'ya expect?" Leon said. "They've all got it too soft these days."

"That's the truth," Parker agreed fervently.

Harry glanced at Josh. "Make sure Leon doesn't embarrass himself."

"I'll give it my best shot." Josh's grin faded. He searched Harry's face. "Anything wrong?"

"No," Harry said. "I'm ready for bed, that's all." He started to close the limo door.

"Let's hear it for the groom-to-be," Leon yelled. "Man's never gonna be the same again, once he's married."

Harry shut the door on the good-natured cheers.

He watched the limousine cruise off into the night, and then he turned and went swiftly toward the lobby door.

Halfway there, he broke into a loping run.

Something was wrong.

*Danger. Be careful. Be careful.*

The riveting sense of wrongness had slashed through his good mood a few minutes earlier. His first instinct, born of long habit, had been to repress it.

But the realization that the chilling sensation was some how connected to Molly crept insidiously into his mind. He had been unable to ignore it.

*Danger. Danger. Danger.*

Molly's advice came back to him in an overwhelming rush. She had told him not to fight his own nature. She had warned him that the battle would tear him apart. For the first time, Harry acknowledged that she was right. The one sure way to drive himself crazy was to refuse to accept the truth.

He forced himself to relax and cautiously open his senses.

*He's here. He's here. Murder. Murder.*

Harry staggered under the impact of the silent, screaming blow. He recovered awkwardly and fumbled with his keys. Chris, the night doorman, emerged from his small office and opened the lobby door.

"Evening, Mr. Trevelyan. Late night, huh?"

"Bachelor party," Harry said tersely. He fought for control even as he tried to leave all his senses on full alert.

Chris winked. "Congratulations."

"Thanks." A wave of dizziness hit Harry as he started toward the elevator.

"Anything wrong, Mr. Trevelyan?"

Harry missed the elevator call button on the first attempt. Panic shot through him. *Too late. I'm going to be too late.* "Chris, have there been any visitors to my place while I was out?"

"Just Mrs. Stratton."

"Olivia?" Harry shook his head, trying to clear it.

"Yes, sir. But she left several hours ago."

"No one else?"

"No, sir."

"Do me a favor will you?" Harry said hoarsely.

"Sure."

"I'm going to play a little joke on Molly."

"A joke?"

"Bachelor party joke."

"Oh. Right. Got it." Chris grinned. "What do you want me to do?"

"Give me a few minutes to get upstairs and then call me on the intercom. When I answer, tell me that Detective . . ." Harry rubbed his forehead and forced himself to think. "Tell me that Detective Foster of the police department is on his way up. Say he's told you it's an emergency."

Chris's brow wrinkled. "Emergency?"

"Yes. Just a joke. Will you do it for me?"

"You bet."

"Thanks, Chris." The elevator door slid open. Harry managed to get himself inside and punch the right button.

As the doors closed, he leaned back against the wall, shut his eyes, and concentrated on finding his balance on the glass bridge that stretched above the abyss.

He was not going to fight the conflicting sensations this time, he promised himself. He would try Molly's suggestion. He would simply sink into his senses. The way he did when he was with her.

*Too late. Too late.*

A rat named panic was trying to eat into his awareness. Harry forced the creature back into its dark hole.

Just another sense. No different than sight or touch or smell. Just another one of his natural abilities. Like his reflexes. Perfectly normal, Molly had said. For him.

Perfectly normal. All he had to do was accept it. Use it. Be at peace with it. Molly's life might depend on his acceptance of his own natural abilities.

*Molly's life.*

Harry took a deep breath. He steadied himself on the glass bridge.

From out of nowhere an alert calm stole over him. Harry began to breathe more easily. He knew without experimenting with them that he had regained control of his reflexes. He had stopped trembling. He straightened away from the elevator wall.

The elevator door opened. Harry drew another deep, steadying breath.

He stepped out of the elevator and went down the carpeted corridor to his front door. He shoved the key into the lock and turned the knob.

"Molly?" He slurred his voice and stumbled deliberately as he let himself into the hall. The feeling of impending danger threatened to crush him. "Honey, I'm home. Hell of a party. Should have seen the fight at the tavern."

"Well, well, well. Blind drunk." Cutter Latteridge smiled as he came around the corner into the hall. He grasped Molly's arm in one hand, chaining her to his side. In his other hand he held a silenced gun that was leveled at Harry's chest. "How very convenient."

# 22

"**H**arry, I tried to warn you." Molly's eyes glittered with tears of despair. "I'm so sorry. I'm so sorry."

Harry peered at her, as though having a problem focusing on a moving image. "What the hell's he doing here?"

"I'm here to set the stage for a proper departure, Trevelyan," Cutter said.

"I'm not going anywhere." Harry staggered toward him, allowing the momentum of his awkward movement to send him careening into a wall. He fetched up against it and started to slide gently toward the floor. "Put that gun away, Latteridge. You can't shoot anyone here. Not your style."

"My style has changed, thanks to you, Trevelyan."

"Harry." Molly tried unsuccessfully to shake herself free of Cutter's grip. "Are you all right?"

"Haven't felt this good in a long time." Harry scrabbled around on the floor. His fingers brushed against his ankle sheath. He made a show of heaving himself back into an upright position. The knife was now tucked into his shirt sleeve. "What's going on here?"

"He wants to make our deaths look like a murder-suicide," Molly whispered. She searched his face as if trying to see past the facade of drunkenness. "Harry, he's going to kill us."

"Nah. He won't do that." Harry floundered forward. "Will you, Latteridge or Laxton or whatever your name is?"

"Stay where you are," Cutter ordered quickly. He backed away, dragging Molly with him.

"Can't shoot me in the chest," Harry explained cheerfully. "Wouldn't look like a suicide, now would it? Got to go for the head or mouth or something."

"Damn you," Cutter hissed. "You really are crazy, aren't you? Your sister-in-law is right."

Harry shook his head sadly. "And here I thought a shrink was supposed to maintain confidentiality."

"Keep your distance or I'll kill Molly right now," Cutter warned. "Right *now,* do you understand me?"

"Sure, sure." Harry massaged the back of his neck as he lurched to a swaying stop. "I hear you."

Cutter frowned. "I'm delighted to see you drunk, Trevelyan, but I must admit this is beyond my expectations."

"I make it a practice never to live up to other people's expec ... expectations," Harry said.

Molly's eyes widened with sudden comprehension. He knew then that she had finally realized he was not drunk. He willed her not to give the game away.

"Stay right where you are, Trevelyan." Cutter started to raise the gun.

At that instant the intercom buzzed. Cutter froze.

"Hey, we got a visitor," Harry said brightly. "Party time."

"Don't answer it," Cutter ordered.

"Got to." Harry lifted one shoulder in an elaborate, what-can-I-do shrug that sent him reeling off-balance once more. "Doorman knows I'm up here. He saw me get on the elevator. Knows Molly's here, too."

Cutter scowled furiously, clearly torn. "All right, answer it. But tell him you're going to bed and don't want any visitors. Got that?"

"Sure thing. Headed for bed."

Harry stumbled toward the intercom. As he stretched out a hand to punch the button he gaged the distance to his target. Cutter was holding Molly directly in front of him.

From this angle Harry knew that he could hit Cutter's shoulder. But that was not good enough. He needed a shot that would bring Latteridge down before he could fire the gun.

"Yeah, Chris?"

"Sorry to bother you at this hour, Mr. Trevelyan," Chris said in portentous accents, "but there's a Detective Foster from the police department on his way up to see you. He says it's an emergency."

"*Police.*" Cutter, already disconcerted by the interruption, exploded with rage. "Goddamn you, Trevelyan. What's going on here? What have you done?"

"Beats me," Harry said as he turned away from the intercom. He smiled at Cutter. "Looks like we've got company from the police department. Now what do you suppose the police want at this hour? I wonder if I forgot to pay a parking ticket."

"Damn you."

"Don't think the old murder-suicide scenario's going to work tonight," Harry said. "Be a little tough to explain to Detective Foster on your way out, eh?"

Cutter's face worked. He abruptly released Molly, shoved her out of his path, and glanced wildly at the door. "I've got to get out of here."

"There are two elevators," Harry volunteered helpfully. "With any luck you won't get into the same one Detective Foster is about to arrive in."

"Stay back." Cutter swung the gun frantically between Molly and Harry and then concentrated on Harry. "Don't move. I mean it."

Harry raised his arms in a wide arc. "I'm not going anywhere."

"You son-of-a-bitch," Cutter snarled. "This isn't over."

"You sound like my cousin Josh. Kid's got a similar flare for melodrama."

Cutter ignored him. He whirled and ran for the door.

The blade slipped eagerly out from beneath Harry's sleeve. The hilt fit his hand perfectly. He waited for the right moment, knowing beyond a shadow of a doubt that it would come. It was as if he could read Cutter's mind before Cutter himself knew what he was going to do.

There was no paranormal sense involved, just logic and observation. Cutter was in a panic. He was acting emotionally, not logically. Fury would overrule his common sense. He would be unable to resist taking vengeance for all that had gone wrong.

Harry knew that Cutter would turn and try to kill him before he fled.

Sure enough, Latteridge swung around as he wrenched open the door. Rage had screwed his face into a grotesque mask. "You've ruined everything, Trevelyan. Damn you."

He aimed the gun.

Not at Harry. At Molly.

In that instant, Harry was sure that he did go a little crazy. *Too late.*

His reflexes took over. The knife left his hand as though it had a will of its own.

It struck Cutter in the center of his chest. The impact jerked him back a step. A strange, uncomprehending expression replaced the rage in his eyes.

He dropped the gun and clawed at the hilt of the knife. "But I planned it all so carefully," he said hoarsely as he fell to his knees. "Nothing could go wrong this time."

Cutter sprawled facedown on the tile. He did not move.

Harry pulled Molly close. She buried her face against his shoulder. She was crying when she said, "You saved us. You saved both our lives tonight."

This time he had not been too late.

"You knew, didn't you? Before you came through the door, you knew he was here."

Harry tightened his grip on Molly as they watched the soft light of dawn wash away the last of the darkness outside the windows. The police had finally left a short while earlier. Latteridge's body had been removed. The blood on the hall tile was gone.

Neither Molly nor Harry had felt much like going to bed.

"I knew . . ." Harry hesitated, uncertain how to put it into words. "I felt that something was wrong."

"You sensed more than that. You realized that Latteridge was here."

"It was a logical deduction, given the fact that he was the only real source of danger we had encountered recently."

"Don't give me that logic stuff." Molly turned in the circle of his arm. Her emerald eyes gleamed with a knowing expression. "You knew he was here because I'd warned you."

"Did you?"

"Yes, I did, and what's more, you heard me. In your mind, Harry."

He bent his head and brushed his mouth across hers. "Let's just say that I got one of my insights."

"It was a lot more than that." She wrapped her arms around his neck and kissed him soundly. When she was finished she moved her head back a couple of inches and smiled. "One of these days I'll get you to admit it."

"You're safe." Harry eased her back onto the sofa and covered her body with his own. "Dear God, Molly, that's all that matters."

She touched the edge of his mouth with the tip of her finger. "And you're safe, too. That's all that matters to me." Her eyes glowed.

An all-consuming passion exploded within Harry without warning. The rational part of his brain knew that it was very likely a reaction to the aftermath of violence and the fact that he had come very close to losing Molly. But the reasoning was swept aside by the powerful need that seized hold of him.

"Molly," he whispered. *"Molly."*

"Yes." She pulled his mouth down to hers.

Desire roared through both of them, an elemental force that could not be stopped. Harry fumbled with Molly's clothing and then with his own.

Half undressed, they came together in a storm of need.

Need was everything in that moment. Harry did not question its demands. He accepted it, welcomed it, surrendered to it.

He needed to feel the boundless warmth and life and energy in Molly. He needed to experience the incredible sense of sinking into her, of touching the deepest part of her while she touched the deepest part of him.

Molly opened herself to him. He surged into her, seeking arcane mysteries that could not be learned in any other way. He craved the secrets of her soul and yearned to show her his own.

He stepped boldly out onto the glass bridge, knowing that Molly waited for him on the far side of the abyss. As long as she was there, he would not fall.

He was no longer alone in the whirling darkness.

When it was over, Harry lay sprawled in Molly's arms, allowing the warmth of her to seep into his bones, all the way to his soul.

*I love you,* he thought.

Molly cradled his face between her hands. "I love you, Harry."

It was then that Harry realized that he had never spoken the words aloud. Not once. Incredible. He could not imagine life without her. It was time to tell her what was in his heart.

"I love you, Molly."

She smiled, her eyes bright with laughter and love. "I heard you the first time."

# 23

Harry brought Molly and their newborn son home to the Abberwick mansion on a fine day in spring. He settled both onto the grand Victorian fainting couch in the front parlor and prepared to limit visitors to a reasonable number. It wasn't going to be easy. A long line of Trevelyans, Strattons, and Abberwicks had announced their intention to call upon the new mother and baby. The hall was already filled with gifts.

Harry stood near the couch and gazed down at his son. Awe and a sense of wonder that exceeded anything he had ever felt for the laws of Newton and Einstein soared through him.

"Incredible," Harry whispered. "He's absolutely incredible."

"That's just what I was thinking." Molly gave Harry a tired, but thoroughly satisfied smile. "What do you think of the name Sean Jasper Trevelyan?"

"A little awkward, but what the heck. He'll be able to handle it." Harry gingerly reached out to touch Sean's tiny fingers. "Amazing."

"If you think this one's amazing, wait until you see the next one," Molly said.

"The next one?"

"There will be a little girl, too, you know," Molly predicted happily. "In about two years, I think."

"You've got plans?" Harry asked indulgently.

"I saw her, remember? The day she and little Sean, here, saved my life by reminding me of my father's giant toys down in the workshop. We'll call her Samantha Brittany after our mothers."

Harry grinned. "Anything you say, my love. I certainly don't have the strength to argue with you. I know the doctor insisted on discharging you and Sean today, but I'm still recovering. It's going to be a while before I can go through that again."

"You were wonderful," Molly assured him.

"I was a basket case."

"Not true. You never left my side." Molly touched her son's tiny nose with the tip of her finger. "Or my head," she added very softly.

Harry pretended not to hear that. But the part of him that had once dreaded such comments and the implications buried in them no longer reacted with instant alarm.

Footsteps sounded in the hall. Harry looked toward the door. "I told Ginny to keep the visitors to a minimum today."

"Hi." Tessa stuck her head around the edge of the door. Heloise Stickley hovered directly behind her. "We came to pay our respects to the new member of the family."

"Come on in," Molly said. "Hello, Heloise."

"Hi, Ms. Abberwick. I mean, Mrs. Trevelyan." Heloise smiled shyly. She clutched a large, unwrapped box in both hands. "Cute kid."

"We think so." Molly glanced at the large box. "How nice of you to bring a present, Heloise."

Heloise flushed. "Yeah, well, this isn't exactly a present. I finished my prototype. Thought you'd like to see it."

Harry groaned. "Not today, thanks."

"But it works," Heloise said, enthusiasm replacing her shyness. "At least, theoretically. I haven't had a chance to actually test it yet. I need to find a suitable subject. Someone who gives off the right brain waves."

Harry took a step back, scowling. "Don't look at me."

"Huh?" Heloise cast him a quizzical glance. "I wasn't thinking of using you, Dr. Trevelyan. I need someone who has a history of manifesting some sort of psychic abilities."

"Right." Harry smiled blandly. "Well, I guess that lets me out."

Molly gave him a laughing glance. Then she looked at Tessa. "How's the hotshot espresso bar consultant?"

"We're opening a new Gordon Brooke Espresso Bar in Bellevue in June," Tessa said complacently. "This time it will be done right. Going to make a killing. And I get a chunk of the profits."

"I think it's time I hired a new assistant," Molly said. "Something tells me I won't be seeing much of you in the future."

"I'll never abandon my roots," Tessa assured her. "But I'm considering having my eyebrow ring removed. What do you think?"

"Don't do anything rash," Molly advised. "You've got an image to maintain."

"True." Tessa looked thoughtful.

A soft knock announced another visitor.

"Okay if I come in?" Josh asked.

"Sure," Molly said. "Meet Sean Jasper."

"Sean Jasper? Great name." Josh ambled into the room and came to a halt near the bed. "Looks like he's going to take after his old man."

"What's that supposed to mean?" Harry asked.

Josh grinned. "Let's just say he's not the best-looking little dude in the Trevelyan clan."

"He's gorgeous," Molly said firmly. "Just like his father."

"Thank you," Harry murmured.

"Beauty is in the eye of the beholder, I guess," Josh allowed. "Maybe when he loses some of those wrinkles he'll look a little better."

More footsteps. Kelsey appeared in the doorway. She was

wearing a small backpack. "Molly, I just got in. Plane was a little late. Ginny tells me that I missed the whole thing. Are you okay?"

"We're both okay," Molly said.

"Oh, he's adorable." Kelsey started forward and then came to a halt when she saw Josh. She blushed. "Hi."

"Hi." Josh appeared to be having trouble deciding what to say next. "Haven't seen you since Christmas."

"When you spilled the punch on me," Kelsey agreed.

"Couldn't have been me," Josh said. "I've got great reflexes. Runs in the family. How's school?"

"Terrific," Kelsey said. "What about you?"

"Good," Josh said. "Just fine."

An awkward silence fell. Josh and Kelsey continued to stare at each other as if they were alone in the parlor.

Molly glanced at Harry and raised her brows.

Harry didn't need mental telepathy to know what she was thinking. Things had been like this between Josh and Kelsey since they had met shortly before the wedding.

"There, I've got it all set up," Heloise announced, oblivious of the sudden hush. "Stand back, everyone, while I turn it on."

"What?" Harry spun around to see that Heloise had removed a strange-looking apparatus from the large box. It consisted of several dangling metal cuffs, a sophisticated electronic control panel replete with various meters and dials, and a long cord. The cord was plugged into a nearby outlet.

"All set?" Heloise asked brightly.

"Hold on just a minute here." Harry started toward the plug with grim determination. "This is no place for that kind of thing."

Heloise flipped a switch. The control panel lit up like a Christmas tree.

"Oh, wow," Heloise breathed. "It's actually registering something. This is the first time I've ever picked up this kind of reaction."

"Holy cow." Kelsey shucked her backpack and went toward the machine. "What is it, what's going on?"

"I'm not sure yet." Heloise began twisting dials and making adjustments.

Josh went to stand behind Kelsey. "What is this thing?"

"It's a device designed to pick up paranormal brain waves." Heloise hunched over her control panel. "I've been working on it for months, thanks to the grant I got from the Abberwick Foundation. Whew. Someone in this room is really emitting some strong vibes."

Harry halted halfway to the plug. "Get that idiot device out of here, Heloise. This is neither the time nor the place for a demonstration."

"Wait, Harry." Cradling Sean Jasper in her arms, Molly pushed aside the blanket and sat up on the edge of the couch. "Let's see what Heloise has come up with."

"You're supposed to be resting," Harry muttered.

"I'm fine. I want to see how Heloise's machine works."

Harry briefly cursed the Abberwick curiosity. He took another step away from the machine. The lights on the control panel did not dim.

"Hang on, everybody." Heloise busied herself with some dangling wires. "I'm definitely getting a reading. This is so exciting. Someone in this room is putting out paranormal brain waves like crazy."

"I hope it's me," Kelsey said. "I'd love to have paranormal brain waves."

Heloise held one of the meters close to her. "No. Sorry. It's not you."

"Try Harry," Josh suggested. "Everyone in the family says he's got the Second Sight."

Heloise looked at Harry.

"Don't come near me with that thing," Harry warned. "You got that grant from the Abberwick Foundation against my professional advice. It was a waste of money, as far as I'm concerned. There is absolutely, positively no scientific rationale for this kind of research."

"Come on, Harry," Molly said. "Let Heloise attach the meter to you. What harm can it do?"

"Yeah," Josh said. "What's the harm?"

"The harm is that it violates every basic principal of the laws of science," Harry said. "And I will not be a party to any such damn fool experimentation."

"Now, Harry, be a sport." Molly paused as Heloise came to an abrupt halt in front of her. "What is it, Heloise? What's happening?"

"I'll be darned." Heloise gazed at the meter with a rapturous expression. "The reading is very strong right here."

"Me?" Molly was delighted.

"No, I don't think so." Heloise cautiously moved her meter around in the vicinity of Molly and little Sean Jasper. "Not you."

"Shoot." Molly grimaced. "I was hoping I might have a few psychic powers."

"The baby," Heloise announced. "The paranormal waves are coming from Sean Jasper."

"Good heavens," Molly whispered. Awe shone in her eyes. "It's hereditary."

Harry stared at his infant son. Then he smiled slowly. "Don't blame me. Something tells me it runs in both sides of his family."

Molly laughed.

And in that moment Harry did not need any special psychic power to catch a glimpse of the love-filled future that lay ahead. He could see that future very clearly in Molly's brilliant eyes.

He was absolutely, positively certain of it.